OUT OF THE DEEP

TITLES BY THE SAME AUTHOR

A Good Liar
Forgiven
Fallout
Cruel Tide
Fatal Reckoning
Burning Secrets

OUT OF THE DEEP

RUTH SUTTON

HOAD
PRESS

First published in United Kingdom by Hoad Press in 2019
2 Lowther Street, Waberthwaite, Millom, Cumbria LA19 5YN
www.ruthsutton.co.uk

ISBN: 978-0-9929314-5-2

A CIP catalogue record of this book is available from the British Library.

Editorial: Lynn Curtis
Typesetting and Page Layout: Chris Moore
Cover Design: Kevin Ancient
Proofreading: Sharon Keeley-Holden
Typeset in Adobe Garamond Pro 11.5/14.5pt
Printed and bound in UK by TJ International, Padstow, Cornwall

Acknowledgements

The motivation to write my seventh novel was boosted by attending an Arvon writing course at the Hurst Centre in 2018: thanks to the tutors and my fellow writers for their support.

Thanks are also due to Lynn Curtis, my editor, Chris Moore for typesetting, Sharon Keeley-Holden for proof-reading, and yet again to Kevin Ancient for another striking cover.

For his detailed knowledge of the Florence Mine in Egremont, thank you to Mr Finlinson.

As ever, my partner Mick Shaw has been a constant source of encouragement and feedback, for which I am very grateful.

Author's Note

Some of the places mentioned in this novel are real, while other places are not.

All of the characters are fictional. Any resemblance to real characters, living or dead, is purely coincidental.

RS, Waberthwaite, August 2019

PROLOGUE

No moon. Above the black profile of the fell, stars turn slowly in the dome of sky. No wind. Ripples in the wake of a small boat wink with reflected light: tiny diamonds on a rumpled sheet. Silence broken only by the soft splash of oars, and the occasional grunts of the rowers.

One of them speaks. 'Bloody dark out 'ere. I hate it.'

Another voice answers: deeper, less local, less anxious. 'Of course it's dark. That's why we're here. No light, no one around.'

'How far do we 'ave to go?'

'Right across to the far side, where the scree hits the water... where it's deepest. Once he's down there, he'll never come up.'

'Serves 'im right. Creepy bastard! He knew.'

'They all did.'

'Even Ma?'

'Her too.' The splash of oars stops for a second. 'Just a bit further.'

'How we going to get 'im out? It was hard enough getting 'im in, when the boat was tied up.'

The deeper voice has authority. 'You hold us steady, I'll push him out.' The boat rocks violently. 'Shit, it's stuck! Caught on something. Lift your end.' The voice rises, hissing with anger. '*Lift*, I said, not push! For God's sake...'

With a burst of cursing, the heavy load is heaved over the side and slides quietly into the water. A few bubbles burst on the surface. The dark shape turns over and spirals out of sight.

For a while they sit, holding the sides of the boat, heads down, breathing hard. Above their heads the skyline is glowing gold.

The deeper voice reacts. 'Christ, the moon's rising. We'll be lit up. Get rowing – quick, quick!'

They turn the boat and head back, into the shadows, away from the past.

Chapter 1

Anna Penrose woke suddenly, her face wet with tears. Night after night since September 11th, it had been the same dream: planes, blue sky, smoke, flames, bodies falling, clouds of dust enveloping people on the ground as they ran in panic.

She sat up, pushed back the damp covers, put her feet to the floor and shook her head to dislodge the unforgotten images. It was early on an October Sunday morning. Soon the sun would rise. Clear your head, she thought, don't give in. She pulled on running clothes, tethered her thick hair into a ponytail and went downstairs, ignoring the unwashed dishes in the sink and the unopened boxes that littered the house. All that could wait. For now, she wanted to feel the air on her face. A large tom cat curled on the sofa raised his head as she passed, but he could wait too.

The Land Rover standing outside the small semi had seen better days, but it was cheap to run and started every time she asked it to. In less than twenty minutes she was pulling into an empty car park, from where the path led down to Ennerdale Water. There was no one else around. Daylight strengthened as the sun began to climb. Soon it would pierce the trees behind her and beam across the lake, lighting up the fell tops.

Anna stretched, pulling her muscles into shape, before setting off along the path, past the remains of the old hotel and on under the trees. Her breathing was easy as she ran; the old ankle injury niggled for a while then disappeared. It always reminded her of that night in Whinlatter Forest when she'd thought she was going to die. She ran a little faster to prove that she'd survived the attack.

The flat road along the west shore of the lake was her favourite place to run faster, really push herself. Trees cast islands of shade onto the wide track. The lake glistened beyond, ruffled by a wind on the far side. Just down to the Youth Hostel and back again would be enough for today. Where the lake met the river that fed it, she rested for a few minutes, watching the water tumbling over the rocks before it split into a delta of smaller streams.

A wave of loneliness hit Anna then, as it always did after the nightmare. It was three years since Mark had died and she had left the Military Police; she wanted someone to tell her that things would be all right, someone she could lean on. For a while, she had leaned on Tony Wong, a colleague from the Forensics team. He was young and funny and good at his job, but the misery of the past few months had taken its toll on them both. When the murder case against Rose Heslop collapsed, Tony took it hard, though it wasn't his fault. The police team at Workington CID all knew Rose was guilty, but the forensic evidence just wasn't enough to satisfy the Crown Prosecution Service, and that was that. Now Tony was making noises about moving back to Carlisle. A long-distance affair was not what Anna wanted.

What she wanted most of all was a friend, someone to confide in and laugh with, but there was no one. She was heading towards forty and was part of many people's lives, but not really important to any of them. Was this all there was to be for her? Was the pattern set for the rest of her life? Mark had been the one, but he was gone. She could replace the physical side of their relationship, but that wasn't enough for her, not now. She wanted more.

Work was no better. DI Bell had never wanted a woman sergeant and still didn't; he made no bones about letting Anna know it. She'd got quite close to DC Maureen Pritchard, once she'd been forgiven for getting the job that Maureen wanted, but they had little in common beyond a shared hostility to 'Dinger' Bell, and now Maureen was moving back to the Drug Squad and being replaced by yet another man, who would probably take his cue from Bell and behave accordingly. Great. What was it with West Cumbrian men, or at least those in the police? If she'd known it would be as bad as this Anna would never have left the Red Caps, no matter how much she yearned for a new life, close to the mountains of the Lake District.

She looked around. Sunlight was glinting off the lake's ruffled surface and the fell tops gleamed. This was a beautiful place, just minutes from her home. Maybe it was worth a bit of loneliness.

By the time she turned the Land Rover back into her street, Anna was looking forward to the quiet day to come. A full day off was a blessing and she could use it well, making the small house feel more like a home. Still smiling at the thought, she noticed the large motorcycle parked in front of the house, and a figure sitting on the front doorstep, a helmet between his feet and a newspaper obscuring his face. The smile froze and her heart bumped in her chest. She knew at once who this was. What was he doing here?

The man looked up, folded the newspaper and got to his feet.

'Here you are,' he said, smiling at her. 'I hoped you'd come back before it started raining.'

'How long have you been here?'

Tony Wong shrugged. 'Half an hour or so. I was giving it another few minutes, before the neighbours called the police.'

She laughed. 'That could have been embarrassing. Do you want to come in?'

'Thought you'd never ask,' he said, stepping aside to follow Anna into the house.

'Drink?' she asked.

'Coffee, great, thanks.'

'I've only got tea, and no milk.'

He laughed. 'Won't come to this café again. Black tea is fine.'

Tony settled himself onto a stool at the breakfast bar. 'It's good to see you, Anna,' he said. 'I've missed you.'

Anna was glad that her back was turned, hiding the flush she could feel on her face. She hadn't seen Tony for a couple of months, since they'd argued about the Heslop case for the last time. The misery of that business had hung between them, although for a while the sex was so good that it didn't matter. But recriminations festered, and she already knew that sex wouldn't be enough to hold them together. And now he was here, and she was feeling low, and still fancied him like the first time…

'I'm going to take a shower,' she said, turning towards him while the image of him in her bed still lingered in her mind. She patted his shoulder as she passed. 'Make yourself at home, I won't be long.'

In the shower she ran the water hot and stood quite still, letting it splash on her shoulders and the top of her head before she soaped herself and watched the suds at her feet. Suddenly the shower curtain was pulled back. Tony was standing quite close, naked, smiling. His body so white, his hair so black. He held a hand over his groin, but there was no mistaking what he wanted.

'Tony,' she said. 'No, that's not… Go away, get dressed!'

His face fell. 'But you… I thought…'

'Well, you were wrong.'

'Please, Anna. We used to shower together all the time.'

'Well, that was then. Get dressed. I'll come down in a minute. We need to talk.'

She pulled the shower curtain across and sluiced off the last of the soap before stepping into the empty bathroom, drying herself and putting on fresh clothes. There was no sound from downstairs but she knew he was still there.

In the kitchen, Tony was standing at the sink. He turned towards her, wet hands dripping onto the floor.

'What are you doing?' Irritation bubbled up and out. 'I don't need you to do my washing up. Leave it.'

'Sorry,' he said. 'I got that all wrong. I thought now you've moved house, we could, you know, pick up where we left off.'

Anna shook her head. 'But that was why I moved – to make a fresh start,' she said. 'We tried to keep it going, didn't we? But everything was such a mess, I wanted a clean break from the Whinlatter house and everything about it.'

'I loved that house,' he said.

Her voice rose in irritation. 'But I was attacked there, don't you see? I didn't want to be afraid anymore. I wanted neighbours and street lights.' She paused, took a deep breath. 'Being with you reminded me of things I had to get away from. It just took me a while to realise it.' She paused. 'And anyway, you're going back to live in Carlisle, aren't you?'

'Maybe. Dad's not well. And it would be cheaper living with him, but I'll have to sort out the job transfer first.' Tony looked at her, hesitating before he said, 'I thought maybe we could carry on... at a distance?'

She shook her head again. 'That's not what I want, not really.'

He looked around for a towel to dry his hands on. She handed one to him. 'Anyway,' he said, 'you all blamed me when the Heslop case fell through, didn't you? I heard what Bell used to say. Called me "that chinky kid", didn't he?'

'No,' she began, then stopped. 'Well, yes. Bell is a git. And maybe we did blame Forensics. If you could have found gunshot residue, fingerprints, DNA… anything to prove beyond doubt that Rose Heslop shot the poor bastard, we could have made the case. But we didn't.'

There was a rattle as she spoke and the cat flap in the back door lifted. The large brown and black cat poked its head through and stepped carefully into the room.

'This is Khan,' said Anna. 'I think he belonged to the previous owners, from the way he treats the place. Maybe they didn't want to take him. I didn't ask him to stay, but he does.'

They both watched as Khan looked at them for a moment, before he stepped over to Tony and pushed against his legs.

'Well,' said Anna, 'you're very privileged. The man who fixed the washing machine got hissed at.'

Tony gently pushed the cat away. 'I shouldn't have come,' he said, picking up his helmet from the floor. 'I'm not going through all that business again. Rose Heslop was clever. There was nothing to find. Not enough evidence, sympathetic defendant, and the CPS pulled the plug. End of story. It happens. Why should it come between us when what we had was so good?'

'Sex isn't always enough,' she said.

'Obviously.' He forced a smile. 'Worth a try though. And it was pretty good, you can't deny that.' Anna felt herself weaken, but he moved first, towards the door.

She listened to the grunt of the motorbike accelerating down the quiet street while she leaned against the inside of the front door. Tony was a lovely man, but it would never have worked.

Something buzzed on the kitchen table. It was Anna's pager: a callout for the Mountain Rescue Team. Thank God, she thought. Something to do that would be more useful than emptying boxes and fanning old flames.

❖ ❖ ❖

The Wasdale Mountain Rescue Team was assembling in the car park of the pub that stood at the top end of the valley, beyond the end of Wastwater. They sorted out their kit quickly and listened while the operation details were relayed. Anna looked around and realised with pleasure that Simon Buttler, the newest member of the team, was in the group. She'd only seen him once before, but after the difficult encounter with Tony, she fancied some cheerful conversation with a good-looking man who wasn't going to make assumptions about her. He was tall and broad, which she liked, with hair the colour of ripe corn. He had long fingers, with well-manicured nails, and even when dressed for the outdoors he looked stylish.

There was a familiar-sounding incident to deal with this Sunday morning. They were looking for a missing hiker, one of a group of young men who had attempted Scafell Pike the previous night as part of the 'Three Peaks Challenge'. The 'Three Peaks' was notorious in the western Lake District: it involved climbing Ben Nevis in the Scottish Highlands first, then driving directly down to Cumbria to climb Scafell Pike in darkness, before ascending Snowdon in North Wales, all within twenty-four hours. For some reason, it seemed to be the challenge of choice for young men who over-estimated their own fitness.

'Here we go again,' said one of the team. 'What's the betting? He's half asleep, not got the right boots or proper clothing, and no idea where he is or how to get down.'

There was a general shaking of heads. 'All of the above probably,' said the team leader, 'but let's not jump to conclusions. Some of these groups know what they're doing. The rest of last night's walkers are in the pub. Ten young men, on a stag do.

The driver's sober, but I'm not sure about the others. Anna, you're the policewoman, right?'

'Detective Sergeant, no less,' said someone else.

Anna nodded recognition of her proper title and noticed the broad smile crossing Simon Buttler's face.

'OK then, Superintendent Penrose,' said the leader. 'Get as much detail as you can about when and where they last saw the missing lad – whose name's Ben, by the way.'

Even with all her interrogation skills, the only worthwhile information Anna could glean from an exhausted and embarrassed young man called Ian was that they'd all reached the top of the mountain around midnight, but the cloud came in then and he wasn't sure whether they were all together when they started the descent. Ben had gone off beyond the summit cairn to relieve himself and maybe he'd got lost. Ian shrugged, saying, 'Ben's a bit of an idiot,' with a faint smile. Anna didn't smile back.

The usual descent route taken by these feckless night-time walkers was the obvious place to start. If idiot Ben had set off behind the rest, he might have slipped or fallen without being able to alert the others. If he took the wrong route off the summit, he could be anywhere. The team split, each taking one of the main routes up the mountain. Anna noticed with pleasure that Simon was with her group as they set off into the fine drizzle that was by now blowing into their faces.

What was it about this man that she found so attractive, she wondered. Maybe it was his voice, educated and confident. Whatever made him so, Simon was clearly self-assured, and she admired that quality in others; envied it too. She lengthened her stride to catch up and walk alongside him.

'It's Simon, isn't it?' she said, glancing across. 'I'm Anna, by the way.' She stretched her hand towards his and he took it briefly.

'Yes,' he said. 'The Superintendent. Congratulations, that's quite a promotion.'

She laughed. 'The others are still not used to me being in CID. At least the jokes about "coming quietly" have stopped now. And what's your line?' she asked.

As soon as the words were out of her mouth, she realised they sounded a bit too nosy. Sometimes she couldn't stop herself from asking questions, and it made people wary. She didn't want to put this one off, but he didn't seem to mind.

'I own an estate agency, Buttler and Lilley. We've got an office in Whitehaven, one opening soon in Maryport, and another planned for Carlisle. We're doing well.'

'Must have been tough, though, the past few months, with the Foot and Mouth emergency?'

'Different, yes, but not completely flat. And now the worst is over, things are getting back to normal. We'll be fine.' He smiled at her disarmingly. 'Estate agents aren't always loved, I know. But it's great work and fits in well around a family.'

Family, thought Anna. Of course there is. Every attractive bloke around has to have a wife and kids somewhere. Or else he's gay. She'd need to find out a bit more about this one, without asking too many direct questions, but it was odds on he was out of the running.

The group climbed steadily, all of them used to the ascent and fit enough to maintain a good pace without having to stop. There was precious little to see as the cloud swirled around them, blotting out the black shape of the lake below, but the base of the cloud was rising fast, like the safety curtain at a theatre. Below, the lake winked into life. Above their heads the outline of the fell stood out against the clearing sky.

By the time they reached the summit, where the large round cairn stood like an Iron Age fortress, the cloud had finally lifted, revealing the usual litter that the night-time walkers frequently left behind them, and which the MRT members routinely picked up when they got the chance. They sat for a while, waiting for the other group to join them.

'Coffee?' Simon proffered a steaming cup. 'Caroline always makes more than I can drink.'

'No, thanks,' said Anna. So the wife has a name, she thought. But she was wrong.

'Caroline's my daughter,' Simon went on. He studied Anna over the rim of the metal cup. 'She looks after me since my wife left.'

Anna looked back at him and smiled. OK. Message received and understood.

Teams from the other valleys, Eskdale and Langdale, would check the other slopes of the mountain, leaving the western side to the Wasdale team. Simon suggested that 'idiot Ben' might have taken the wrong route off the summit. 'You and I could head towards Mickledore,' he said, showing Anna the map. 'He'd have to be an idiot to take that route, but then he is, by all accounts.' Before she had the chance to agree, Simon had checked with the team leader and the two of them were setting off together, at right angles to the other path.

Decisive, she thought. I like that.

Anna was pleased to have him to herself, and they talked as they walked. It wasn't long before she told him about serving in Bosnia, and being a Red Cap.

'I joined up, too,' he said, 'straight from school.'

Anna turned to face him. 'Really! What regiment?'

'Oh, never mind about that,' he waved the question away, 'I got out again as soon as I could. You obviously did much better there than I did. Keep going and tell me about Bosnia.'

She was happy to share some of the experience without having to explain much about army life, because she knew a fellow ex-serviceman would understand.

They were descending a steep path covered in loose scree, with Anna in front. Simon had taken a walking pole from his rucksack to use on the descent, and she could hear it tapping just behind her. Suddenly her toe caught on something and she lost her balance, lurching forward. She began to slide sideways, one foot stuck under her body, and was immediately aware of the pain in her ankle. It was the same one she'd injured on that awful night, tripping on a tree root in the dark. When she stopped sliding, she was lying with her head below her feet on the steep slope, winded and struggling in vain to turn over and get up.

Almost at once, Simon was at her side. Anna was very conscious of how close he was. 'I'm OK, really,' she said, 'I just need to…'

'It's OK,' he said. 'Let me help.' He took her shoulders and pulled them gently round. 'Don't move that ankle, let me look.' He started to unlace her boot, easing the foot out to hold it gently, feeling the joint with his fingers.

'Nothing broken,' he said. 'Just a sprain. I'll strap it up and we can get down together. It'll be fine.' Anna watched as he found strapping in his rucksack and bound the ankle expertly to hold it steady, then replaced the woollen sock to keep it warm. 'There,' he said. 'How's that?' He stood up. 'Now, we'll pull you up, put your arm around my shoulders and get you down to the valley. OK?'

On the radio he was clear and authoritative, explaining the situation, what he'd done and what they would do next. 'Slight sprain,' he said. 'Just needs ice and elevation and it should be fine.'

That natural decisiveness again. 'No sign of the hiker, by the way,' Simon went on, looking around as he spoke into the radio.

'What's the betting he'll turn up under his own steam? Over and out.'

Little more was said as they struggled together down the path to the valley and onward to the campsite, from where someone offered them a ride back to the pub. When they reached the yard where the team's cars and vans were parked, he helped her out of the back of the vehicle, thanking the driver for his help. Anna stood by Simon's side, leaning on him. She wasn't used to accepting help, but this felt all right and she found she was happy to let him take charge.

'I'll drive you home, in your car, then get a ride back here to pick up mine,' he said. Once he'd helped Anna to ease herself into the passenger seat, he asked, 'OK, where to, ma'am?'

She smiled. 'Thank you, driver. Frizington, please.'

He looked at her. 'Frizington? That's where you live?'

'Yes, just moved in. It suits me,' she said, but then began to worry about the half-empty boxes in the small house, the dishes in the sink, the unmade bed. He was an estate agent; he knew about houses and probably had much higher standards than she did. But never mind that, she told herself. This is the most interesting man I've met in a while, and if he's not put off by a bit of domestic chaos, he could be even more interesting.

'You've hurt that ankle before, by the look of it,' Simon said, as they drove slowly down the winding road along the lakeshore.

She hesitated. How much to tell him?

'It was a few months ago. A suspect attacked me in my home... the house where I used to live... in the Whinlatter Forest, and I hurt my ankle getting away from him.'

Simon looked across at her. 'You were attacked? That's awful. And you were alone? Was that why you moved?'

She smiled, pleased that he understood. 'Yes, I needed to be less isolated, for a while at least. I was pretty freaked out by it, actually.'

'Not surprising,' he said. 'But why Frizington?'

'Why not? Close to the hills, shops, takeout food, pubs. Ennerdale just twenty minutes away. I know it was a mining village once and they all look a bit grim, but I like it, and it was what I could afford. Even now the mortgage is a stretch.'

He nodded. 'Fair enough.'

When they arrived at the house, Khan the cat rose from his favourite kitchen chair, stretched and stood quite still for a moment before he bolted for the cat flap and disappeared. Simon helped Anna to sit down and looked around quite openly. He said nothing about the mess in the kitchen but commented approvingly on the layout and the colours of the tiles and work-tops, noticing the specific details that had appealed to her too. When he offered to wash the dishes, she was pleased to let him do so while she sat with her foot resting on a chair and a packet of frozen peas on her ankle.

'I'll be fine, Simon. Really.'

'You need to rest. Will you go to work tomorrow?'

'Oh, yes. Hard enough to prove myself as a Detective Sergeant without taking time off. Someone will pick me up if I can't drive. No problem. And thanks for all your help today.'

'Hall Brow, is it, where you work?' he asked.

'That's right, on the outskirts of Workington. Not far from here as the crow flies, but a bit further by car. I like a bit of space between work and home.'

'Yes, good idea in your line of work,' he said. 'How's it going, by the way?'

'The job, you mean?' She hesitated. 'OK. You know how it is, establishing yourself in a new place. I've been here less than a year. It takes a while to settle in.' She hesitated. 'And it takes a while for them to get used to someone new, from a different background.'

'Who happens to be a woman?'

She nodded. 'That too.'

'Well, if you ever want to talk things through, with someone from the outside, I'm a good listener.' Simon got to his feet and pulled a small phone out of his pocket. 'And now I need to sort out a ride. Caroline will come and take me back to Wasdale for my car. I'll make the call outside – better signal.'

Anna watched as he stood in the driveway outside the house, talking into the phone for a few minutes.

'OK?' she said when he came back into the house.

'Fine. She'll come straight here.' He stayed standing. 'Would you mind if I had a look at the rest of the house? Never seen these properties before, and it could be useful information for some of my clients.'

The question took her by surprise, but she couldn't really refuse, after he'd been so helpful and while she was stuck with her foot up. She heard him pacing from room to room above her head. The footsteps stopped in the room over the kitchen, her bedroom, and then moved again. She wondered what he was looking at. Then she heard him on the stairs and he walked back into the kitchen.

'Interesting,' he said. 'Good storage space, and the views at the back would attract some buyers too. Mind if I ask how much you paid for it?'

Anna told him: he could find out easily enough if he wanted to. It was the most interest anyone had taken in her in a long time and she rather liked it.

When a car horn sounded in the street outside about half an hour later, she'd been chatting away comfortably about work and running and the new house, without realising how the time was passing.

'That'll be Caroline. Don't get up,' said Simon. 'And I'll see you again soon, I hope. Can I call you, to see how you're doing? Your phone number's on the MRT list, isn't it?'

Before she had time to respond, he was gone.

As the front door closed, the cat flap rattled at the back and Khan strolled towards her, pressing his big head against her legs. Anna put down her hand and rubbed his ears. 'Well,' she said. 'One door closes, another one opens. This could be fun.'

In the car on the way back to Wasdale, Simon could see that Caroline wasn't pleased to be summoned like a taxi, but his mind was on other things.

CHAPTER 2

'Ey up, Hopalong's here,' said a loud male voice as Anna pushed open the door to the CID squad room the following morning and limped towards her desk. Detective Inspector 'Dinger' Bell got to his feet and pointed at her. 'What's up with you?'

'Slipped,' said Anna, offering as little information as possible. 'MRT shout, yesterday.'

'Bloody do-gooders,' Bell went on. 'Another Three Peaks moron, was it? Don't know why you bother. I'd leave the daft buggers out there. Didn't find 'im, did you?'

Anna shook her head.

'Well,' said Bell, 'guess what? He's turned up. Call came in half an hour back. He walked into the pub in Langdale looking like death warmed up. Said he got lost, slept out and wanted them to give him breakfast. Didn't even know where he was. Stupid bastard.'

Anna sighed. It was no surprise that the walker had turned up, but trust Bell to make some mileage out of it. She eased herself into her chair and looked around. The large functional space was empty apart from herself and the DI, although other officers might have been hiding until the boss's customary early-morning rant was over.

'Bring back National Service, I say,' Bell went on. 'Waste of tax-payers' money all this mountain rescue stuff, stopping idiots killing themselves.'

'Tax payers don't pay for it,' said Anna. She'd told him this before but he rarely listened to anybody. 'It's a charity. People donate, we volunteer.'

'Well, more fools the lot of you,' said Bell. 'And now you've got a bad leg, so you're not much use to anyone.'

'I'm still here, aren't I? Ready to work.'

Bell snorted. 'Someone needs to be. Pritchard's clearing out next week, back to the Drug Squad, and we've got two new buggers coming in. Talk about revolving doors.'

As if on cue, the door opened and a familiar figure entered. DCI Sam Tognarelli had been in the Cumbria force for almost as long as DI Bell. They were both short of stature and grey of hair, but there the similarities ended. Anna sometimes thought of Tognarelli as the antithesis to Bell, thoughtful and quiet rather than careless and noisy. The DCI was not alone. Behind him loomed a figure almost a foot taller, with black curly hair and a striking angular face, like a statue from the South Pacific, Anna thought. The third person looked like a child by comparison, slight and pale, with small round glasses and short mousy hair scraped back unnaturally from a straight parting.

Bell sat still, watching, as Tognarelli turned and ushered the newcomers into the room. 'Good,' the DCI said. 'Two key people already here for you to meet straight away.' He nodded at Bell. 'DI Stanley Bell,' he announced. Anna hid a smile: she'd never heard Bell's proper first name before and doubted whether it would ever be used again. 'And DS Anna Penrose,' Tognarelli went on. 'Not been with us long, and a great addition to the team.' Anna half rose out of her seat, holding on to both arms of the chair to take the weight off her ankle. Tognarelli noticed, as she knew he would.

'Sit down, Anna, please, you're obviously struggling. What is it?'

'Injured while helping some idiot down off the fells, sir,' Bell chipped in.

Sam looked at Anna, not at Bell, which would shut him up for a few moments. 'Mountain Rescue team,' Anna added. 'It's nothing, just a bit of a sprain. It'll be fine.'

The DCI turned to the tall man. 'You'll know all about sprains, I expect, Brown. Must be an occupational hazard for a rugby player.'

Before the tall man could speak, Sam went on, 'DC Henare Brown, late of Workington Reds Rugby league team, then into uniform, now with us.'

Brown smiled and spoke in an accent quite different from the usual tones heard around the office. 'Been a while since the Workington Reds,' he said. 'Don't play much these days.'

'Aussie, right?' said Bell. Anna noticed he'd stayed in his seat, probably aware that he might look a little taller sitting down.

Brown smiled again. 'Not quite. New Zealand. Came over in 'ninety-five to play in Workington, and I'm still here.'

'Lucky you,' said Bell. 'I'd be off like a shot if there was anywhere else to go.'

Sam interrupted, again without seeming to notice that Bell had spoken. That was one of the things Anna admired about him: he never lost his cool or reacted to Bell's frequent interruptions. She wished she could learn to do the same.

'DC Brown will be replacing DC Pritchard, when she goes back to the Drug Squad. And we have another introduction.' He turned towards the boy still hovering by the door. 'Jason Quigley, a civilian IT expert who's joining us here. Not before time, I reckon. We're a bit behind when it comes to technology here, Jason. Born too early, probably. We've got a lot of kit, but I'm not sure we use it as well as we could.' The DCI turned back to Anna. 'So, Jason will be helping get us up to speed there, as well as doing all computer-based work. That will save us so much time.'

Anna wondered what Bell would say to this, but there was a merciful silence before Tognarelli went on, 'DC Carruthers will be here for a few more days, then he's off to HQ in Penrith.' Still no response from Bell, but Anna had to suppress a smile. Bell's expression was a picture as he tried to work out how on earth his feckless sidekick had managed a transfer to HQ without him knowing. All this entertainment so early in the day was taking Anna's mind nicely off her aching ankle.

'DS Penrose,' said Tognarelli, 'can you show Brown and Quigley around the place while I have a word with DI Bell?'

'Certainly, sir,' said Anna, pulling herself up again. Brown stepped towards her and offered his arm, which she held on to. As soon as she was steady, she let go and he stepped away. When the two senior officers had left the room, Jason Quigley looked relieved and walked across to shake Anna's hand. She noticed his palm was slightly damp. The poor lad was nervous. For his sake, she hoped he was really good at his job.

Tognarelli was gone and Bell was back in the room before they'd had a chance to do more than find the right desks and observe the stained coffee table, littered with empty cups and the single teaspoon that someone had chained to it. Bell stood just inside the door and looked across at them. He was obviously annoyed and Anna wondered what the conversation with Tognarelli had been about.

'You lot might as well know,' said Bell, 'I asked the DCI to have another go at the CPS about taking the Heslop case to court, but no joy. We just have to suck it up.' He shook his head in irritation. 'Missing kiddy case, in the spring,' he explained to the newcomers. 'Kid's abducted by mother's boyfriend, to try and force her to leave her husband. Nice, eh? Kid escapes, boyfriend follows her back to the family farm, after a short detour via Penrose's place, and ends up with a bullet in his brain, put there – we're positive – by mother's fair hand. She claims he did it himself, and no one in our splendid Forensics team could find anything to prove she's lying. Bloody ridiculous! Crown Prosecutor still won't take it on, and now the DCI tells me Rose Heslop's upped and left with the two younger kids, and disappeared. Couldn't stand the gossip, apparently. Well, well.'

'Tough on the kids,' said Anna, remembering Helen Heslop and her little brother, whose evidence could have sunk his mother's story if anyone had been prepared to allow it in court. Unsurprisingly, the CPS had decided not to rely on the evidence of a six year old, however skilfully Pritchard had winkled the damning statement out of him. Anna wondered how the Heslop children's lives would be affected by what had happened.

Bell harrumphed back to his desk, leaving Anna to get on with the introductory explanations. 'Call me Henny,' Henare Brown said. 'Henare's the Maori version, but most people get it wrong. My mother's Maori,' he added. 'From the East Cape – know where that is?'

'New Zealand?' said Quigley. They laughed. 'North Island, east coast,' Brown explained. 'First place to see the sun in the morning. When the millennium was being celebrated, that was a big deal. They had an orchestra playing on the beach at Gisborne at sunrise on New Year's Day, but I was over here then. Missed it all.'

'Long way to come to play rugby,' said Anna.

'Better money, and then I met the wife, and the kids came along, so I'm still here.' He smiled, revealing very white teeth in a brown face. 'Always wanted to do police work, so it turned out OK.'

'Still a long way from home, though,' Anna said.

He smiled. 'Yup. But home's here now. We've got the sea close by, and mountains. At least I'm not stuck in London or Birmingham. Couldn't cope with that.'

The phone jangled. Bell picked it up, scribbled a few notes and called Anna over. 'Did you lot get close to Wastwater looking for that idiot yesterday?'

'Not really, why?'

'Call from a bloke in Preston, part of an amateur diving group that splash around in Wastwater looking for stuff. They must be crazy, it's cold in there.'

'What about it?'

'He says someone told him the Rescue team were out in Wasdale yesterday and it made him remember something, from a week or two ago.'

'About the lake?' Anna asked. Bell was taking his usual circular route around information he was meant to share. 'We were there yesterday, not two weeks ago.'

'I told 'im that, but the bloke said he realised he should have reported it earlier.'

'Reported what?'

'Seeing something in the lake – that's what he said. Not him, but someone else who was there at the time, said he saw something on a ledge, below the scree.'

'It's hundreds of feet deep there,' said Anna.

'Aye, but they reckon the thing was caught on a ledge.'

'What thing?'

'A bundle, so he said.'

'Big? Small?' Getting the facts from Bell was like getting water out of a stone. Not for the first time, Anna wondered whether this slow drip feed of information was because he couldn't actually get the facts out in a proper order, or was a deliberate attempt to make the listener look foolish.

'Big,' said Bell.

'Possibly a body, you mean?'

Bell nodded. 'Anybody missing that we might find down there?' he said. 'Get that new kid to take a look.'

'Misper's a missing person, right?' Jason whispered, when Anna went to speak to him. 'How far back do you want me to check?'

'A year or two, for a start,' she said. 'Let me know what you find.'

A few minutes later he was at Anna's desk. 'There's quite a few,' he said. 'Over the past two years, Silloth down to Millom. Four males and one female, but the female was only on the list for a few days. She must have turned up. So, four males, aged between seventeen and seventy-three. I could look wider, if you want. Someone might end up in the lake who's come from anywhere, right?'

'Few million visitors to the Lakes every year,' said Anna. 'But if it is a body, it didn't just fall in, did it? A bundle, the Preston bloke said. That means someone's wrapped it up.'

'Or it could be an old carpet, or a dead dog, or a kitchen sink,' Brown chipped in. 'I've got a wetsuit somewhere. I could go in and have a look if you want?'

He's new, Anna told herself. Maybe they do things differently in New Zealand. 'If it turns out to be something serious, we'd have to have followed procedure,' she said. 'That would mean getting the police dive team in first off, doing it by the book. If we need evidence later, we have to have it all properly gathered and logged.'

'Right,' said Brown. 'How long would all that take?'

'And how much would it cost?' said Anna. 'It's up to Bell or Tognarelli to decide if it's worth it.'

Brown looked across the room at the DI and lowered his voice. 'Those two are quite different, aren't they?'

Anna smiled. 'Bell and Tognarelli – you noticed?' she whispered. 'Chalk and cheese. First thing you learn is how to navigate between them. Tognarelli's the DCI, so we don't see so much of him. Both good coppers. Just different styles.' She paused, thinking. 'Actually, there might be some politics to deal with on this lake thing. We had another case, not so long ago, with a woman's body in a lake. Buttermere that time, further north. The press called it the 'lady the lake' case, of course, and it was in the papers for weeks. The husband was accused of doing her in, and there was a lot of fuss at his trial about evidence... pathology, forensics, why it took so long to find the body. Tons of questions. That might be on Bell's mind. He likes to keep his nose clean with the big bosses, even though he slags them off all the time. And you didn't hear that from me.'

Anna took Jason's findings across to DI Bell and waited for instructions on how to proceed. Bell leaned back in his chair, sucking the end of his pen. 'Well, we know it's not the bloke you were looking for yesterday, but it could be anyone or anything. Nothing to show yet that it's actually a body.'

'But we have to check, don't we? What if it is a body and we just left it there? Could be another 'lady in the lake' debacle.'

Bell thought a little longer, weighing up the risks. 'Call the police dive team' he said, sitting up straight. 'See if they're available, check how long it would take them, and how much to budget for. I'll have to kick this upstairs... I'm not taking the decision on my own.'

Just half an hour later the decision was made: what the diver had seen would have to be investigated, whatever the cost, and the police dive team would be on site first thing on Tuesday. 'Take Forensics with you,' Bell said to Anna, 'and that new bloke, the big one. Let's see how he handles himself with a proper case. Where did he train?'

'Here,' said Anna. 'Same as all of us.'

'That's something at least. God knows how they train their coppers in Australia.'

'New Zealand,' said Anna.

'Wherever. Go on, sort it out,' said Bell, turning back towards his office. 'I'm still trying to work out who Carruthers knows at HQ. How the hell did he wangle that?'

CHAPTER 3

As the car crested the rise on the last stretch of the road into Wasdale from the coast, Henny Brown gasped at the view ahead of them: a wall of rock two thousand feet high that plunged into the black water of the lake. He stopped the car and Anna glanced across at him.

'Never been here before?' she asked.

'Never. I had no idea. I've been to Windermere and Coniston with Celia and the kids, but nothing like this. It's wild. Stunning.'

She followed his gaze. 'Those screes go straight down for another two hundred and fifty or so feet below the surface. It's the deepest lake in England.'

'And people dive down there? What are they expecting to find?'

'Commandos were trained here during the war. Maybe they left stuff behind.'

'The odd body, I shouldn't wonder. Two hundred and fifty feet – that's eighty metres!'

Anna checked her notes. 'The report said that a diver had seen something on a ledge, not far below the surface. Must have got caught on the way down. Let's hope it's still there, or we'll never find it.'

They'd reached the crossroads where a road turned left towards the head of the lake. Sunlight winked on the water and low white cloud streamed westwards on a fast breeze over the tops of the screes. 'There they are,' said Anna, looking to her right. 'Down there, on that stretch of shore.'

Two vans were parked high on a green bank that sloped down to the water's edge. Several men were standing around, at various stages of donning their wetsuits and equipment.

'They've got a Zodiac,' said Brown, pointing to the black rubber boat resting behind a Jeep at the top of the bank. 'Haven't seen one of those for a while. It'll do the job.' He looked across to where the scree met the water. 'No chance of getting vehicles down the other side of the lake?'

Anna shook her head. 'There's a narrow path that runs along the bottom of the rock fall. You can see it if you know where to look. And there's a big house and a farm to our right, beyond those trees at the end of the lake. There's a track to the main road, but no way to get close with a vehicle. If something has been dumped in there it would have to have come from a boat.'

As they stood watching the team manoeuvring the Zodiac down to the water's edge, another van drew up behind them. Anna glanced at it and then looked away. 'Forensics,' she said. 'I'll introduce you and then we'd better check in with the dive team.'

Tony Wong emerged from the van and went around to the back, to start unloading his gear. Anna and Henny walked up to meet him.

'Henny, this is Tony Wong, Forensics.'

Brown put out his hand. 'DC Henare Brown, rookie.'

Tony squinted up at the man, who was several inches taller than him. 'Henare? Maori name, right?'

Henny beamed, 'Right! You're the first person who's recognised it. Do you know New Zealand?'

'One of my uncles lives there, in Petone. I went once, years ago. Loved it.'

Anna interrupted. 'OK, gentlemen, that's enough reminiscing. Work to do. Dive team leader's called Clegg apparently.'

'Bernard Clegg?' Tony said. 'Good bloke. Worked with him before. I can see him, by the boat.'

They walked down, Anna trying to look like the senior CID officer present, rather than someone shorter than one of her side-kicks and less knowledgeable than the other. She made sure she reached Clegg before the other two and introduced herself first. Clegg smiled at Tony, but with Anna he was all business.

'We talked to the diver who said he'd spotted whatever it is. Gave us pretty good coordinates, so it shouldn't take long. We're heading straight across from here, just to the right of that large rock at the bottom of the scree.' He handed Anna a pair of binoculars. 'Apparently, we're looking for something roughly triangular, with dark wrappings. Odd shape for a body, but it could be. Won't know till we get it out.'

Anna nodded. 'We've alerted the pathologist, just to save time in case we need him. He'll have to come from Lancaster. Forensics will take a preliminary look.'

Tony said, 'If it is human remains, I'll do as little as possible, avoid disturbing things before we get into a more controlled environment.'

'Right,' said Clegg. 'OK, we'll take it from here.' He handed the binoculars to Anna. 'You keep an eye on things with these.'

Tony began taking pictures, while Anna and Henny leaned against the car. Anna's ankle was starting to throb, but she didn't want to be the first to sit down. Sometimes being the only woman on site made her feel very self-conscious.

'You OK standing?' Henny asked.

'Fine,' she said. 'Bet there's no phone signal round here.' She checked. 'Nothing. That'll be another delay in getting the pathologist, if we need him. One of the frustrations of working out here.'

'Oh, but look around,' said Henny. 'Would you trade all this for a decent phone signal? I wouldn't. This place is magical.' He borrowed the binoculars and took a long look around. Handing them back to Anna, he asked, 'Were you born round here?'

She shook her head. 'No. Down south. Don't think there's anywhere like this in the south of England. They say it's the deepest lake in the country, with the smallest church in England too, down at the head of the lake. And Scafell Pike, under that cloud, is the highest mountain. Quite a place.'

The Zodiac's outboard engine sputtered into life and the boat moved slowly across the black water towards the spot Clegg had pointed out. The red jacket of the man steering was the only spot of colour in a monochrome landscape. Within a few minutes the boat slowed to a stop. Standing on the shore, Anna and Henny could hear the men's voices carrying across the water. Tony had humped his bags down to the water's edge and was waiting with arms folded. Anna was grateful for his reaction to her, as if they were no more than colleagues. But she still wondered why she'd been so quick to take him into her bed a few months before. He was attractive, no doubt about that, but it was a risk she shouldn't have taken with a work colleague who was younger than her. If he wanted to embarrass her, she'd given him every chance to do so.

They heard the splash as one of the divers went into the water, then the other, and for a while there was nothing to see. Anna trained the binoculars on the spot where they had disappeared. A head broke the surface briefly and then went down again. Suddenly, several metres to the left of the original dive, the head reappeared, an arm was raised, and they heard a shout. The second diver emerged onto the lowest rocks of the scree, and between them the two men hauled a large black shape from the water.

'They've found something,' said Anna. 'Look.' She handed the binoculars to Henny. 'It's big,' he said. 'Too big to get in the boat maybe.'

Tony called up from the water's edge: 'Can you see it?'

'Black, big, hard to see the shape,' Henny called back. 'They'll have to tow it back if they can't get it into the Zodiac.'

For a while the watchers on the shore could hear voices and see splashing as the object was secured to the side of the Zodiac. Slowly, with the outboard leaving only the faintest wake, the boat and its mystery escort came back towards them. As it reached the shallow incline of the pebbles, Tony, who had donned Wellington boots in the meantime, waded into the water to help steer the black object gently onto the bank, where he'd spread out a tarpaulin like a picnic blanket. Henny and Anna made their way down, the ache in her ankle forgotten. Once the bundle was laid onto the tarpaulin the divers stood back, taking off their equipment and keeping well out of the way, as Tony looked carefully at the gift they had brought him.

Wearing his usual bright blue gloves and resting his hands on his hips, he stood to one side for a while, staring intently at the triangular shape at his feet. The bundle was wrapped in black plastic, and rope was looped around it. One side of the triangle was shorter than the other two, and bisected by the indentation caused by the rope, the beginnings of a V-shape. There were no obvious lumps or bumps, indicating a depth of wrapping underneath the outer layer.

Tony looked up at Henny and held out a pair of gloves. 'Put these on and help me turn this over,' he said.

Henny glanced across at Anna, as if seeking permission. They both knew it was his strength and reach that Tony wanted. 'Go on,' she said quietly. Together the two men turned the bundle over onto its other side and stood up. Tony gestured to Anna to join them.

'There's a fair amount of wrapping, by the look of it, and the ropes have been knotted by someone who knew how to make them hold. I'll have a proper look at them later. Why take such care with something unimportant? It could be a body that's bent over at the waist, which would mean the feet and head are both at this end.'

Tony stepped back. 'If this is a body, and someone's gone to a lot of effort to conceal it, I'm not going to disturb it by trying to check here. We need to get it into the lab first, examine the wrapping from the outside in. That could tell us a lot. I'm worried about the effect of air, if there is a body in there.'

'Are you saying we need the pathologist?' asked Anna.

'Yes, definitely,' said Tony. 'I know, there'll be a lot of grumbling if it's not a body after all, but we can't afford to compromise the evidence if it is. Remember that last case? Check with the boss if you need to, but my recommendation is that we don't open it up here, but take it back to the lab and call in the pathologist.'

He was right, and there was no way to check with Bell from this isolated spot. 'OK,' Anna said. 'Can you get it in the back of the van as it is?'

Tony scratched his head. 'With a bit of rearrangement of my gear, yes. I'll take it straight down to our lab and wait for you there. Leave the pathologist call until then, if you want. A few hours' wait won't make much difference, if we can keep it in relatively stable conditions in the meantime.'

'I'll talk to Bell when I can get a signal,' said Anna. 'Wait for us. I want to be there when you open it up.'

❖ ❖ ❖

'How sure is he?' Bell asked, when Anna was able to get him on the phone from Gosforth. 'Do we trust him not to stuff this up?'

Anna moved away from the car, out of Henny's earshot. She didn't want the boss's snide remarks about Tony Wong to be overheard. 'He's being super careful, obviously,' she said. 'After the Heslop mess, he'll want to get it right.'

'Well, wait till we're sure there's a body in there before we get grumpy guts Henshaw up from Lancaster. He's a miserable git but he has a lot of pull, and he's been even more full of 'imself since he got that gong. OBE indeed. "Other Buggers' Efforts" more like.'

Anna waited for the rant to end. 'Do you want to come down yourself?' she asked.

'Stand around with that smell making me gag? No thanks! I'll tell Nelly what's up, and you can report to me if and when we need to call Neville bloody Henshaw OBE.'

Bell rang off. Anna wondered whether DCI Tognarelli knew how many officers still referred to him as 'Nelly', and whether it bothered him. She guessed he was past caring.

In the Forensics lab it was like a bizarre party game, where you take it in turns to cut a piece out of the parcel and then guess what's inside, except that only one of the group standing in a circle around the table in the morgue would actually be doing any cutting. Tony had asked Anna to take detailed notes and Henny to do the photographs while the process continued. Even Jason Quigley was there as part of his 'induction', hoping he wouldn't feel sick and make a fool of himself.

Tony began by examining the knots, explaining how they had been made and waiting while Henny took the necessary pictures. Once the rope was removed, Tony examined the bundle to find the best place either to unwrap the plastic or cut into it, to ascertain what lay inside. He mumbled to himself, debating the implications of various options, and Anna asked him to explain the main choices for her notes. After feeling the underlying shapes carefully, Tony finally decided to cut into a section of the bundle where he guessed the feet would be, if a body lay within.

There was absolute silence in the soulless room as Tony made the first incision, a few inches long, cutting away a small section of the plastic and drawing it back. Crouching down to see what lay underneath, he drew in his breath. 'Cloth of some kind,' he said. 'And it's intact. Extraordinary.' He looked around. 'Do we know how long this thing's been in the water?'

'No way of knowing,' said Anna. 'No reports of it being down there until just a couple of weeks ago. Why?'

'Well, if it's been there for any length of time, you'd expect the fabric to have rotted unless...' He stepped back and looked again at the bundle. 'Unless it's been wrapped so tight that all the water has been kept out, and possibly the air too. If it was kept relatively dry in there, things might have been preserved.'

'Like a mummy?' Jason's boyish voice came from close to the door, where he'd positioned himself in case he needed to escape.

Tony nodded. 'Yes, a kind of mummification.' He poked at the patch of fabric with his gloved fingers, lightly at first and then with greater purposefulness. He turned to Anna. 'Feel here,' he said. 'Tell me what you think.'

Anna stepped forward, pulling the gloves more tightly onto her fingers, and pushed two forefingers into the space. She looked up, then moved her fingers further to one side. 'Toes,' she said. 'Is that what you think?'

He smiled. 'I think it's time to call in the pathologist.'

'You'd better be right,' said Bell, when Anna reported to him. 'You know what Henshaw's like. He'll charge for every minute

32

from when he picks up the phone to when he gets home again, and probably his dinner on the train too. I'll call him myself. Ten-thirty now, what's the best way to get him here?'

'Probably up to Carlisle and then down to Workington. Getting up from Barrow takes longer. We haven't let any air into the bundle, and Tony's got it in a cold store. Morning would do, then we get the PM done the same day if it is a body.'

Bell groaned. 'If? It better bloody *had* be, after all this farting around. How's that new bloke shaping up by the way?'

'Good,' said Anna. 'It was handy having someone as big as him today.'

'Bigger than that shrimp Quigley,' said Bell. 'He'd better be good at his job, that lad. Have you talked to him about the set up in the office?'

'I did,' said Anna, 'and I didn't understand half of what he started talking about.'

'That sounds promising,' said Bell. 'Get him started on the misper file.'

'Already done,' she said, but Bell didn't respond.

It was the following morning when Neville Henshaw OBE strode into the lab like a ship in full sail. He was a heavy-set middle-aged man with an overbearing manner and a voice straight out of an Evelyn Waugh novel. Anna took an instant dislike to him, compounded by his insistence on addressing her as 'my dear'.

She caught the look of dismay on Brown's face when this happened for the first time, but there was nothing that he or anyone else could do to stop it. Anna resolved that when she got an opportunity, and in private, she would explain to this moron that she was a Detective Sergeant who'd seen active war service and deserved to be treated as such. But that would have to wait.

For the moment they needed his expertise, and to get the job done as quickly as possible.

Henshaw stood with scalpel raised, like Mr Bumble about to eat his dinner, but he instructed Tony Wong to make the first incision and to cut open the bundle from end to end, first the plastic, and then the cloth underneath, which now appeared to be a dark grey blanket. After that Tony stood back, awaiting the next instruction.

'You thought the feet were here, right?' said Henshaw. 'So let's go for the jackpot, shall we? If the body's folded over at the waist, that means the head should be here,' he said, pointing. 'I'll do this. Don't want any accidents.'

Anna, Tony and Brown leaned forward to watch as Henshaw peered closely at what lay in front of him. Jason hovered by the door as before. For a few minutes the pathologist snipped and tugged, working so minutely that the others couldn't see what he was doing. Finally, he stopped and stepped back. 'Well, well,' he said. 'Fancy that.'

Anna looked down and gasped. On the table, framed by black plastic and shreds of blanket, was a pale face, perfectly preserved. Parchment yellow skin, sunken cheeks, grey stubble. The face of an old man.

CHAPTER 4

Sam Tognarelli pulled his front door closed, checked it was locked, and looked at the car keys in his hand. Day after day it was the same routine. For reasons he never understood, it was at this time every day that he missed his wife Judith most acutely. For a year or two, as her condition had worsened, the carers had arrived at 8.30 a.m. and he had left the house feeling a dreadful mix of relief and guilt. When it was finally clear that she would never recover, he'd taken leave from the job and had devoted all his time and energy to her, until the final stroke had ended her life nearly two years ago.

Sam often wondered whether Judith's health had been affected by the trauma that she'd experienced thirty years before, held at gunpoint by a deranged coward, who had then shot himself while she watched, trussed and helpless. She had seemed to bounce back afterwards, which was one of the things Sam had loved about her, but she'd lost her confidence, and the nightmares went on for years. When the first stroke happened, she had faded very quickly; the second had left her more dead than alive. He kept a picture in his wallet of Judith as a young woman and looked at it as he thought of her: the red hair she'd inherited from her mother Maggie, pale skin, bold eyes. In the picture she was laughing, and that's how he tried to remember her.

Sam put the picture away and started the car, forcing himself to think about the day ahead, not the long-dead past. The recovery of the body from Wastwater the day before had led to the immediate formation of a dedicated investigation team, and he wanted to see how DI Bell would get the job started, now that the pathologist had finished the post-mortem. With any luck, Bell would slip into the sloppy working methods Sam knew he was prone to, and there would be yet more pressing reasons to persuade the man to take early retirement. It was nearly thirty years since the legislation that tried to clean up policing, but still some of the old guard were clinging on. Bell was a good copper in some ways, but his archaic attitudes and corner-cutting habits could easily derail a prosecution.

The drive to CID HQ in Workington was so familiar that Sam's car almost got there unaided. He and Judith had moved north to Parton from St Bees many years before, to put some distance between Judith and her mother, and to be nearer to her work, and now Sam was reluctant to move again, even though the house they'd bought when they married was too big for a man on his own. They'd wanted room for children, but the children never came, and the spare rooms with their closed doors reminded him of that sadness until Judith's illness had blotted out one regret and replaced it with another. He wished they'd worked less hard and had more time for each other. He still missed her, every day.

The car park at Hall Brow was full and Sam was grateful for the space reserved for the DCI, one of the most useful perks of the job. He recognised Maureen Pritchard's smart Audi in its usual spot. Funny how some people cared passionately about their cars, while for others they were just a means of getting around. Maureen's car was always spotless, changed for a new model every two years. She'd been with the team for a while, but Sam knew how angry she'd been that DS Penrose had been appointed over her head, as Maureen put it. Her imminent return to the Drug Squad was no surprise to him. Their gain, our loss, Sam thought.

He was less sure about Penrose: she was bright enough, ambitious, capable, but lacked any real feel for the area, and that counted for more here than it might have done in other parts of the country. West Cumbria was special, and Penrose didn't understand that specialness. It would take time and a willingness to open herself up, which he hadn't seen much of from her, so far. DS Penrose was still very self-contained, prickly even, and her working with Bell didn't help the situation.

When DCI Tognarelli entered the briefing room, Bell had just started the meeting. It was the usual scene: people standing or sitting around the open space, arms folded, waiting to be called on to make a contribution, or else scribbling notes about the work to come. On one wall was a large space where details of the investigation would be posted up as they came in. For now, there wasn't much on it.

Bell stopped what he was saying and looked across at Sam. One or two of the seated people started to get to their feet, as if Sam were royalty. He gestured to Bell to carry on and stood by the door, listening. After the calamitous investigation surrounding a previous submerged body, found in Buttermere, he was hoping they would do a better job this time. Bell asked Penrose to explain the results of the post-mortem, and Sam was pleased to see that she was taking a central role in the early stages.

Anna stepped towards the front of the room where Bell was standing, beside the noticeboard. She was holding a sheaf of notes.

She nodded towards Bell, and Sam too, before she began to speak.

'The body was recovered from the south-western end of Wast-water at eight-forty-five yesterday morning, close to the spot indicated by the amateur diver, who'd reported seeing a bundle on a ledge about ten metres below the surface. Forensics did a preliminary examination on site, but it was decided to preserve the integrity of the wrappings until they could be removed in a controlled environment. The bundle was then examined by Professor Henshaw, Home Office pathologist from Lancaster, and the post-mortem was conducted.'

She paused and looked up from her notes. Go on, Anna, Sam thought to himself. You're doing fine, just keep going. No one spoke, and Anna looked back at her notes.

'Professor Henshaw's first finding was that the body had been preserved by an unusual process called adipocere.'

'Addy who?' Bell said. Sam groaned to himself. As the senior investigating officer, Bell shouldn't be the one trying to make jokes.

Anna took no notice of the interruption and kept her eyes on her notes. 'It's sometimes called "mortuary wax", and occurs when a body is kept in an environment that is damp but deprived of oxygen. In this case, the body had been folded over at the waist and then wrapped so tightly that air couldn't penetrate the wrapping. The body's own fats then caused a kind of mummification.' She looked up, expecting questions. 'It makes identification easier because some of the features are preserved, but it's harder to pin down how long exactly since death occurred.'

'So we know what this person looked like? That's a bonus.'

Maureen spoke from her desk at the far side of the room. Sam was pleased that she was obviously interested, even in the last few days of her assignment to the team.

'Yes, the face was well preserved,' said Anna. She took a photograph out of her file and turned to pin it up on the noticeboard behind her. As she stepped back, Sam peered across, but he was too far away and the room was too dark for him to see the image properly.

Anna went on. 'Professor Henshaw examined the body. His report indicates that the man was probably in his seventies, with a weak heart and some pre-existing kidney problems. These would probably have killed him in the end, but the immediate cause of death was severe dehydration.' She looked up again, but still no questions. 'There were some signs of physical violence on the face, and restraint marks on the wrists and ankles. The pathologist's conclusion is that the man had been attacked and then restrained, or else physically abused while restrained. He had been deprived of fluid for some time, but death had resulted from organ failure, and occurred earlier than might have been the case in a healthier person.'

She stopped and looked up. 'Thanks, Anna,' said Bell. 'Any thoughts or questions, anyone, before we get on to the Forensics?'

'We're sure he was dead before he was dumped in the lake?' Sam heard the accent and was pleased to see the newcomer speaking up, even though he was on probation with CID. Anna responded quite formally.

'Yes, DC Brown. No sign of suffocation or drowning.'

Another new voice spoke up. 'Is there any estimate as to how long the body had been there?' Jason Quigley. His voice was strong for such a small man, Sam thought. No trace of an accent either, although he was local. Sam wondered where he'd gone to school.

Anna said, 'Apparently, once this process happens, the mummification can last for many years, but it takes a while to develop. Professor Henshaw reckons at least several months, but he can't be more precise than that at present. We might know more when the test results are complete.'

Bell intervened. 'Who's been checking the misper file?'

Quigley raised his hand. 'Me, sir. I checked for men in their seventies reported missing over the past five years, just for a start. It's quite a long list. I was surprised.'

Sam asked, 'Was this the Cumbria database, or the national?'

Jason Quigley looked nervous. 'National. I reckoned someone could have come to the area from anywhere.'

'Stick to Cumbria. How many there?'

Jason looked at his notes. 'Over the past five years, four men aged sixty and over are missing and unaccounted for, sir.'

'We'll come back to that,' said Bell. 'Is Wong here?'

'Here, sir,' said Tony. He'd been sitting at the back of the room, keeping his head down.

Bell asked him, 'Before we get back to the ID, anything useful from the materials the body was wrapped in?' Tony got to his feet.

'Up 'ere, lad,' said Bell, 'so we can all hear you.'

Tony worked his way forward and began to read from his notes. 'Outer wrapping was heavy black plastic that you could find in any DIY place or builders' suppliers. Nothing distinctive about the cut edges, but it might be possible to match with another piece of the material that this was cut from. Several metres of plastic were used to wrap the body. Underneath was a blanket or covering of some kind, synthetic not wool, which probably helped the preservation. Nothing unusual about it, but again it could be matched by the characteristics of the fibres.'

Sam asked, 'Anything to indicate where the wrapping of the body might have taken place?'

'Ah, well,' said Tony, grateful for this question. 'That's more promising. Sand grains found in the wrapping will be helpful there. Early examination shows this is sand from a saltwater environment, with traces of haematite more commonly found along the west coast of the county, down to the Furness peninsular.

The rope also shows traces of saltwater, as well as the freshwater of the lake.'

'Weighting?' asked Henny Brown.

'Four big boulders that also indicate a seashore setting. And something else too.' Tony looked towards the back of the room. 'DC Pritchard, could you pass over the item on the desk where I was sitting? It's in a large brown evidence bag.'

Maureen reached for the bag and had to lean forward to lift it. 'Let me,' said Brown, taking the bag from her and walking over to Tony with it. He reached in and pulled out something that looked like a large bullet. 'There were fishing weights,' he said, holding up an example, 'ten of them, worked into the folds of the blanket. Each weighs a couple of hundred grams. Those plus the boulders would be enough to sink the bundle, but it snagged on a rock ledge ten metres down and stuck there. Not much movement in the water to dislodge it. The weights themselves are common, but only in the same kind of marine environment that the boulders and the sand came from.'

'Would the weights on their own have been heavy enough to submerge the body?' Brown asked.

Tony shook his head. 'Don't know why he bothered with them. Another boulder would have done the job properly.'

'Doesn't sound very well organised,' Brown went on. 'Maybe done in a panic.'

'OK, Wong,' said Bell. 'That information narrows it down nicely. We'll need to focus on the coast, and where people are fishing, probably commercially.'

Tony stepped back as Sam turned around to the light switches behind him and flicked them all on, flooding the crowded space with a white fluorescent gleam. 'Now let's have a better look at the victim,' he said.

They all turned towards the photograph and Sam took his glasses from his pocket to get a better view of it. The details clicked into focus. He put his head on one side, then took a few steps closer. There was something very familiar about that dead face.

'Excuse me,' he said, pushing past Bell and walking towards the wall, until he was standing looking closely at the photograph.

Suddenly it came to him, like a blow to the stomach. He could picture the dark book-lined room, hear the petulant voice. Sam turned around and took off his glasses.

'I know this man,' he said. 'Thirty years ago, I interviewed him in connection with the death of a child in a boys' home. He was on the Board of the home and had oversight of the health of the children there. His name is Dr John Graham, from Broughton-in-Furness, near Ulverston.'

'Bloody 'ell,' said Bell. He called across to Quigley, 'OK, computer man, look it up for us.'

'No need,' said Sam. 'I remember most of the details.' He cleared his throat, noticing that his mouth felt dry. 'It was nineteen sixty-nine,' he began. 'A boy called Steven Stringer was found drowned in quicksand, near the coast road between Barrow and Ulverston. Just eleven years old. Turned out he was from a boys' home: Montgomery House at Attercliff. Dr Graham was one of the trustees of the home, which was a run by a chap called Captain Edwards. We believed that the boy's death wasn't an accident, and I interviewed Dr Graham as part of our investigation.'

He stopped talking, memories crowding into his mind. The CID room was quiet, all eyes on him. 'I was a young DC then. I should have done more.' He hesitated. 'We should all have done more.' He struggled to find the right words to explain why they'd failed, but it was too complicated, too painful.

Sam straightened his back and looked around the room. 'Some of you will remember my wife Judith,' he said. No one spoke. 'She was a young reporter at the time, on the *Furness News*. She and I worked on the case together for a while, and then again a couple of years later.' He hesitated, feeling a lump in his throat. 'There were... difficulties with the inquiry. I left the force for a while, moved up here, then rejoined CID.'

An image of his wife suddenly appeared to him then, as he had first seen her, looking out over Morecambe Bay in 1969: long strands of red curling hair had strayed across her face, green eyes challenging him. He looked down, felt for a handkerchief in his pocket and blew his nose.

The room was tense and silent, watching. One of the newcomers spoke. 'Sir,' said Brown, 'are you saying that a thirty-year-old case has something to do with this man being in the lake?'

'It was a long time ago. No charges were brought against Dr Graham at the time. Obviously, we need to keep an open mind about any possible connection to the old case.'

Jason Quigley said, 'Sir, there was a John Graham on the misper list I found. Reported missing by his son in April 1999, never found.'

Sam nodded, as if this confirmed what he had seen. He urgently wanted to get out of the room, away from their curious stares, to shake off the regret and confusion that fogged his mind. 'DI Bell, I'll leave this to you for now, OK? Plenty for you to be getting on with, and I'll make my preliminary report to the Super. Get in touch if you need further information, but everything about Montgomery House is on file, I'm sure. Carry on.'

He turned and left the room, closing the door quietly behind him.

Bell stood up and clapped his hands. 'All right, you lot. You heard the DCI. Plenty to do. Quigley, you're on everything we can find about that case the DCI mentioned. Wong, we want more information on the rope, the blanket, anything to locate where this man had been attacked, held, whatever happened to him. Penrose, Brown, check next-of-kin, neighbours, and how the body got into the lake. We need to know when the bloke went missing, what avenues were explored at that time. He was posh by the sound of it, not some loser no one cared about. Let's get on with it.'

Bell retreated to his office and a hum of activity began in the room. Anna was on her computer when DC Brown loomed beside her desk. 'Sit down,' she said, pulling up a chair. 'I get a crick in my neck looking up at you.'

He laughed. 'Celia says that all the time. Sorry.' He sat down and leaned towards her. 'What's the story with the DCI's wife? He looked pretty upset when he was talking about her.'

Anna hesitated. She wasn't sure how to put this and lowered her voice. 'I only know what people have told me. Bell's been around the longest, but he and Sam have never been close. All I know is that Sam's wife was quite a high flyer, editor of one of the local papers, before she got ill. Stroke, I think. When she was really bad, he took time out to look after her, months off the job before she died.'

'No family?' Brown asked.

'No kids, apparently. I think Sam has a sister somewhere, but there was no one else to look after Judith, and he wouldn't put her in a home.' She lowered her voice to a whisper. 'Bell was really pissed off about the DCI being off work. In the pub one night, he started going on about "people who put family ahead of the job", as if that was the wrong thing to do. I reckoned he was talking about Tognarelli.'

'Family comes first for me,' said Brown. 'It's the most important thing to my people. *Whanau*, we call it, not just Mum and Dad and the kids, but the whole extended family – aunties, cousins, grandparents. Can be dozens of people, all interconnected, supporting each other. You don't just dump a sick person in a home, you take care of them.'

'Sam's a good bloke,' Anna whispered. 'But I'm not sure his heart's in the job anymore. He must have enough years' service to retire. I just wonder how much longer he'll stay.'

Henny gestured towards Bell's office. 'He's next in line, right?'

Anna nodded, but realised she might have said too much to the newcomer. 'We need to get on,' she said. 'You heard none of this from me, right?'

'Right,' said Brown.

'Penrose! Get in 'ere.' Bell's voice vibrated out of the open door of his office and jarred in Anna's ears. She got to her feet. 'Oh, God, what now?' she said to herself, and tapped unnecessarily on the doorframe. 'Sir?'

'Come in and close the door,' said Bell. She entered warily, unsure what was bugging the boss, although clearly something was.

'What did you make of all that?' he asked, leaning back in his chair.

'All what, sir?'

'All that stuff about our revered boss and his saintly wife chasing pervs together thirty years ago.'

'You mean, what the DCI said about the boys' home linked to our body? You reckon it was a sexual abuse case?'

'Abuse of some kind, most likely. Happening all the time, then and now. Some blokes can't keep their hands off little boys – dirty buggers! And anyway,' Bell continued, 'how could Nelly remember a face so quickly from so long ago? Even if this Graham bloke has gone missing, that doesn't prove our body is 'im, does it? He could be anywhere, run off with one of his patients for all we know. Even Nelly's memory might play tricks. I don't buy it, not as the only ID.'

'Why didn't you say anything then?' asked Anna.

'He's the DCI, isn't he? Can't challenge him in front of the whole team.

'And what was all that about him leaving the force and coming back? I 'eard he had a rough time as a young copper in Barrow, but that stuff was news to me.'

That's why he's annoyed, Anna thought. Bell likes to know everything in advance. He doesn't like surprises. 'The DCI's obviously kept this case quiet,' she said out loud. 'It was the first I'd heard of it too.'

'Well, people wouldn't tell *you* things like that, would they?' said Bell. 'But I should know about it. And now he's telling us that our body is this bloke Graham, but that's only *his* view. Not enough to build a case on.'

'What do you want me to do?' Anna asked.

'Get the Boy Wonder on to it. We need photos of this Graham bloke, recent enough to match to the body in the morgue. And we could do with some DNA too, just to make sure. Can't afford to take this for granted, whatever Nelly tells us. And hurry it up. We need to know who this bloke really is, pronto.'

'Yes, sir,' Anna responded, turning to leave.

'And shut the door,' said Bell. 'I've got some calls to make.'

Anna went to Jason's desk. 'We need some recent photos of this Dr Graham that the DCI mentioned. Bell wants more proof of ID before we start digging. Search for stuff about the Montgomery House boys' home too – near Attercliff, wasn't it? Tognarelli said Graham was one of the trustees, something to do with the management of the place. If you can't find anything on the computer, go down to the archives and check out the local press for – what year was it?'

'Nineteen sixty-nine,' Jason replied, without looking at his notes. 'Ten years before I was born.'

It didn't take long. Within an hour he was back at Anna's desk. 'I checked with the collator in Barrow,' he said. 'There's a lot of stuff in their files linked to this boys' home. Took him a while to find anything on Dr Graham, but there are some photos and he's faxing the best ones over, although he says they're quite old. No prints for a John Graham on file, but he wouldn't have a police record, would he, being a doctor?'

Anna raised an eyebrow. 'Don't be fooled by the title, Jason,' she said. 'All sorts of people do all sorts of things. If there was something going on at that boys' home, how do we know he wasn't involved?'

Jason stared. 'Involved in... fiddling with little boys?'

'If that's what was happening there, yes. Look at all the rumours about that MP in Rochdale.'

Jason's mouth was open in disbelief. 'I'll check the fax machine,' he said.

It was a while before the expected photos arrived, and Anna took them straight through to Bell. Together they peered at the blurry images. 'I hate faxes,' said Bell. 'Never give you a clear image. Look at this one, must be from donkey's years ago. Is there a date on it?'

Anna looked carefully at the picture. 'There, on that poster, at the side,' she pointed out. 'It says, "Barrow Tennis Club fixtures, nineteen seventy". And the man standing with the trophy does look like the body we've got. The caption says, "Men's singles winner, Dr J. Graham, Broughton".'

Bell sniffed. 'One of the anyone-for-tennis brigade. That figures. Pretty thin start to a murder investigation, an ID from decades ago and a thirty-year-old photo. We need more than this.'

Anna went back to Jason. 'We need something more recent,' she said.

He shook his head. 'Nothing so far. I asked the chap to keep looking.'

Bell appeared at her shoulder, peering down at Jason's screen. 'Can't you find anything else, lad? We could be off on a wild goose chase if we're not careful.'

Anna said quietly. 'What are you going to say to the DCI about this?'

'Nowt, not yet,' said Bell. 'And you won't either, right?' He pulled Anna to one side and looked around, making sure they weren't being overheard. 'Look, you saw how he welled up, talking about that case. If this bloke in the morgue is Dr Graham, then Nelly's too wrapped up in it to be objective. Means too much to him. He won't take himself off the case, so we'll just have to work around him, for now at least.'

Anna went back to her desk. Sometimes it felt like office politics affected police matters far more than they should, and if she wasn't careful she'd end up trapped in the middle.

CHAPTER 5

Henny Brown stopped by Anna's desk. 'Whoever the body actually is, someone put him in the lake, right? And we know they must have used a boat, as there's no access to the spot where the body must have gone in, on the far side, away from the road.'

Anna nodded.

'So why don't I go and check for boats on the lake – Wastwater? It doesn't look like a place where they have them for hire, like they do at Coniston and Windermere. Either whoever dumped the body brought a boat with them, or they got hold of one some other way – most probably nearby. Worth a look? I know the way up there now.'

He was right, she thought. Properly identifying the body would have to happen, but this was a separate way in to the investigation.

'Bell's put me on confirming the ID,' she said. 'Could you handle this on your own?'

'Piece of cake. I've got a map, and I can always ask the locals.' He grinned. 'I'll see you later. Thanks, Sarge.'

Brown was delighted to have made a suggestion that took him out of the office for a while: the tension in the place was getting to him. Bell seemed to be at the bottom of it all. Some people thrive on drama, he thought, and being the centre of attention.

He'd met senior officers like that before in uniform, constantly playing power games, setting the whole place on edge. The best thing was to get on with the job and keep out of their way.

When Wastwater came into view Henny stopped the car, as he'd done the first time. The day was sunny and almost windless. On the screes across the lake patches of grass and bracken showed green and brown; the rock itself had a pinkish hue. Chevron stripes of these colours were picked up in reflections on the water that appeared and disappeared, as ruffles of breeze came and went. He parked the car where the dive team had stopped, got out and looked around. To his right, the road wound along the lakeshore towards the coast.

Henny opened up the Ordnance Survey map and spread it over the warm bonnet of the car. The map was of the south-west quadrant of the Lake District, which gave him a detailed look at the road from Gosforth and the spot where he was parked. Now he could see the packed contour lines of the screes. The mass of Scafell rose beyond them to the north-east. There was another mountain at the northern end of the lake. He checked. Great Gable was the name, taken he assumed from its triangular shape, on the top of which a wisp of cloud was clinging.

One place on the map that indicated habitation was at the top of the valley, beyond the end of the lake, and he turned the car to follow the road in that direction. Soon he could see a large white building ahead of him, with the word 'Inn' painted large on the facing wall. He parked in front of the granite-clad building and pushed open the door into a dark porch lined with wood panelling. A young man appeared from a door behind the reception area.

'Can I help you?' he said. The accent was definitely not Cumbrian.

Brown brought out his warrant card and introduced himself. 'Is it possible to hire a boat anywhere on the lake?' he asked.

The young man smiled. 'A boat? For fishing maybe?'

Brown nodded. 'Yes, maybe. I didn't see any as I drove up, but...'

The young man had already turned away to open the door behind him. 'Bob,' he called. 'There's a policeman here, asking about a boat.'

Another man, older, dressed in a blue boiler suit, stuck his head round the door. 'A boat?'

'Look,' said Brown, 'we need to know where someone who needed a boat round here might get one from.'

'What for?' said the man.

'For any reason,' said Brown. He certainly didn't want to start talking about bodies at this stage. 'A small motorboat, or a rowing boat.'

The man shook his head. 'Not up here,' he said. 'But there's a boathouse at the other end of the lake, near where the river runs out. No idea whether there's a boat in it, mind you. Don't even know who it belongs to, but the Youth Hostel people might know. That's the big place, down by the lakeside. Can't miss it. Far end, past the road to Gosforth. The drive goes down to the left.'

The Youth Hostel looked deserted, but Brown could hear noises round the back of the building and followed them.

'The boathouse?' said the young woman busy packing laundry bags into a van. 'Doesn't belong to us. Could be the big house further down the road. Never been down to the lake myself. Why would you?'

Why wouldn't you? Henny thought to himself. He was always amazed that people who lived in beautiful places often didn't appreciate what surrounded them.

A few hundred yards further down the road a very fancy set of wrought-iron gates barred a driveway that wound down through shrubberies towards the lakeshore. The sign on the gate read 'Holme Hall'. Brown rang the bell in the gatepost and waited. A voice squawked, 'Yes?'

'DC Brown, Workington CID, I'd like a word about the boathouse.'

There was a pause before the gates swung open.

The house was large and imposing, made of slate and granite in the same style as the Youth Hostel and the inn, but with signs of expensive renovations. Scaffolding was still standing at one end of the building. A smartly dressed woman stood at the open front door, watching while Brown got out of the car and walked across, his boots crunching on the slate chippings.

'DC Brown?' she asked, without a smile. Henny got out his warrant card, which she took from him and inspected with care, squinting up at him. 'Not from round here, are you?'

'New Zealand originally, ma'am,' he said, judging that this woman would expect the utmost politeness.

'Ah, yes,' she said. 'I'm Madeline Jeffers.' She stretched out her hand, which Brown shook respectfully. 'Now, what's all this about the boathouse?'

Clearly she was not about to invite him into the house and Henny decided to go along with it, for the time being at least. He adopted his most formal tone of voice. 'We are investigating a possible crime at this end of the lake and have reason to believe that a boat of some kind would have been needed.'

'What kind of crime?' she said sharply, as if he had accused her of involvement in it.

'I'm not at liberty to disclose that at present, ma'am. Do you own the boathouse down where the lake meets the river?'

'Yes, it belongs to the house.'

'And is a boat kept there?'

'It used to be, but no longer. We have no interest in keeping a boat.'

'We?'

'My husband and I. He's away at present, in London.' She looked sceptically at him. 'I really need to know what this is all about.'

Brown hesitated, not sure how much he should reveal. He smiled his best smile. 'Do you think we could go in the house, Mrs Jeffers, and I'll explain some of the details?'

To his surprise, the woman smiled back at him and put up a hand to tuck a strand of hair behind her ear. Then she turned into the open doorway and walked ahead of him to a large light room at the back of the house. Beyond the long windows a lawn sloped down to the edge of the lake. He stood for a moment, staring out at the colours and the sunlight on the water. 'What a wonderful spot,' he said.

She stood beside him. 'Yes, we love it. I just wish we'd lived here when the children were small, instead of in the city. But what with work, and schools, you know how it is. Living here wasn't really an option then.' She turned towards him. 'So what's this about, officer? A crime, you said?'

'Yes, ma'am. We have reason to believe that something has been dumped in the lake, and that a boat was used.'

'What kind of something? Not another lady in the lake case, surely?'

'I can't say, but we do need to know whether a boat might have been used. I'm sorry, I can't say more than that.'

Madeline Jeffers shrugged. 'Very well.'

Brown went on. 'So, I guess the boathouse is beyond those trees,' he said. 'Can you reach it from the house?'

'Yes, it's on the path that runs around this end of the lake. The public footpath starts a bit further down the road. Anyone could walk down there.'

Brown made a note. 'You said there was a boat kept there before you arrived?'

'Yes, it was there when we moved in. Must have been left by the previous owners… we were surprised to find it. But it was pretty old and rickety, and we never used it.'

'When was that?'

'We moved here three years ago.'

'And what did you do with it?'

'We gave it away, last year. One of my husband's cousins runs a Scout troop in the Midlands. They come up here to camp and so on, and when we asked if they wanted the boat, they were happy to take it.'

'Last year, you said?' Brown was making notes, although he suspected he could be wasting his time.

'Yes, in the spring.'

'And do you have the name of the people who took it away?'

'One moment,' she said. 'I'll get it for you.'

She was away a few minutes and Henny had time to look out of the windows again, at the dark lake to his left and the top of the screes. What a place this was.

'Here we are,' said the crisp voice, and Mrs Jeffers held out a piece of headed notepaper with a name and number written on it. 'The Scout master is my husband's cousin, here are his details.'

'That's very useful, thank you,' Brown said. 'And if I might ask, do you remember anything unusual taking place on the lake in the years you've been in the house, especially while the boat was still here?'

Mrs Jeffers looked thoughtful. 'Not offhand, no. And you can't tell me what your investigation is about?'

'No, ma'am. But thank you for your help. If anything does occur to you, here's my card. Please call me. I'll go and have a look at the boathouse now, if I may?'

'Certainly,' she said, 'and I'll show you the way, officer.'

'I'd prefer to go alone, if you don't mind,' he said. 'I'll take the public footpath you mentioned.' It was highly unlikely that anyone with a body to dispose of would have taken the risk of approaching the house. A flicker of disappointment appeared on Mrs Jeffers' face, but she led him back to the front door without further comment, and shook his hand as he left. She's lonely, Henny thought, as he drove back down the drive.

A hundred yards or so further down the road was a gate and a public footpath sign. Brown parked the car in a lay-by and walked back. The gate wasn't locked. The footpath was wide and sloped gently down the hill before turning into the woods that skirted the river and led towards the end of the lake. Brown took some pictures with the small camera he'd brought with him. There was no chance of driving down here, he thought, but using a wheelbarrow would be easy. It would be conspicuous, but who else would be down here in the early hours of the morning?

Five minutes' walk down the path he spotted the small stone boathouse to his right behind a clump of bushes and walked towards it. The door was locked but the lock looked quite new. There was also a bolt that had clearly been in place for some time. On the far side of the boathouse was a small window, green with dirt. Henny rubbed a gap big enough to peer through, using his torch to illuminate the dark interior. It was empty. If there had been a boat in there, he thought, it wouldn't be difficult for someone to access it, but it must have been someone who knew the area well.

The far end of the boathouse had access to an enclosed stretch of water, with a narrow passage into the main body of the lake. If the lake was high and the water flowing fast out of it, it might take more than one person to manage a laden boat up towards the deep area below the screes. Two people, he thought. If this was so, the case suddenly seemed more complicated.

Driving back to the office, Brown had a satisfying feeling of a morning well spent. He'd taken the initiative and suggested that the boat would be worth investigating, and felt he was right. He was used to being part of a team, but if the team didn't gel he was happier on his own, and that's how it felt right now.

Back in the office, Anna and Jason were still trying to get a recent photo of John Graham to allay Bell's doubts about the DCI's ID, but to no avail. Anna was clearly frustrated, and ready to be distracted by Brown's report of his findings.

'I think we need to track down this boat, if we can,' he said. 'As far as I can see, it was the only boat that could have been found at the lake. Otherwise whoever had the body would have needed to bring a boat with them and to launch it somewhere close to the road. That's a much more public space. The boathouse is hidden away, but still accessible to anyone who comes down that path to the lake.'

'OK,' said Anna. 'Let's contact the people who took the Jeffers' boat and see whether it's still around. It's a long time ago now, but there might still be some physical traces if it was used to transport our big bundle. But before you do that, I need to fill you in. Sit down a minute.'

Henny pulled a chair across and sat down. Anna flicked through her notes. 'While you were out, Jason and I dug around in the misper file and located Graham's next-of-kin, a son, who lives in Lancaster. Neill Graham, he's a doctor too. Barrow police handled the case, and apparently the son complained that they hadn't done enough, let the trail go cold. I called the DI in Barrow who handled it and he says there was some talk of debts, or a scandal, either of which could have prompted the doctor to take himself off, although the son said that was just village gossip. The police found nothing, no bank account movements, no car, no note, nothing. If the doc did want to disappear, he did a good job. Anyway, they're sending the file over, and I called the son at the number we have.'

'Good stuff,' said Brown. 'Does Bell know?'

'He's been out most of the morning. All he wants to find out is whether this body is really Dr Graham. In fact, between you and me, he thinks that the DCI could be chasing old shadows. Those two have history, as you've probably realised. I reckon we should just get on with it and secure the ID before we start building a case on straw.'

'So what now?'

'Get your jacket on again,' said Anna. 'We're going to meet the son at the doctor's house in Broughton. Neill Graham looks after the place. He can't assume his dad's dead, even after all this time.' She glanced at her watch. 'By the time we get there and talk to him we'll be late back. That OK with you?'

'I'll call Celia. She knows how much this job means to me. It'll be fine.' Henny smiled. 'It's been a good day so far,' he said. 'And I reckon it's going to get better.'

Anna's ankle felt so much easier that she offered to drive to Broughton, just over an hour away, down the coast to the very edge of the Lake District and then east up the Whicham Valley.

'So what do you want me to do about the boat?' Brown asked as they drove, wondering if Anna had forgotten what he'd told her earlier.

'Oh, yes, the boat. Where is it now?' she asked.

'Well, it's a year or more since it was moved.' He fished in his pocket for the paper Mrs Jeffers had given him. 'The bloke who took it lives in the Midlands, apparently, but his Scout troop camps here.'

'When we get back, call that number and check it out. It'll keep till tomorrow. First priority is to get this ID sorted.'

Brown said no more. He had to remember that he was on probation, and Anna was his boss.

Dr Graham's old house was on the edge of the small town, set back from the road. All the curtains were drawn, making the place look abandoned and lifeless. There was no car on the gravelled drive at the front.

'The son must be on his way,' said Anna. She checked her phone but there was no signal. Nothing to do but wait. 'Go and have a look round Broughton,' she said to Henny. 'You won't see anything in New Zealand like this place. It's had a town charter for hundreds of years. The square is just down there,' she said, pointing to their left. 'Such a small place, you can see how gossip would thrive once someone started it off.'

Before Brown could get out of the car, another vehicle pulled into the drive. It was large and black and much more shiny than Anna's tattered Land Rover. 'Too late,' she said. 'He's here.'

A tall man emerged from the driver's side of the black car and watched as Anna and Brown walked towards him. He put out a gloved hand. 'Neill Graham, John's son. Thanks for coming. It's been months since anyone took any interest in my father's case. Those idiots in Barrow seemed to find one reason after another to say there was nothing more they could do.' He paused. 'Sorry, you can't comment on fellow officers, I'm sure. But I have to say, I'm glad you're from a different area.'

Neill Graham took a bunch of keys from his pocket and went up the three steps to the impressively large front door. 'We don't visit the house much,' he said, unlocking it. 'A neighbour comes in to check the place every now and then, but we've not been here since August.'

They followed him into the dark hall.

'Not sure what you're looking for,' he said. 'The police went all through the place when Dad disappeared. They looked at bank statements and such like, but nothing ever seemed to help. I still can't believe he would just leave without a word to us, even if he did want to get away. Come in the lounge, I'll open the curtains.'

Anna and Henny sat carefully on the large sofa, but Neill stood by the mantelpiece, looking down at them.

'Did he want to get away?' Anna asked.

Neill shrugged. 'I don't know, really. He hadn't been himself for a few weeks, seemed anxious. He was usually pretty relaxed about security, leaving doors unlocked and such. This is a very safe place. But then he started locking up all the time, even when he was in the house. I asked him about it and he said he was being careful, but never said why. I should have asked him more about it, but we try not to pry. He's an independent man, always has been. That's why I wasn't worried when he didn't pick up the phone for a few days. He had friends all over the place, didn't have to ask permission if he wanted to go off somewhere.'

'So when did you start to worry?' Anna asked. Brown sat quietly beside her, making notes. Neill Graham had obviously been asked this before and answered quickly.

'It was early April, nineteen ninety-nine. We were coming up to stay in a week or so, me and the family, for the second half of the Easter holiday, like we always did, and I'd talked about it with Dad a number of times. When it got to a day or two before, and he still wasn't answering the phone, I called Mrs Tyson, who lives in the square and used to be Dad's housekeeper when he was working. She said she hadn't seen him for over a week, and he'd not mentioned that he was going anywhere. The car was gone, but he usually shut the scullery window if he was going away. I asked her to check and it was open. I called his friends. No one had seen or heard from him, and that's when I decided to call the police.'

Neill Graham shook his head. 'Right from the start,' he said, 'I got the feeling that they really didn't care.' He looked hard at Anna. 'So why are you here, why now, after all this time?'

She hesitated. 'A body has been recovered. We have reason to believe it might be your father's.'

Dr Graham stood up straight, as if called to attention. 'What "reason to believe"? What do you mean?'

'One of our officers thinks that he recognised the face, but we don't have a definite identification, as yet. Would you be able to come with us and provide one?'

Neill Graham looked puzzled. 'But it's been over two years. Surely, after all this time...'

'The body is unusually well preserved,' said Anna. 'Our Forensics people can explain. We can drive you up to Workington, if you're free to come with us now. Or else at your earliest convenience.'

Graham breathed out and shook his head. 'This is a shock, you understand. Give me a minute.'

They waited. He said, 'I need to know, obviously, but I have to check in at home. They're expecting me back.'

'Of course,' said Anna.

It didn't take long for him to agree to accompany them. Neill Graham drove his own car, following as they took him first to the CID office and then to the mortuary. The remains were partially uncovered. He looked carefully at the waxy face, put a hand to his mouth. 'It's him,' he whispered. 'That's my father, John Graham.'

Chapter 6

It was nearly seven when Anna got back home, and the phone was ringing as she walked into the house. It was Simon. Her stomach lurched. She'd been hoping he would ring, and now he had.

'You're just home?' he said, when she explained why the phone had rung for so long. 'That's a long day, you must be exhausted.'

She sighed. 'I am. And my ankle's throbbing. I drove down to Broughton and back, probably wasn't the best idea.'

'Why Broughton?' he asked.

'Just a case,' she said. 'Can't discuss it, sorry.'

'No, of course. None of my business. But making you feel better *is* my business. How about I come over and make you dinner, or else bring something in?'

She hesitated. It was couched as a suggestion but felt like an instruction. For a moment she struggled: part of her felt railroaded, but part of her was delighted to have a decision made for her at the end of a long day. The passive part won. 'You know,' she said, 'that's the best idea I've heard all day. Bring something in, Chinese or fish and chips, anything you like. I'll do my bit and warm the plates.'

While she waited, Anna unpacked two more boxes and piled the remaining ones tidily by the back door, so the kitchen looked less like a warehouse. She showered and changed her clothes too, fervently hoping that the queue in the takeaway place would be long enough that she'd feel more prepared when he arrived. As it turned out, the timing was perfect: when Simon rang the doorbell she was feeling good and was pleased with her surroundings, for the first time in days. Fish and chips were exactly what she needed too, with a bottle of cold white wine that must have come straight from Simon's fridge and tasted more expensive than the plonk she normally drank.

When the plates were empty, Simon cleared the table after insisting that Anna put her bad ankle up on a spare chair. She watched him carefully, wondering. How come he fitted so comfortably into her life? What had happened to his wife, presumably the mother of his children? Was he as well off as he appeared to be?

'Do you mind if we stay here, in the kitchen?' she said, as Simon filled their glasses. 'This is the best room in the house at the moment, until I get the living room sorted out.'

'No problem,' he said. 'It took weeks in our new house before we all felt comfortable.'

'Where do you live?' she asked.

'It's not far away, actually, if you're a crow. By road, you go towards Egremont and then east, towards the hills. There are some lovely villages up there, and we live in one of them, Hilton, in an old Victorian vicarage. Needed a lot of work, but I'm happy with it now. Quiet, big enough for all three of us to have our own space. Quite different from where we lived before, more to my taste.'

'Not like this,' said Anna, aware of the functional box in which she'd chosen to live.

'No, but this is a good space for you, isn't it?'

'I think so. And what about your children? Are they OK living in a quiet village?'

'They're fine,' Simon said. He took a small photograph out of his wallet and held it out for her to see. 'Here they are, looking reasonably cheerful, wouldn't you say?'

Anna looked at the photo of two young people. The girl was tall and very attractive, with long blonde hair and a smile perfected for the camera. 'That's Caroline?' she asked, remembering the name from the last time they'd met.

'It is, and the boy is Rory. He's a couple of years younger.'

He looks much younger, Anna thought, much less confident.

Simon put the photo away. 'Caroline will be twenty-one in the New Year, Rory's eighteen. He wasn't happy at school, and he's not sure yet what he wants to do. Caroline already works in the estate agency with me and I'm hoping Rory will join us. We'll see.'

'They're fine-looking young people,' said Anna.

'Thanks,' he said.

'Do you mind my asking,' she ventured, 'what happened to your wife?'

Simon looked away, towards the window. 'She left us, two years ago. Just walked out.' He looked back towards Anna. 'We haven't heard from her since.'

Anna's police brain buzzed but she quelled the immediate questions that came to mind. 'I'm sorry,' she said.

Simon was still looking out of the window, remembering. 'I came home one day and her car was gone. So was she. I called around her friends, but no one had seen her. I could tell that some of her clothes and personal things were missing, so I thought she must have decided to go away for a few days. We hadn't been getting on, I thought she might have needed a break.'

'But where would she go?'

He shrugged. 'I had no idea.'

Anna leaned forward. 'Simon, did you report her missing?'

He looked at his hands. 'I did,' he said. 'Didn't know what else to do, so I rang the police. They said to check with local hospitals, anybody I could think of where she might have gone. And they said she couldn't be considered as missing until she'd been gone for longer than a day.'

Anna nodded. 'As an adult, that's the norm.' Suddenly she recalled that Jason had included a woman on his misper list, but had said that the name had been removed. 'So did you actually report her missing?'

'Yes, when the forty-eight-hour limit came and went, I called and they put her on the missing persons list, but then something else happened.' He ran his hands down his face and took another long drink of wine. 'We got a letter.'

'From her?'

'Yes, from Wendy. She said she'd gone to live with someone called Clive, in Sunderland of all places. It was bizarre. I'd no idea she'd met someone else. I was shocked.'

'Are you sure the letter was from her?'

'Oh, yes, it was her writing, not an email or anything. Her handwriting, on a sheet of paper, no address, not even a date.'

'Do you still have the letter?'

He shook his head. 'I burned it.'

Anna stretched across the table and put her hand over his. 'I'm so sorry to hear all this. It must have been dreadful for you.'

He frowned. 'I don't think about it much now, but it still hurts.'

'Have you heard anything from her since then?'

'Nothing. I wondered about her money, but a letter came from the bank saying her account had been closed. No other post arrived for her, so I guess she must have had it diverted. Maybe she changed her name. I thought of paying someone to find her, but what's the point? If she wanted to come back, she would have done so by now.'

Anna's professional mind was racing. She knew this was probably not a police matter: people leave relationships all the time and start new lives, without anything sinister having happened. But she was still curious. 'What about the children, how did they react?'

'They've been wonderful,' Simon said, smiling. 'So loyal, so strong.' He paused. 'It's strange, the three of us are more together than we were when she was with us, and I'm not even their father.'

Anna's surprise must have registered on her face.

'I met Wendy when her children were very young,' he explained. 'I knew her father. He's the Lilley in Lilley and Buttler, our company. He founded it and then took me on when I came out of the army. He's died since then, but I kept the name.'

So, you married the boss's daughter, Anna said to herself. And now she's gone. What complicated lives some people lead.

Suddenly Simon got to his feet. 'I'd better go, before I drink too much. Two glasses of wine. I should be OK to drive, shouldn't I, officer?'

'Only just,' said Anna. You could stay, she thought, but that would make life far more complicated. No rush. She now knew he was fit, solvent and unattached, which was all good, so best not blow it by being too eager.

She struggled to get up, putting her bad leg gingerly to the floor. 'Thank you so much,' she said. 'For the supper, and the wine.'

'And the sob story?' he said. 'Sorry. I didn't mean to burden you with all that.' He leaned down and kissed her cheek. 'You're easy to talk to, and I get lonely sometimes.'

She smiled up at him. 'Me too.'

As Anna stretched to open the front door, Simon put both his arms around her and held her very close for a moment. 'It's been lovely,' he said. 'Next time, you come to my house, have dinner with us, meet my kids.' He looked at her. 'Is that OK? Can I call you?'

For a while after he had gone, she sat at the kitchen table finishing the rest of the wine. Khan reappeared from somewhere and jumped onto her lap. 'You missed him,' she said to the cat. 'He's lovely. This could be really good.'

The following morning it didn't take long for the afterglow of the evening to fade. Bell had called an early-morning update meeting just after eight. There was no sign of DCI Tognarelli. Anna reported on Neill Graham's positive ID of his father. Brown gave details of his theory about the boat and the next steps necessary to check its current whereabouts. They were beginning to identify priorities for the coming day, when Maureen Pritchard raised a laugh with a story from the Drug Squad about a flock of sheep that had broken into a cannabis crop at an abandoned farm on the fells near Longtown.

'High as kites, apparently,' she said. 'Someone spotted them charging down the lane, then they spilled out onto the road and butted a man who was trying to herd them into a field. Knocked him down and trampled all over him, poor bugger.'

'You've got stoned sheep,' Bell said, joining in the general merriment, 'and we've got a perv in a pond. Probably serves him right, I say. Dirty old git.'

A voice rose over the general hubbub. It was Tognarelli. He'd been standing unnoticed at the back of the room. Now he walked slowly towards the front where DS Bell was standing. He turned to the group of officers who had quietened down and were looking at him, unsure what to do. 'You've all got work to get on with,' he said. 'Carry on.'

Sam gestured to Bell, and the two of them went into his office and shut the door. Once inside, Sam waited until Bell was standing close to his desk, away from the door. 'Can you explain to me what you just said out there?'

Bell looked puzzled for a moment, then raised his chin. 'I expressed a view that this Dr Graham, whoever he is, probably got what was coming to him.'

'Meaning?' Sam's voice was harsh.

'Meaning, that if he was involved in molesting little boys, well, we shouldn't be wasting too much time on him.'

'DI Bell,' said Sam. 'You can think what you like, but what you said out there was unprofessional and a very bad example to any of our officers, never mind those who've only just joined us.'

'Well, they'll have to get used to it, won't they?' said Bell. 'No room for bleeding hearts in this job.'

Sam waited, but not for long. 'I need you to be very clear on this,' he said. 'The man found in the lake is a victim of crime, not – what did you call him? – the perv in the pond.'

Bell stared at his boss, his face reddening. Sam continued speaking, keeping his voice low. 'You seem to be approaching this case as if it doesn't matter that Dr Graham ended up dying of thirst, trussed up and left to rot. And you're encouraging other officers to take the same line.' He paused, choosing his words with care. 'As of now, I'm taking charge of this case. I've checked with the Super. He insists that you cannot leave the team until the case is sorted out. You will stay here for the time being, but you'll be assigned to other duties as soon as you can be replaced.'

Bell gasped. 'What other duties?'

'The Drug Squad have asked for an additional senior officer. They are investigating something much more serious than stoned sheep, involving hard drugs being brought into our area from abroad. They've asked for someone with local knowledge.'

Bell sat down behind his desk, calculating the implications of what he was hearing. 'Is this a temporary transfer?'

Sam shrugged. 'No decision on that yet. For the time being, you just need to do your job here but I take command as of now.' He looked around the untidy office. 'And get this place tidied up. It's a shambles.'

Bell nodded. 'Yes, sir.'

Sam said no more. He turned and went back into the main room, where he stood for a moment until he was noticed and a hush fell.

'I'd like you all to report back here at two this afternoon,' he said. 'Slight change of direction in this case and I need you all on board. Carry on, everyone.'

As he left the room there was a moment's silence before the noisy speculation began. Five minutes later, Anna answered the phone and heard that she was required by the DCI, in his room, at once.

CHAPTER 7

Anna knocked on Tognarelli's door and waited. She expected to hear him call her in, but instead the door opened and he personally beckoned her into the room and to an armchair by a low table. He sat himself down in the matching armchair opposite. She was discomfited by the informality and perched awkwardly on the edge of the chair, unsure what to do. The room was scrupulously tidy, and the polished desk clear of any papers. A computer sat on a side table. The contrast with Bell's office was stark.

'So,' Tognarelli said, leaning forward, but not looking at her. 'I'm taking over as SIO on this case, and DI Bell will be reassigned to the Drug Squad as soon as he can be spared here. They need another senior officer, but that's not the reason I'm taking charge of the Graham case.'

Anna said nothing.

'You know DI Bell and I have had our disagreements in the past about how to approach the job, but we can live with that. This is a bit different and I want you to understand why I'm concerned about it.'

Anna still stayed silent. She had no idea what the DCI wanted to tell her.

Sam leaned back a little and looked out of the window. Yellow leaves were floating past on the wind. He stroked his chin. 'Now that we've confirmed the identity of the body, one central line of inquiry has to be opened up.'

'You mean Dr Graham's connection with that boys' home you mentioned?'

Sam nodded. 'Yes. Granted, it was a long time ago, but some of the impact of what happened there.... Well, the effects of being in a place like that could last a lifetime.

'If you and I are to work together on this case now, which is what I want, you need to understand something about this background, things I may not share with the whole team. Do you understand?'

Anna nodded.

Sam went on. 'The case was complicated. Some of the investigative work was done by Judith Pharaoh, who later became my wife. We uncovered a network of abuse of the boys. And we also found a conspiracy to cover up what had happened, which included senior police officers and the editor of the local newspaper, who was also Judith's boss. I was a junior officer at that time. I was warned off, told I was sacrificing my career.'

'You mean, you were warned off by a senior officer?'

'Exactly so,' said Tognarelli. 'You might find that hard to understand, DS Penrose, but those were different times. I had no choice but to resign. It was another two years before I decided to rejoin and then in a different team, not back in Barrow.'

Anna looked puzzled. 'What's this got to do with DI Bell?'

Sam looked at his hands. 'I've taken him off this case because I'm not sure I can trust him. Don't get me wrong, he's a good copper in his way, but he has a weakness. We got sight of that today, in the meeting.' He looked directly at Anna for the first time, as if his mind had cleared. 'Actually the problem is twofold. First, Bell is clearly unsympathetic to anyone who could be suspected of, as he would call it, fiddling with little boys. But the other problem is Bell's – what can we call them – "connections?"' Sam used his index fingers to indicate the quotation marks. 'DI Bell, like some other senior officers we could probably name, belongs to an organisation that occasionally undermines his integrity as a police officer.'

'You mean, the Lodge?' she said, beginning to understand what Sam was trying to explain. 'Did that have a bearing on the original conspiracy?'

'Very likely. And old loyalties die hard. DI Bell has been a police officer for a very long time, most of it in this region, but it's highly likely that he knows other officers who were then or are now based in Barrow. West Cumbria is a small world, Anna.' Sam got up. 'I need a coffee, do you want one?'

'No, thanks,' she said. 'May I have some water?'

She watched him as he followed the routine demanded by the Italian coffee machine in one corner of the room.

'So it's this case in particular that you're concerned about?' she asked.

Sam waited before replying, finishing off the coffee production and bringing her a bottle of water from a small fridge. 'As soon as I recognised Graham, I wondered if Bell was the right person to lead this inquiry or if maybe I should do it myself. There are a lot of people still around who worked hard to keep a lid on the Montgomery House business, and some of them will know Bell, one way or another. The Lodge, Rotary, the golf club, the pub… who knows? Maybe I'm being unfair, but I couldn't take that risk, not with this case.' He sipped his coffee. 'You're an outsider, Anna. That can be a problem for you, I know, but it's what this case needs.'

'And I certainly wouldn't be in the Lodge,' she added.

'Obviously.' Sam smiled for the first time. 'Plus I've seen you at work… your energy, your courage.'

Anna could feel her face reddening. She looked down. 'You can count on me, sir.'

'I know that. And one more thing – I want you to keep all this to yourself. As far as the team is concerned, I will take Bell's place as SIO, plain and simple. OK?'

She nodded, 'Of course.'

'Good. Now I want you to tell me more about your meeting with Neill Graham. Did you ask him about how and when his dad went missing?'

'Yes, he seemed to remember the details quite well. He'd obviously been asked about them before.'

'What did he tell you?'

'I think he was trying to justify to himself why he didn't report his father missing earlier, but he said the old man led an independent life, despite his age.'

'Yes,' said Sam. 'Dr Graham was in his mid-forties when I met him, although he seemed older than that to me at the time. The pathologist said there were some underlying health issues, didn't he, but nothing that meant he couldn't look after himself.'

Anna wished she had Henny Brown's notebook or had made more detailed notes herself. She went back over the first conversation with Dr Graham Junior. 'He did say his father had seemed upset about something in the weeks before his disappearance… got a bit paranoid about security. More than was usual for him.'

'Did you follow that up?'

She shook her head. 'The first priority was to confirm the ID.'

Sam smiled. 'Bell didn't believe me, did he?'

'No, he insisted we get confirmation. And…' She hesitated.

'And what?'

'He said you were obviously too close to the case and might need to be kept away from it.'

'That's rich.' Sam stood up. 'So, when we meet the team this afternoon, I'll be suggesting certain lines of inquiry, which I hope make sense to you. If they don't, or if you think I'm going off track because of my history with this case, I expect you to say so, loud and clear.'

She nodded. 'What are you going to tell the team this afternoon?'

'Not as much as I've told you, that's for sure,' he said.

At the meeting later that day, DCI Tognarelli was all business. The change of team leadership was presented, and apparently accepted, as a logical adaptation to changing circumstances. Neither Pritchard nor Bell was present, but Sam didn't comment. Some findings were repeated, at his request, but nothing appeared to have changed significantly, apart from the clear understanding that Dr Graham's past history was now part of the investigation.

When Sam finally left work quite late that evening he felt it had been a good day and was looking forward to getting back to some real policing, rather than the bureaucratic rut he had been stuck in for some time. He wondered what Judith would have made of the return of the case that had brought them together.

As he opened his car's driver's door, someone emerged from another vehicle further down the line. It was Bell. He opened the passenger door of Sam's car and sat down. Sam hesitated for a moment, then got in. They sat, side by side, facing into the dark hedge that surrounded the car park.

'What do want?' Sam asked.

Bell snorted, clearly very angry. 'What do you think I bloody want?' He turned towards Sam. 'How about an apology for showing me up in my own station, in front of my own people?'

Sam shook his head. 'I've done no such thing. I'm taking charge of this case. It happens all the time.'

'Don't give me that shit.' Bell spat his words, making Sam lean away from him. There was a distinct whiff of whisky in the confined space. 'I know what you're up to. Bloody typical, getting rid of me, sneaky like! You've been after me for years, everybody knows that.'

Sam opened the car door. 'Have you been drinking?'

'What if I 'ave? Off duty now, aren't I? Want to breathalyse me too, do you, just to put the lid on it?'

For a moment Sam thought about going back into the station, instructing someone to remove Bell's car keys and call him a taxi to get home. But this time he wasn't going to do the sensible thing. Something in him boiled up and over. He turned towards Bell and poked the snarling man in the shoulder.

'Look,' he said. 'For years I've put up with your sneers and your sloppy habits. I've watched good young coppers come in here and crumble within weeks, ending up careless and cynical, corrupted by you. Do I want you to get out? Yes, no question. When I get the chance, I'll push a bit harder. It won't take much. Drink driving, that should fix it.'

Bell pushed Sam's hand away. 'Don't point your finger at me, you pompous git! Just because you and your precious wife chased a few pervs around Barrow years ago...'

'Don't you dare!' Sam spat back at him. 'Don't you dare mention my wife. You're off the case. Don't even think about getting your fucking Lodge mates to back you up. That doesn't work like it used to, thank God. Now, get out of my car before I come round and pull you out.'

For a moment Bell didn't move. The two men sat facing each other, faces inches apart, the air between them sharp with loathing. Then Bell turned away and got out of the car, slamming the door shut behind him. As he walked away, Sam leaned his forehead on the steering wheel, pleased with what he'd said, but not how he'd said it. Bell had snapped first. Sam had faced him down. He was in charge of the case. Bell would do as he was told or risk the disciplinary action that Sam would take if he had to. For the first time that day he smiled.

CHAPTER 8

'I'm looking for information about DI Harry Grayson, probably retired,' said Sam into the phone. The sergeant in Barrow police station couldn't help and put him through to someone else. 'DS Hattie here,' said a woman's voice. 'Desk Sergeant says you're looking for Harry Grayson. Who's speaking, please?'

'This is DCI Tognarelli, Workington CID,' said Sam. Silence. 'Hello,' he said. 'Are you there?'

'Tognarelli,' the woman repeated. 'Sam Tognarelli?'

'Yes. Who are you?'

'I was Kath Tunnicliffe, sir,' said the woman. 'At Barrow nick when you were there, years ago. I was a WPC, uniform.'

'Good God,' said Sam, remembering. 'You worked for DS Morrison.'

'Deceased,' said Kath Hattie. 'Disgraced, then deceased.' She hesitated. 'No regrets about either of those, from me at least.'

'Nor me,' said Sam. He wanted to hear how WPC Tunnicliffe had become DS Hattie, but stopped himself. 'Kath, I'm looking for Harry Grayson. He could have retired.'

'He has,' said Kath. 'Last year. Did well, got to DCI. He was a good bloke.' She paused. 'Mind me asking what this is about?'

'We found Dr Graham's body in Wastwater. You lot tried to trace him a couple of years ago. Well, now we have.'

'You mean the old chap from Broughton who was mixed up with the Monty House business? Grayson led on the search for him. We never found him, and it really bugged Harry. Hang on, I'll get you his number.'

As he waited, Sam pictured young Harry Grayson in his mind's eye, from when they'd first worked together. Good-looking… ambitious. Too ambitious, Sam had thought for a while, and too keen on Judith.

'Here's his number,' said DS Hattie. 'Near Ulverston, I think. I'm sure he'd be pleased to see you. Old times and all that.' Another pause. 'How long were you off the job, after?' she asked.

'Two years or so,' said Sam. 'It wasn't easy.'

'At least those bastards didn't finish you,' she said.

'No.' There was too much to add, so he didn't. 'Thanks, Kath. All the best.'

Sam rang off. The police have moved on, he thought. And about time too.

In the squad room, he went to talk to DC Brown. The man had promise and Sam wanted to give him a chance to show it. 'Any progress on the boat?'

Brown reached for his notebook. 'I found the man that the Jeffers gave it to, a relation of theirs who runs a Scout troop. They keep it at a campsite, somewhere near Windermere. It's a long shot, but we might find something there. I'm going to have a look at it later today. If it seems promising, I'll get Forensics on to it.'

'Is Wong still with us?' Sam asked.

'He's moving back to Carlisle to live with his dad, but still working out of here for a while yet.'

Sam wondered if Wong and Penrose were still seeing each other. He'd heard the rumours about them.

'Let me know what you find,' he said to Brown. 'Good work, by the way.' He looked around. 'DS Penrose in?'

'Canteen, I think. She'll be back in a minute.'

'When she is, ask her to come and see me, OK?'

Two hours later, Anna and Sam were driving back to Broughton. It had taken a while to get Neill Graham on the phone, and he'd agreed, a bit reluctantly Anna thought, to meet them at the house again. 'What more do you want, Sergeant?' he had asked. Anna had said something vague about further inquiries, needing to have a proper search through John Graham's papers. She shared Neill Graham's reaction with her boss.

Sam's response was quite emphatic. 'We need to chase this up. John Graham was a respectable elderly bloke, living in the same safe community for decades, nothing to worry about. And then all of a sudden something spooked him, by the sound of it. Something or somebody made him lock his doors... seriously affected his mood. Isn't that what Neill told you last time? And a short while after that, the doc takes off in his own car and disappears. We need to know what happened to him next.'

Sam looked across at Anna, 'Right. The original misper file should reach us tomorrow, and I'm going to see the officer who was in charge of the search. That was DCI Harry Grayson from Barrow, by the way. He and I worked together there years ago. He retired last summer but he's not far away, worth a personal visit. And I want to go through Graham's papers, even if someone looked at them before.'

'I'm not sure they did,' said Anna. 'Neill Graham claimed that no one really cared enough, just went through the motions. That can't be right, can it?'

Sam shook his head. 'That's my worry. Someone might have been quite happy to see the doc drop out of sight, not want to stir anything up. People have long memories. No one wants their reputation spoiled by things that happened years before. Things were so different then, before PACE.'

'Doesn't that apply to Grayson as well?'

'I don't think so. He had his chances to cover up things like the rest of them and chose not to. I think he's OK.' Sam hesitated and added, 'At least, I hope so.'

As they pulled into the drive of the Graham house, Neill's smart car was already there and the front door stood ajar. He must have heard the crunch of wheels on gravel and appeared in the doorway. Anna thought he looked annoyed and was curious to see how Sam would handle him.

Sam extended his hand. 'DCI Sam Tognarelli, Workington CID,' he said. 'I believe you've met DS Penrose. We've had a bit of a switch around and I'm now heading the investigation into your father's death. My condolences, by the way.'

'Bit late for that,' said Neill. 'After the first few weeks I was sure we wouldn't see him again, even though it felt, you know, unfinished. I suppose you want to come in?'

'Yes, please, and thanks for taking time to come over again.'

In the dark hall Neill stopped and turned to face them. 'Tognarelli?' he said. 'Why's that name familiar? Have we met before?'

'We haven't, sir,' said Sam, 'but I met your father, as part of the Montgomery House investigation, thirty years ago. I interviewed him in this house actually.' Sam looked to his right and pointed to a closed door. 'In that room, as I recall. Was it a study? I remember lots of books.'

Neill frowned. 'So that was you,' he said. 'Dad said a young policeman had been impertinent to him. I think that's the word he used. He must have mentioned your name – it's not an easy one to forget. And now you're a DCI.' He turned to Anna. 'There's a lesson for you, Sergeant. Impertinence pays.'

Neill opened the door Sam had indicated, and they followed him into the room.

'Yes, this is it,' said Sam. 'He must have kept it just as it was.'

Neill said, 'Dad didn't like change. Always stuck to routine. That's why I knew things weren't right when he got jittery, started doing different things.'

'Can we sit down?' Sam asked.

Neill looked at his watch. 'I don't have long. This was very short notice. I've an appointment at five o'clock, back in Lancaster, and it's nearly three-thirty now. I can give you half an hour, no more.'

Sam ignored this sudden time pressure. Anna noticed yet again how the DCI seemed to know what he wanted and just went for it, avoiding any distractions. 'Just a few questions, Dr Graham. Won't take long. And then my sergeant and I will need to have a look through any papers that relate to your father's connection with Montgomery House. With your permission, we could leave the detailed examination of the papers until we get back to the office, rather than delay you here.'

'Can't imagine what you think you're going to find. And are you sure it's connected to Montgomery House? That was so long ago.'

'It's possible,' said Sam. 'But for now, I want to know a little more about what might have upset your father shortly before he went missing. You said a few weeks before, can you be more precise?'

Anna sat to one side, making notes, while Graham screwed up his eyes in an effort to remember.

'He went missing in April nineteen ninety-nine.'

'Early April, you told us,' Anna interjected.

'Yes, yes, I know what I said, thank you. It was maybe a week or two before that I noticed he seemed agitated about something

– tetchy. He stopped going out, said he was tired all the time. I thought he was ill but he insisted he was fine, just didn't want to go anywhere. Not like him.'

'Did he mention anything that had happened, or anybody?'

Neill looked up suddenly. 'He didn't, but I asked his neighbour, the woman who kept an eye on him. When I rang her while I was looking for him, she said he'd had a letter, something by hand, no stamp. She'd found it on the mat and had given it to Dad. She wasn't sure about the date, I think she said several days before, whatever that means.'

'Her name?' Sam asked.

'Mrs Tyson, lives in the Square,' said Neill. 'She's still around, you could ask her.'

'We will,' said Sam. 'Your father never mentioned this letter himself?'

Neill shook his head.

'Any mention of someone watching the house, or calling?'

'Nothing.'

'Do you know what happened to the letter?'

Neill threw up his hands in exasperation. 'No! Look, I told your sergeant here, we saw Dad at holiday times, but not much in between. He had his own life. I've no idea what he might have done with something that came through the door.'

Again, Sam didn't react. 'And where did your father keep his papers. In here, I would guess?'

Neill pointed to a large desk that stood under the curtained window. A shaft of light lay across its dusty surface where a crack in the curtains invited in the afternoon sun. 'We went through his papers, obviously. We probably took anything that related to us as a family, or his financial affairs. The rest, well, you can't throw away someone else's papers, can you? Unless... until... you're sure they've gone.' The man's voice tailed away. Neill took out a large hankie and blew his nose. Specks of dust moved slowly in the shaft of light.

Sam stood up. 'With your permission, sir, my sergeant and I will have a look now for anything that might help our investigation. We won't detain you here while we sort through it. We can do that back at the office and return anything to you that we don't need, as soon as we can.'

He makes it sound so reasonable, Anna thought. She felt for the latex gloves that should be in her bag.

'While I do that,' Sam went on, 'could you show my sergeant where Mrs Tyson lives? That's something else we could confirm while we're here.'

Neill looked up at him. Anna knew he was calculating whether this man could be trusted. 'Don't you need a warrant or something?'

Sam smiled benignly at him. 'Not if you give us permission, sir. We could always get one, though, if required.'

Neill looked at his watch. 'Oh, get on with it. The desk's unlocked. I'll show the sergeant where Mrs Tyson lives and then I'm afraid I'll have to go. I'll need to lock up. You've got ten minutes or so, OK?'

'Fine,' said Sam. 'Thank you.'

Nicely done, thought Anna, as she put away her notebook and followed Neill Graham out of the house. She slowed things down as much as she could to give Sam more time, and it was fifteen minutes later that they returned. Neill had his keys in hand and Sam was already standing by the car, as unruffled as before. He held up a brown evidence bag. 'This is all I need for now, thank you, Dr Graham. I hope we won't need to trouble you again.'

Neill looked at him for a few seconds. 'Fine, fine,' he said. 'I expect to be kept informed, Chief Inspector. And, frankly,

I'm also expecting a more thorough job than last time. Too late for Dad now, but we need justice for him. You understand?'

'Of course,' said Sam.

Anna began to walk towards his car. Behind her, Neill caught hold of Sam's sleeve. 'May I have a private word, Chief Inspector?'

Sam turned towards him. 'Of course.' He already knew what Graham Junior might be concerned about.

'This is a bit awkward,' said Neill. 'You were part of the original Monty House case, weren't you?' Sam nodded. 'Well,' Neill went on, glancing up to make sure Anna was out of earshot, 'you'll be aware of the accusations that were flying around then about...' he paused '... improper relationships with some of the boys.' He raised his eyebrows, as if to avoid saying anything more explicit. Sam said nothing.

'I was just a lad then,' said Neill, his voice still low, 'but I know how upset my mother was about it all.' He sighed. 'Well, when you look through my father's papers, you may find something we missed, something maybe a bit incriminating about... you know.'

Sam decided to help him out but kept his voice low. 'You mean, we might find something that indicates your father had an interest in young boys?'

Neill nodded, looking embarrassed. 'I suppose it's possible.'

'As I recall, Dr Graham, we found nothing at the time to show that your father participated in the abuse of those boys. My suspicion was that he might have known from his medical care of them that something wasn't right but had not taken any action. There were other people, not just your father, who were in a position to know what was going on, but whose loyalty to the principal of the home, Captain Edwards, overrode their doubts. Does that ease your mind at all?'

Neill nodded. 'Yes. I appreciate that, thanks.'

On the way back from Broughton, as they crossed Duddon Bridge, Sam said, 'You can tell me about Mrs Tyson, but not yet. Something I want you to see first. Do you know the Corney Fell road?'

Anna shook her head. 'Is it special?'

'You'll see,' said Sam. 'Might be busy with Sellafielders coming off shift, but worth a look on a clear afternoon.'

And it was. The narrow road rose through woods for a while and then crossed a cattle grid onto the open fell. As they climbed, the Duddon estuary and the wide sweep of Morecambe Bay came gradually into view to the south with the unmistakable outlines of Barrow and Walney Island. The single-track road snaked across the pale brown treeless fell. From time to time they dodged on-coming cars in which only the driver was awake while the passengers slept. 'Sellafielders,' said Sam. 'They use this road as a short cut, and they don't take any prisoners.' On a sharp bend near the first summit he pulled in and they both got out of the car to look up the Duddon Valley toward the high fells.

'DC Brown would love this,' Anna said. 'He was very taken with Wasdale, and this view is even bigger.'

When they reached the final summit, she gasped. Below them, stretching to the western horizon, lay the Irish Sea, low tide revealing the sandy coast. To the south, Black Combe rose in a rounded arc. To the north were the Sellafield towers, then the cliffs of St Bees Head, and beyond, across the Solway, the faint blue line of the Scottish coast. Out to sea, a cap of white cloud sat on the highest point of the Isle of Man.

'Impressive, isn't it?' said Sam. 'Judith always loved this view.'

'I can see why,' said Anna.

When they turned north once more on the main coast road, Sam asked Anna about her meeting with Mrs Tyson.

'She was more help than Graham Junior,' said Anna. 'Noticed more. But women often do, don't they?'

'I couldn't possibly comment,' said Sam, smiling. 'What did she notice?'

'Well, it was she who found the letter that arrived and seemed to kick off Graham's anxiety. It was on the mat when she called one day and she picked it up. No stamp, no address, just Graham's name. And in a very childish scrawl, she said, someone unused to writing, or else deliberately disguising their handwriting. Either way, it was quite hard to read. She said she put it on the desk in the study, where she normally put his post. He never mentioned it, and she didn't ask. But Graham did seem upset by something after that.'

'Neill said his father was worried about security,' said Sam.

'Yes, Mrs Tyson said the same. He was constantly checking that doors and windows were locked. Kept the downstairs curtains closed too, which was most unlike him.'

'Anything else?'

'Apparently he asked her if she'd seen anyone hanging around, in the village or near the house.'

'Just anyone or someone specific?'

Anna checked her notes. 'Yes, he asked about a man... middle-aged.'

Sam was quiet, thinking.

Anna glanced across. Beyond her boss's profile, the coast was lit by the long rays of evening sun. She broke the silence. 'What did you find in the desk?'

'Not sure yet,' he said. 'I just picked up everything in the drawers. It needs more time than we had today.'

'You think there'll be something that the Barrow police missed?'

'Who knows what they found? We'll know more when I talk to Harry Grayson.' He paused. 'Wouldn't be surprised if they missed something. I told you, some of our Barrow colleagues would want the case to fade away with the minimum of fuss.'

At Hall Brow, the car park was almost empty.

'I'm staying a while, to make a start on these papers,' said Sam. 'Write up what you learned from Mrs Tyson and I'll see you in the morning early. Eight?'

'Fine,' said Anna. 'See you tomorrow.'

She was pulling out of the car park when her mobile phone rang. She stopped, pulled out the phone and checked the number. It was Simon's.

'Where are you?' he asked.

'Just leaving work, why?'

'Don't go home to an empty house. Come here instead, meet my family, eat with us. If you want to stay over, there's plenty of room.'

She hesitated.

'I know you'll come,' he said, and she knew he was smiling.

CHAPTER 9

Anna followed Simon's directions and was at the house within half an hour. She hadn't been sure what to expect, but in the event was surprised by the size of the three-storey Victorian mansion, which stood on a slight rise outside the village of Hilton. There was still enough light in the western sky to burnish the sandstone and reflect off the windows. Three cars were parked neatly to one side of a gravelled area to the left of the front door. One dark blue Mercedes, nearly new, one low-slung white sporty number and an older hatchback. From her short experience of house hunting in the area, Anna had an idea of what this house might be worth: Simon must be doing really well. For a second, she imagined what it would be like to live here, with a man who loved her, and never again have to worry about office politics or how to pay the bills.

A light came on in the porch and Simon appeared in the open doorway, silhouetted against the shining hall behind him. As she got out of the car he came to meet her, smiling and holding out his hand. 'How's that ankle?' he asked. 'Can you manage?' She laughed and took his hand, leaning in for the kiss on her cheek. He smelled good.

'Come in,' he said, leading her towards the house. 'Dinner won't be long. You made good time. Not breaking any speed limits, I hope.'

'As if,' she said.

She'd left her workbag locked in the car. He took her jacket to hang in the cloakroom. They were standing in a large square hall, with a fireplace on one wall, opposite a wide staircase with carved banisters. Under her feet was a circular rug, deep red, contrasting with the polished floorboards.

Anna looked around. 'What a lovely space,' she said. 'How long have you been here?'

He thought for a moment. 'About three years. We hadn't been here long when Wendy,' he hesitated, 'moved out. Come and meet the kids, we spend most of our time in the back room.'

This was a large kitchen diner that ran across the back of the house, the exterior wall a miracle of glass engineering that incorporated a near-invisible door. Anna wanted to take a closer look, but Simon held her arm and turned her around just as a young woman walked towards them from the kitchen end of the room. She was tall and striking, with long blonde hair that hung to her shoulders. The tight blue jeans and white blouse she wore were at once casual and elegant. Anna was surprised and a little intimidated by the beautiful room and the beautiful girl. She'd not expected Simon's daughter to be so glamorous.

'Caroline,' said the girl, extending her hand, which Anna took and shook lightly.

'Anna,' she countered.

'Nice to meet you,' Caroline replied, with a flicker of her eyes that took in Anna's untidy hair and second-best trouser suit.

'Straight from work,' Anna said, feeling Simon's warm hand on her shoulder.

'Anna's a detective sergeant, Caroline,' he said.

The girl's blue eyes widened. 'Heavens. Not in trouble, are we?'

Anna laughed. 'Not yet,' she said.

'Rory upstairs?' Simon asked.

'Where else?' Caroline responded. She turned to Anna. 'My brother spends an extraordinary amount of time online, but he usually turns up for meals. Dad said you were coming, so he's had time to adjust. He's not great with new people.'

'Anna's not people, Caroline, she's a friend,' said Simon. 'What would you like to drink, friend? I put a bottle of bubbly in the freezer when I knew you were coming – should be cold enough now.'

'Wake me up, someone,' said Anna. 'After a day like I've had, this is heaven.'

Simon opened the bottle, picked up a champagne flute and led her to the far end of the long room, where a sofa faced the evening light that streamed through the wall of glass. He opened the Prosecco and poured it expertly into the flute, handed it to her and tinkled the ice in his glass of Scotch.

'Caroline's in charge of dinner and Rory will magically appear when it's ready. Have a drink, relax, tell me about your day.'

Anna took a sip of the cold wine and relaxed into the chair. 'It was OK,' she said, 'better than many others actually. I spent most of it with my boss, and we drove down to Broughton and back over Corney Fell, which was a treat in itself.'

'Broughton, again?' said Simon. 'Bit far from your patch, isn't it?'

'Just some inquiries about an old case. Nothing very interesting. And what about your day?' she asked. 'A profitable one, I hope?'

'Busy as always. We do OK,' he said.

'Clearly,' said Anna, looking around the room. 'What a wonderful house you found. Makes mine look even more like a shoebox.'

'One of the perks of the job,' he said. 'This place was pretty rundown when I found it. Caroline has a great eye for décor. Her mother did too.'

A second glass of wine and the glow of the evening sun made Anna feel quite detached from normality, suspended in a different space. An unexpected question emerged from her mouth. 'So, what happened with Wendy? How could she want to leave all this?'

Simon looked down at the glass in his hand. He shook his head. 'I was shocked,' he said. 'I didn't think things were that bad. Still don't understand why I didn't see it coming.'

'I did,' said a voice from the other end of the room. Caroline turned towards them, wiping her hands on a towel. 'I knew something was up. I told Dad, but he didn't believe me.'

Simon looked up, puzzled. 'You said you thought Wendy had a boyfriend. That's a far cry from saying she was going to walk out.'

Anna felt awkward, caught between the two of them. She struggled to get out of the deep armchair. 'Look,' she said. 'Maybe I should leave. It was a kind offer, but…'

Simon put his hand on her arm. 'No need, Anna. Sorry, this is something we need to discuss in private,' he emphasised, looking hard at Caroline, 'not in front of guests.'

Caroline shrugged and went back to the cooker. Anna sank back into the chair. Prosecco on an empty stomach had certainly hit her hard. She'd either need to stop drinking right now or spend the night here. She didn't feel ready for that.

The door opened and a young man came in. Simon looked relieved and got to his feet. 'Rory, you've come down! Come and meet our guest. Anna, this is my son, who's torn himself away from whatever the latest game is, probably because he could smell food.'

Anna shook the boy's hand. He was shorter than his sister and he looked a lot younger too, although Anna thought there was only two or three years between them. The same fair hair, but without the lustre of his sister's, and the boy's face was pockmarked with adolescent spots.

'Anna's with the police,' Simon explained. 'And she's in the Mountain Rescue team. That's where we met.'

Rory nodded. 'Can I have a beer?' he asked his father.

'Help yourself,' said Simon. Rory picked up a bottle from the fridge and took it down to the far end of the kitchen, to inspect what was being prepared. Words passed between him and Caroline. Anna couldn't hear what was said.

'It must have been difficult, taking on someone else's children,' she said in a low voice. 'Especially when they hit adolescence.'

'Well, legally they're my kids,' Simon said quietly. 'I adopted them when Wendy and I got together. They have my name, and it feels as if we're a proper family.'

Anna nodded.

'What about you?' he said. 'Ever been married?'

She shook her head. 'There was someone, but...' She hesitated, reluctant to say more.

He leaned closer. 'I just wondered about, you know, whether you're committed.' He paused, looking embarrassed. 'That sounds awful. You know what I mean.'

She smiled. 'I wondered about you, too.' She raised her glass. 'Here's to us,' she said, 'and "just wondering". It makes the world go round.'

Dinner was excellent. Anna refused a third glass of Prosecco and told herself to be more careful, aware of the three of them looking at her.

'So how come you're in the police?' said Rory. He'd been sitting silent, watching and listening as the meal progressed, and the sudden question from him came as a surprise.

'Rory,' said Caroline. 'Don't be so nosy.' She turned to Anna. 'Sorry, he does blurt things out sometimes. And we don't see many of Dad's friends here.'

'You see loads of people at the agency,' said Rory to his sister.

'But they're clients, not friends,' Caroline said firmly.

Anna felt she needed to break the tension between them. 'Would you like to work in the agency, Rory?'

He shook his head. 'No, thanks! Don't like all the paperwork, and having to butter people up. Dad and Caroline are good at that, I'm not.'

Simon interrupted, 'But you're good at other things, aren't you? Practical, outdoors things.'

'I've got ADHD,' said Rory. 'That's what they said at school. I'm not thick, I just don't like sitting still.'

'Unless it's in front of a screen,' said Caroline. 'Then you sit still for hours.'

'But I'm busy too,' the boy protested. 'Do you play computer games?' he asked Anna, not waiting for a reply. 'You have to make decisions all the time. Not like school. They don't let you decide about anything there.'

Simon reached across to pick up some empty plates. 'Don't get me started about Rory's school,' he said. 'He'd have been better off learning at home, but...'

'Mum made me stay on,' said the boy. 'When she left, I left too.'

There was an awkward silence. Simon sat down again. 'Anna goes running,' he said. 'Tell her about your running, Rory.'

'Just started,' said the boy. 'Got myself some new trainers.'

Caroline laughed. 'But you still wear the old ones for running, don't you? The new ones are just for posing around in. Show us, Rory.'

He glared at his sister and tried to hide his feet under the chair.

'Look at them,' said Caroline. 'Shiny white, about as practical as high heels for running around here. And they cost a bomb.'

'They're only Adidas,' Rory complained. 'Could have bought Gucci.'

'That's enough, you two,' said Simon. Caroline raised her hands in a silent gesture that read, *See what I have to put up with*? She picked up some dishes from the table and carried them back towards the kitchen end of the room.

When the two young people had left them, Simon smiled at Anna and shook his head. 'Anyway,' he said with emphasis, 'to go back to the adult conversation – the road by Wastwater is a good running route, at the right times of the day. You know it, don't you? I heard you lot were out there earlier in the week – with a dive team, wasn't it?'

For a moment Anna wondered how Simon knew about that, but of course his job was perfect for hearing local gossip, and plenty of people had seen them by the lakeshore that morning. She decided to be vague about the operation. 'Yes,' she said, 'the divers were trying out a new Zodiac and found something caught on a ledge. Nothing much.'

Rory interrupted from the far end of the room. He'd obviously been listening to their conversation. 'A Zodiac?' he asked. 'That's what we want, isn't it, Dad?' Before Simon could respond, Rory went on, 'We've got a proper boat, of course, but a Zodiac's handy for getting in close to things.'

They've got a boat as well, Anna thought. Maybe Simon's won the Lottery and is keeping quiet about it. Simon raised his hand, as if signalling Rory to stop. 'Anna doesn't want to hear about that, I'm sure,' he said. 'Now where's that coffee?'

'There're some chocolates, too,' Caroline said, coming back to the table with a fancy gold box, which she placed in front of Anna. 'One of Dad's clients bought them. We don't eat much chocolate, so help yourself.'

Anna forgot her usual careful eating momentarily and picked one of the chocolates out of the box. It tasted strongly of brandy and she wondered how many it would take to put her over the limit.

'Time I was going,' she said. 'It's been a long day and a delightfully unexpected evening. Thanks so much for a lovely meal, Caroline, and to you, Simon, for the invitation.'

'Are you OK to drive?' he asked. 'You can leave the car here if you want, pick it up tomorrow? Rory could drive you, now he's passed his test.'

'I'll be fine,' Anna persisted. 'Thanks.'

Caroline held out the box of chocolates to her. 'These are for you,' she said, smiling. 'You'll enjoy them far more than we do.'

Anna wavered, then laughed and accepted the attractive box: it would look churlish to refuse. 'Strictly rationed,' she said. 'I'll look forward to my daily wickedness.'

Driving the short distance back home, she wondered about the Buttler family. Caroline was clearly very competent. How did she feel about having another woman in the house? And was Rory as feckless as he seemed to be? Anna didn't know many young people and wasn't sure how to react to them. Back in her own kitchen, she hid the box of chocolates away in a cupboard, so it wouldn't tempt her all the time, and poured herself a nightcap. Khan jumped up on her lap, keen for attention after an evening in the empty house. She rubbed his ears. 'Missed me, have you?' The cat nuzzled into her. Anna spoke softly to it.

'Well, with any luck, I might be stuck in the house with you a bit less often, so get used to it.'

The following morning Anna went in extra early to finish her report on the conversation with Mrs Tyson. She put it on Sam's desk before he arrived at eight. Shortly afterwards, he appeared beside her.

'We'll check on what's happening with the boat, and I'll get Jason started on background checks on some of the Monty House people I remembered from the photos we took from Dr Graham's. Then you and I need to talk to Harry Grayson. 'I called him last night. Offered to go to him, but he said he fancied a trip to Whitehaven, so we'll meet him at the Beacon Museum by the harbour. There's a little café there, or we can get a drink and sit outside if there are too many people around.'

At the early-morning briefing, Sam noticed that Bell was standing conspicuously at the back of the room, arms folded across his chest, determined to distance himself. The rest of the team must have noticed too, Sam thought. For now he had to make things look as normal as possible. And he might need to have a word with HQ about moving Bell on as soon as possible. Clearly they couldn't work together for much longer.

Sam asked Anna to lead. She shared what they'd learned about the hand-delivered note Dr Graham had apparently received before his disappearance, and how it had upset him. Mrs Tyson believed the original note had been destroyed, but she did remember its curiously clumsy lettering.

DC Brown reported that the boat from the Jeffers' boathouse had been relocated near Windermere and he was going to inspect it himself. Towards the end of the meeting, Sam put up his hand.

'May I add something, DS Penrose? I'm interested in Dr Graham's involvement with the Montgomery House inquiry thirty years ago. It's a long gap, but some of the boys who were mistreated there will now be in their forties. It's possible that one of them might have tried to blackmail Dr Graham, putting pressure on him about his connection to the scandal. He asked Mrs Tyson, his neighbour, if a middle-aged man had been seen hanging around.' Sam paused, aware of the unasked questions. Anna looked at Bell, who was playing with his phone, ostentatiously taking no notice.

'I know what you may be thinking,' Sam went on, looking around. 'Why now, after all these years? DS Penrose and I are compiling a list of possible names to check up on. Who knows where a young man with such a bad start in life might have ended up? In prison, overseas, or just leading a normal life until something untoward happened that made him desperate, looking for a source of easy money.'

'Or it could have been revenge,' said Jason, for whom the very idea of an abusive boys' home was anathema.

'That too,' said Sam. 'We're meeting one of the original inquiry team today, to see if we can find out anything useful. In the meantime, Brown, check any evidence from the boat. Go back and see the Jeffers, jog their memories about the time when Dr Graham went missing. Any reports of suspicious activity, lights on the lake, unfamiliar people hanging around... anything at all. Report back to DI Bell. Sergeant Penrose and I will be out until this afternoon.'

Anna glanced again at Dinger Bell, who was still playing with his phone. She was wondering if everyone had noticed that the two senior officers were barely speaking to each other.

'There's a file on the back seat,' said Sam when Anna got into his car a little later. 'I haven't brought all the photos I found in Graham's desk, but I'll be asking Harry about some of them. There were quite a few of groups of lads and people involved with Monty House, and I picked the clearest ones. I'm just not sure whether all the boys who were around in nineteen sixty-nine are in them.'

Anna glanced at one of the images, at the faces of the boys. Even though they'd have been relatively well looked after in the home, in terms of food and rest, most of them still looked pinched and haunted, and probably younger than their years.

'What were they like, the lads?' she asked.

Sam peered ahead at the road, thinking. 'Like any other group of boys, I reckon, although they'd all had disturbed childhoods. Youngest was about ten, oldest maybe fifteen. Some of them had been taken from home for their own protection; some because their families couldn't cope, for a variety of reasons. Then Stevie Stringer was found drowned and that kicked the whole case off. He was a sad case. Told his mates he was going to find his mam who lived in Morecambe. He was found in quicksand in the Bay.'

'Accident?' Anna asked.

Sam shook his head. 'He'd been drugged and it killed him. Doesn't take much to overpower such a small body. Someone dumped him in the quicksand to make it look like an accident, but it wasn't.'

Anna thought about what she'd just heard. 'You believe that whoever was in charge of the health of those kids should have known they were being abused?'

'Of course. And that was Dr Graham. I interviewed him in the same study we were in yesterday. He swore black and blue that he knew nothing about it, trusted the principal, Captain Edwards, and the home's matron, denied there was any cause for concern. The matron's name was Iris Robinson. She admitted finally that she thought the boys were being harmed but didn't blame Edwards for that. Misguided loyalty I suppose. She supported him right to the end.'

'What happened, finally?'

Sam shook his head. 'Long story. I try not to think about it. I'll tell you when we've got more time.'

Anna knew she needed to change tack. 'So what do you want to find out today?'

'Mostly, what happened to the boys after they left Monty House. If one of them has re-emerged wanting to harm Graham in some way, that's a good place to start. Whatever happened to cause his death, someone took a lot of trouble to cover it up. I'm sure this wasn't just a random abduction or a case of mistaken identity. I think someone tracked him down and sent him a note demanding something, or else just to frighten him.'

Anna glanced again at the faces of the boys. 'It could be one of these lads, you mean?'

Sam looked across. 'Is there a woman in the photo you're looking at? Quite smart-looking, in her forties, wearing a hat?'

'Not in this one, no, why?'

'She must be in one of the others. Don't bother looking, it won't mean much to you. That's Irene Thornhill, wife of the editor of the local paper then. She was one of the prime movers in the whole sorry business, making money by blackmailing the men who abused Monty House boys.' He paused. 'It took us quite a while to work out what she was doing. In the beginning, she was very friendly to Judith, supported her at the newspaper office. Judith even went to live with the Thornhills when her flat was trashed.' He shook his head. 'And Irene got away with it, all of it.'

Anna put the photos back in the file. 'Bell thinks you just want to relive an old case. Put things right.'

Sam nodded. 'For once, he could be right. It still bothers me.'

CHAPTER 10

The café at the Beacon Museum was quiet. Sam looked around, saw a man sitting in the far corner and smiled. Anna followed him, noticing that the other man also smiled broadly as he got to his feet. The two of them shook hands and then hugged each other. Sam pulled back. 'DS Penrose, meet DCI Harry Grayson, retired.'

For a while Anna felt like a mere spectator, watching from the sidelines as two old friends reminisced about former times. Grayson's a charmer, she thought, even with grey hair and a slight paunch. She wasn't surprised to hear later that Sam had once wondered whether Harry's advances to Judith would be reciprocated. It was strange to think of her esteemed superior as a gauche young man, at the start of his career.

Eventually, the two men got down to the serious business of the meeting. Anna, it had been agreed, would take a back seat, observing their conversation and taking notes as Sam dictated them to her. He produced the photos he'd taken from Dr Graham's desk and, sitting close together opposite her, he and Grayson began to pore over them, identifying people Jason would now have to track down, if Sam's theory about the case was right. On that point, Harry Grayson wasn't convinced.

'It's been thirty years,' he said. 'Why now? If Graham were a paedophile – and we didn't think that at the time, did we? – would he pay up just to avoid someone accusing him now? Do we know what he's been up to since then?'

'I've got someone checking,' said Sam. 'And let's think some more about those boys who were let down by Graham and everyone else. Let's say they tried to get on with their lives, but reached a point when they stopped blaming themselves and wanted to hit back at someone who was still around. They can't go after the dead. Thornhill and Edwards topped themselves. Thornhill's missus ran away. Morrison's dead. What happened to ghastly Inspector Cardine?'

Harry shook his head. 'Mikey Bennett bashed him up pretty well, but he survived. Checked out of the hospital as soon as he could walk then disappeared. Bosses swore they had no idea where he'd gone... all the usual cover ups. Cardine had no reason to go after Graham, had he?' Harry looked back at the photos. 'Is Mikey Bennett on your list?'

'Oh, aye,' said Sam. 'And a few others like him. There was a lad called Leonard, another nicknamed Spud, and Stevie Stringer's family might want to punish Graham as well. Should be able to get some of the other names from Social Services.' He gathered together the photographs and stacked them roughly. 'Anna, can you chase that up, please? Names and any contact information for lads who were placed at Montgomery House around the time it all kicked off. Nineteen sixty-nine to seventy-one for a start.'

Anna made a note. She looked up, pen poised. 'Some of them might have changed their names maybe, to make a fresh start?'

Sam nodded. 'Could have. It's not going to be easy to track them down.'

'You've got some spotty adolescent computer whizz on the job, haven't you?' said Harry. 'They seem to be everywhere these days.'

Sam smiled. 'Not spotty, but we've got one of those. Works wonders on the computer – and so fast! But when did Jason get to be a suitable first name for a Cumbrian lad?'

'Somebody on *Neighbours* called Jason, wasn't there?' said Harry, and they both laughed.

Sam tapped his finger on the stack of photos. 'These all came from Graham's desk… still there after all these years. We met the son at the house in Broughton yesterday.'

Harry nodded. 'I remember him from when the old man went missing. Grumpy git, as I recall. Kept saying we weren't doing enough, but we followed every lead we had. There was nothing. We know John Graham drove away in his smart BMW one evening, and there was no trace of him after that. Nothing taken from his bank account, no activity on his credit card.'

Anna asked, 'Did you check with his former housekeeper at that time?'

'Mrs Tyson?' Harry frowned. 'Of course we did. She said Graham Senior had asked her about seeing someone hanging around, but the house to house turned up nothing.' He paused. 'I do remember there wasn't much love lost for Graham in the village. Nothing specific, but people kept their distance from him. I often wondered if they were glad he'd left.'

Sam nodded. 'Mud sticks, doesn't it? Neill Graham was bothered about what might turn up from his dad's past, probably about his connection with Monty House. That might have affected the village's view of him too. But we never suspected John Graham of involvement, did we?'

Harry shook his head. 'Being negligent, yes. Corrupt, possibly. But not actually fiddling with the lads himself. There certainly wasn't enough for us to bring charges.'

'Charges?' Sam's voice was unexpectedly loud. He leaned forward and spoke very close to Harry's face. Anna could see the anger in his eyes. 'None of those bastards was ever charged with anything, were they? You lot dropped the case like a hot brick after Edwards and Thornhill topped themselves. I was warned off in no uncertain terms. Why else do you think I quit? The whole thing was a stitch up.'

Harry sat back, inching away from his friend's distress. 'You're right.' He shook his head. 'Things were different then, mate. We did what we could, which wasn't much. You left. I stuck around. We all moved on.'

'Except for Stevie Stringer.' Sam looked away, out towards the harbour, telling himself to calm down.

Harry broke the silence. 'So, what line are you taking, now that Graham's finally turned up?'

'Various forensic leads. Looks like the body was wrapped up by the sea somewhere, even if Graham died elsewhere. There were some minor injuries, not enough to kill him. Pathologist reckons he died of thirst.'

Harry frowned. 'Thirst? Could it have been an accident?'

'Yes, it could, but he didn't wrap himself up and chuck himself in the lake, did he? That was planned, and it could have worked. If the body hadn't stuck on a ledge, we'd never have found it.'

'All finished, are we?' said the waitress, stretching between them and picking up crockery. It occurred to Sam belatedly that they should have found a place to talk where they couldn't be overheard. He looked around, to make sure that there was no one close enough. Harry didn't seem to be bothered. Maybe that's what happened when you retired.

He asked, 'Are you thinking it was one of the lads? Delayed revenge?'

Sam kept his voice as low as he could. 'Could be, or just someone looking for easy money from threatening an old man. Graham wouldn't have been hard to find and obviously had money – big house, posh car. They might not have meant to kill him, but his health wasn't good apparently.'

'What about someone else from Monty House?'

'The only person I could think of was Irene Thornhill, but again the time gap is a puzzle.'

Harry looked across at Sam. 'She got someone else to do her dirty work thirty years ago.' He hesitated. 'Judith was very lucky.'

Sam stared back, remembering.

'I was so sorry to hear about Judith,' Harry said quietly. 'She was a wonderful woman.'

'She was,' said Sam. 'I miss her every day.' He shuffled in his chair. 'Anyway, back to now. I'll check up on Irene Thornhill. But I still don't understand why she would think Dr Graham was worth bumping off. What difference would it make to her?'

'We're assuming she's still alive,' said Harry.

'Or she might have passed on the job to someone else,' Sam said. 'She always was a schemer. Look how she sucked Judith in and then spat her out. I wouldn't put anything past Irene.'

He closed his eyes, thinking. 'One more thing, Harry,' he said. 'What happened to Mrs Robinson?'

'The Monty House matron? She quit after Edwards died. She had an elderly father and went back home to look after him, I heard. Now she must be ninety odd herself.'

'I want to see her too,' said Sam. 'She loved those boys, and some of them might have kept in touch with her.'

'Kath Hattie might know where she is,' said Harry. 'She's good on things like that. Give me a minute.'

As Harry went outside to find a better phone signal, Anna scribbled down notes about names and details they'd discussed.

'You can see why I wanted this case, can't you?' Sam said. 'Even now, it still feels raw to me. Coppers hate unfinished business. I just hope I'm not completely wrong about the cases being connected.'

'Roselea Rest Home, near Bardsea,' said Harry when he came back in. 'Kath says she would have heard if the old girl had died. Don't know how much she'll remember though. She's pretty ancient.'

'Worth a try,' said Sam. 'Thanks. And give Kath a hug from me when you see her.'

'That's if, not when, now that I've left the job,' said Harry. 'I'm more likely to see her when she retires herself. How much longer are you going to give it?'

'Not sure,' said Sam. 'I'll take this one through, and then we'll see.'

This could be his last case, Anna thought. He needs to get it right, not let it go cold, again.

Before they left, Sam and Harry took another close look at the photos together, noting all the names they could remember. There were some they didn't recognise, and Sam kept those to show to Mrs Robinson. Anna left them to it. Clearly Harry Grayson thought Sam's line of inquiry could be fruitful, and this time the case wouldn't be dropped as fast as possible by an embarrassed police force. The two old mates parted amicably, promising to meet again soon, but Anna doubted that Sam would want to remind himself of old pain.

The need to speak to Mrs Robinson took them south again, almost to Barrow, before they turned east along the coast road that skirted the north shore of Morecambe Bay. As he drove,

Sam pointed out where various parts of the original case had unfolded, and Anna let him tell her as much as he wanted to.

The Roselea Rest Home was close to the church in the centre of Bardsea, an old stone-clad house looking out across the flat expanse of the bay. They found a parking spot and Sam turned to Anna. 'I think I'd better do this alone,' he said. 'If she remembers the last time we met, it could be distressing for her to talk about it in front of a stranger. I won't be long. Can you amuse yourself for half an hour? If you're into birds, walk down to the shore. I'll see you back here.'

The heat and the sour smell of old bodies struck Sam as soon as he was standing in reception, waiting to see if Iris Robinson was willing and able to talk to him. The warrant card gave him access, but there was little point in pestering someone who was too weak to respond. Just a few minutes later, Sam was ushered into an empty room and went to a window that was filled with the blue of sky and a lattice of branches. On the pale green walls were pictures, saccharine and tasteless, of cats and bunches of flowers. Sam thought about his own old age and vowed to avoid incarceration for as long as he could.

'She'll be so pleased to have a visitor,' said the smart woman in uniform who showed him in. 'But she gets tired quite quickly, mind. Just a few minutes, all right?' Sam nodded, wondering how long 'a few minutes' could be teased out. 'I'll go and fetch her,' said the woman.

When the door opened again, he turned and there was Iris, older and smaller and hunched over to one side in the wheelchair, but unmistakable. The uniformed woman leaned over to speak into the invalid's ear. 'Here's your visitor, Iris. I'll bring you both a cup of tea soon, OK?'

The nurse smiled at Sam and left them alone, but the closed door didn't block the sound of a wailing voice outside, complaining about a lost handbag. Iris squinted up at Sam's silhouette against the bright window. He moved across and leaned down so that she could see his face more clearly.

Iris Robinson's first reaction was puzzlement. Sam kept quite still, waiting to see if she recognised him. If she didn't, there was little chance that she would remember anything else. He waited. Then he said, 'It's Sam Tognarelli, Mrs Robinson. Remember me?'

The old woman looked hard at him, then smiled. 'But you're too old to be Sam. He's such a nice young man, how is he?'

Sam's heart sank. 'He's fine, thanks,' he said. 'And he'd like you to look at some photos of the old days. You always had a good memory for faces, and he'd like to know who some of these people are. Is that OK?'

As he held out the photos towards her, she brightened and tried to sit a little straighter. A wisp of hair fell over her eyes. Sam brushed it gently away.

'Are you comfortable?' he asked.

She nodded.

He picked out one of the photos and held it in front of her face, sitting beside her so that he could check what she was seeing. She pointed a bent arthritic finger at Captain Edwards, standing in the middle of a group. 'That's the Captain,' she said. 'He was a real gentleman, always so good to me.'

'Anyone else you recognise?' Sam asked, cheered by her quick reaction to one familiar face.

'Dr Graham, next to him.' She looked up at Sam. 'I never liked him, you know. Never looked me in the eye... very rude.' Peering again at the photo, she put her head on one side. 'And that man, on the end, he was a newspaperman.' She looked more closely. 'And there's his wife, see. Look at that hat! And she's standing at the back – not like her at all. What was her name?

No, don't tell me.' There was a short pause. 'Thornhill,' Iris said, triumphantly. 'I think it was Irene.'

Sam smiled at her. 'What a memory,' he said, with genuine respect. 'After all these years, I wonder if you remember any of the boys?'

'My boys,' said the old lady fondly. 'They all called me Ma, you know. There were some bad ones, of course, but mostly they were just... lost. Let me see them.'

Sam picked another photo, with faces that he and Harry couldn't put names to. 'How about these fine young men?' he asked.

This time Iris took the photo out of Sam's hand and held it close to her face. 'Ah, yes,' she said. 'Now *he* was a bit different. Always very polite to all the adults, very chatty. Now what was his name?' Sam kept very still but no name emerged and he sensed the old woman's mind wandering.

'Which boy was it?' Sam asked. 'Show me.'

'There,' said Iris. 'Good-looking lad, a bit older than the others, and very grown up for his age.' She pointed to a tall figure, standing at the edge of a group of boys. Sam looked hard at the image but the face wasn't familiar to him. Maybe he was already at work when Stevie Stringer's death had sparked the whole thing off.

Sam pointed to the image. 'Can you remember his name, Iris?'

She stared at him, dredging the dark pond of memory.

Suddenly the door opened and the nurse, whose name Sam couldn't see without peering at her chest, was pushing a trolley into the room. 'Here's your tea,' she said, brightly. 'You must be getting tired now, Iris, aren't you? I'm sure your visitor doesn't want to wear you out. Do you?' she said pointedly to Sam.

He stepped away from the wheelchair and stood for a moment looking out of the window as the woman fussed with the tea.

His mind was far away, remembering the last time he'd spoken to Iris, when she'd finally acknowledged what had happened to 'her boys'.

'We're having a good chat about old times, aren't we, Iris?' he ventured, picking up the required tone of concern and kindness. If Iris was taken away, he would learn nothing more. He needed her to stay, just a little longer.

'Are you sure now?' the woman asked, looking at Iris carefully. 'Your tea's on the side here, in your special cup. The kind policeman will call me if you need help.'

'Thanks,' said Sam, holding open the door. 'We'll be fine, just a few more minutes.'

When they were alone again, Iris pointed out a few more of the boys, but he had those names already. Now he had one last question, the most important one, but maybe he'd left it too late. 'Where did any of those boys go, Iris? Do you remember that?'

She shook her head. 'The Captain never told me anything like that. The boys just disappeared.' She pointed again to the boy at the edge of the group. 'Except for that one. He was different. He wrote me a letter, saying he was going away somewhere. The letter came just after... after I left. Someone sent it on to me. I was so pleased for him.'

'Do you still have the letter?' Sam asked, without really knowing why. He just longed for something concrete, anything to reinforce an old woman's wandering memory.

She smiled. 'Oh, I couldn't possibly give you anything so personal, could I?'

'Could I see it, perhaps?'

She shook her head. 'I keep letters in my special drawer, in the desk in the living room.' She paused. 'I have to go now. So much to do. And I have to make Dad's tea. Shall I see you out?'

Sam had to give in. There was more, he was sure of that, but it was locked away in a mind living in the past, lost to the present.

'Thank you,' he said. 'It's been lovely to see you, Iris.' He held out his hand and she held it in her dry fingers.

She said, 'Tell that nice policeman with the funny name that I was asking after him, won't you?'

'I will, of course,'

'Oh,' said the old woman suddenly. 'That boy, the one who wrote to me, he was a lovely lad. Very friendly with Mrs Thornhill.'

Sam looked at her, hoping for more, but the moment passed.

Outside Anna was standing by the car. 'Any luck?' she asked.

He shook his head. 'Not really. She's amazing though. Doesn't know what day it is, told me I couldn't be Sam Tognarelli because I was too old, and then reeled off the names of some of the kids on those photos as if it had all happened yesterday. One boy I didn't recognise. I need to know his name.'

'Well, maybe she'll remember that too,' said Anna. 'I wonder how Brown's getting on with the boat.'

CHAPTER 11

DC Henare Brown looked at the smouldering pile of wood and the smoke that spiralled gently up into blue sky. 'Is this it?' he asked. He'd driven for nearly two hours to find the Scouts' campground near Lake Windermere, explained himself half a dozen times, and now, finally, had tracked down the boat, just two hours too late.

He turned to the man in khaki shorts standing next to him. 'I rang you yesterday, left a message about needing to see this boat. I could have saved myself the journey.'

The man shook his head. 'No signal, that's why we're here. Not exactly wilderness, but we need to get our lads away from what they're used to. Anyway,' he went on, 'the boat was useless. We put it on the water and it leaked like a sieve. Never been properly looked after. Wood was so wet we had a hard time getting the fire going, but it burned in the end. What did you want it for?'

Brown shook his head. 'Doesn't matter now, does it?' he said, smiling at the Scout master. 'The case is two years old, and we have other leads.'

'What case?' asked the man, waiting for more information. Brown didn't reply. He poked at the remains with a long stick. 'What about the rowlocks?' he said. 'Where are they?'

'Oh, we took those off,' said the man. 'And the oars were OK, so we kept them too. Do you want to see them?' He turned towards one of the sheds that stood at the edge of the clearing where they were standing.

'Is the shed open?'

'Sure,' said the man. 'I'll show you.'

'Let me go in on my own,' said Brown, pulling on his latex gloves. 'I might need to take them with me.'

The man shrugged. 'Help yourself. The rowlocks are on the shelf, at least that's where I put them. Oars standing up, at the side.'

Inside the shed, Brown found the oars and took them out into the sunlight that had managed to penetrate the canopy of the trees. They were old and had seen better days. The handles were bound with cord for a better grip, the chance of finding usable prints slim to none. He went back inside and found the heavy metal rowlocks on the shelf. These too he carried out into the light, where he looked at them carefully while the man in shorts watched.

'What are you looking for?' he asked.

Brown didn't respond. On the pointed end of one of the rowlocks he could see a shred of black plastic. From an inside pocket of his jacket, he took an evidence bag and put both the rowlocks into it, smiling at the prospect of what his mates would say when he got back: the rhyming potential would be irresistible.

'I'll take the oars too,' he said. 'Not sure you'll get them back.'

The man shrugged. 'No matter. They cost us nothing.' He waited, still hoping the policeman with the Kiwi accent would tell him what was going on, but in vain.

'Thanks,' said Brown, stretching out his hand. 'You've been a big help.'

It was little enough to show for a long trip, but at least he wasn't going back empty-handed. Brown sat in the car for a while, wondering about the job, and home in New Zealand,

and whether he'd made the right choice in staying here when the injury finished his rugby career. He longed for home, but he knew that Celia would never leave her family. He might persuade her to make the trip when the children were older, but how could they ever afford it? He needed to stop wishing he was somewhere else. New Zealand would always be home to him, but this place was almost as beautiful.

The road back to Workington took him north past Rydal Water, on to Thirlmere and along the shore of Bassenthwaite Lake before the final eastward run towards the coast. There were sheep and cattle in some of the fields along the way, as farms slowly recovered from the ravages of Foot and Mouth that had left pastures empty and the landscape deserted. He wondered how many farmers had given up during that dreadful time, driven to other jobs to survive or lured into a different life by compensation cash from slaughtered animals, cash like they'd never seen before. They could restock and restart but some wouldn't want to. There must be farm buildings standing empty all over the county. He remembered Maureen's report of the stoned sheep and smiled, but if the sheep hadn't drawn someone's attention, the cannabis farm could have been left undisturbed, making someone a tidy profit.

It was dark by the time he pulled into the car park at Hall Brow, and he called Claire to tell her that he'd be back in time to put the kids to bed. As he finished the call he noticed Maureen Pritchard heading towards her car, carrying a box. He ran across, offered to carry it for her and stood back while she opened the car and hefted the box into the boot herself.

'Thanks,' she said. 'DC Brown, isn't it?'

'Henare, call me Henny,' he said, and then paused, wondering about something. 'Have you got a minute?'

'Yes, just heading up to see my dad.' She checked her watch. 'He'll be working for another hour yet.'

'What does he do?'

'Hairdresser,' said Maureen. 'He owns a salon in Carlisle. I keep telling him to take it easy, but he loves it, doesn't want to give up.'

'Good on him,' said Brown. He hesitated. Should he mention what he'd been thinking about? Might as well. 'You know your story about the stoned sheep? The cannabis was being grown in an old farm building, wasn't it?'

She nodded. 'Yes, way up on the north-east fells. The farm was abandoned during Foot and Mouth.'

'That's what I was wondering. There must be quite a few farms that are standing empty right now, some of them pretty isolated, big sheds unoccupied, right?'

'It'll take a while to get farming back to normal,' she said, 'whatever normal turns out to be.'

'So in the meantime,' Brown pressed on, 'those properties could be useful to people who need space and privacy, like those cannabis growers, or anyone who wants to store stuff out of sight. Didn't someone say there were concerns about drugs being brought in from Europe?'

Maureen nodded again, not sure where the new DC was heading with all these questions. 'We've worried about that for years. This coast is close to Ireland, with isolated beaches and good harbours.' She looked at him. 'So what's on your mind?'

Faced with the direct question, he doubted himself and shrugged. 'I'm just the new boy, right? But someone will know about these abandoned properties, won't they?'

Maureen thought for a moment before she turned to open the car door. 'Yes, I suppose so. Is that it?'

Brown nodded, feeling foolish.

'Thanks for the hand with the box,' she said. 'See you around.'

It was only when he got back to his desk that Henny remembered another lead he should have checked. What time was it? Nearly six, not too late for a phone call. He checked through his notes for the Jeffers' number and dialled, hoping that he'd get more from this conversation than he had from his previous chat with Mrs Jeffers. This time a man answered. Henny asked if they could remember anything more about unusual activity on the lake.

'Ah, yes, my wife told me about your visit and we had a chat about it all. There was only one odd thing we could think of in connection with the lake, but it doesn't amount to much.'

Let us be the judge of that, Henny thought to himself. Out loud he said, 'Any detail would be useful, sir.'

'Well, we had some people staying here – my wife thinks it was April or May of nineteen ninety-nine. One of them went outside for a smoke quite late one night. In fact, it could have been past midnight. The next day he asked us whether people went night fishing on the lake and said he'd heard voices. He couldn't see anything, pitch black out there before the moon rose, but he was certain he'd heard a voice, maybe two. Sound does travel easily across the water. Sometimes we can hear people on the track below the screes on the other side.'

Henny began to scribble. 'You said one or two voices, sir. Can you recall what your friend actually said? And I'll need this person's name, if that's OK?'

'Can't see why not,' said Mr Jeffers. 'James Houghton's the name. I can get you his phone number.'

'Thanks. And is there any way you can pin down the date more precisely?'

'Give me a minute, will you? I'll just have a word with the wife.'

Henny heard him call, then there was silence for a few minutes, before Jeffers' voice began speaking again.

'You still there, officer? Sorry about all that. My wife found her old diary, to check when Houghton was actually staying with us. It was the weekend of April the fifteenth and sixteenth, nineteen ninety-nine. Does that help at all?'

'It certainly does, Mr Jeffers. Thanks.'

'Busy day?' said Celia when Henny finally arrived home, tired but triumphant. He nodded. 'Good, though. I won't have to sit in the meeting tomorrow with nothing to say.'

Anna Penrose was worried about the following day. She'd felt like a spare part on her trip down the coast with Sam. Why had he wanted her with him when they'd spent all their time on an old case that he knew inside out and she didn't? He'd even insisted on driving, and when they finally got back around seven she felt sick, with a pounding headache. They went back to Hall Brow to pick up her car. Driving back to Frizington seemed to take her forever, with full beam headlights constantly in her eyes along the twisting road.

Back at home, Khan wanted attention but she couldn't respond. Anna slumped at the kitchen table, her head down, trying to summon the energy to make herself a drink. Food was out of the question but she managed just one of the chocolates that she'd brought back from Simon's. The shot of brandy was welcome, and she had another.

She was about to struggle upstairs when the phone rang, loud and insistent, the noise jangling her tired brain. Picking it up was the easiest way to get the noise to stop. She held the receiver to her ear but said nothing.

'Anna?' It was Simon calling. 'Are you there? Are you OK?'

The sound of his voice was the last straw, and her discomfort spilled over. 'Yes, I'm here,' she managed to say. 'Not feeling good… sorry.'

'What's the matter?' he asked, concern in his tone.

'Not sure,' she said. 'Banging headache… stomach ache. I was just on my way to bed. It's been a long day.'

'I rang around six, but there was no one in,' he said.

'No, we had to go to Barrow, and then to Bardsea. Don't know why I went really, Tognarelli did all the work.'

'Tognarelli? I thought Inspector Bell was your boss,' Simon said.

'He was, but Tognarelli's the big boss, and he's taken over the case. Not sure why.' Silence. 'Are you still there?' she said.

'Of course. Look, I can be with you in a few minutes. Sounds as if you need some help.'

Anna wanted to say she didn't need help, and that she'd be fine, but those weren't the words that came out of her mouth.

'Are you sure?' she said. 'Don't want to bother you.'

'No bother,' he said. 'Leave the front door open. I'll be round in a few minutes. You need some TLC.'

Simon was as good as his word. Fifteen minutes later he tapped lightly on the front door and came into the house, calling her name.

'In the kitchen,' she called back as the cat fled from the intruder. Her head was throbbing and she couldn't get up, but she didn't need to.

'Don't know what's up with me,' she said. 'Feel awful.'

'Have you taken anything?' he asked, kneeling beside her. He felt her forehead, then her pulse. She shook her head. 'Any painkillers in the house?'

'In the bathroom cupboard.'

A minute later he was by her side again, with pills and a glass of water. 'When you've taken those, we'll get you upstairs,' he said. 'Don't worry, I won't undress you, just need to get your feet up and your head down.'

She lay back on the pillow and he pulled the covers around her.

'I thought I was just car sick,' said Anna. 'Not used to being a passenger.'

He smiled. 'Long way down to Barrow and Bardsea. That's off your patch, isn't it?'

'Tognarelli's got a thing about this case... He's sure it's got something to do with an old scandal at a boys' home.' She shook her head. 'Shouldn't be telling you this.'

'Means nothing to me,' Simon said, stroking her hair. 'All I know is that someone's been working too hard. You need to sleep. I'll call you tomorrow, OK?'

Anna felt the stresses of the day ebb away, but one thing lingered in her mind. 'He really loved her,' she said.

Simon smiled down at her. 'Who really loved who?' he asked.

'Sam, my boss. He really loved his wife. Her name was Judith. He says he thinks about her every day.'

Simon hesitated. Finally, he asked, 'What happened to her?'

'She died. He looked after her at the end, took time off work and nursed her himself. Not many men would do that.'

'No,' said Simon. He straightened the covers. 'Come on, stop thinking. Time to rest.'

Anna nodded drowsily. 'Thanks. You're a life-saver.' She heard his steps go down the stairs and the front door close before she turned over and fell asleep.

By the morning it was worse. Her stomach was cramping but her period wasn't due for a week or more, unless she'd got her dates wrong. It was already light. After she'd persuaded her eyes to focus, the bedside clock said seven-thirty. She was late already and felt wretched. Driving to work seemed impossible, and she'd be no use to anyone even if she were there. She reached for the phone to call in sick, and it was just bad luck that DI Bell was standing beside Sam's phone when it rang.

'Christ, woman,' was his cheerful response. 'What's up with you now?... What – stomach ache? Pull yourself together, for God's sake. We're short-staffed here already, without people crying off with the collywobbles.'

He listened for a moment.

'I should bloody well hope you'll be back tomorrow. We've got a murder investigation on, in case you'd forgotten.'

When Sam came back, Bell told him about Anna's call, relishing the chance to stir things up. 'That's why we don't need women as senior officers,' he added. 'Just not reliable enough. Can't have people off every month with women's problems, not at this level. Don't get me wrong, nothing against women, not their fault, but it just doesn't work.'

Sam listened. He knew what Bell was doing and longed to see the back of him, but for the time being they were stuck together, like it or not. 'So,' Sam said, rising to the bait despite himself, 'you're saying that women shouldn't have senior posts because they might have an occasional day off, are you?'

Bell saw the look on his boss's face and began to backtrack. 'Well, no, not that exactly... it's just, you know, we managed OK without the women all this time, didn't we? They're not built for it. Just makes things more complicated, that's all I'm saying.'

Sam looked at him, knowing there was no point in a public row.

'If my wife was here, she'd have your guts for garters,' he said, keeping his voice low. 'And it's time you were off, isn't it? We've all got work to do.'

Bell turned and left without another word.

By the end of the morning's briefing, the information board on the wall was beginning to fill up. Sam summed up what was being revealed.

'So, if Forensics can match the black plastic on the rowlocks to the wrapping on the body, we know that the boat used to carry it out onto the lake was taken from this boathouse.' He pointed to a map of the western end of Wastwater. 'DC Brown can confirm that this boat has since been destroyed by the Scout troop who took it over.' 'DYB, DYB, DYB,' came a voice from the back of the room, which Sam ignored. Someone explained to Brown that it was a Scout motto, meaning 'Do Your Best'.

'No report yet about the oars,' Sam continued, 'but we're not expecting too much from them.' He pointed to Henny Brown. 'Thanks to DC Brown's persistence, we also have a possible time-frame for the dumping of the body, April fifteenth or sixteenth, nineteen ninety-nine. Can you explain that, Brown?'

'Yes, sir. I spoke to someone staying there at that time, a Mr Houghton, who says he heard a voice, or voices, out on the lake very early one morning, but he didn't see anyone. No light.'

'Just one voice or two?' said Sam.

'He wasn't sure,' said Brown, 'but if someone's on their own, why would they be talking? There's no signal out there, so it wouldn't be on a phone.'

'True,' said Sam. 'And it's unlikely that someone on their own could have managed the job. It's quite a challenge to get a body from a car to a boathouse, into a boat and then over the side, without capsizing.'

Sam checked his own notes. 'The wrapping tells us that the location of Dr Graham's death, or at least where his body was trussed up, was by the sea, probably around the haematite area of the Furness peninsular, so we'll need to follow that up. And Jason will check the names of people associated with Dr Graham that DS Penrose and I identified yesterday.'

Sam looked around the crowded room. 'Where is Jason?'

Brown raised his hand. 'His computer was running slow. He was expecting something and went to find another computer to check it.'

'OK,' said Sam. 'Anything else we need to be thinking about, until Jason gets back?'

Brown asked, 'We've ruled out anyone from Dr Graham's family or people in his village, have we?'

Sam nodded. 'No one had anything to gain from harming him. Dr Graham wasn't well liked in the village by the sound of it, but there wasn't enough animosity to lead to this.' He hesitated. 'I'm still convinced that his death is linked to his involvement in the boys' home scandal. And at this stage, I'm also prepared to guess that whoever abducted the doctor didn't necessarily mean to kill him. The pathologist has told us that the old man was frail. The shock of whatever happened might have made him ill and there could be accidental reasons why he became dehydrated, which caused the organ failure that killed him. Any thoughts on that?'

Brown had another question. 'Could someone have been trying to get money out of him?'

'Quite possibly. And that brings me back to the boys whose lives were ruined by the home Graham was supposed to be supervising…'

Jason came into the room, holding his files and smiling. 'Got it, sir,' he said. 'I've been looking for something to explain the long gap between the boys' home scandal and the time that Graham disappeared. On that list of names you gave me, one came up positive.'

He gave Sam a piece of paper. Sam read it and closed his eyes for a moment. 'OK,' he said. 'Michael Bennett, known as Mikey in nineteen sixty-nine when I knew him. To keep a long story short for now, he attacked a police officer and afterwards escaped from Montgomery House. The officer survived; Mikey couldn't be found.' He looked up. The group looked back at him, wondering how all that could have happened. 'It was a long time ago,' he went on, 'and things were different then. From our conversations yesterday, I'd say it's possible that Barrow police didn't try too hard to find him. They wanted the whole business closed down with as little investigation as possible, to protect their own.

'What Jason's now discovered is that Mikey Bennett was discharged from the Merchant Navy early in 1999 with a drink problem. Not sure where he went, but if my hunch is correct, he came back to Cumbria, got in touch with Dr Graham to tap him for money, and we can guess the rest.'

Sam turned to Jason, standing beside him. 'Good job,' he said. 'How far have you got with the other names on the list?'

'Still working on it, sir. Computer's playing up but I've got someone coming from Penrith to sort it out. Should be properly online again by lunchtime.'

'And what about Graham's car?' asked Brown. 'They never found it when he went missing, did they?'

Sam shook his head. 'I'm afraid that fits the pattern on this case. There were too many skeletons in the closet for Barrow police to bust a gut. All the details were circulated, obviously, but it must have been like a needle in a haystack.' He thought for a moment. 'I'll make a few more calls,' he said. 'If Bennett is top of our list, we need to be able to link him to this case. Anything back from Forensics about the boat?'

Brown checked his notes. 'Black plastic on the rowlocks was the same type as found on the body, but that doesn't tell us who wrapped the body or took the boat out. No prints on the oars. They're checking for DNA. Lab isn't…'

The squad room phone rang, interrupting Henny's report. Jason was closest and picked it up. He turned to Sam. 'For you, sir,' he said.

Sam reached for the phone and listened. 'Where? When? Don't let anyone near it – and get Forensics.' He looked up. 'Jason, I want all you can find on Michael Bennett. Any prints, DNA, medical history, dental records, anything. You've got my mobile number. Call me when you have something. And, Brown, you're with me.'

CHAPTER 12

They were in Sam's car, with Brown driving, before it was clear where they were headed. 'Wasdale,' was all Sam said, and Brown had to visualise the map in his head to be sure which route to take without having to ask.

Sam was quiet for a few minutes. 'Graham's car, the BMW,' he said finally. 'It's been found, not far from where they took the boat out.'

'Better late than never,' Henny ventured, and then regretted sounding so trite. This was his chance to impress the big boss and he couldn't blow it. He also guessed there was more information to come, something that was making Sam think hard.

'There's a body in the car,' he said quietly. 'No ID yet, but I think it's Bennett.'

Henny nodded, and Sam went on talking, without taking his eyes from the road ahead. 'Thirty years ago, Bennett attacked a senior police officer I watched him do it.' He hesitated, the memory clear in his mind. 'Judith, my wife, she was there too. We knew that the police officer had been involved in abusing those boys, and Judith felt sorry for the lad.' He stopped, knowing what Brown must be thinking. 'I know, it was a serious offence, and I should have stopped her, but I didn't. She told

Bennett to run and gave him her purse, to help him escape. That was the last time I saw him.'

Brown was puzzled. 'She gave him money, after he attacked the officer?'

'I told you,' said Sam, 'she felt sorry for him.'

'What happened to the police officer?'

'Judith looked after him until the ambulance arrived. She probably saved his life. He survived and later on discharged himself from hospital and disappeared.' Another pause then Sam said, 'I hope he's dead.' He looked across at Brown. 'His name was Cardine and he was a bastard. I'm not surprised Bennett went for him.'

Brown was piecing together what he'd heard. 'Was Cardine part of the cover up, about what was happening at the boys' home?'

'Yes,' said Sam. 'Him and several others. I never knew how many other police officers were involved, but they were going to protect each other. They didn't want the details coming out then. Thirty years later they probably still don't. The linen's well and truly dirty, even if it's old.'

'And now Bennett's dead, in Graham's car?'

'That's my guess. We'll see when we get there.'

They drove towards Wasdale, down narrow country roads, past abandoned farm buildings up for sale. When they reached the place where two roads met by the river that flowed out of Wastwater, sun had broken through early cloud, picking up the autumn colours of the trees. Two cars were parked on the grass verge; Brown pulled onto the patch of grass on the other side.

Down a green track through the trees they could see movement. Sam showed his warrant card to the uniformed constable who stood guarding the entrance to the site, which was marked by yellow tape. 'Go round by the markers on the ground, sir, away from the tyre tracks. Forensics haven't got here yet. Doctor's here though.' He pointed through the trees.

Sam led the way towards the dark blue car, where a figure in crime-scene overalls was leaning into the open driver's door. As Sam and Brown approached, the woman straightened up.

'What have you got for us, Dr Sutherland?' Sam said. 'This is DC Brown, by the way. Not been with us long.'

Sutherland nodded. 'Middle-aged male, mid-forties, possibly older. No prizes for cause of death. Have a look.'

Sam and Henny peered into the interior of the car. The body lay slumped over the steering wheel with the face turned towards them. It was bright pink.

'Well, Brown?' said Sam.

'Carbon monoxide poisoning,' said Henny.

Sam walked towards the back of the car. A plastic hose ran from the exhaust pipe into a back window, which was rolled up to hold the hose tightly in place. Crumpled newspaper was stuffed around it, to block out the air.

'Any note?' asked Sam.

Dr Sutherland took a plastic bag off the dashboard and handed it to him. Inside was a single piece of lined paper, torn at one end. Sam held it up to read what was written.

'"Sorry",' he read, turning it over, but the other side was blank.

'Is that all?' said Brown. 'Just "Sorry"?'

'Writing's pretty bad,' said Sam. 'We need to show this to Graham's neighbour in Broughton. She said he'd had a note delivered, before he disappeared. That was scrawled too.'

Sam handed the plastic bag to Henny, then leaned in to look at the dead man's face more closely. 'It looks like him,' he said.

Sutherland raised an eyebrow. 'You know him?'

Sam nodded. 'Think so, but we'll have to check to confirm. Michael Bennett. He'd be in his mid-forties. Heavy drinker, liver's probably shot.'

Dr Sutherland pulled off her latex gloves. 'We'll see all that when I get him back to the lab. DC Brown's right about the carbon monoxide, but sometimes these deaths are more complicated than they appear.'

Sam said, 'I'm already trying to find his medical and police records, and any prints or DNA samples from here will confirm the ID, but I'm pretty sure it's him. People change as they age, but not that much.'

'How long since you knew him?' asked Dr Sutherland.

'Thirty years or so,' said Sam. 'He was just a lad then. If it's him, he's been away until recently, Merchant Navy.'

'Is this his car?'

Sam smiled. 'Oh, no. Way out of Mikey's league. We think he may have abducted the owner. That man died and his body was dumped in the lake.'

Sutherland nodded. 'Yes, I heard about that.' She studied Sam's face. 'Is that why you're on this case, because of the history?'

Sam nodded, but said no more.

'Right,' said Sutherland. 'As soon as Forensics have finished, I'll have the body. Anything you think I should be looking for?'

'Sedatives,' he said. 'I reckon there was someone else in on the body in the lake job. He might have wanted rid of Bennett as well and tried to make it look like suicide. I'll need to know what you can find about that, OK?'

'That's a tricky one. Suicides sometimes take sedatives to make them go through with it. Should have the results by tomorrow.'

As Sutherland walked back to her car, another vehicle appeared. It was a van this time. One of the men who emerged from it was Tony Wong, black hair flopping over his face as usual.

'Graham's car?' he asked. There was no need for introductions.

Sam nodded. 'I want to know how long it's been here and any trace evidence linking it to Graham, especially in the boot.'

Tony said, 'You think Graham was killed somewhere else, wrapped up and then brought to Wasdale?'

'From the sand and weights in the body wrappings, I'd say so,' Sam confirmed. 'But we need to know how long this car's been here. It was found early this morning, by someone looking for a place to relieve himself, apparently. He gave us a statement, but that doesn't help us pin down how long the car's been here.'

Sam pointed at various marks on the grass between the car and the road. 'See if you can tell us more from the tyre tracks and ask at the house over the bridge. Hard to believe it's been here all the time since Graham's body was dumped, without anyone seeing it. But if it wasn't here, where was it? And have a look for evidence of someone else involved in this death. Bennett could have topped himself, but he could have been helped, or forced, with or without sedatives before death. So any traces of another presence you can find, prints, anything. OK?'

Tony nodded. He knew what to do. Sam glanced at his phone. No signal. 'By the way, Tony,' he said, 'if this is Mikey Bennett, and if he abducted Graham, then I've an idea where Graham might have been held before he died of dehydration and whatever else killed him. Do what you can here. I'll check that out. It's near Barrow, so I'll use their Forensics team if I need to. That OK with you?'

'Fine, as long as they let us have everything they find.'

'Oh, they will,' said Sam. 'I'll make sure of that.'

Back in the car, he said, 'OK, Brown, you'll need to check that note with Graham's neighbour. Bennett could have written it himself, or someone else have forced him into it. But it would help to know that this writing and the note Graham received are from the same hand.' He thought for a moment. 'When we find a signal, I need to make some calls. And can you call Penrose at home? Don't want her to think I'm pulling rank, but it's not like her to be away. Need to check she's OK.'

He pointed across to where Tony was organising the examination of the area around the car before it was disturbed by the removal of the body. 'Wong and Penrose were an item for a while, but I suppose you heard that already.'

'Really?' said Henny. 'I didn't know that.'

'Well, you didn't hear it from me,' said Sam. 'That's their business.' He shrugged. 'But sometimes it helps to know these things.'

When they were away from the shadow of the mountains, the phone signal magically reappeared and Brown pulled the car over so they could both make their calls. His didn't take long. There was no response on either the landline at Anna's house or her mobile. Both were switched to voicemail, and he left messages asking if she was OK, whether she needed anything, and asking if she could get in touch with work.

'Have you tried at Hall Brow?' Sam asked. 'She could have gone in, just forgotten to switch her mobile on.'

Sam's call was more productive but his mood had darkened by the time it was finished. It had taken a while, being passed from one extension to another, before he could speak to the officer who'd organised the search for Dr Graham when he first disappeared.

'Yes,' Sam said, 'we found his body in Wastwater. Signs of foul play, and someone put him in there. In your original search for Graham, did you go out to Lowsy Point?' Henny listened while his boss had to spell the name out. 'It's opposite the northern tip of Walney Island. Look at a map... Why?' Sam asked after a pause. 'Because that's where one of the Monty House boys used to hang out... Bennett, Michael Bennett. What do you mean, he wasn't on your list? ... No, we can't pick him up. He was found dead this morning. What?... Look, just get me the DCI... yes, now, Sergeant, right now.'

'So you're sure it's Bennett?' said Brown while Sam held the phone away from his mouth and cursed under his breath.

'I'm sure enough to put the wind up those lazy gits who stuffed up the search in the first place.'

Sam put the phone back to his mouth. 'Yes, good. My DC and I need to check the huts at Lowsy Point. Can you send a couple of officers out there to assist? We might need Forensics help too, but I'll call in if we do... Possible homicide, and the victim was known to have a bolt hole there. It was a while ago, but still a lead we need to follow up.' Sam checked his watch. 'About noon? We'll meet them down near the railway crossing, where the road starts round to the point. I won't keep them long. Thanks.'

By the time Henny steered the car gingerly down the potholed road over the railway crossing the sky was clear and blue, with a sharp wind from the west that ruffled the reeds along the shore-line. Ahead of them the muddy strand curved around towards a headland. They got out of the car and looked around. No sign yet of the local officers who were being sent to join them.

Sam pointed across towards the far end of the curve to the outline of low sheds set back from the shore half a mile away. 'That's Lowsy Point,' he said. 'All this area is some kind of nature reserve – dunes, ponds, and the Irish Sea round the other side. Most of the huts are used for fishing. Pretty bleak out here in winter, but on a day like this, it's a joy. Barrow's just over there, but it could be light years away.' He held up his hand. 'Hear it? Curlews, oystercatchers, out there on the mud, feeding.'

Brown shaded his eyes with his hand, peering into the light that bounced off the distant water. 'Our oystercatchers are all black,' he said, 'and bigger.'

They turned at the sound of a car engine. A dark green Range Rover bounced down the track towards them and stopped, the engine idling. A young woman in Wellington boots and waterproof jacket climbed from behind the wheel and shook Sam's hand. She had blonde plaits pinned round her head like a garland, which made her look more like a Scandinavian pop star than a Cumbrian detective. A young man appeared from the passenger side. Sam thought they both looked impossibly young.

'DC Spears,' said the woman, 'and DC Atkins. The DCI said you're looking for someone at Lowsy Point?'

'Not someone, something,' said Sam, having introduced himself and Brown. 'Years ago when I was in the Barrow force there was young man who used one of those huts as a hideout. He's a suspect now in the abduction of Dr John Graham from Broughton two years ago. Graham's body was found last week and I'm guessing this was where he was kept, before his death. Your boss said it wasn't searched when Graham first disappeared in April ninety-nine.'

The two DCs looked at each other. 'I was based in Lancaster then,' said the young woman.

'And I'm new here too,' said the other.

'Doesn't matter,' said Sam. 'I know this place, and it hasn't changed much. We'll take your four-wheel drive, the road's in a bad state.'

The young man rubbed his hands, smiling. 'That's why we brought it. Don't often get the chance to drive this baby.'

There was an old van parked by one of the huts as they approached. A figure in overalls appeared, wiping his hands on a rag. He stopped when he saw the four strangers, guessing who they were. 'Bloody 'ell,' he said. 'I'll come quietly. What's brought you lot out 'ere mob-handed?'

Sam produced his warrant card, introduced himself and Brown. 'We're from Workington CID,' he added, 'and these two officers are from Barrow. We're inquiring about Michael Bennett – mid-forties, used to come out here as a lad. And you are?'

'Youdell's my name,' said the old man. He looked at Sam, his head on one side. 'Mikey Bennett, you mean?'

'You know him?' said Sam.

'Me cousin's lad. He were in care as a young 'un, down the coast. He went to Merchant Navy. What d'ye want him for?'

'We just need to know where he's been the past year or two,' said Sam. 'He had a place out here, didn't he, years ago?' He turned and pointed to one of the low black huts behind them. 'That one, if I remember rightly. We need to take a look.'

'Private property that,' said Mr Youdell. 'Can't just walk in, can you?'

'We can get a warrant if we need one,' said Sam. 'And while we're here, we could have a good look at all the other places out here where folk keep stuff they don't want us to see.'

Mr Youdell put the rag back in his pocket and thought for a few moments. 'Nowt going on out here,' he said finally. 'If you can get hold of Mikey, he could let you in himself.'

'Not possible right now,' said Sam. 'Is it locked?'

'Aye.'

'Do you have a key?'

'Aye.'

'Well, Mr Youdell, you have a decision to make. Let us into one shed, or we can come back later and search them all. Your choice.'

'I'll get the key,' said the old man.

The shed had double doors. Youdell opened one side to let them in.

'Is it possible to open the other door too?' said Brown. Youdell nodded. 'Big enough for a car, sir,' Brown added.

'It's a bloody boat shed,' Youdell chipped in. 'What d'ye expect? We go fishing from here – big boats, not poncey canoes.'

Sam ignored him and called out, 'Officer Spears?' DC Spears appeared at the door. 'Give Mr Youdell a seat in the back of the Range Rover. We'll need a statement from him, and your torch, and tell the other officer to stand by the door. If there's anyone else around they need to be kept away.'

The inside of the shed was dark and smelled foul. Brown put his hand over his mouth. Sam switched on the torch and they watched its beam penetrate the darkness at the far end of the shed. The floor was covered in brown rushes and old newspaper.

Sam bent and looked at one of the pieces, then another. 'Nineteen ninety-nine,' he said.

'Sand all over the floor too,' said Brown. 'This could be it.'

'Don't tread anywhere there might be tyre tracks,' said Sam.

He turned to the dark shape of PC Atkins now standing guard in the doorway. 'Does your radio work out here?'

'Yes, sir,' said Atkins.

'Are you thinking what I'm thinking?' asked Brown.

Sam nodded. 'It's all here. Sand, and there'll be haematite in it,' he said. 'Fishing's the main activity here. Have a look for any lead sinkers like the ones weighing down Graham's body. Take the torch and check the far end. We'll call Forensics, but see if there's anything obvious first.'

Brown trod carefully to the far end, squatted on his haunches and began to peer at the ground. 'Over here,' he said, almost immediately. 'Faeces. Dry, could be a dog's, could be human, down in that corner.'

He stood up, almost hitting his head on a narrow shelf that ran along the back wall. 'And look here... a hat.' He picked up a tweed flat cap with his gloved hand and held it in the beam of the torch. 'Can't see Mr Youdell or his mates wearing this, can you?'

'This is it,' said Sam. 'Bag it up. This is where Graham was held, I'll swear to it.'

The two men retraced their steps carefully towards the door.

'Radio this in, will you?' Sam said to Atkins. 'Log it as a potential crime scene in the abduction of Dr John Graham in April ninety-nine. Seal it off and get a Forensics team out here, quick as you can.

'Stay here with Atkins,' he said to Henny Brown. 'I'll take a statement from Mr Youdell, then we'll leave it to Forensics. They'll have a field day out here.'

Sam walked across to the Range Rover and joined Youdell in the back seat. 'Can you take notes, DC Spears? Mr Youdell and I are going to have a little chat.'

'What about?' said Youdell. 'I've nowt to tell you.'

'Well, that's a pity,' said Sam, 'because in the absence of any other explanation I will have to arrest you on suspicion of abduction, for a start, with possible murder charges to follow.'

'You what?'

'We need to know exactly who this shed belongs to, when and how it has been used, and everything you can tell us about Michael Bennett.'

Youdell shook his head. ''E's family,' he said.

Sam hesitated. 'Mr Youdell, I'm sorry to have to tell you that a man we believe to be Michael Bennett was found dead this morning, in a car that belonged to a person whose body was taken out of Wastwater last week. We also have reason to believe that Bennett was involved in that business. You're going to tell us everything you know about him and this shed or I can only assume that you're covering something up. Do you understand?'

'Bloody Nora,' said Youdell. 'Have you got a cig?'

The old man's statement, when it emerged, wasn't particularly helpful. The shed had belonged to Bennett's father, now deceased, and Youdell had seen Mikey there just after he came out of the Merchant Navy. It looked as if Bennett had been living there, having nowhere else to go. 'Drinking a lot,' said Youdell. 'He were pissed the last time I saw him, in the Feathers in town. Couldn't get much sense out of him, but he said he had something going. I took no mind. He were always going on about making deals and such. Lies mostly. He were a bit touched.'

Sam pushed him to remember back to April ninety-nine, but Youdell struggled with the details. 'Mikey were 'ome by then, but not long, mind. Drinking. Said he 'ad a plan to get money, but 'e always said that.'

'Did you see him or anyone else out here at that time?'

'Not me,' said the old man with relief. 'Me and the missus were away, one of her coach trips, down south somewhere. We go every April, cheaper than summer. Don't get out 'ere much till June usually.'

'So you don't know who was here?'

Youdell shook his head. 'Weren't 'ere, was I?'

'What about the other huts, and the boats?'

Youdell shrugged. 'Don't ask me.'

'Who should we ask?'

The old man reeled off a list of names and Sam interrupted him. 'DC Spears, can you take all this down: names, addresses, any contact details? I've already spoken to your DI about all this. If he agrees, I'd like you to follow this up, take statements, and send them to me at Workington. DC Brown will give you all the details, dates, background. Can you handle that?'

DC Spears beamed at him. 'Yes, sir, if my DI gives the word.'

'He will,' said Sam. 'I think your DI will want to help in any way he can.'

It would be a while before the Forensics team arrived. Sam decided to leave the two Barrow officers at the scene while he and Brown walked back to their car. As they set off along the track, a flock of dunlins rose in perfect formation from the whispering edge of an incoming tide and wheeled away towards the open sea.

'We need to check with Mrs Tyson in Broughton,' said Sam, mentally ticking off items on the list he carried in his head. 'She might recognise the writing on the note in the car, from the one that Graham got before he disappeared. It's a long shot, but worth a try. Anna will know where to find her. By the way, did you check with Hall Brow about her? Has she appeared yet?'

'Damn,' said Brown. He checked his phone. 'I'll do it now.'

The call didn't take long. 'No one's seen her,' he said to Sam.

Chapter 13

Simon opened the door to the spare bedroom as quietly as he could and looked at the figure lying in the bed. It had been easy so far. Her unhappiness and insecurity was obvious: all he'd had to do was find the vulnerable spots, fan those embers until they glowed and then add a little kindness. As her trust in him grew, so did his control. Now the information he was coaxing from her was useful but troubling. Reading the notebook he'd found in her bag had confirmed his fears. Things weren't looking good. The past that he'd strived to put behind him was threatening to rise like floods after a storm. He could hear it, feel it lapping around his feet. He had to act soon before he drowned. He closed the door carefully and left the house.

Anna opened her eyes, wondering why the sunlight was coming in at a different angle. She looked around the unfamiliar room and gradually remembered. Details came back to her slowly. She'd told work that she wouldn't be in. That must have been the day before, and she must have gone back to sleep for a while, but for how long? At some point she'd tried to get up, heading for the bathroom, but had fallen, hitting her head on something hard.

What happened after that was a blur. She must have made a phone call, and then Simon appeared. Had she called him?

She couldn't be sure. But he'd definitely arrived, she remembered that, and had checked her over before helping her out to his car. The fresh air must have cleared her head; she remembered the conversation they'd had while they were driving to his house.

'I think it's the job that's making you feel like this,' he'd said. 'You're not happy with it, I can tell.' He glanced across at her. 'You're a strong capable woman, and they don't appreciate you.'

'It's OK,' she'd said. 'And I need to work.'

'Maybe,' Simon had answered. 'But not like this.'

And now here she was, in a spare room at his house, half-dressed and feeling helpless. There was a clock on the bedside table and she blinked until it came into focus. The digital numbers said 8.24, and it must be morning because of the light. She propped herself up on one elbow, the one that wasn't bruised, and noticed her clothes folded neatly on a chair in the corner of the room.

Oh, Christ, she thought. I need to go home. I shouldn't be here. Sitting up was difficult, but she did it, and managed to put her feet to the floor. As she did so, there was a light tap on the door. It was Caroline Buttler, long blonde hair gleaming in the early-morning light.

'Thought I heard something,' she said, still standing by the door. 'How are you feeling?'

'What happened?' asked Anna.

'Dad says you fell at home so he brought you back here.'

Anna glanced across at the clothes on the chair. Caroline followed the look. 'Don't worry. I undressed you. Dad's too much of a gentleman. He had to go out for something this morning, so he left me in charge here.'

'When did all this happen?'

'Yesterday, about lunchtime. Dad was here for his lunch when you rang. He said you were hurt and went straight out to find you.'

'I don't remember any of that,' said Anna in a worried tone.

Caroline shrugged. 'You'd hit your head. Maybe you had our number on your phone or something. People do funny things when they're concussed. Dad said you were mumbling away about something. How's your head now?'

'Took me a while to focus, and my face hurts but...'

'Headache? Blurred vision?'

'Not now. Actually, I feel really thirsty.'

'Of course. Stay there, I'll bring you a drink. Tea, coffee?'

'Tea, please. No sugar, thanks.'

Caroline disappeared and Anna tried to stand. She took a few tentative steps across to the chair and found the trousers she'd been wearing. Wanting to feel less exposed, she'd managed to pull them on before Caroline reappeared.

'Careful,' she said. 'Dad said I had to look after you until he got back.'

'What about work?' said Anna. 'I need to call in. What if they've been trying to contact me?'

'I'll bring the phone up,' said Caroline. 'Dad picked up your bag for you but couldn't find your mobile.'

It was Jason who was in the office early and answered when Anna rang in. 'Where've you been?' he said. 'There's been a right flap on here when we couldn't find you. Thought you'd been kidnapped or summat. Brown rang both your numbers, and I think someone was going round to your place last night.'

'I had an accident,' said Anna weakly. 'Fell... hurt my head. I'm at a friend's house. I'm OK. Tell the DCI I'll be in later. And tell them I'm sorry for the worry. I'm fine now, really. Got to go.'

'See you later then,' said Jason cheerily, and rang off.

'Everything OK?' said Caroline.

Anna forced a smile. 'Thanks for the tea,' she said. 'I should have told them at work where I am. They've been trying to contact me. I'll have to go in.'

'Are you sure? Dad said you needed twenty-four hours' rest.'

'Well, I feel OK actually. Is your dad around?'

'He left a while ago. Said he'd be back at lunchtime to see how you are.'

'Can't wait that long,' said Anna. 'And I need my car. Could you call me a taxi to take me home?'

'No need for a taxi, I can take you, but let me check with Dad first, OK? I'll call him, won't be long.'

Left alone again, Anna felt as if her life was being run by someone else. She needed to pull herself together. Caroline came back. 'OK,' she said. 'Here's the deal. Have some breakfast here with me and then I'll take you home. Dad says that's fine, as long as you're OK.'

Anna wanted to say that it was her decision, not theirs, but she thought better of it. When Caroline had gone again, Anna got dressed slowly and checked herself in the mirror. What a mess. Her right eye was bruised and puffy, hair all over the place. She found a brush in her bag and pulled the hair down over her forehead to cover the damage. As she put the brush back, she checked that her notebook was there. Losing it would have made her embarrassment at work even more acute. She would need the notes about their conversations in Barrow, and the details she'd got from Sam about his meeting with Mrs Robinson. That would give her something concrete to do when she got to work, making up for lost time. And her phone... where was it? Must be at home if it wasn't in her bag.

The light in the west-facing kitchen diner was mercifully low. Anna put her head around the door, guessing that Caroline would be in the back room that seemed to be the centre of the house. She was reading the paper, but put it down when she saw Anna come in.

'Here you are,' she said, standing up. 'Now then, what can I get you to eat? Fruit, yoghurt, porridge, bacon and eggs, toast? Whatever you fancy.'

Anna laughed. 'Too many decisions! Fruit and yoghurt perhaps, and some toast, maybe? Have you eaten yourself?'

'No, not yet, so we can eat together,' said Caroline. 'Very civilised. Make yourself at home.'

She pulled out a chair for Anna and turned away to find the makings of their breakfast.

A few minutes later one end of the oak dining table was laid out with all the things they wanted. Caroline brought two glasses of fresh orange juice. She put them down and looked across at Anna. 'Actually, I know it's all a bit accidental, but it's really nice for me to have another woman in the house. It's been a long time.'

'Since your mum left?' said Anna. 'How long?'

Caroline looked away for a moment. 'Nearly three years, but it feels longer. I was only eighteen then, and it felt like I had to grow up really fast, you know? I wanted to go to college but I couldn't leave Rory, not with Dad working so hard.' She hesitated before she added, 'Rory's had a hard time. Dropped out of school. And now...' She shrugged. 'He does some work for Dad, not sure what. But apart from that, the only thing that gets him out of the house is volunteering at the old iron ore mine, just down the hill. One of Dad's clients helps run the place, and he took Rory on. Dad thinks keeping busy might help him... he's had some problems.'

Anna wanted to ask more about these but stopped herself. Instead she said, 'Is that the Florence mine?'

Caroline nodded. 'It's only part-time, but Rory seems to like it. They take visitors into the mine workings. He helps with that.'

Anna shuddered. 'I wouldn't like that. Can't stand confined spaces. The dark… claustrophobia. Nightmare.'

They shared fruit and yoghurt and ate in silence for a while. Anna was thinking about Wendy Buttler, wondering if this would be a good time to ask about her. Why did she leave? Was it a permanent break? Had she and Simon divorced? How attached were the children to their mother? Did Simon still care for her?

'Do you still see your mum?' Anna asked.

Caroline shook her head. 'She's got a new life now. Dad says he didn't know she was seeing someone else, but I did. I saw them together once, just by chance. And then she wrote to us, after she left. Said she had a new life and wouldn't be coming back.'

Anna looked up. 'When was that?' she asked.

'About a week later. Dad had reported her missing, but then he rang and cancelled it.'

'Rang the police, you mean?'

'Yes. They weren't bothered. It probably happens a lot. People often need a break from each other. Sometimes they come back.'

'But your mum didn't?'

'Not a word since then. We don't know where she is.'

'That must be hard for you,' said Anna.

Caroline looked up, her eyes wet. 'If you want the truth, I was glad to see the back of her. She and Dad were rowing all the time. It's a big house, but we could hear them. And I saw her throw money at him once. She said it was dirty. Dad said she was having a breakdown.'

'I'm sorry,' said Anna. 'I didn't mean to…'

'It's OK,' said Caroline. 'Don't often get the chance to talk about it. Dad won't have her name mentioned, and Rory – well, he doesn't say much, but I know he feels the same as me.'

'So what happened in the end?'

'Came home from school one day and she was gone. All her stuff had gone too, wardrobe empty. No note, no car, nothing. Then the letter came and we just carried on.'

Anna could feel her policing instincts kick in. 'Still got the letter?' she asked, not looking up from the breakfast bowl.

Caroline said, 'It was addressed to Dad. I don't know what he did with it. Doubt he kept it though, why would he?'

'And what about your other dad?' Anna asked.

Caroline shrugged again. 'No idea where he is. It's just the three of us now. I run the house for Dad and work in the office too. Rory could have a proper full-time job with Dad too, if he ever gets his head out of his… backside. Sorry. It makes us cross when he doesn't pull his weight.'

Anna wanted to ask what difference her presence might make to this cosy threesome, but that would be a question too far. Instead she said, 'You're very loyal to your dad, aren't you?'

'Of course,' said the girl. 'He's everything to us. And he says we might be going to live somewhere else soon… make a fresh start.'

'Oh,' said Anna surprised. 'I thought things were going well here, with the business?'

'They are,' said the girl, 'but Dad's always making plans. He says we have one life and we've got to live it to the full.'

Anna wanted to ask more about all this, but now was not the time. She pushed back her chair and pulled herself up, feeling the twinge in her ankle. 'Thanks for breakfast,' she said. 'You can tell your dad you were the perfect hostess.'

'You can tell him yourself,' said Caroline. 'You're seeing him again, aren't you?'

Anna smiled. 'Could be,' she said.

Back at her house, Khan was desperate for food and attention. The phone rang while Anna was opening a tin with the cat buffeting her legs.

'I'm here,' she said, in her brightest tone, guessing that it would be someone from work fretting about her absence.

'Thank God for that,' said Sam. 'I was beginning to wonder whether we should get a search started. Are you OK?'

'Sorry about all this,' Anna began. 'I was feeling pretty awful when we got home from Bardsea, spent the day in bed with... Well, it could have been anything. Something I ate maybe, or just monthly stuff. When I got up in the night, I fell in the bathroom and banged my head. Nothing serious. I must have pushed the wrong button on speed dial and a friend came over and took me back home to keep an eye on me.'

'Good friend to have in a crisis,' said Sam, wondering whether Tony Wong was back in the picture. 'Anybody I know?'

'A chap from the Mountain Rescue Team,' said Anna, 'so he was really good in a crisis.' That at least was true. 'Sorry to have caused such a fuss. I've had a good sleep and I'm just getting ready to come in. I look a bit rough.'

'Nobody cares how you look, Sergeant, we just need you here,' said Sam. 'Quite a few developments. Update at four, you'll be in by then?'

'Absolutely,' said Anna. 'And I'll have that report written up about seeing Harry Grayson and Mrs Robinson. Has Jason dug up anything more on those lads?'

'Not so far as I know. We've been focussed on Bennett today. I'll tell you why when you come in.'

'Tell me now,' said Anna.

Sam hesitated. 'We found a body this morning, in Dr Graham's car, in Nether Wasdale. Looked like a suicide. Sedatives in his system, but he could have taken them himself.'

'Or someone might have doped him first?' Anna asked.

'Indeed. Hard to tell. Anyway, it was definitely Michael Bennett, I've just had confirmation. So things are pretty busy here and we need you back. It's not a good time to let Pritchard go off to the Drug Squad either. Might have to ask her to stay with us for a while.' He paused. 'How do you feel about that?'

'Fine by me,' said Anna. She meant it, but wasn't sure that DC Pritchard would feel the same. Maureen's resentment of Anna's status was still pretty raw.

Yet again, it was the politics not the police work that raised Anna's blood pressure. She put on her most authoritative outfit and set off for work.

CHAPTER 14

DCI Tognarelli's annoyance was obvious as soon as Anna knocked on his door and went in. He seemed much more irritated than he'd sounded on the phone.

'I'm pleased to see you back,' Sam said without a smile, 'but you still have some explaining to do, DS Penrose. We've wasted too much energy and time wondering where you were. Whatever you've been dealing with, all it takes is a phone call to keep me in the loop. Doesn't look good when I have no idea where my senior officer is.'

'No, sir. Sorry,' she said, trying to find an excuse that would sound reasonable. There wasn't one. 'After we got back from Broughton yesterday…'

'But it wasn't yesterday, was it, Sergeant? We've not seen you for thirty-six hours. Quite apart from the uncertainty, there's a lot to do here, and not enough people to do it.'

Anna was surprised by Sam's bad temper, but knew she needed to grovel. 'Yes, I apologise, sir. It was the accident… I must have lost track of the time. I called in this morning as soon as I realised how long it had been.'

'What about your mobile phone?'

'I didn't have it with me, sorry.'

'Is this friend reliable?'

'Absolutely, sir. He's not in the force though, so he might not know about the need to keep in contact.'

Sam looked up at Anna, whom he hadn't invited to sit down. 'And the accident you had was...?'

'Hit my head,' she said, pulling her hair aside so Sam could see the bruised eye. He said nothing. She could see that he was weighing his words and still didn't ask her to sit down, which was a bad sign.

'How long have you been with us, Sergeant?'

'Just over a year, sir.'

'I've told you before that I admire your energy and your courage,' he went on. 'But this may be time to make something very clear to you. We are a disciplined force. Energy and courage aren't enough. We have procedures that need to be respected. Your army background should have taught you that.'

Anna nodded. 'Yes, sir.'

'I've no idea what caused you to fall, but there's really no excuse for failing to let us know where you were. I've already had DI Bell telling me that women aren't reliable enough for senior responsibility. I disagree, but I have to apply the same standards and expectations to everyone in my command. You understand that?'

'Sir,' Anna said, standing as straight as she could while the reprimand continued.

'Are you ready for duty? Recovered from your accident?'

'Yes, sir.'

'Well, you'll need to pay particular attention at this afternoon's briefing and pick up whatever duties follow from that. Understood?'

'Yes, sir.'

'We're convening in ten minutes. You may go.'

Anna sat at her desk for a few minutes, trying to focus and aware that this was the closest she'd come to an official reprimand that would go on her record. She hadn't felt right for a week or so but Sam would be watching her closely now. She'd have to pull herself together, fast.

During the briefing Anna sat quietly at first, not wanting to draw attention to herself, but it made her feel even more out of touch and she realised she'd have to be more visible. Things had certainly moved on. The report from the police doctor said that sedatives and traces of cannabis in Bennett's system might have made him incapable of setting up the exhaust hose that carried the fatal dose of carbon monoxide, although that was an open question and the pathologist couldn't be certain. Forensics reported that the car had been thoroughly cleaned and only Bennett's prints had been recovered. No evidence of Dr Graham, alive or dead. There was a small scratch on the rear passenger side, and some paint would have been transferred. They were waiting on the Barrow Forensics report for more details about the paint and any other trace evidence.

Anna hadn't noticed Maureen, but it was her voice that raised a question. 'Could Bennett have set up the hose and then taken something and just waited?'

'I asked that question too,' said Sam. 'But there's no way of making a definitive timeline, apparently. So, this could be suicide or someone could have set it up to look like one. The car was wiped clean, according to Forensics. No traces of anyone other than Bennett. That tells us someone else had been in there and wanted to cover their tracks, and that person knew enough to make a proper job of it.'

There was an audible snort. Sam looked across to where it had come from. Bell, of course. 'Something to add, DI Bell?' he asked.

Dinger shrugged. 'Wouldn't be the first time our expert Forensics team have missed something, would it?'

'Maybe you'd like to take that up with them yourself,' Sam replied. Dinger shook his head and Sam continued. 'Even if there had been evidence of someone apart from Bennett in that car, it doesn't necessarily tell us that someone pushed him into suicide, or doped him first and then set up the hose to finish him off.'

Brown said, 'We think someone helped Bennett to get rid of Graham's body. Could he have been killed by that other person, who was hoping to protect himself?'

Sam nodded. 'Could be.' He hesitated. 'But it's all speculation. And going back to the original crime against Graham – to be honest, my experience of Bennett makes me doubt he was a killer, or a suicide come to that.'

Anna was surprised to hear that Sam was still wedded to a theory based on what he'd known of Bennett thirty years before, when Mikey was just a boy. People change, she thought, surely he knows that. She looked round, wondering if other people in the team were thinking the same thing, and who would have the guts to challenge Sam when he seemed to be in such a bad mood.

Jason certainly wouldn't challenge the SIO, Anna thought. He was young and new, and would do as he was told. Sam was keeping Jason busy. He'd been instructed to check the names and current whereabouts of all the Monty House old boys, which was proving to be a slow and tedious process. And there'd been another name on the DCI's list to be checked. This was Irene Thornhill, one of the adult visitors to Montgomery House who'd been central to the conspiracy there. Tognarelli had told Jason that the woman was thought to have escaped to Spain in 1971, after her disgraced husband had shot himself, but Jason hadn't found any record of that name when he checked with the Spanish border authorities.

Anna expected Sam to be annoyed when Jason reported his lack of progress, but the DCI didn't take much notice. Instead he seemed fixated with the information he'd picked up from Mrs Robinson, the matron at the time of the scandal thirty years before. 'When I interviewed Iris Robinson,' Sam said, looking intently at the faces of the team around him, 'she told me that one of the boys – whose name we still don't know – was very friendly with Irene Thornhill.'

'Oh, aye, how friendly?' It was Bell speaking. Anna wasn't surprised to hear his reaction. The man seemed obsessed with people having sex. Again, Sam didn't respond, but continued to talk about Mrs Robinson, adding that the old woman's memory had gone and she would not be able to testify. 'But,' he added, 'I can personally vouch for enough of the details she remembered from thirty years ago to believe what she told me about the older boy.' He looked around the room, waiting for a response.

No one spoke. Anna was not the only one who wondered if the DCI's obsession with this old case was warping his view of the current one. She was still smarting from Sam's reprimand, but she needed to take this chance to reassert herself in front of the team.

'Irene Thornhill must be getting on a bit by this time, mustn't she, if she was doing all that thirty years ago?'

Heads turned towards her, aware that this was the first time she'd spoken. Sam nodded. 'She'll be least seventy. Jason, did you get her date of birth?'

Jason looked at his notes. 'Born June nineteen twenty-six. That makes her seventy-five now.'

Anna asked again, this time to Jason: 'And do we know that she's still alive?'

'No, ma'am, I'll need to check that further.'

This time Sam was clearly irritated. 'Well, do it, Jason. That's what we pay you for.'

Jason blushed, and Anna was pleased that she wasn't the only victim of the DCI's bad mood. Going back to her desk, she felt sidelined. Maureen was well established and trusted, with local knowledge that Anna could never aspire to. The new boy, the Kiwi rugby player, seemed to have established himself in Sam's good books, while she was having to prove her commitment all over again. And then there was Quigley the computer whizz. He'd be able to find Wendy Buttler's present whereabouts, but Anna couldn't ask, and he couldn't help, not unless it was centrally relevant to the investigation.

One thing she could do was make clear to DC Brown that she, and not Sam, was his immediate boss. She asked him to come to her desk, on her turf, to review what he'd been working on in her absence.

Anna referred to the notes she'd been making during the briefing. 'Have you checked the handwriting on the message they found by Barrett's body?' was her first question.

Brown sat down without being invited to do so, but Anna couldn't look up at him comfortably so she let it go. 'I took it to Mrs Tyson yesterday afternoon,' he said. 'She couldn't swear it was the same writing as the note to Dr Graham. They were both scrawled, no clearly formed words that a handwriting expert could use. And anyway,' Brown went on, 'if Barrett was drugged, he could have been forced to write that note, before someone finished him off.'

'OK,' said Anna. 'So what about Graham's car? Do we know how long it had been in the spot where it was found, near the bridge?'

'The people who live on the other side of the bridge said they didn't think it was there the previous day, but they weren't sure. Neither of them had crossed the bridge in that time, and it's quite hard to see the road from the other side.'

'And Forensics?'

'You heard what they said about the inside of the car having been wiped down. From the tyre tracks they reckon the car had been driven down there after the heavy rain the previous evening.'

Anna sat back in her chair. 'You've made a good start with us, haven't you?'

Brown smiled. 'Hope so. Chucked in at the deep end, but that's OK. I like being busy, and the DCI's a good bloke, I reckon.' He paused. 'Bit rough on Jason this morning, though.'

And me too, Anna thought.

'What's Pritchard like?' he asked. 'I had a word the other night and got the impression she doesn't rate me much.'

Anna smiled. 'That's fairly standard, don't worry about it. Pritchard's local roots go very deep. She didn't rate me either, as an outsider. "Offcomers" they call us, and you're a double "offcomer" – from the other side of the planet. It'll take her a while to adjust.' He nodded.

'Did she tell you about her dad, the hairdresser?'

'She mentioned it, yes.'

'Get to meet him, if you can. He and Maureen, I reckon they know everyone's business between here and Carlisle. Maureen says people use her dad as an alternative to reporting someone direct to the police. The salon's like a clearing house for criminal intelligence.'

'Really? That's rich,' said Brown, laughing. 'Mind you, that's how small towns work everywhere, isn't it?'

Anna tutted. 'Carlisle a small town? Don't say that too loudly. Anyway, where's this investigation going now, do you reckon?'

Brown shrugged. 'The DCI is sticking to his theory about the boys' home case.'

'Do you think he's right?'

'Not for me to say, Sergeant.'

'Right,' said Anna. The new boy was learning all the time.

A few minutes later, in the corridor outside the Ladies, Anna met one of the admin girls, who greeted her and handed over a file. 'These came for the DCI from Barrow,' she said. 'He said they had to go to DC Pritchard when they arrived.'

'I'll take them, thanks,' said Anna, wondering why Pritchard and not her. It was a sure sign of being in the doghouse, at least for now, unless Sam had another reason for involving Maureen in the Barrow end of the case. Maybe there was a Drug Squad interest. They were notoriously quiet about their operations. There was one way to find out.

Maureen wasn't at her desk in the corner of the office and there was no one around, so Anna resolved to sneak a peek at the reports. The Forensics report was on top of the pile in the folder. She glanced through it. Drugs – she'd guessed right. In a dark corner of the messy shed at Lowsy Point they'd found a block of cannabis resin that had presumably fallen out of a larger consignment. Tyre marks were not consistent with Dr Graham's car. So where had it been all that time? She turned the page. Prints were identified on the cannabis plastic wrapping and matched those taken from the dead man in the car, Michael Bennett. Well, well. All the sheds at Lowsy Point were now being searched by the Drug Squad and findings would be forwarded in due course.

Anna's mind was racing. All of a sudden the Graham/Bennett case had turned a corner and threatened to veer off in a different direction, back into the grasping arms of the Drug Squad, who were a county-wide force and could easily outgun Workington CID at Cumbria HQ. It made Anna feel even more jaundiced about the job than she did already. There was nothing she could do. She put the papers back in the folder, left it on Pritchard's untidy desk and retreated. How would Sam handle this one?

Chapter 15

Maureen Pritchard wished she'd paid more attention at the computer training course she'd been on last year. Finding the information she wanted was taking far longer than she'd expected, but she was not going to ask that spotty adolescent at Hall Brow to help, or give the rookie DC the satisfaction of thinking that he'd given her an idea. She was trying to find out who owned the land where the stoned sheep had revealed the cannabis farm.

They were pretty sure this wasn't an isolated case. Cumbria was a huge area and currently even more empty than usual, until the ravages of Foot and Mouth had been cleared away and normal life was fully resumed. There were whole swathes of the county unvisited, unsupervised, uninhabited, where all sorts of illegal activity might be going on. It was strange, she thought. Carlisle during the Foot and Mouth outbreak had been thriving, teeming with hundreds of people drafted in to help, all of whom were paid a daily allowance and needed accommodation and meals and nights out. But beyond the bustling city, the county had been in lockdown, frozen in fear and paranoia, breathing in the stench of slaughtered animals.

Finally, after interminable clicking and scrolling, Maureen found what she was looking for. She could identify the exact boundaries of the farm where the sheep had broken into the cannabis shed, and the properties that stood around it. Hesketh Farm was up on Carrock Fell, east of Carlisle, and belonged to a Mrs Hannah Salkeld. So far, so good. A few more phone calls revealed that the farm house had been unoccupied for six months, since the flock had been culled. Mrs Salkeld apparently had run the place single-handed. Must be quite a woman, Maureen thought, but where is she now?

The local village policeman was the best source of information, and the news was exactly what Maureen wanted to hear: Mrs Salkeld had moved off the farm and into Carlisle, to live with her daughter and family, and was still there. If Maureen wanted to check what had happened to the farm since it was abandoned, she could find the best person to talk to with relative ease. If that Kiwi bloke was right, they might find the link to other properties that were being used for the same purpose. She left a message for DI Bell and set off towards Carlisle, feeling a surge of satisfaction about going back to the Drug Squad where she'd always felt at home.

Within minutes of meeting Mrs Salkeld, Maureen realised the task might not be as easy as she'd hoped. Finding the tidy bungalow on the outskirts of Harrowby wasn't a problem, and she'd rung ahead, hoping that Mrs Salkeld would be at home and ready to talk. The phone had rung for a long time, but eventually a brusque voice had said 'Hello'. Maureen had explained who she was and what she wanted. 'OK' had been the only response, but that was at least more promising than 'Piss off'.

The house was in a quiet street and Maureen drove slowly down it, looking for the right number. There were net curtains at the windows and a small neat garden in the front. Rain had begun to fall out of a leaden sky and Maureen pulled up the hood of her anorak as she approached the front door and pushed the bell. After a few minutes, when there was no response, she pushed the bell again. This time a voice on the other side of the door said, 'OK, OK, keep your wig on. I'm coming.'

A key was turned and a bolt unfastened. The door opened slowly. Maureen took out her warrant card and held it up. The woman looking out at her from the dark hallway was about the same height as herself, but a good twenty years older. A navy blue headscarf was knotted under the chin, with grey curls protruding on either side. A brown lined face and bright blue eyes peered first at Maureen, then at the proffered warrant card, and then back at Maureen. Mrs Salkeld shuffled backwards. She was wearing thick red woollen socks in place of shoes, and a long brown coat, tied at the waist with something that looked like string.

'Mrs Salkeld?' said Maureen cheerily, trying to work out whether this bizarre appearance heralded a useful conversation, or a complete waste of time.

'Hannah – call me Hannah, everyone else does.'

'DC Pritchard, call me Maureen.'

'Aye, come in then. And tek them shoes off. Our Susan keeps a tidy 'ouse.'

Hannah shuffled down the cold hall and into a room at the back where a small fire was burning in the grate. 'Susan says to put the heating on, but I can't be doing wi' it. She allus puts it on when she gets in, but it goes off as soon as she goes out of a morning.'

Maureen was glad of the fleece lining in her anorak. 'Shall we sit down, so I can ask a few questions about your farm?'

Hannah snorted. 'What farm? Nowt left. They killed the sheep, and I shot the dogs. They were going mental with nowt to do. Dogs 'ave to work.' She shrugged. 'So do I. Can't be doing with all this. Wish someone had shot me, like, when the sheep went. What's the point?'

Maureen took a deep breath, trying to get the scenes of farm-yard carnage out of her head. 'It must have been very hard for you, Hannah. But you got compensation for the sheep, didn't you?'

Hannah snorted again. 'Money. What's the point of that? Can't buy more sheep, not yet, and they won't be hefted, so how will I keep 'em properly?'

'Hefted?'

'Eeh, you know nowt,' said the old woman. 'Herdwicks know where they belong, that's hefting. They stick to their own patch, teach the lambs so they don't stray. New sheep won't be hefted, won't know where to go. Them London buggers don't ken all that, do they? And you don't, neither. Where are you from then?'

'Carlisle, born and bred,' said Maureen.

'City folk, they know nowt. Not farming?'

'No. Dad's a hairdresser, in town. Has his own salon.'

Hannah laughed. 'We could 'ave done with him last year. Shearers let us down. Does he do sheep?'

Maureen shook her head. She needed to take back control of this conversation.

'It's about the land and the buildings, Hannah, not the sheep.'

'What about 'em?' she answered, angrily. 'Got the land from me dad, and him from 'is dad. Bred our own sheep for fifty year, that's how they get hefted.'

'Yes, but there aren't any sheep there now, are there?'

Hannah leaned forward. 'Our Susan said there was summat about sheep getting onto the land from over the fell. Their farm weren't touched, lucky buggers. And our flock was OK, not in-fected. But they were killed anyway. Firewall, they called it, stop the spread. Next farm were OK, just outside the limit. And their sheep got out, our Susan said. That right? Going to prosecute them, are you, for letting the fences go, using our farm as cheap fodder? Serves 'em right, I say.'

Maureen abandoned politeness and interrupted this flow with the questions she needed answers to. 'Who knows you're not on the farm anymore, Hannah, apart from the family?'

'Eh? Who knows I'm 'ere, not there?'

'Yes. Who did you tell?'

Hannah thought for a moment. 'Eeh, now you're asking. Don't see folk much, except at auctions and such.' Her face brightened. 'Oh, aye, the man from the auctioneers. He was out when the sheep were culled, doing valuation and that. He asked if I were staying and I told 'im I were coming 'ere. Nice bloke. What's 'is name…? Suppose he's back at work, now it's mostly over. Terrible job that, seeing all them animals just before they died.'

'Yes, terrible,' said Maureen. She was beyond sympathy, just trying to get the job done.

Hannah looked at her. 'Nice hair,' she said. 'Does your dad do it?'

'What?' Maureen saw the conversation sliding away from her again. 'Yes, he does actually.'

'I want a haircut,' said Hannah. 'Would 'e do mine? You could ask 'im for me, couldn't you?'

'Well, just now, I need to know some more about what happened to your land.'

'Help me think, a haircut, wouldn't it?' said Hannah. 'Without all this weight on me 'ead.'

Maureen closed her eyes. Whatever it takes, she thought. 'Would you like me to take you to my dad's salon, and then you might remember?'

'I'll get me boots on,' said Hannah, smiling broadly. 'Just fancy a trip into town.'

An hour later, after Hannah had been dropped at the salon with a hasty explanation and a promise to return when the job was done, Maureen had a chance to carry on looking for the link they needed. The valuer's name was Brian Berry and he was back at work at the auctioneers, even though regular auctions hadn't yet started again. He remembered Hannah Salkeld well, unsurprisingly.

'I doubt she'll be back. I've already had Susan, the daughter, inquiring about the best way to sell the land. After the stoned sheep embarrassment, she wants rid of the place as fast as possible.'

'She can't have known what those empty sheds were being used for, can she?' Maureen asked.

'Susan? Doubt it, straight as an arrow. Just like her mam, although Hannah likes to keep this air of mystery. Susan told me they'd notified an agent to keep an eye on the place, and then assumed it would all be OK.'

'Agent's name?'

'Can't help you there, sorry. You'd need to ask Susan yourself. I have a number for her, if you want it.'

Another call, another message left, another delay, but finally Maureen had the agent's name, and a number to ring. Before she did that, she checked and the agent appeared to be clean, or at least there was nothing on record about any dodgy dealing. If he was part of a chain setting up an illegal business, she would have to dig a little deeper.

Maureen rang the agent's number. 'Mr Dreghorn? You'll be busy, I'll bet,' she said. 'Lots of farms unoccupied, lying idle.'

'Too many,' said Dreghorn. 'I reckon this'll change Cumbria farming, for good. So many livelihoods lost. The ones who survived will be trying to diversify, make themselves less vulnerable.'

Maureen smiled at the idea of cannabis growing as a fallback for hard-pressed farmers, but this was not the time to start that rumour.

'Do you think estate agents are keeping track of places that might be coming on the market?'

'I'd be surprised if they weren't,' he replied. 'They all know each other, and word gets around. Now the golf has started up again, and the Rotary, and the Lodge, you know how it is. The gossip will be flowing free.'

'Can you think of anyone who might have a particular interest, specialising in farm properties?'

Mr Dreghorn thought for a moment. 'Let me have a think. I can fax you over a list, so long as you're clear it didn't come from me. And I'm not going to ask why you want to know.'

'And I'm not going to tell anyone else about this conversation, OK?'

She didn't hear the mumbled reply before the line went dead.

When Maureen got back to the salon, the transformation in Hannah was striking. 'Miracle worker,' Maureen whispered to her father. 'Her own daughter might not recognise her.'

'No chance of getting paid, I suppose?' he ventured, smiling.

'Put it down as an act of charity,' said Maureen. 'And the price of civic responsibility.'

Hannah spent most of the short ride back to Harrowby looking at her reflection in the little mirror above her seat. 'He did a good job, your dad. That'll be the annual shearing until next Christmas.' She paused and glanced across at Maureen. 'And I remembered a bit more about what happened while I was packing up to leave the farm. I 'ad a phone call, see. Some bloke... didn't catch 'is name. He said he were from electric, asking whether we 'ad power in the sheds. Told 'im to mind his own business. Never trust anyone on t'phone, me dad always said.'

'Quite right,' said Maureen. 'And did you have power in the sheds?'

'Aye, for when we were lambing. But it was cut off when we left.'

They'd need power to grow cannabis up there, Maureen thought. Someone could have reconnected it. Something else to check.

Dinger Bell was in a jovial mood when Maureen got back to the office, pleased that Sam's irrational obsession with Monty House was now clear to everyone. He beckoned Maureen into his room and shut the door. The file of reports from Barrow was on his desk. 'Nelly sent this to you, but that's just his way of telling me to keep my nose out.' He lowered his voice. 'Always was a pompous git, better than us proles. We had a right ding-dong the other night. I told 'im, to 'is face.'

'Told him what?' asked Maureen.

'That 'e's a pompous git.' Bell laughed and tapped the file. 'Well, the Drugs boys are right up his arse on this case now. They've found cannabis at Lowsy Point, that place near Barrow, and Bennett's prints all over it.'

'Bennett who was found in Graham's car?'

'The same. He had a shed at this place, owned a boat, and there are other boats all around. Way off the track, straight out into the Irish Sea, perfect spot for a bit of illegal importing. We could 'ave found where they're bringing the stuff in. Can't wait to get off this case, but Super says I can't get to the Drugs Squad until we've got the Graham death sorted.'

'So looks like we're both stuck here. I'm still chasing the cannabis farming angle,' said Maureen, keen to share what she'd learned.

'Chickenfeed,' said Bell, dismissively. 'Might make a bit of local cash, but it's the big boys we should be after. Someone's bringing in the hard stuff, and that's where we need to focus. Pity it's Barrow, never did trust them buggers, but it's a start. They're checking all the other sheds and boats out there.'

He looked at his watch. 'Should have something back from there by the end of the day.'

'Do you want to hear my line on the cannabis farms?' Maureen asked.

'Later,' he said. 'We need to go through this file before more shit hits the fan.'

Back at her desk, Maureen found the list of land agents that Mr Dreghorn had faxed through. She folded the list and put it in her pocket.

CHAPTER 16

Anna was wondering what Sam would find for her to do when he arrived in the office, looking annoyed, and called her in.

'We've had the reports back from Lowsy Point,' he said, needlessly tidying his already tidy desk. 'I've passed some of them on to the Squad.'

'Drug connections?' Anna asked, innocently. She didn't want to admit to what she already knew from sneaking a look at the report.

Sam nodded. 'Cannabis resin found at Bennett's shed, and other evidence too, indicating fairly clearly that Graham was held there, and possibly died there.' He paused. 'And they found prints that link Bennett to the cannabis. Drug Squad are interested in that, obviously.'

'They think Bennett's involved?'

'They might think that, I don't,' he said. 'Doesn't add up.'

'Why not, sir? That could explain why someone topped him – if he was getting to be a liability?'

Sam shook his head. 'That's not his game,' he said. 'Not the Bennett I knew.'

Anna had thought about what she wanted to say to him next. 'You remember, a few days ago, you said that I was to say if

I thought you were going off track, making too much of the link with the boys' home?'

Sam looked up, frowning. 'Did I?' He leaned back in his chair. 'And do you think that?'

'Well, sir,' she said. 'You met Michael Bennett when he was a lad, thirty years ago.'

'Yes, I did.'

'And you think he wouldn't be involved with a drugs racket.'

Sam nodded. 'Right, he's not. I know it.'

Anna's voice rose a little, despite an effort to keep it low. 'But that was thirty years ago. People change. It's a different world now, and it looks as if he's been up to his neck in this stuff, from what we know so far.'

The DCI stared at her without speaking.

'Isn't it possible,' she ventured, 'that you're reading this wrong? You and your wife…'

'Who's mentioned my wife?' Sam shot back.

'No one has,' said Anna quickly, 'but it meant so much to both of you back then. You told me so yourself.'

Sam turned his chair round and stood up. Anna could see how angry he was. She wished she hadn't started this.

His tone was hostile. 'Is this because I had a go at you about your carelessness?' he said. 'Have you been talking to Bell?'

'Bell? No, I've not seen him.'

'Well, don't talk to him about any of this, OK? This is my case and you're my sergeant, at least for the time being.'

Anna was too shocked to speak.

'I thought I'd been very clear, DS Penrose,' said Sam, facing her down. 'It's my belief, based on thirty years' experience, that Bennett had reasons for abducting Dr Graham that had nothing to do with drugs. I can't explain yet how this latest evidence fits in, but I don't want Pritchard and the Drugs boys trampling all over our case.' He pointed at her. 'And I expect loyalty from you on this.'

Anna nodded. 'Yes, sir.'

'No contact with Bell and Pritchard, except through me, understood?'

She nodded again.

'You've made your feelings about this case, and my conduct of it, quite clear.'

'But you said…' Anna began, trying to protect herself.

'Whatever you heard me say, Penrose, I'm still in charge of this case. We need to know who was helping Bennett with his disposal of Graham's body, how that car got to Wasdale, and how Bennett died.' Sam sat down again. 'In pursuit of that case, and no other, I have something I want you to do.'

'Sir,' said Anna, reverting to the curt response that had always served her well when dealing with unreasonable authority.

'Remember we went to see Mrs Robinson, the former matron at Montgomery House?'

'In the home in Bardsea?'

Sam nodded. 'I've had a message from them saying that she's asking to see me again. I can't go down there right now, too much going on here. I want the name of an older lad who was friendly with Irene Thornhill. She won't talk on the phone. If you go now, you should be there before she gets too tired to talk. They're expecting you.'

'Yes, sir.'

'And, Penrose,' he said, 'I need to see some results. You're my sergeant, but you seem…' Sam searched for the word he wanted. 'Detached. As if you'd rather be somewhere else, doing something else. It's not what I want, and not what we're paying you for.' He sat down, gathering papers into a neat pile and not looking at her. 'Carry on. I'll be here late, so let me know what she tells you.'

Someone knocked on the door. 'You asked us to hold your calls, sir,' said the young uniformed policewoman, handing him a note. 'There was a call from Barrow a few minutes ago, from a DC Spears. She said it was urgent, that's her number.'

Anna couldn't wait to get away and turned to leave, but Sam held up his hand to stop her. 'Wait, this could be important. And stop hovering by the door. Sit down.'

Anna watched as he dialled the number and waited, then he pressed the loudspeaker button on his phone and a young woman's voice said, 'You asked me to make some further inquiries, sir, about Lowsy Point and the connection to your investigation. Mr Youdell gave us a list of names – people who might know more about Michael Bennett?'

'Yes, yes,' said Sam, looking at Anna. 'Anything useful?'

'It took a while to track down one of Bennett's mates, but he told us that Bennett owned a lock-up in Barrow.'

'What sort of lock-up? A storage place?'

'No, sir, a lock-up garage. DC Atkins and I went straight there. Tyre tracks and an old tarpaulin, as if a vehicle had been covered. Been there some time, by the look of it.'

Sam was taking notes. 'Anything else?'

'Some paint marks on one side of the entrance. We looked up the files on Dr Graham's car, and the paint was the same colour. We could get Forensics to confirm a match. Do you want us to organise that?'

Sam looked up at Anna and smiled. Thank God for good news, she thought. Might put him in a better mood.

'Yes, as soon as you can. Good work, DC Spears. Tell your sergeant to give me a call.'

But Spears hadn't finished. 'That got me and DC Atkins thinking about the logistics, sir.'

'Go on,' said Sam.

'Well, Bennett didn't have a car. If he abducted Dr Graham in his own car, the BMW, and took him to Lowsy Point, then there should be traces of it out there, not necessarily in the shed. Then Bennett took the BMW to the lock up. When Graham died, Bennett must have used it to transport the body up to Wasdale.'

Sam was taking notes. Even Anna was impressed by the logical process that DC Spears was following.

Sam interrupted. 'I'll talk to your Forensics people. We need a wider search for BMW tyre tracks at Lowsy Point, even though it's so long ago. And they need to go over Graham's car again, looking for any trace of prints apart from Bennett's and Graham's. Leave that with me.'

'Right, but that's not all, sir,' the young woman went on. 'Mr Youdell, the man we met at Lowsy Point – I thought he was holding out on us and I made some inquiries about him.'

'Go on,' said Sam expectantly.

'Turns out he and Bennett go back a long way, as mates, not just because they're related. I went to see him again, told him he had more to tell us and he'd better make it quick if he didn't want us turning his place upside down. Bit of a risk, sorry, but I wanted to push him. I had him down the station, just to wind him up, and took a formal statement. I'll send it through, but can I read you what he told us?'

'Keep going, I'm listening,' said Sam. 'Don't read the whole thing, just pick out the important bits.'

'OK, well, Mr Youdell said that he'd seen Bennett at Lowsy Point one Monday morning in April ninety-nine.'

'That's when he said he was away with his wife.'

'On the coach tour, right, but I checked with the bus company and that tour started a week after this incident. Anyway, he said Bennett was in a terrible state, shaking. Youdell thought it was a hangover. Bennett said he was in trouble, and that Mr Youdell…

George his name is… wasn't to tell anyone that he'd seen him. Bennett said he had to get to a phone fast, and George Youdell dropped him at the phone box, the one near Steele's on the main road. Youdell didn't ask what it was about, and Bennett didn't tell him. George went off on holiday after that and didn't see Bennett again for several weeks.'

'When did that coach tour start?' Sam asked, scribbling on his pad.

'Friday, April the twenty-first. George Youdell saw Bennett at Lowsy Point about a week before that.'

'Brilliant. Thank you, Spears. An excellent piece of work, and I'll say so to your sergeant. Fax that statement to me here. Send a hard copy too. I'll arrange for your Forensics to check the lock-up as well, so you go with them. See if there's any CCTV nearby and let me know if so. Thanks again.'

Sam looked up at Anna after he'd ended the call. 'Now *that's* good police work,' he said. 'We could do with some more of that round here. You'd better get off to Bardsea. Make sure you have your report to me by the morning.'

'Sir,' Anna said, before turning and heading out of the office.

She was furious. He'd as good as told her that she wasn't up to the job, taking it out on her when his precious boys' home victim turned out to be a hardened criminal, and had been killed for it. Then he'd made sure she knew that the Barrow DC, who sounded like a teenager, was doing a great job, while Anna was sent off on another wild goose chase to talk to some old biddy who didn't know what day it was. An hour and a half each way, it was going to take her the rest of the day to drive there and back.

Anna stopped in the car park before she set off and rang Simon's mobile number. She was very pleased to hear his voice. 'Can you talk?' she asked.

'To you, any time,' he said. 'How are you doing?'

'Honestly?' she said. 'I wish I'd stayed in bed. Got a right rollocking when I got in, and now Sam's given me a shitty little job to do, back to Bardsea again.'

'What's down there?' he asked.

'Just some old dear away with the fairies. Sam thinks she's got information, but it would never stand up in court so I don't know why he's bothered. Feels more like an errand concocted to keep me on my toes.'

Simon's tone was sympathetic. 'Well, when you get back, it's dinner here. You obviously need cheering up. Come over whenever you're ready.'

'Are you sure?'

'Absolutely,' he said. 'Come and dump some of the stuff that's weighing you down.'

'You're very good to me,' she said.

'You're worth it. See you later.'

Anna smiled as she rang off. Now she had something to look forward to.

It was lunchtime when she arrived at the Roselea Care home and the smell made her gag. What was it exactly… overcooked vegetables and a slight hint of burning? Not for the first time, Anna hoped she would die suddenly, not end up somewhere like this.

'I thought that nice policeman was coming back,' said the nurse that Anna introduced herself to. 'Iris was very taken with him. She might not want to talk to anyone else.'

'That's my boss,' said Anna, with all the patience she could muster. 'He couldn't be here today, but we got your message and I came straight here.'

'Well, don't hold your breath,' said the nurse. 'Iris can be quite, well, stubborn at times. And she's having her lunch so can you wait, please? Better still, come back in half an hour or so. We're all a bit busy right now.'

She pointed towards the door that Anna had just entered by and practically steered her out again, into a steady drizzle that drifted in off the bay. Anna pulled up the hood of her anorak and set off towards the shop in the village that she'd seen last time she was there. At least she could buy something to eat while she waited for the unappetising lunch at Roselea to be consumed.

By the time Anna got back to the over-heated reception area the aroma of food still hung heavily in the air. She was shown into a large room in which the residents sat in armchairs or wheelchairs lined up around the walls, looking at each other or at their own knees. In the far corner of the room, in a wheelchair, sat a bent white-haired figure. The nurse leaned down to speak directly into her face.

'Here's your visitor, Iris,' she said, with loud deliberation.

Iris looked up and frowned. 'Where's that man, the one who came before?'

Anna followed the nurse's example and leaned down to speak close to Iris's face, but the woman recoiled from her. 'Get away! Who are you? Where's that man?'

The nurse, who'd been watching this encounter from a discreet distance, pulled a chair over. 'You'd better sit down,' she whispered to Anna. 'She can be a bit awkward. Give her a minute.'

Anna sat down, smiled at Iris and waited. When the old lady's expression cleared a little, she said, 'Sam couldn't come today, so he asked me to come instead.'

'Sam? He's the young policeman, isn't he? Do they have the same name, the two of them?'

Just go with it, said Anna to herself. She smiled again. 'Yes, it's funny, isn't it? The old Sam, who came here before, he's my boss. He sent me.'

170

Iris nodded.

'And he said you had something to tell us, something you'd remembered. Is that right?'

'Did I?' Iris asked, looking at the nurse.

'Yes, dear,' said the nurse. 'It was the name of someone from Montgomery House – one of the boys.'

'Who? What boy?' said Iris blankly.

'Let me try,' said the nurse. She kneeled down in front of the wheelchair and took Iris's hand in hers. 'You looked at some photographs, of your boys.'

'My boys,' said Iris, smiling. 'Yes, I remember.'

The nurse looked up at Anna, as if to say, *My work here is done*, and went to talk to another of the residents who was calling to her. Anna moved so that she was directly in Iris's eye line, kneeled down, and said, 'There was one boy. You said he was special – older than the others, more grown up.'

'Oh, yes, that was Stuart,' said Iris. Anna blinked and tried not to react too much. 'Yes, Stuart,' she said. 'And what was his other name?'

'I've got some new slippers,' said Iris, holding up one foot to show Anna.

'Aren't they lovely?' she said. 'I'm sure Stuart would have liked them too.'

Iris nodded. 'He was such a nice boy,' she went on. 'Came from Kendal. A bit posh,' she added. 'He went out to work. Irene liked him. They used to talk a lot.'

'Irene Thornhill?'

Iris pouted, as if in disapproval. 'Thick as thieves, those two,' she said. 'I thought it was a bit, well, you know, not right.' She lowered her voice. 'Old enough to be his mother she was.'

Anna made a sympathetically critical face. 'Really? And what was his other name, do you remember?'

'Billings,' said Iris suddenly. 'Stuart Billings, do you know him?'

Anna shook her head. 'Would I like him?'

'Everybody liked Stuart,' said Iris. 'Except his mother.'

'Is that why he was in Montgomery House?' Anna asked. It was the first time she'd thought about what had brought these boys into care.

Iris looked down. 'Of course, but we can't talk about that, can we?'

Anna shook her head. 'That wouldn't be right, would it? No.'

'Have you got the photograph?' said the old lady.

Stupid, thought Anna. Of course I should have brought it. 'No, I'm sorry,' she said. 'Sam, my boss, he has it still. Would you like him to send it to you?'

Iris smiled. 'Yes!' She raised both her hands from her lap and clasped them together. 'They were all my boys, you know.'

Suddenly, Anna saw the old woman's face darken. 'The Captain,' she whispered. 'He died, you know. It was a terrible day.'

Anna took both her hands. 'I know,' she lied. 'And you did your best, for all of them.'

As Anna looked into the agonised face, Iris gripped her hands and began to cry, tears welling out of her eyes. Anna looked around for the nurse, who'd noticed and came hurrying over. She eased Anna's hands away and replaced them with her own. 'You go now,' she murmured. 'She gets upset sometimes. I'll stay with her a while.'

Anna stood up slowly, leaving the nurse wiping away the tears and talking softly.

'I'll go then,' she said, leaning down so that the nurse could hear. She nodded, and Anna walked carefully across the room and through the open door into the hall. She leaned against the wall and breathed out then hurried to the front door, desperate for fresh air, and waited until someone came to release her.

She'd got the name that Sam had wanted. Thank heaven. The mention of Kendal, and the fact that Stuart Billings was out working while he lived at Montgomery House, they were extra pieces of information that Sam might be pleased about, something to offset his disapproval of her. Results, that's what he'd asked for. It wasn't much, but Anna hoped it would be worth the long drive.

She checked her watch. Three o'clock: she could drive back, write her note for Sam, go home to change and still be at Simon's in time to spend a long evening with him and clear her head of the terrors of old age.

Three hours later, showered and changed and feeling excited, Anna waited for someone to open the door of the Old Vicarage and invite her in to the spacious comfortable house. She'd thought about this moment during the long drive back to Hall Brow. Sam hadn't been in his office, so she'd written a short account of her visit to Iris Robinson, the name he'd wanted, and notes about where the boy's mother had lived – assuming Iris had remembered that correctly. She left the report on his desk, so he would see it first thing.

The whole episode confirmed Anna's doubt about her boss's judgment in this case. And at the back of her mind a feeling was growing that her own move to the Cumbria force had been a mistake. The place was stuck in the past with misogynists like Dinger Bell, and local expertise was valued higher than modern policing. Anna wondered whether she would ever be accepted or feel comfortable here. Simon thought that she was being taken advantage of, and maybe he was right.

The front door opened and Simon was there. He held out his arms to her and she walked into his embrace. It felt like coming home.

He laughed. 'Bad day?'

She laughed too. 'Long drive, for a few words and a vision of the hell that could await us all.'

'Heavens,' he said. 'You need a drink.'

Simon went ahead of her into the wide back room, which was warm and softly lit, and smelled of roasting chicken. They stood side by side at the kitchen counter, looking out at the fading glow of evening, wine glasses in hand. 'It's just you and me tonight,' he said. 'Caroline and Rory are at the flicks in Workington, *Lord of the Rings*. Rory's passed his driving test and I think he just wanted to go out, because he can. It's hard for kids out here with no way of getting around.'

'Hard on you too,' said Anna.

'True. I've felt like a taxi driver for years, but now I can send them off and have the house to myself for a change.' He leaned across and kissed her gently. 'And it feels good.' She closed her eyes for a moment, savouring the touch.

'Tell me about this dismal day you seem to have had,' he said, topping up her glass.

She groaned. 'Where to start? Well, I got a right grilling about being away for a couple of days. Then I suggested that my boss is too concerned with an old case and it might be affecting his judgment.'

Simon winced. 'Not a great plan,' he said.

'But he asked me to say if I thought he was wrong,' Anna protested. 'And when I did, he got really angry. Said something about me being his sergeant, "for the time being", as if my job was on the line.'

Simon shook his head. 'That's no way to get the best out of you, is it?'

Anna went on, feeling even more aggrieved, 'And then he said he wanted "results", so he sent me all the way down to Bardsea to see an old lady in a care home. That was the vision of hell.'

'And what were the few words you got in Bardsea?' Simon asked, after taking a long sip of his drink.

'What? Oh, just someone's name and a few details from thirty years ago. I told you, he's obsessed with it.'

There was a pause. Simon turned and walked down the room towards the range stove where he checked the chicken in the oven. 'I'll put the spuds on,' he said. 'You must be hungry.'

She nodded, following him to savour the sight and aroma of the food. 'I didn't have much lunch. The smell in the old folks' home put me off eating. Don't think I've ever been in a place like that before. It was depressing.'

'And who was it you went to see there?'

'Just someone who used to work at a boys' home in the area. Mrs Robinson, her name is. She's old and almost completely off with the fairies, but Sam insists that she has useful stuff to tell us.'

'Mrs Robinson,' Simon repeated. 'Well, you're here now. We'll eat soon and then you can forget all about it.' He put his hands on Anna's shoulders and smiled down at her. 'It's a job, just a job, not your whole life.'

'But I have to work,' she sighed.

'And there are plenty of other things to do. Someone with your skills could do really well in a business like mine, for instance. You've got the energy, the people skills, charm... everything it takes.'

'Charm?' she laughed. 'That's a first for me.'

A little later, when the chicken and a chocolate mousse and some local cheese had all been despatched with relish,

Anna leaned back in her chair and looked at Simon. 'Where did you learn to do all this? In the army?' she asked.

He shrugged. 'Round and about, picked up a few useful things. Do you want coffee now or would this be a good time for you to see the rest of the house? I had a poke around yours, remember, so you should have a look at mine. And you're not doing a search, Sergeant, you're taking an interest in the property. I need to get you thinking like an estate agent.' He must have had a bad time in the army, Anna thought. He never wants to talk about it.

He led her from room to room, from the basement where he kept an impressive array of wine; around the ground floor, including an enviable utilities room; and then up the wide stairs to the landing. 'Never get landings like this in new builds these days,' he said. 'It's considered a waste of space, but it mirrors the hall downstairs and makes the place feel so different.'

'Palatial,' said Anna. 'I love it.'

'And the space gives us all some privacy,' he said. 'Rory has the big front room and his own bathroom, Caroline is upstairs, and I have the huge room at the back, with my own en suite, of course.'

'Of course,' she said. 'May I see?'

He looked at her. 'Certainly, madam,' he said. 'Come into my boudoir.'

He stepped into the bedroom behind her and leaned over her shoulder as she took in the colours, the soft lighting, the west-facing windows. 'Like it?' he asked.

She turned and looked up at him. 'Love it,' she said.

'Well, let's stay here then,' he said, putting both arms around her, and pushing the door shut with his foot.

For Anna, the sex felt different, delightfully so. Simon was quieter than her previous lovers – more patient, less demanding.

'Just one thing missing,' she said finally, turning towards him and resting an arm across his chest. 'We should have brought the bottle up. Now I need a drink.'

'Wait right there,' he said, clambering out of the big bed. She watched appreciatively as he walked out of the room, and again when he returned with a bottle of Champagne and two glasses. 'The Chablis was nearly finished,' he said, 'and I want to celebrate.' He uncorked the bottle and they giggled as the bubbles trickled down onto the duvet. 'Here's to us,' he said. 'And the best sex I've had for three years.' He took a gulp of the wine. 'In fact, the only sex I've had for three years, and definitely worth waiting for.' He kissed her, holding the glass over her head.

'You're welcome,' was the only response Anna could think of. And it was true. Right at that moment, she was as happy as she'd been in a very long time. But only for a moment. Suddenly she thought of Wendy, the wife, not the ex-wife, and still out there somewhere. Her shadow haunted the house.

'Are you leaving the dismal day behind you now?' Simon asked a little later, as they snuggled down into the bed and were lying side by side.

'Oh, yes.'

'So, what was the rest of the story? You mentioned a vision of hell and a name?'

'Oh, just one of the boys in the home, where Mrs Robinson had been the matron.'

'Why that boy?'

'Iris said he was special. And my boss wanted to know what he was called.

'And what was he called?'

'Stuart,' she said. 'Stuart Billings.'

Simon closed his eyes and leaned deeper into the pillow.

'Just an ordinary name.'

'Agreed,' said Anna. 'Heaven knows why Sam's so interested.' She turned towards him. 'But that's work and I can't talk about it, so let's do something else, shall we?'

Later, in the quiet of the night, Simon lay on his back listening to Anna's steady breathing. He remembered Irene, and Wendy. Sex seemed to matter to them, and to Anna. He knew what to do and to say, but the whole rigmarole left him cold. It was just biology, nothing more. What mattered to him was money and control over his life. He tried to picture the future he'd worked for all his life, but now all he could see was Tognarelli, standing in his way.

CHAPTER 17

DCI Tognarelli finished reading the report, closed the file and looked up. 'I knew it,' he said. 'Drugs at Lowsy Point? Bennett as dealer, a Mr Big? Never made any sense to me. And they found nothing.' He picked up the file and brandished it at Bell, standing on the other side of the desk. 'No trace of anything in any of the boats or sheds except for that one block of cannabis with Bennett's prints conveniently on it. Doesn't prove a thing.'

Bell folded his arms. 'Oh, sit down, Inspector, for heaven's sake,' said Sam. He looked at the DI, wishing he didn't have to, but for the time being they had to put up with each other. Might as well try to be civil, before Bell transferred to the Drug Squad and out of his hair. Bell seemed to have forgotten their altercation in the car park, unless he was storing up his anger for another attack. He was just as full of himself as ever.

The DI leaned back in his chair, paunch straining at the buttons of his shirt. 'One good thing,' he said. 'We won't have to deal with those Barrow buggers. Like to do things their own way, always have. So, if Bennett wasn't master-minding the whole thing and getting bumped off for his pains, then what's going on?'

Sam leaned forward. 'Well, here's an alternative theory. It's got nothing to do with drugs. Bennett comes back from the Navy, skint. He comes across Graham somewhere, reckons he might be good for a few quid, to avoid any accusations about what went on at Monty House. Graham refuses, dies in that shed, then Bennett gets someone to help him get rid of the body. Two years on, overcome with remorse, he drives the car that he's hidden all this time to a place where it'll be found and tops himself.'

'So why was the car cleaned of all prints and traces, as far as we know?' said Bell. The tone of his voice betrayed his continuing doubt about the lack of forensic traces. Sam didn't respond and Bell went on, determined to make the connection that would bring the Drugs Squad into the picture. 'And we still have no idea where these drugs are coming from, or how they're being moved. Pritchard's getting all worked up about who's growing cannabis up on the fells, and how much more there is that we 'aven't found yet.' He hesitated, remembering. 'She thinks that someone's keeping track of the properties left empty and making use of them, while all those farmers are off in Barbados with the compensation from Foot and Mouth.'

Sam rolled his eyes. 'Yet more rumours. Pritchard spends too much time with her dad at his hairdresser's. She needs to deal with stories like that, not start them.'

'But she's got a point,' said Bell. 'We had a good laugh about the stoned sheep, but we need to know how that happened. She's on to it. She's a good copper.'

'How come she's not a sergeant by now?' Sam asked.

'She said it wasn't worth applying.'

'And then we gave Anna the job,' said Sam.

'Exactly,' said Bell. 'No love lost there. How's Penrose doing, anyway? I thought she might quit after that bloke attacked her.'

'She moved house,' Sam said. 'Told me she couldn't stay in such an isolated spot after the attack on her.'

'She still banging our little Chinese friend?' Bell enquired, with his usual decorum.

Sam scowled. 'None of our business.'

Bell shrugged. 'It is if she's not concentrating on the job. Someone needs to tell 'er.'

As if on cue, there was a tap on the door and Anna responded to Sam's 'Enter!'

'I'll be off then,' said Bell. 'Villains to catch.' He walked past her without a word, closing the office door behind him.

'Did you see it?' Anna asked. 'I left it on your desk last night.'

Sam looked blank, then nodded. 'Oh, the visit to Iris Robinson.' He shuffled some papers around and picked up one that had got buried under the Barrow Forensics report. 'This it?' He opened it up and glanced through it. 'You got the name, that's good, and he was from a family in Kendal. Had a job and... look at this, very close to Irene Thornhill. Now that's interesting.'

'I still don't see...' Anna began.

'No, I know you don't,' he interrupted. 'Irene may be dead, or otherwise off the scene, but this business would have been just up her street, believe me. Have a seat, I'm going to find Jason.' He passed the Forensics report to her. 'Read this while you're waiting.'

A few minutes later he was back, with Jason Quigley behind him. 'Right, Jason,' Sam began. 'More inquiries for you. New name, Stuart Billings. He had a job somewhere local but still lived at Montgomery House in the late sixties. Don't know what happened to him after that. There's a photo of him somewhere.' Sam shuffled the papers on his desk again. 'Did you take it, Sergeant?'

'No, sir,' she said. 'I should have done really when I went to see Iris. Luckily she didn't need it.'

'It must be here somewhere,' Sam said. 'I'll let you have it later, Jason. We need anything you can find on this person: home details, anything about why he was in the home, where he was working, where he went when the home was closed, any connections to the Thornhill woman.'

Jason looked puzzled. 'What's he supposed to have done, sir?'

Anna was feeling tired but more confident than she'd been the day before: confident enough to add, 'And do we have any evidence that he's connected to Bennett?'

'Of course he's connected!' said Sam, losing patience very quickly. 'Those boys in Monty House were all connected with each other, and with the adults who ran the place and farmed them out to their mates. No physical evidence, not yet, but I know it, in here.' He tapped at his chest. 'We'll find the link to the Graham case, it's just a matter of time.'

Anna wanted to argue, but there was no point.

At two different computers in the Hall Brow CID squad room, Anna and Jason were busy pursuing different inquiries. Anna's approach was slower and less confident, and it was a simpler search, even though it would have been hard to justify if anyone knew what she was doing. She typed 'Wendy Buttler' into the DVLA search engine and waited. There it was: the right name, the right address at the Old Vicarage, a blurred picture, no endorsements. She checked police records for any mention of the same name, but there was nothing. She checked the telephone records in Sunderland, where Caroline had said her mother had gone with the new boyfriend. Nothing.

A young woman appeared by her desk. 'DCI Tognarelli sent these over, Sergeant,' she said. 'Some photos?'

'OK, thanks,' said Anna, quickly closing the window on the computer screen. She tapped an empty space on her desk. 'Just leave them there.'

They can wait, she thought, and went over to watch Jason at work, hoping to learn something from him. He was on the phone and smiled as she sat down next to his desk. He put his hand over the mouthpiece. 'Kendal Social Services,' he whispered. 'Trying to find more about Stuart Billings.' A voice squawked at him. 'OK, I'll hold, thanks.'

'Hope this isn't another wild goose chase,' said Anna. 'The boss thinks this Billings had something going with a woman who hung around Monty House in nineteen seventy-one. Sounds unlikely to me.

Jason listened to the voice at the other end of the line and began to scribble in tiny handwriting. 'OK. And what happened to Stuart after the scandal, when they closed the place?' He frowned. 'Abroad? Are you sure? And you haven't heard of him since?'

'Well,' said Jason, when he'd asked all the questions that the woman from Social Services could answer, 'there's a turn up. The DCI might be right.'

'The matron at the home said Stuart and the Thornhill woman were very close,' said Anna. 'Could have been a mother and son thing.'

'Or every young man's dream,' said Jason. 'What was he… a teenager and she was in her forties?' He nodded slowly. 'All this and foreign travel too.'

'Really?' said Anna. 'You reckon a young man could go for an older woman like that. Leave home, everything?'

Jason thought for a moment. 'Depends how bad things were there for him, doesn't it? And if she was keen, and on offer, yes, I can see it.'

'Have you checked anywhere else for that name?' Anna asked.

He shook his head. 'Not started the detailed stuff yet, but nothing came up initially. No DVLA or police records.

He might have changed his name, of course, got a new passport, changed his appearance even. Better get on with it. Did you want anything in particular?'

Anna shook her head. 'Just a question, Jason. Do people sometimes just disappear without trace, completely?'

'It's possible,' he said. 'But if they're alive, they usually leave some kind of a trail. Why?'

She shook her head. Caroline had said that Wendy and Simon had been fighting before Wendy left. Something about 'dirty money'? For the first time, it crossed Anna's mind that Wendy hadn't just left for her own reasons. She could have wanted, or needed, to disappear completely. Or there was always the other possibility: that she was no longer alive.

Back at her own desk Anna sat thinking for a moment. She picked up her mobile phone and saw that someone had left a message. Simon had called and asked her to call him back. His voice sounded odd, clipped and irritated.

'Hi,' she said. 'You called me?'

'Where are you?'

'At work, why?'

'I need to talk to you. Meet me on the north side of the bridge in half an hour.'

'Why? What's the matter?'

'Half an hour,' he repeated. 'I'm in the car.'

Anna felt sick as she left the office and walked over the bridge, looking for his car. Simon was clearly annoyed about something. What had happened? She opened the passenger door and sat down. He didn't bother with a greeting.

'Who's DC Pritchard?' he said. His voice was so different. She wondered what had happened to make him sound so fierce?

'She's one of our team, but when this case is closed she's going to the Drug Squad. Why?'

184

'She called the office in Workington this morning and left a message for me.'

'What about?'

'I thought you might know. What's going on? Why are police sniffing around me?'

Anna shook her head. 'I've no idea.' Why would Pritchard be calling an estate agent? 'Oh, wait,' she said. 'Might be something to do with a cannabis farm the Squad found up on the fells a week or so back. Pritchard was checking who would know which farm properties were empty, on the market, after Foot and Mouth.'

'Well, she got my name from somewhere. Was it you?'

'No! Nothing to do with me. It's Pritchard's line of inquiry, not mine.'

'Well, you all talk to each other, don't you? Have you been gossiping about my business?'

Anna looked around, wondering who might be watching them. 'No!' she said, as quietly as she could. 'I don't gossip about your business, Simon. Why would I?'

'Well, don't,' he hissed, 'ever. OK?'

'I won't,' she said. 'And I didn't. I told you, Pritchard has her own investigations, they don't involve me.'

He said nothing, refusing to meet her eye and staring out at the river.

'Maybe this was a bad idea,' he said finally.

'What was?' she asked.

'Us getting too close,' he said. 'You'd better go. Can't be seen talking to me, can you?'

'Simon, please. It's not like that.' She could see how angry he was and it made her feel sick. 'Will you call me later?'

He shrugged. 'You'd better go.'

She got out of the car, watching as he drove away. Back in the office, she sat down at her desk, feeling upset and confused. Pritchard's message to the agency sounded like a routine inquiry, and probably was. Why would Simon think that the woman he'd just slept with had been gossiping about him at work? For a while she sat, pretending to be busy, turning over in her mind what had made Simon so defensive. He was obviously a private man, nothing wrong with that. But why such anger?

Suddenly, she realised how little she really knew about him. Using the pretence of fleshing out Maureen's interest in local property ownership, she checked with Jason about the procedure, made some calls, and an hour later was feeling more confused than ever. There was no record of anyone called Simon Buttler or Stuart Billings having joined the army between the years that he would have done so. Had he lied to her about that, or said he'd joined up just to make a connection with her? Either way, it was a bit odd. Having a birth date would help.

Guessing that Simon wouldn't be at home, she called his home number.

'Hello?' said a voice she recognised.

'Rory?' she said, pleased that it was he who had picked up and not Caroline. 'It's Anna, your dad's friend.' No response. She tried again. 'Sorry I missed you and Caroline the other night. How was the movie?'

'OK,' he said. 'Do you want to speak to Dad?'

'No, he's at work, isn't he? I wanted to ask you or Caroline something actually.' She tried to sound casual, less official. 'Is it your dad's birthday soon?'

'No,' Rory said, after a short pause. 'Not till March the sixth.'

'And is it one of the big ones next year?' Anna asked, keeping her voice as light as she could.

'No, not yet. He'll be forty-seven next year. Not fifty for ages yet. Why?'

'Oh, just something he said. Sounded like he was heading for fifty soon.'

'Well, he isn't,' said Rory. 'Is that it?'

'Yes. Yes, thanks. Won't keep you, 'bye.'

She worked it out. Now she had something more specific from which to search. 'Simon Charles Buttler, dob March the sixth, nineteen fifty-four.' She turned back to the computer, with no idea what she would find.

An hour's work, hoping that no one would ask what she was up to, rendered plenty about Simon as an adult, from around 1980, but before that, nothing. If he wasn't in the army, as he'd said, then where had he been during those missing years? She was mystified, still hoping that all was well, that the man she had begun to feel so settled with was really someone she could trust. 'Reliable?' Sam had asked about him. Was Simon reliable? She truly hoped so. So he'd lied about being in the army, did that really matter?

It took Anna a while to track down Maureen Pritchard. She'd worked out beforehand how to approach the question, so as to keep some things to herself.

'Something Brown mentioned to me,' she said, when she finally got Maureen on her mobile phone. 'He said he'd talked to you about checking on empty properties, where the cannabis operation might be going on. Did you follow that up?'

Maureen made a sound that indicated all was not going well. 'I saw this crazy old lady who owned the land where the sheep got stoned. There had been some thought of selling up, and the agent they'd contacted gave me a list of estate agents who'd shown an interest in similar properties – farmhouses and such. That's as far as I've got, just checking around, to see if any of them might be connected. Nothing so far.' She paused. 'And I'm not sure why I'm bothering, as my esteemed DI thinks I'm wasting my time.'

'Bell being as helpful as ever, is he?'

'You know him.'

Maureen sounded more friendly than usual. Anna took a risk. 'One of the names you've contacted is a friend of mine,' she said.

'Oh, which one?'

'Simon Buttler, of Buttler and Lilley.'

'Hang on, let me check my list. Oh, yes, left a message with him this morning. You know him, do you?'

'Yes, he's in our Mountain Rescue Team,' said Anna. It was the truth, if not the whole truth.

'So he's on the level, is he?'

'I'd have thought so, yes.'

'Well, you'd be wary of him if he wasn't, wouldn't you?' Maureen asked. 'Anyway, I thought you and Tony Wong were an item.'

Cheek! Anna thought. 'I didn't think my personal life was anyone else's business,' she said, annoyed that it had even been mentioned. 'And if we were an "item", as you call it, we're not now.'

'Good,' said Maureen, unabashed. 'Something a bit sleazy about him, I think.'

'Sleazy?' Now Anna was really irritated.

'Well, you know… the motorbike leathers, the floppy black hair. Anyway, if you're not together anymore it doesn't matter, does it? Are you and Mr Buttler an item now then?'

'If we were, you're the last person I'd discuss it with.' Anna regretted ever starting this conversation. Her annoyance boiled over. 'You happily married people can be so smug!'

Maureen snorted. 'Well, maybe we've got something to be smug about. You'd better be careful, Anna. It's a small place. If you're seeing someone dodgy, it won't stay private for long.'

'Obviously, when there are gossips like you around,' Anna said, and slammed down the phone. For a moment she sat fuming, wishing she had the courage to jack in the job and all her nosy colleagues and just enjoy herself, before middle age took a grip.

Jason appeared at her side. 'You OK?'

She smiled. 'Fine, thanks. Just a conversation that went wrong. It's personal, nothing to do with work. Do you want something?'

'The DCI says he sent some photos over this morning. Now I need them for this search he's got me on. Something to do with that boys' home?'

'Oh, yes.' Anna remembered shuffling the papers around on her desk to find the file. 'Here they are. Not had time to look at them myself, but that's OK. It's a bit late now anyway.'

She handed over the file and Jason returned to his desk.

Anna's phone rang. Sam had another job for her, and yet again it meant a long drive in a Land Rover that wasn't built for comfort. She wondered if this was further punishment for not living up to his expectations.

'DC Spears is doing a great job, chasing up the Bennett connections in Barrow,' Sam said, 'but she needs senior back up and her DI says we should help out. So you need to get down there, just for a day or two.'

'OK,' said Anna.

'Call me if there's anything interesting.'

'Will do.'

Anna wasn't sorry to be out of the place for a couple of days. The drive to and from Barrow wasn't a bad commute, if she could avoid the Sellafield shift change mayhem. She wouldn't see Simon for a day or two either, but that was probably just as well. She had some serious thinking to do.

Chapter 18

It was one of those dark grey days when the wind slices in from the west, straight off the Irish Sea, and beyond that the stormy Atlantic. Barrow police station was close to the centre of town, in an old building that looked well past its shelf life. Anna's hair escaped its tether and danced around her head as she ran across from the car park. DC Jasmine Spears was ready and waiting for her and she was all business, not a hair out of place, blonde plaits firmly fixed in their strange wreath.

'Glad to have some back up, Sergeant,' she said. 'It's Jasmine, by the way, but everyone calls me Jas. Don't know what my parents were thinking of, sounds more like a perfume than a police officer.'

'Mine's easy,' said Anna. 'You can even spell it backwards. What have you got for us? My DCI's dead impressed with you, by the way. If ever you want to move north, he'd take you on, no question.'

Jas Spears smiled and blushed slightly at the unexpected compliment. 'Might think about that. Born and bred in Barrow but it wouldn't do me any harm to get out. Not yet, maybe. Don't want to look too, you know…'

'Ambitious?' Anna anticipated the end of that sentence. 'Nothing wrong with ambition. Don't let the old boys tell you otherwise.'

They were in the main room of Barrow CID, where Jas had set up a board with all the details of the Bennett case. 'You didn't come out to Lowsy Point that first time, did you?' she asked.

'No, the DCI took the new DC, Henny Brown.'

'Dishy Brown,' said Jas. 'He's from New Zealand, isn't he? A rugby bloke, someone said.'

'That's him. You reckon he's a looker?'

'Just my type,' said Jas. 'Anyway, here's the map that shows you where Lowsy Point is, right out on the coast north of the town centre, at the top end of the Walney Channel. Fishing boats are kept out there, it's less affected by the tide, and there's quite a community – the usual crowd of misfits. It's a long way down a track that gets covered by a high tide, but that's what some people like, to get right away, for whatever reason.'

Anna looked carefully at the map. 'So that's where they think Dr Graham was kept, in one of the sheds?'

'That's what Forensics thought, certainly. But you're not sure how he died, is that right?'

'PM said he died of dehydration,' Anna explained, 'but it affects people differently, depending on how healthy they are to start with. And Dr Graham was already pretty sick – heart issues apparently.'

'So he could have died unexpectedly, accidentally even?'

'Could have,' said Anna. 'If he'd been left for too long without water, even if that wasn't intended.'

'Nasty way to go, though,' said Jas.

They looked at the photos that the Forensics team had taken of the inside of the shed. Jas pointed. 'Human excrement, apparently. No doubt that someone was kept there for a few days at least.'

'OK,' said Anna. 'So, let's say the old man dies, and Bennett panics. He has to get rid of the body and he needs help. What does he do?'

Jas picked up a list. 'These are the names George Youdell gave us, the man we questioned out there. He's Bennett's second cousin, or third. Anyway, he didn't want the police poking around so he coughed up this list of Bennett's mates. All locals. I've worked my way through them. This bloke here,' she pointed to a name, 'he told us Bennett had a lock up, and that's where Atkins and I found the paint fragments that made it look like Graham's car had been kept there.'

She looked up. 'There's still one bloke I haven't managed to see, and I've just found out he's in Haverigg nick, which isn't far. We'll see him later today. From what I've got so far, no one can place Dr Graham at Lowsy Point, not directly. I'm still hoping the one in the nick might have something useful.'

'What's he in for?'

'Drug dealing. Two years. Could be out in less.'

Anna raised her eyebrows. 'There's a drugs connection we're following up too,' she said. 'Well, I should say the Squad thinks there's a connection, because of the cannabis found in Bennett's shed, but my boss isn't convinced.'

'The DCI?'

'Tognarelli, yes. He has a theory about Bennett.'

'Didn't your DCI work here in Barrow, years ago?'

'Thirty years ago, yes. He was a young DC then, and keeps harking back to the case he worked on at a boys' home called Montgomery House, where Bennett was as a lad.'

'This bloke in Haverigg was there as well, from what I've found out.'

'Name?'

'John Chipping. Nickname Spud.'

They looked in detail at the statements that Spears had taken so far. All of them mentioned that Bennett had a drink problem, and that he was very short of money when he came out of the Navy. 'Looks like he drank his earnings away,' said Spears. 'Sad, really. He didn't give himself a chance. Wouldn't be surprised if he topped himself. Nothing much ahead of him, no family, no money. Is there any doubt that it was suicide?'

'The DCI doesn't think it was, but he's living in a world of his own on this one. Forensics couldn't be certain, but it looks pretty clear to everyone else.'

'Well, I've arranged a Haverigg visit for this afternoon,' said Jas. 'Hope that's OK. Never interviewed anyone in the nick before, so I'll be learning from you on this one. I just hope he's got something to tell us, when you've come all this way.'

'I'd like to look at the lock up as well,' said Anna. 'Any CCTV close by? If anyone else was involved in Bennett's last trip up to Wasdale, that might help. Could we check that before we go to Haverigg?'

The lock up was in a row of old garages near the Barrow football ground. Litter swirled in the wind. There was yellow tape across the entrance. DC Spears produced the key for the rusty padlock and together they lifted the metal roller door, which screeched into place above their heads. Dull light filled the empty space. The wind found its way in to swirl dust and litter around.

'There's the paint transfer,' said Jas, pointing to the edge of the doorframe. 'The BMW's probably the biggest car Bennett ever drove.'

'Might not have driven much at all,' said Anna. 'If he abducted Graham in his own car, he would have dumped him at Lowsy Point and brought the car back here, out of the way. Nobody overlooks this place. Who owns the lock ups?'

Jas checked her notebook. 'Mr Patel, lives in Preston. He owns all sorts of property out here. Seems on the level. Says he rented the garage to Bennett from the beginning of 1999, after he got back from the Navy, and he paid six months ahead, in cash. Always late with the money.'

'Why didn't Bennett get rid of the car and let the lock up go?' Anna wondered aloud.

Jas shrugged. 'Not very bright maybe. His mates said he was always thinking that something would crop up, and he would need the space. He could have been keeping other stuff in here too, although Forensics didn't find traces of anything suspicious.'

'No sign of drugs?'

'Nothing,' said Jas.

Anna added, 'Tognarelli says Bennett wouldn't be into drugs, but he's basing that on thirty-year-old memories. Doesn't make sense, but I got my head chewed off for saying so.'

'He seemed like a good guy to me,' said Jas.

'He is,' said Anna. 'It's just, well, complicated. Where's the CCTV, by the way?'

'Closest is on the corner with the main road. Do you want to have a look?'

Back at the station they found the right tapes from the time period twenty-four hours before the car was found in Wasdale. Looking at the grainy footage was taking too long, they had to get to Haverigg. Just when they were about to give up, there it was, on the jerky film. A figure walked towards the lock up, and a few minutes later the BMW appeared, being driven slowly towards the main road before it turned the corner and headed to the right. 'That's it,' said Anna. 'Anyone in there apart from the driver?'

They peered at the screen. 'No,' said Jas. 'I reckon it's just Bennett. Could have picked up someone on the way north, but he was alone when he left here. That's definitely him walking around the corner before that, is it?' she asked.

'Right height, right age, hard to see the face, but I'd say it was Bennett. Looks like the clothes he was wearing when they found him. So we now have him alone when he left here.'

Jas glanced at the clock. 'Better go,' she said. 'I said we'd be at the prison at two. Your car?'

'No, thanks,' said Anna. 'My backside hasn't recovered yet from the drive down.'

Getting into the prison involved a tedious process of checking bags and pockets, showing ID and being escorted through various locked doors. The buildings were old, brick-built, and spread out over a wide flat area, exposed to the worst of the wind off the sea.

'Beach is just over there,' said Jas, pointing into the wind. 'They have trouble sometimes with people standing on the shore, chucking stuff over the fence.'

'What a place,' said Anna, out of earshot of the officer who was escorting them. 'Wouldn't want to get marooned in here. Feels like a gulag in Siberia.'

'Not meant to be a holiday camp, is it?' said Jas. Anna saw the officer smile: he could obviously hear them.

John Chipping, prisoner number 6489, was waiting for them in a grey room, sitting by a metal table on a metal chair. Both table and chair were screwed to the floor. He looked up as the two women entered, smiled at them. He was dark and thin, with a stubble shadow around his chin and glasses held together at the side with pink tape. He pushed the glasses higher with his forefinger. 'Well, well, my lucky day. Welcome, ladies.'

Jas remembered the advice Anna had offered her as they drove up from Barrow. 'Some of the young blokes are really smarmy to women officers. They obviously think they can charm their way into some kind of deal. Take no notice, don't smile, and don't whatever you do respond. Just blank them off and keep on with what you want to say. You'll have met dozens of blokes like that on the outside but being inside seems to give some of them a sense of being on their own turf. Pretty pathetic actually, and that's what they are, for all their bluster. I'll start things off, OK?'

Jas nodded. 'Thanks.'

As she'd advised the younger woman, Anna took absolutely no notice of Chipping's opening gambit. It was as if he hadn't spoken.

'DS Penrose, DC Spears,' was all she said. They sat down and Anna took out a file, which she left unopened on the table, and a notebook.

'John Chipping, right?'

Chipping nodded. 'People call me Spud. Don't know why.' He smiled at Jas, who stared straight back at him.

Anna continued, her voice quite flat. 'We're investigating an incident involving an acquaintance of yours, Michael Bennett.'

'What kind of incident?' Chipping asked. 'What's he done?'

'Our records show that you and Bennett were in care together as boys, is that right?'

He nodded. 'Monty House. With that bastard Edwards.'

'And did you keep up an acquaintance after that?'

Chipping shrugged. 'Saw him around. Barrow's a small place. People know each other. Then he went off somewhere. Navy, I think. Hardly saw him after that.'

Anna opened the file and looked at a piece of paper. Jas could see that it had only a few words on it, which didn't appear to be relevant to this conversation. 'Our records show that you started your sentence here in December last year.'

'Right,' said Chipping. 'Two years and for what? Nowt.'

'Before that, you were on remand?'

He nodded.

'So when was the last time you saw Michael Bennett?'

'Mikey? God knows.'

'Think, Mr Chipping. It's important.'

'How important?'

'When was the last time you saw Bennett?' Anna repeated. Jas sat still, learning how not to get dragged into anything.

Chipping sat back in his chair, staring at the ceiling. Jas guessed he was trying to work out what advantage to him there might be in cooperating. He shrugged again. 'Dunno. Could have been not last year, year before.'

'Nineteen ninety-nine?' Jas said.

Chipping turned to look at her. 'Good girl,' he said. 'Not just a pretty face, are you, love?' Jas tried hard not to react, regretting what she'd said and concentrating on her notes, head down.

Anna brought the man's attention back to her. 'What did Bennett say to you, at that time?'

Another shrug. 'He were in a right state. Said he needed help with summat.'

'With what?'

'No idea. Looked dead rough. Been on a bender, he said. I told 'im, whatever it was, he was on his own. I was in enough trouble meself, didn't need any of 'is.' Chipping paused. 'Then he said he'd seen one of our old mates from Monty House. Saw him on the street somewhere, but the bugger didn't let on. Well, he wasn't a proper mate, even when we were all in there together. Older than us – right up the arses of the people who ran the place, and the other pervs. He 'ad a job outside. Edwards even gave 'im driving lessons. Bet 'e got a sore bum as the price for that, smarmy git!'

Anna looked up. 'Where did Bennett see this man?'

'Didn't say, did he? But he said our mate had changed his name and got rich, by the look of it. Big car, all that.'

'Name?'

'What's it worth?' said Chipping. 'I reckon I know some stuff you could do with. Hear all sorts in here.'

'Name?' Anna repeated.

Chipping leaned forward. 'That's it, love. Name means nowt, does it? He'd changed it. And Mikey reckoned the bloke was up to summat.' He leaned back, hands behind his head. The smell of stale sweat hung in the room. 'That's what I mean. You 'ear things.'

'What was his name when you knew him?' Anna said again. 'We'll work out the rest. And it's worth nothing, by the way. You're just confirming something we're investigating, nothing new.'

'So you know this bloke's into drugs then?' said Chipping. 'That's what I heard.'

Anna looked hard at him. 'I want the name. Haven't got all day, Mr Chipping.'

He dropped his arms and leaned forward again.

'Bitch,' he said quietly. Anna didn't blink. 'Stuart Billings,' he said. 'Bilko, we called him. Allus out for himself, just like Sergeant Bilko on the telly.'

Jas scribbled assiduously in her notebook. Anna asked, 'And what have you heard, about Mr Billings and drugs?'

'That he's got summat big going. Not small stuff like most blokes in here. We get caught; blokes like him get away with it. Know how to butter up the right people, see. Bastards.'

'Is that all?'

'Hard stuff,' said Chipping. 'Comes in by sea. Mikey could have done stuff like that, if he'd 'ad the guts. Boats and that. Harbours all up the coast here. Coastguards can't keep eyes on them all, can they?'

Anna closed the file and put her pen away. 'So this was gossip, nothing more?'

Chipping shrugged. 'No smoke and all that.' He smirked at them. 'And if I knew owt for sure, I wouldn't tell you lot. Not without my brief and a proper deal.' He snorted derisively and banged on the table top. 'Policewomen? You're just a joke.'

Anna got to her feet and waited while the door to the room was opened. Jas followed her lead. As they walked back down the dismal corridor, Jas said, 'Who's this Bilko anyway?'

Anna laughed out loud. 'Too hard to explain,' she said. 'Before your time.'

'OK,' said Jas, 'but we got something from him, didn't we?'

Anna put her finger to her lips. 'Say nothing until we're outside,' she said quietly. 'Walls have ears in a place like this. As you heard, information gets traded, like everything else.'

The exit formalities over, they went back to the car and drove out of the gates, back down the road towards the village and reality. Jas said, 'I need a few minutes to get that place out of my system. There's a café near the beach. Cuppa?'

A short while later they sat in the car, looking out towards the ebbing tide, steam from their takeout tea clouding the windscreen.

Anna was thinking aloud. 'Same name I got from the matron at Montgomery House. She said this Billings character was close to the adults in the place. Too close, she said. Sounds as if he's done all right for himself since then.'

'What about all that drugs talk?' Jas asked.

'Could be just that,' said Anna, 'talk. It's an easy way to explain someone's success – easier than admitting that a kid with a rough start in life can do well by working hard and staying out of trouble. Especially if you came from the same place and ended up in prison.'

She remembered something. 'There were photos of Billings and the other lads, in Monty House. The DCI showed them to the old lady who was matron there and now they're in our office, but I never got to look at them properly.'

'We've got a set too,' said Jas. 'Sent down from Hall Brow. They're on my desk somewhere. I was going to put them on the board but haven't done it yet. I'll dig them out when we get back. Black-and-white and pretty blurred, but I've seen that Chipping bloke's face before. People don't change that much, unless they want to, with surgery and such.'

Half an hour later, back in the Barrow CID room, Jas handed the photos to Anna, who leafed slowly through them. She recognised Bennett, sitting cross-legged on the ground, and Chipping at the other end of the same row. Standing to one side, detached from the main group of boys, next to a woman wearing a hat, was another figure. Not an adult, but he looked older than the other boys. Anna stared at him.

'Jas, have you got a magnifier?'

She fumbled in a drawer and handed over a round magnifying glass. Anna cleaned it and held it over the image.

She looked, looked away, then looked again. She stood up, pushing the chair back so suddenly that it clattered over.

'Toilet?' she asked, looking around.

Jas pointed. 'You OK?'

Anna said nothing, stumbling across the room, her hand to her mouth. In the safety of the Ladies, she vomited into the toilet bowl and stayed leaning over it, breathing heavily, as tears ran down her cheeks.

CHAPTER 19

The next few minutes were a blur. Anna flushed the toilet, cleaned herself up, waited until her breathing returned to normal. She walked slowly back to the office, feeling as if she'd been hit in the stomach.

Jas tried not to fuss, using what she'd learned about not reacting. 'You OK?' was all she said. 'Sit down for a bit. You look rough.'

Anna took the proffered chair and sat down, facing away from the younger woman's concern. 'Don't know what happened then,' she said, as she found a tissue in her bag and blew her nose. 'That place must have got to me more than I thought.' She blew her nose again. 'Or something I ate, maybe.' She smiled. 'Not looking forward to driving that shaky Land Rover back up north.'

'No rush, is there?' said Jas. 'You can phone from here if you want to, and take your time going back. What are you going to tell the DCI?'

Anna thought as carefully as she could. 'Confirmation of that name, and that Bennett had obviously encountered him about the same time as Graham went missing.' How much more could she say? 'We think Bennett needed help to dispose of Graham's body. Maybe he asked Billings, like he asked Spud.'

'Do you know where Billings is now?' Jas asked. She was cutting images out of the photos, to put on the display.

Anna shook her head. 'Looks like he's changed his name. Could be anywhere.'

'Well, it's a start,' said Jas. 'And the drugs link might be useful.'

Anna shrugged. 'Maybe. One of our DCs is working with both our team and the Drug Squad. They're chasing up some cannabis growing up on the fells, and think there are drugs coming in somewhere on the west coast, but that's about as vague as the story Chipping was telling us. Not sure whether this stuff will help them much.'

Talking was helping. Anna's mind was racing, but she appeared calm and rational.

'Are you OK to drive back?' Jas asked.

'Fine, thanks. Being sick helps, doesn't it? I feel much better now. Thanks for taking me round, very valuable.'

'And thanks for the lesson in how to deal with creepy guys,' said Jas. 'I hate men like that. I just have to learn to freeze them out, like you did.'

'Don't forget,' said Anna, shaking Jas Spears' outstretched hand, 'Workington could do with some more good women coppers. You'd do fine with us. Think about it.'

'Thanks,' said Jas.

Anna walked carefully to the Land Rover in the car park, aware that she might be being watched from the office. Once inside, she started the engine and drove out into the street, away from the police building, found a space by the side of the road, and pulled in. She'd already decided what to do, and there was a good enough mobile signal here in town for her to make the call.

The number rang and rang. 'Pick up,' she whispered.

The ringing stopped and a woman's voice said, 'Buttlers, Caroline here.'

'Caroline,' Anna said, as brightly as she could. 'Is your dad at home?'

'No,' said the girl. 'He's had to go out.' There was a long pause. 'He and Rory had a row early on. Rory went storming off. I think Dad's gone to look for him.'

'What were they rowing about?'

Another pause. Then: 'Same old stuff,' said Caroline. 'I told you, Rory doesn't pull his weight round here. I get cross with him and so does Dad.'

'Do you know when your dad will be back?'

'No,' said the girl. 'Wish I did. I feel stuck here, waiting for one of them to ring. I thought we were going away for the weekend, but I've probably got that wrong.'

'OK, I'll let you go,' said Anna. 'When you see your dad, can you ask him to call me? On the mobile, not at the office.'

'Sure. Bye then.'

Anna put away the phone and hung her head. He wasn't there. She couldn't say or ask anything else, and part of her was relieved about that. But she had to know for sure. Maybe Simon had a brother, or a cousin, someone who looked just like him and had been in Monty House all those years ago...

There were too many coincidences for her to be hopeful about it. The rational part of her brain wouldn't allow her to evade the likely truth. Stuart Billings... Simon Buttler. The same initials. Then there was his doubtful claim to have been in the army, the over-zealous interest he had taken in her work, and his fury with her when the police contacted him. And the way his wife had disappeared, seemingly without trace. It all added up to a picture that filled Anna with despair at her own gullibility.

She breathed in and out slowly, cleared her head, and set off slowly, away from the busy town.

❖ ❖ ❖

The office at Hall Brow was deserted when she reached it towards the end of the afternoon. She checked with the desk sergeant. 'Where is everybody?'

'Big flap on,' he said, without looking up. 'Call came in,' he checked his watch, 'couple of hours ago, and everyone buggered off.'

'Where?'

'A fire, up Pardshaw way.'

'What sort of fire?' she asked, leaning down to draw his attention away from whatever he was doing. 'A house... a car?'

The sergeant looked up at her. 'A big blaze, on the fell. One of the PCs said it was a crop of cannabis, but they've all got their knickers in a twist after them sheep were found stoned last week.'

'Do you know exactly where they are?'

'That geeky lad of yours'll know. He's still around.'

'Jason? OK, thanks.' She ran to the office.

'Oh, you're back,' he said, raising his eyebrows when he saw how distraught Anna appeared, not like her usual unflappable self. 'Sam said to tell you they've gone up to a fire.'

'Why all of them?'

'Firemen said they'd found a body. Sounded like arson or an accident. Anyroad, they all shot off there and I haven't heard much since.'

'Bell and Pritchard too?'

'All of them. Cannabis involved again, apparently. The DCI left a note on your desk before he went out.'

The scrawled message on Anna's desk gave the coordinates and underneath Sam had written: *Body. Badly burned. Looks like accident or arson, or both. May not be a phone signal. Call Cockermouth nick for info, or the fire station. Sam.*

Anna sat down and tried to process this latest news. It had to be coincidence. Yes, Simon and Rory were both away from home. So what? They could be anywhere. But something nagged at her. She picked up Sam's note with the coordinates, double-checked that the OS map was in the Land Rover, worked out the route, and set off.

It wasn't difficult to find. As soon as she got to Pardshaw she could see smoke streaming away towards the high fells. Anna followed the twisting lanes to find the spot that Sam had indicated. It was obvious from the presence of three cars parked randomly across the road. A uniformed young woman flagged her down.

'Pull off here, ma'am,' she said. 'Follow the track down to those sheds on the right, where the fire engines are. They're all in there.'

As soon as Anna got out of the car she could smell the sweet heaviness of the burning crop in the smoke that was swirling around. Cannabis didn't burn by accident. This stuff must have been lit deliberately, but why? No way to hide it, not in the daylight.

She ran towards the sheds. As she rounded a corner, she could see Sam's short figure standing with Bell and Pritchard. Brown was there too, head and shoulders taller than the others. It was he who looked up and saw her, before the others turned their heads.

'Who's minding the store?' Bell asked. 'No need for all of us to be up here. Show's over.'

'What happened?' Anna asked. She'd been practising ignoring difficult men today and carried on doing so.

Pritchard took over the explanation. 'Looks like someone tried to torch the crop in the shed, using petrol. Wind's easing but earlier on it was fierce up here. Stuff must have blown back, caught whoever it was. Lit match or static electricity… something sparked it off and the fire raiser went same way as the plants.'

Sam pointed to markers laid out on the ground, which led to the edge of the scorched area inside the entrance to the shed. 'Looks like whoever it was ran back and forth, probably looking for something to put the flames out. But it didn't work. Nasty way to go.'

'Where's the body?' Anna asked.

Sam pointed to the shed door. 'In there,' he said. 'Shed didn't catch, or we'd have had trouble finding it. Just a lad, by the look of it.

Someone must have told the poor bastard to get rid of the crop, and it went wrong. Badly wrong. Forensics are in there now.'

'Any ID?' Anna asked. She was starting to feel sick again.

Pritchard shook her head. 'Not yet. Timing's interesting though. I've been working down that list of estate agents dealing in abandoned farms like this one, and now this. Someone's trying to get rid of the evidence, I reckon.'

Bell shook his head. 'Just a sideline, all this. Real stuff's coming in somewhere on the coast and we're still no nearer to it.'

Anna pulled herself together. 'Might have something for you on that, from a bloke in Haverigg prison. Rumour mostly, but he was talking about boats bringing in hard stuff. Not through Barrow, maybe one of the other local harbours – smaller, probably. Doesn't know which one though.'

'Not much use then,' said Bell. 'It has to be someone far more organised than this poor bugger.'

There was a call from the doorway. 'Sir?' Bell and Tognarelli both looked up, then at each other, working out whose job it was to respond. Anna walked between the two of them, something propelling her to see what lay inside.

Tony Wong was there, kneeling by the shrouded shape on the scorched floor. He looked up at her and nodded. 'Not a pretty sight,' he warned. 'Accelerant splashed back somehow and then caught. He's burned from the knees up. Didn't stand a chance – no one here to help, nothing to cover the flames. He tried rolling by the look of it, but probably too late. No ID to tell us who he is, or what the hell he was doing up here.'

Anna looked down. Incongruous white shoes protruded from under the shroud, gleaming in the semi-darkness of the shed. Tony followed her gaze. 'New trainers,' he said. 'Fresh out of the box. Adidas. Just a lad.'

Anna turned away. Words eluded her. Pieces of a puzzle she didn't want to see jostled against each other in her brain.

'Anna?' she heard Tony say, but no reply seemed possible as she walked slowly out of the shed and into the gloom. Outside, she kept walking. Bell and Tognarelli were arguing with each other about something. It was Maureen who saw Anna's expression and took her arm, pulling her gently to one side.

'What is it?' she said. 'You've seen a burned body before, haven't you?' Anna nodded. Still the words didn't come. 'You need to sit down, over here, lean on the fire engine.'

Anna sank to a crouch, sitting on the running board. She took a deep breath. 'I think I know who it is,' she murmured. Maureen leaned down to hear her better. 'How? Who?' she began.

Anna held up her hand. 'Can't be sure but I think his name is Rory Buttler.'

'Buttler?' Maureen made the connection. 'Simon Buttler's boy?' Anna nodded.

Maureen shook her head. 'Christ. What was he doing here, trying to torch the crop? To protect his dad maybe? We were getting close, maybe they panicked.'

'The trainers,' murmured Anna. 'He had new white trainers.'

Maureen had stopped listening. 'Stay here,' she said, standing up. 'Sir,' she called out. 'Over here. Anna's got something. Says she knows who it is.'

But Anna wasn't saying anything. She slipped sideways off the step and fell onto her side on the stony ground.

CHAPTER 20

The body had been in the mortuary for several hours. So far, all Sam's attempts to locate Simon Buttler had failed. There was no one at his office and the number on the answer machine was for his home. At the house there was a young woman called Caroline, who was so upset they could hardly get a word out of her. She had no idea where her father and her brother were, pleading with Sam for more information.

'Is there anyone you could call, to be with you?' he asked. 'What about your mother?'

'She's gone. I don't want to see her... What about Anna? Can I talk to her?'

Sam was confused. 'Anna who?'

'Don't know her surname,' said the girl. 'She's a friend of my dad's. She called him here, this afternoon.'

Sam put his hand over the phone and spoke to Maureen. 'She wants someone called Anna something... must be a coincidence. Has our Anna recovered yet?'

Maureen shook her head.

'One of my officers will come down to see you,' said Sam to the distraught girl. 'You may be able to help us find your dad. Is that OK? She'll be there in about an hour. Will you be OK till then? Give me the address.'

He wrote it down and handed the information to Maureen. 'Caroline's the daughter's name. She might have more to tell us. She's not a child, but I don't want to call her in to ID a badly burned body – not when she's got a dad who could do it. See what you can get out of her about him.'

'What about Penrose?'

'We'll get her home. She might need a doctor. This and the other episode – it's not looking too good, is it? Any idea what's got to her?'

Maureen shook her head. 'She saw the shoes on the lad's body. Wong says she turned away then, didn't want to see any more. She told me she thought it was Rory Buttler, then just keeled over. I think she had a bad reaction once before, during the fighting in Bosnia. PTSD or something? I know she still has to see someone about that, from time to time. She told me 9/11 has been giving her nightmares lately. Maybe the PTSD has kicked off again.'

'OK, leave that with me,' said Sam. 'You get down to Buttler's place, have a look at the girl.'

'Just hope I can get her talking,' said Maureen.

'Watch what you do,' said Sam. 'We don't want the CPS throwing out witness evidence like they did last time. We'll need a proper statement, preferably taken in the station. Bring her in if she's in any fit state, OK? Take Bell's car, we'll get him back. I don't want him interviewing any anxious young woman. And I might not be here when you get back,' he added. 'Going home to get a few hours' sleep. I'll be back in first thing.'

The area around Egremont was unknown territory to Maureen, born and bred in Carlisle as she was: during years with the Drug

Squad she'd seen most parts of the county, but mainly the towns and the coast, not these isolated villages.

It was dark when she left the main road and followed the directions she'd been given to the Old Vicarage in Hilton, an address she knew from investigating Simon Buttler's business. Those checks had started from her inquiries into estate agents buying and selling abandoned farm properties, but she was even more interested in Buttler's finances. The office in Whitehaven was small and there was little evidence of advertising or promotion of the business, or of signboards around the town, though there was apparently talk of opening another office in Maryport and possibly one in Carlisle too. Maybe he'd inherited money, she thought as she drove along an even narrower, darker lane, wondering where the house was.

Must be near a church, she thought, and saw the outline of a spire etched against the twilight glow to the west. Just beyond it was a driveway, and there was the sign she was looking for 'The Old Vicarage', and a glint of light between the trees and bushes screening the property from the road.

The house at the end of the driveway was impressively large. Light streamed from every window, like a palace at party time. As Maureen parked the car she could see that the front door stood open. She got out of the driver's seat and a figure appeared in the hallway. A young woman with fair hair stared at Maureen emerging from the car. 'Who are you?' she said. 'What's happened?'

Maureen stretched out her hand, holding up her warrant card. 'It's the police, Caroline. My boss was the man who rang you, about an hour ago. I'm DC Maureen Pritchard. We know you're worried about your dad and brother, and we're worried about you. Are you alone? May I come in?'

'There's no one here,' Caroline said. 'I've tried everything but I can't find them.'

'It's OK,' Maureen said, putting an arm around her and leading into the house. 'Let's shut the door, shall we? Keep the cold out.'

'No,' the girl cried. 'What if they come home... what if I don't hear them?'

'OK, no problem,' said Maureen.

She let Caroline lead her through to the back and the large open-plan room with its spectacular glass wall. Maureen was adding up in her head what a house like this might have cost, and the financial affairs of Buttler and Lilley estate agents became more interesting by the minute. This wasn't the time for inquiries about them but that time would surely come.

Out in the garden a wisp of blue smoke dwindled in the cold air. 'Someone had a fire out there?' Maureen asked.

'Dead leaves,' said Caroline.

'What a lovely house and garden,' said Maureen. 'Now, let's sit down and you can tell me all about what's happened today. We'll do our very best to find your dad and your brother, but you have to help us do it. A few deep breaths, that's it.' Maureen held Caroline by the shoulders while lowering her gently into a chair.

'Now, pet, can I get you a drink? You've been alone a long time, stressing out. What can I get you? Tea? Water? Something stronger?'

'Tea,' Caroline whispered.

Maureen found her way round the sophisticated kitchen, opening cupboards and drawers to find what she needed. A few minutes later they were both sitting at the big table. Maureen left her notebook in her pocket for now, so she could focus on easing some sense out of the girl.

'So,' she said, 'you live here with your dad and your brother. Your dad's called Simon and your brother is Rory. That right?'

Caroline nodded, holding the mug of tea between her hands. Maureen went on, 'We've been trying to talk to your dad today, that's why we called the house and realised that you were here alone. So my boss sent me to see that you were OK, and if you could maybe help us. How old are you, pet?'

'Twenty-one in January. We're planning a big party.' Caroline looked up. 'Are Dad and Rory in trouble?'

'No, not as far as we know at present,' said Maureen, choosing her words with care. There was no proof of anything at the moment. Suspicions about Simon's business, and a reasonable fear that Rory was dead, but no certainty about either of them.

'Why don't you start at the beginning, pet? Tell me when you saw them last, and we'll do our best to find them. OK?'

Caroline took a deep breath. 'They had a row,' she said, 'this morning.'

'Dad and Rory?'

'Rory wouldn't get up and Dad shouted at him, dragged him out of bed.' The girl lowered her eyes. 'He was really angry, more than usual.'

'He and Rory have argued before, have they?'

'All the time. Dad works so hard, and Rory… well, he doesn't do anything.' She hesitated. 'And he smokes. Makes the house smell awful. Rory says he doesn't, but we can smell it.'

'Lots of young people smoke, don't they?' Maureen said, but Caroline shook her head.

'Not cigarettes.' Further hesitation. Caroline took a sip of the tea and added, 'Cannabis… weed. He got caught for it as a kid but he didn't stop.'

'And he and your dad had a row about that?'

'They were upstairs, in my brother's room,' said Caroline. 'I couldn't hear everything, but Dad said Rory was useless, never helped the family. Just a dead weight, he called him. Dad came downstairs all red in the face. Then Rory came down, and they started again. I shouted at them to stop, but Dad told me to stay out of it.'

'What did your dad want Rory to do? Do you know?'

Caroline shook her head. 'No.'

'You don't know, or you don't want to say?'

The girl pushed back her chair and got up, pushing her hair behind her ears. She looked down at Maureen. 'You don't understand, do you? No one does.'

Maureen kept very still. 'Can you tell me, help me to understand?'

Caroline walked over to the glass wall and looked out into the darkness, her reflected image holding Maureen's attention. 'When Rory was in trouble, he was thrown out of school and no one would give him a job after that. He refused to work in the office, said he wanted to be his own boss. So Dad helped him.'

'How?' Maureen asked. She had to keep the girl talking.

'Bought him some land, told him to make use of it, grow something.'

'Like farming, you mean?'

Caroline turned around. 'A bit like farming, yes.'

Maureen decided to ask a direct question. 'Caroline, did your brother start growing cannabis?'

The girl's face puckered up. She nodded. 'I know it's illegal but they didn't seem too bothered about that. Rory said that was what he wanted to do. I thought Dad would say no, but he just laughed.'

'When was this?' Maureen asked.

'Months ago, a year maybe, when Rory had said he would never go back to school.'

'Did your dad help him get started?'

'They didn't talk about it in front of me, they knew I didn't like it. But it brought them closer... you know, working together. They were getting on well and that was better than before.'

'But today they were rowing again, you said?'

'Something happened a little while ago, something went wrong. Dad was so angry with Rory, said he'd ruined everything. Rory just went back in his shell, wouldn't get up, smoked all the time. I tried to keep things going, but they got worse.'

Maureen kept her eyes on the girl, but her mind was working on what she was hearing, putting the pieces together. Rory had not kept his crop secure and sheep had got into it. That had drawn attention to one of his 'farms', but today they'd found another one, which Rory had tried to destroy. Why?

'Let's talk about today, Caroline. Why did it all flare up again today?'

Caroline sat down again, put her head in her hands for a moment, then looked up at her. 'It was like Dad had told Rory to do something, and he hadn't done it, and so Dad just lost it. He kept saying, "I told you, you have to do it, before we go."'

'Go where?' Maureen asked.

Caroline looked at her, wide-eyed. 'Didn't I say? Dad said we were all going away, for a stay in the sun. Whatever he wanted Rory to do, it had to be done before we went.'

Maureen looked at her watch. 'I promised I'd call in to the station,' she said. 'Let them know you're all right. Can I do that now? You'll be OK for a minute or two?'

Caroline nodded, and took another sip of her tea. 'You're going to find them, aren't you?' she asked, looking up at Maureen.

'Oh, yes,' she said. 'We'll find them.'

'There's no signal in here, you'll need to go outside, where your car is.'

'OK, I'll be back in a minute or two. Finish your tea.'

'Pick up, pick up,' she whispered frantically into the phone once she was safely outside. The ringing tone stopped. Henny Brown's accent was unmistakable. 'You still there?' Maureen said, surprised.

'We all are except Penrose. She's still at home, but someone said she was coming in soon. Who do you want?'

'Put the DI on, will you?'

'Are you bringing the girl in?' said Bell, cutting straight to what he wanted. 'We need to be sure we've got Rory Buttler's body. Bring some DNA stuff too, on both of them, Rory and his dad.'

'Have you found Simon Buttler?'

'No, but we will. DNA probably won't help there, but you never know these days. Anyway, what's the girl saying?'

'Some interesting stuff. Think we've solved the stoned sheep case. The girl has a lot to offer, more than she knows. She's only twenty and seems a bit naïve to me, or else she's putting on a good act. Talking away fit to bust. I don't want her to clam up.'

'What about her ID-ing the lad?'

'What is there to see?' Maureen was whispering now, walking down the drive away from the house, afraid of being overheard.

'Not a lot. Face has pretty well gone. DNA should clinch it if she's not up to the job. Bring a toothbrush, hairbrush... anything with enough for the lab to go on. It'll take a bit longer this way, but we don't want the girl too freaked out to tell us anything else.'

Maureen went on, 'She says they were going away somewhere soon.'

'Were they indeed? I wonder where to?' said Bell. 'I reckon this needs to be put on tape. Don't mention the lad yet. Tell her we don't want to leave her alone in the house. Bring in a few things she might need, and she can sleep here. We'll sort it all out in the morning. Tell her anything you want but get her in here – now.'

The phone went dead. Maureen thought about how she would broach the suggestion that Caroline should come to Hall Brow.

'You know, we're all very concerned about your dad and your brother both being missing, pet,' Maureen said when she had returned to the kitchen diner. Caroline was standing by the glass wall again, facing out.

'What about Anna?' she asked, without turning around. 'Could she come and stay here with me?'

'Anna? Anna who?'

Caroline turned to face her. 'She's a friend of my dad's. She's nice. Could she come here and be with me?'

'They're friends, are they?'

'I think they do the Mountain Rescue thing together,' said Caroline. 'She came for dinner. I think Dad really likes her.' The girl hesitated. 'And I think she might have stayed over one night. Rory said he heard them, in the morning.'

'And how did you feel about that?' Maureen asked, trying hard to look and sound casual as pieces of a picture fell into place.

'OK,' said Caroline. 'She seems like a nice person.'

'I wonder if I know her,' Maureen ventured. 'What does she look like?'

Caroline considered for a moment. 'Bit shorter than me, brown hair, quite thick. She looks fit, you know, like my dad.'

'And you don't know her other name?'

Caroline shook her head. But I do, Maureen thought to herself. Out loud she said, 'Well, never mind that now, pet. My boss has suggested that you come up to Workington with me, to save you being alone here. Bring your mobile phone, in case either of them wants to reach you. There are more people up at the station, all trying to find them, and it'll be a real help to us if you're there as well.'

Caroline frowned. 'But what if they come back here?'

'We'll leave a note, on the door. Otherwise they might worry about you too, and we don't want that. Too much confusion.'

'You're sure that's the best thing?'

'Yes, we'll put you up till the morning, and I'm sure it'll be sorted out by then. Just bring a few things you might need. And can you show me the rest of the house before we leave, just in case there are any clues about where they might be?'

Maureen didn't expect to find anything significant lying around, but she was curious about the Buttler family set up, and even more so about Anna's private life. Ten minutes later, they were driving north. Maureen suspected that the night ahead would be both interesting and difficult for everyone concerned.

CHAPTER 21

It was around ten when Sam got back to his house in Parton. He drove the car to its usual spot by the back door, picked up his bag and locked the vehicle before taking the familiar few steps towards the door. While he felt for his keys in his inside pocket a strong arm slid around his neck, pulling him backwards. Then something was pressed against his mouth and nose. He struggled for a few moments before everything went black.

Must be a dream, a bad dream. He couldn't move, and his head throbbed. Something covered his eyes and there was a nasty metallic taste in his mouth. Wherever he was, it was moving. He lurched from one side to the other of a small space. He must be in a vehicle: not upright in a seat but lying flat, in the boot or on the floor of a van. He struggled to remember. He'd heard something behind him, but after that it was all a blur. He tried to speak but his mouth was held shut. Tape, he guessed, that pulled painfully whenever he tried to move his mouth. Someone had knocked him out, tied him up, dumped him here. But who? Why?

More bumping, then the movement stopped. A moment later, there was a sudden rush of air into the confined space, and a smell of trees and earth. Someone fumbled round his ankles and he could move them, then his knees. He stretched out his legs but stopped when someone pulled at his shoulders.

'Swing your legs round,' said a man's voice. 'Stand up.'

Sam did so, stretching upright, feeling dizzy. He felt himself falling sideways and then being jerked back upright. The tape was ripped from his mouth and he yelped with pain.

'I can't see,' he said.

'Doesn't matter. Stand up straight, use your legs. You can walk OK. I'll lead you.' The voice wasn't local, he thought. A northern accent, but not strongly Cumbrian. 'Who are you?' Sam asked. 'Where am I?'

'It doesn't matter,' the voice replied. 'None of it matters.'

The man pushed and pulled him and Sam went with it. He could tell by the strength in the man's arm that there was little point in trying to fight back. Thin slivers of light seeped under the blindfold – from a torch, Sam guessed. His feet were on a path, bushes catching at his clothes as he stumbled on, up an incline. Then the pushing stopped and he was forced to sit on the ground, leaning against something, a wall or a door. There was the rattle of a chain, something metal, and the voice cursed.

'What's the matter?' Sam asked.

'Nothing. Keep quiet. It's just taking…'

A squeak, and a grating sound. 'Got it,' said the voice. Another metallic whine – a door opening? 'Stand up. Come on.'

Sam was pulled again, up a step. 'Lift your feet,' ordered the voice. 'Now, stop.' The creak of the door again. Then silence, a different sort of silence, interior, with a muffled echo, like a swimming pool or a vault, and a strange smell.

Sam stretched out his arms and hands, feeling for something, anything. 'Don't do that,' said the voice. 'Keep your hands down.' Something scraped on the floor and he was pushed backwards, finding the seat of a chair behind his legs. 'Keep still,' the voice told him. Something was wound around Sam's chest and arms, pinning him to the chair.

'Who are you?' he said again. 'Do I know you?'

There was a small stifled sound of amusement. 'Once upon a time.'

An idea came to him suddenly. 'I knew some people, once upon a time,' he said. 'Iris Robinson, Captain Edwards, Mikey Bennett, Irene Thornhill.'

Silence.

'Is that your once upon a time too?' Sam asked. 'Do you know those people?'

In the silence, he could hear someone breathing heavily.

'You do. I know you do,' he said. 'It's you, the one Iris Robinson told me about. You're Stuart.'

'What did she tell you, whoever she is?'

'That you were different... special.'

'You're guessing. I don't know what you're talking about.'

'Then who are you?' asked Sam. 'What do you want with me? You know what a risk this is, kidnapping a policeman. They'll be looking for me already. You'll go away for a very long time.'

'Yes, I'm going away, and for a long time, but not where you think.'

'How did you find me, Stuart?' Sam continued, relieved they were finally communicating. 'Was it you who helped Mikey with Dr Graham? I always suspected it was, when Iris told me how well you were doing. Who else would Mikey get to help him? Who else could he threaten by telling the truth? But how did you know where to find me?'

'You don't know much, do you?' the voice taunted him.

'We know more than you think,' said Sam, but he was bluffing. The only certainty he felt in his bones was that this man had spent time as a boy at Montgomery House. He was the special one, Irene Thornhill's protégé – the same Irene Thornhill who'd wanted Judith, Sam's Judith, dead. And now that protégé was here, standing close by him in the darkness.

'Take this blindfold off,' said Sam. 'Let me see you. I was there. I'll know you. I'll remember.'

Silence. Somewhere water was dripping. Then there was a sudden whoosh and a different noise, throbbing, rushing. Was the water coming at him? Sam flinched, bracing himself. 'What's that?' he cried out. 'What's happening?'

The unseen man laughed at him. 'Look at you! The big man's frightened of the water. Those are the pumps. If they stopped for good, then you'd need help.'

'But where are we?' Sam shouted. 'Why are there pumps?'

'Guess.'

'A mine or a quarry,' said Sam. 'Somewhere that could flood without pumps. But we're not underground.'

'You could be, in minutes, if I pressed the right buttons and they all worked. But they don't work, not anymore. That's why no one will find you here unless I tell them where I've put you. You need me, Tognarelli. Without me, you're dead. Like that other old man.'

'So I was right,' Sam said. 'You were there, at Monty House, with Mikey and the others.'

'And I knew Doc Graham,' said the man, 'if that's what you want to know. Don't expect me to mourn for the bastard. He was supposed to look after us, but he didn't care. No one did.'

'But Irene Thornhill cared about you, didn't she?' said Sam. He had to keep this man talking. 'She looked after you. You were OK there, weren't you? Did Edwards teach you to drive, like he did the other special boys?'

No response. Sam wanted to goad the man now, to push him. 'You did well, Stuart. Not like Mikey. He never really stood a chance, and in the end it all got too much for him. After all those years, he couldn't take anymore. Or poor Stevie Stringer, dead in quicksand when he was just a kid.'

There was no response and Sam searched for something more to say, to keep talking. 'We found a lad today,' he said. 'Same age as you when you were in that place. Just a youngster. God knows what happened to him. He'll never get the chances you did, to live his life, do well.'

'What lad?' said the voice. Its tone was different now.

'Just someone we found today,' said Sam. 'No one you know. Burned. Terrible way to go, all alone.'

'Where?' said the voice harshly. 'Where was this lad?'

'Up on the fells, above Pardshaw.'

The man gasped. Sam heard him choke. Light from the torch, which had been shining steadily through a chink in the blindfold, suddenly veered away. Sam heard the creak of the door, and the noise as the man stumbled out. The door slammed behind him. Darkness enveloped Sam. He wondered if this was the end for him. Trussed up like Dr Graham, hidden away in darkness, lost.

Maureen was surprised how easy it was to convince Caroline to go with her to Hall Brow. The girl liked being the centre of attention, it seemed, and Maureen played on that. Better to be with us, she said, than sitting here alone in the house, waiting. If Buttler was involved in criminal activity, and Maureen was increasingly sure about that, she wondered how much Caroline knew about her dad's business, the real business that made the money to pay for this house and fancy holidays. The overseas trip that Caroline had mentioned might be crucial, and Maureen needed to know more.

'This trip you mentioned,' she asked casually, as they drove though the dark lanes towards the main road. 'Do you know where you are going, or is it a surprise?'

'Dad hasn't said, but I think we'll be going to Spain. That's where we usually go.'

'Spain, lovely. Whereabouts? Never been myself.'

'Down south, where it's hot. We love it,' said Caroline. 'Started going there when Simon married our mum... been loads of times since then.'

'Oh, so he's not your real dad, then?'

'Oh, yes, he is,' Caroline said firmly. 'He and our mum got together when we were very little. He's the only dad I remember.'

She turned to look at Maureen. 'I wish I knew where he is. Maybe he and Rory went on a trip together, like they do sometimes.'

'A trip?'

'On the boat,' said Caroline. 'Sometimes they go out in it, or else Dad goes on his own.'

'That's nice,' said Maureen casually, fitting more pieces into the emerging picture of Simon Buttler's activities.

Nothing more was said until they reached Hall Brow. Maureen had called ahead and Henny Brown met them at reception. She wanted the girl out of the way for a while, so she could brief DI Bell, and guessed correctly that Caroline would be very willing to go for a coffee with the handsome policeman with the interesting voice.

'Spain again,' said Bell. 'Quigley went looking for the woman Sam mentioned, the one who escaped from that boys' home scandal he's so obsessed with. It took him a while. Apparently, she changed her name to Irene Edwards and got on Interpol's radar a few years ago. They tracked her down to somewhere in Spain, unpronounceable place. She died in nineteen ninety-six, so Quigley says. Give Jason all you know and let him put some more pieces together. He's a genius, that lad. I always knew he'd be useful.'

Maureen couldn't help but smile at yet another example of Bell being wise after the event, and very foolish beforehand.

'Oh, and there's more,' he said. 'That name Penrose got out of the old biddy she went to see. Stuart something?'

'Billings,' said Maureen. 'What about him?'

'Well, this is great – Jason found that this Billings kid had gone to Spain too in nineteen seventy-one, after the boys' home thing. He and the Thornhill woman had something going apparently... doesn't bear thinking of. So now we've got them both in Spain, doing whatever they were doing.'

'Could have been a mother and son thing,' said Maureen.

'And the rest,' said Bell. 'Who cares anyway? We're getting the links. Irene whatever her name is, cosying up to Stuart Billings. And now we've got Simon Buttler heading off there too, if the girl's telling the truth.'

'She's no reason to lie about that, has she? And the family have shedloads of money,' said Maureen. 'You should see that house.'

'Posh, is it?'

'Amazing,' said Maureen. 'The outside is just a big Victorian house, but the inside – like an oligarch's mansion. Must be worth a bomb.'

She had another link to check. 'Is Penrose in yet?'

Bell looked at his watch. 'Said she was coming in soon, about an hour ago. Feeling better apparently. Something about lack of sleep. Hope the doc didn't give her anything too heavy, we need her back on her feet.'

He winked at Maureen. 'I told Sam I wasn't impressed with her, by the way. Told him straight.'

'Why?' said Maureen.

'Well, you know, making sure he knows they made a mistake. Offcomers are no good in this job.'

'And women aren't much better, I suppose,' said Maureen. She knew what Bell was trying to say. 'Thanks for the support, boss, but no thanks, OK?'

Maureen walked away. She'd left Brown minding her star witness too long already and needed to find them, to get Caroline's full story before she grew too tired to tell it. On her way to the canteen Maureen spotted Anna coming in. Brown could wait, but the conversation with Anna couldn't. Maureen walked over, took her colleague's arm and leaned down to whisper in her ear, 'We need to talk, OK, before anyone else does.'

The nearest office door was open and the room was empty. Maureen steered Anna inside, sat her down and closed the door. Anna didn't like being pushed around.

'Get off me, Maureen. What's up with you? I need to check in.'

'Not yet you don't,' said Maureen. 'You need a heads up about what's going to happen, any minute now. I've just brought Caroline Buttler in, for questioning about the whereabouts of her dad and brother.'

'But we know where poor Rory is, don't we?' Anna protested.

'Not for sure, until there's DNA confirmation. Tony said the face was too badly damaged.'

Anna held up her hand. 'Don't, Maureen, please. I can't deal with it.'

'OK, then,' she ploughed on. 'Think how you're going to deal with this. Caroline told me about you and Simon.'

Anna blushed and looked away. 'What about me and Simon? We're friends, OK? Nothing wrong with that.'

'Oh, no? Well, first off, it sounds to me like you're more than friends, according to what the daughter has told me. And second, you knew he was under investigation but you've not said a dicky bird about it, have you? You should be off this case altogether and you know it. What were you playing at?'

Anna stared at Maureen, then lowered her head. When she looked up again, her eyes were wet. 'Who have you told?'

'No one,' Maureen hissed at her, 'that's why we're having this conversation. It's not me who needs to tell someone, it's you. You have to own up, say you're sorry for the mistake and get off this case. If you don't, it's suspension for you – and possibly worse.'

'What did Caroline say exactly?'

'Does it matter? She said that you'd been to their house and she thought you'd slept there. It's enough, Anna, believe me. And what's worse is that you didn't say anything right up front.'

'But he wasn't suspected of anything then. And I still don't think…'

'What? You still think he's good old Simon, fit and friendly, with a big house and lots of innocently acquired dosh?'

Anna said quietly, 'I know more than that about him.'

'It gets worse!' Maureen turned away from her in disgust. 'What else is there?'

'His real name is Stuart Billings. He was at Montgomery House. He knows Sam from there.'

'Oh my God,' said Maureen. 'When did you find that out?'

Anna sniffed. 'Yesterday afternoon, in Barrow. The PC there showed me the pictures of the boys at Montgomery House. I'd not looked at them properly before, and he was there – Simon. He was the one Mrs Robinson identified as Stuart Billings.'

'So what did you do then? You didn't blab to the Barrow mob, did you?'

Anna shook her head. 'Didn't know what to do. It could have been a misunderstanding – his brother or cousin or something. I wanted to check with Simon first, but I couldn't find him.'

227

'Join the club,' said Maureen. 'None of us can. But you should have told us before you checked with Simon. That's your job.'

'I knew I had to tell Sam,' said Anna miserably, 'but I couldn't find him either. And then Rory…' She hung her head. 'I couldn't cope, Maureen. That's why I passed out.'

Maureen pulled up another chair and sat down, running her hands over her face. 'What a mess.'

'I came in now to tell Sam. I know what he'll have to do.'

'Well, you're in luck, he's not here. He told me to go and check on Caroline Buttler while he had a few hours' rest.'

'Is she OK?'

'She was asking for you,' said Maureen. 'That's what sparked off the stuff about you and Simon. She doesn't know your surname it seems.'

'And we still don't know where her dad is?'

Maureen shrugged. 'Caroline said something about them all going away soon – to Spain she reckons. Maybe he's doing something about that.'

'Like what?'

'God knows. You know him. What do you think he's up to?'

'If he knows about Rory, he'll be devastated.'

'And that's the other thing you need to know. Rory was the cannabis farmer, using property bought for him by his dad. They had a blazing row yesterday.' Maureen stopped, realising the unfortunate phrase she'd used. 'Sorry. I reckon Simon told Rory to clear up his own mess and the lad tried to destroy the crop.'

The door opened suddenly and a cleaning trolley was pushed in before the person steering it stopped short. 'Oh, sorry, thought it was empty in here.'

'It is, love,' said Maureen. 'We're leaving. Come on, Anna.'

Anna got slowly to her feet. The cleaner looked hard at her, then at Maureen, who rolled her eyes. 'Man trouble,' she mouthed at the woman, who nodded sagely.

They headed to the only other place where they might snatch a bit of privacy. 'So what are you going to do next?' Maureen asked, as Anna splashed her face and tried to tidy her hair.

'Tell Sam everything,' she said, 'as soon as he comes in.'

'That's going to be a while yet. There's something you can do in the meantime: get some professional credit in the bank. You're going to need it.'

'What do you mean?'

'Use the fact that Caroline knows you. Do the interview I brought her in for. You'll get more out of her than I will – as a familiar face. Do you reckon she's in on all the drugs stuff?'

Anna shook her head. 'Don't know. She's very loyal to her dad, that's for sure. Does some work for him at the estate agency, but I'd be surprised if he'd implicate her in any other stuff.'

Maureen looked hard at her. 'Look, it's not just a bit of cannabis farming here and there. That might have been the lad's sideline, but father, dear father is into much deeper shit than that. I'm sure of it, so's Bell, we just need to join up the dots. The Spanish connection makes perfect sense. Oh, and there's his boat.'

'Oh, yes, the boat,' said Anna, grimacing.

'You knew about the boat?' Maureen was incredulous. 'What kind of copper are you? All that money from a tiny business? Those links with abandoned farm properties?'

'I didn't know about that. And I thought he must have come into money. Properly, I mean. Simon's not the type to...'

'Oh, spare us, please,' said Maureen, exasperated. 'There is no *type*, you should know that. Crime takes all types, not just big blokes with no hair and tattoos.' She shook her head, knowing what a mess Anna was in. 'So, you're going to interview Caroline, right? And if she shops her dad and her brother, that's good police work. Get that under your belt and then tell Sam about the connection, as soon as he gets in. I'll cover for you with Dinger before then, if I need to.'

Anna groaned. 'Dinger? Oh, God.'

'Leave him to me,' said Maureen. 'You just get on and do your job.'

'Why do we need that camera?' asked Caroline. 'I don't like the way the light keeps blinking.'

'Just ignore it,' said Anna. 'Are you comfortable? Had enough to eat?'

The girl nodded. 'Can I leave my mobile on, in case Dad calls, or Rory? If they ring home and I'm not there, they'll call me on this.'

'That's fine,' said Anna. 'And if we hear anything, we can tell you. We've put the word out, if anyone sees them.'

'You mean, you're searching for them?'

'No, not searching officially yet, just asking a few questions.'

'What time is it?' Caroline asked. 'The harbour at Maryport will be open early, someone there might know something.'

'Oh, yes, the boat's there,' said Anna. 'Tell me about that. How long have you had it? What's it like?'

'It's lovely,' said Caroline, smiling. 'Big. Three cabins. It's even got a bar. We can take it to France or to Ireland, as long as there's not a storm or something. Dad says it could cope with most weather, but I wouldn't like it.'

'And do you go to France and Ireland in it?'

'Dad does, just for a day or two. He wouldn't want to leave the business for longer than that, even though he says I'm perfectly capable of looking after things there. Rory goes with him sometimes.'

Anna remembered something. 'Rory said something about getting a Zodiac, do you remember, when we were talking about that poor man's body in the lake?'

Caroline nodded. 'Sometimes they have to get close in to things. Dad said it would be useful.'

Watching her, Anna suddenly realised that it could have been Simon who had helped put Graham's body into the water. Stuart Billings would have known Mikey Bennett. Maybe Bennett had asked him for help... Caroline's voice interrupted that thought.

'Do you want me to tell you more about the boat?' she asked. 'I could tell you where we bought it?'

'No, that's OK, thanks,' said Anna. 'I was just... Could you excuse me for a minute? Just need to check something.'

She pressed the off switch on the camera, got up and left the room. In the observation room next door, Bell and Maureen were watching the interview on a screen. Maureen was still taking notes when Anna opened the door.

'Simon could have helped Bennett with Graham's body,' she said.

'You think?' said Bell, with heavy sarcasm. 'Is it the pills, or are you usually so slow on the uptake?'

Maureen interrupted, seeing the mortified expression on Anna's face. 'Ask her about Spain,' she said. 'You've got that list of questions I gave you, right? Just go through them, get her talking.'

'And next time you come out, leave the camera running,' Bell added.

Anna went back into the room and switched the camera back on. 'OK, sorry. That's enough about the boat, thanks. Tell me more about this trip your dad said you were going on.'

Caroline shuffled in her chair. 'It was just a hint, but that's what he does. Drops a hint, and then it's not quite such a surprise when it actually happens. And we've been to Spain before at this time of the year, when it's not so hot there.' She smiled. 'The house has a pool and we can eat outside. Lovely view, right out to the coast.'

'Did your dad buy it?'

'No, it belonged to a friend of his. She'd lived out there for years, and when she died, we got the house. Wasn't that kind?'

'It was,' said Anna. 'And what was this friend's name, can you remember?'

'Auntie Irene. Dad said she was like a mother to him, when he was a boy and his own mother died... Irene Edwards, she was called. Died about five years ago.'

In the little room next door, Bell punched the air. 'That's it,' he said. 'We've got him.'

CHAPTER 22

Time passed. Sam lost track, conscious only of the throb of the pumps and the increasing numbness in his arms, pulled tight behind him and tied to the chair. He was thinking about the kidnapper's reaction when the dead lad was mentioned. If this man was Simon Buttler, Rory's dad, he didn't know that his son was lying on the mortuary slab, charred beyond recognition. And where had the man gone? What would he do next?

Speculation was cut short when the door creaked open and light sneaked through the blindfold once more. Before Sam could say anything, it was pulled off and he blinked into the light of a paraffin lamp, standing on an upturned bucket by the wall.

Sam looked around, his eyes adjusting to the light. The space was square and high, rusty and red, littered with bits of machinery. To one side of him was another space, like a cage, with hawsers and pulleys. 'Is this a mine?' he asked, peering into the gloom. 'Where are you?'

'Over here,' said the familiar voice. The man was standing in the shadows. He was dressed in overalls, boots on his feet, gloves on his hands. Everything was the colour of dried blood. The man wore a hood of the same colour, through which only his eyes and mouth were visible.

'I can't see you properly,' said Sam. 'Come into the light.'

The man didn't move. He spoke very quietly. 'Tell me about the boy you found. Is he dead?'

'Yes,' said Sam. 'He was dead when we found him.'

There was a long silence before the man said, 'What happened?'

'We think he was trying to set fire to the crop – the cannabis crop. He must have used petrol and it blew back over him. Something sparked it. He had no chance.'

As Sam watched, the man pulled off the hood and covered his eyes with his hands. 'It was my fault,' he said, his voice hoarse. 'I shouted at him… said it was his problem. I should have known he'd do something stupid.'

'Are you his dad? Are you Simon Buttler?' Sam asked.

'I'm his dad, yes. Where is he now? Where's Rory?'

'He's in the mortuary,' said Sam. 'One of our people thought she knew who he was. We've been trying to find you.'

'Was it Anna?' Simon asked. 'Did she recognise him?'

'You know Anna?' said Sam. 'Your daughter mentioned an Anna, but I didn't know she meant my sergeant.'

'Caroline? What have you done with her?' Buttler turned and kicked hard at the side of the cage, which rattled and clanged in protest. 'She's mine, right? She'll tell you nothing. And she knows what to do…'

'She's fine,' said Sam quietly. 'Let me go now and we can work something out about all this. You acted in desperation.'

'No, I didn't,' said Simon. 'I was afraid you'd work it out, that you'd see me and recognise me, that you'd know.'

'Would that be so terrible?' Sam asked.

Simon spat into the red dust. 'You know nothing about the way I am now. I'm not thick, like those other no-hopers at Monty House.'

'Did you kill Dr Graham?'

Simon shook his head. 'Not worth it,' he said. 'Better things to do. And before you ask, Mikey didn't kill him either. He took the old man's cash, but he wouldn't give up the PIN number for the rest, so Mikey left him and went on a bender. Nearly a week, he said, but it could have been longer. When he got back, the old guy was dead. At least that's what he told me. You remember Mikey, Tognarelli. He wasn't a killer.'

'You remember me from then?' said Sam.

'Of course I do. You and that red-haired bitch of yours. Edwards and Irene both hated you. You just wouldn't give up.'

'I did in the end. I gave up being a policeman, for a couple of years.'

'Not long enough,' said Simon. 'I covered my tracks and you didn't really know me at Monty House. Should have been safe enough.'

'There were photos of you back then,' said Sam. 'I showed them to Mrs Robinson.'

Simon shook his head. 'Still alive? That old woman is still alive, and Rory...'

Sam needed to keep him talking. 'It was an accident, you can't blame yourself for his death.' No response. Sam asked another question, hoping he would remember everything that was being said. 'What happened to Rory and Caroline's mother?'

'That was a useful marriage for me and Wendy was keen enough. She loved the money but not where it came from.'

'Did she jump or was she pushed?' Sam asked.

Simon picked up a long piece of metal off the floor and brandished it at him. 'You think that, old man? You think I got rid of my wife because she found out where the money was coming from?'

'Well,' he countered, 'you thought I might give you away, and here I am, trussed like a chicken, in a stinking hole. Why would your wife be any different?'

'She walked out, the stupid cow. She couldn't shop me because I had the kids. They knew they were better off staying with me.' He turned away. 'I don't care where she is, so long as she keeps her trap shut.'

Sam looked at him. Was he still lying? This man had no scruples, no conscience. Maybe he did have, once, but not anymore.

'I could speak up for you even now,' Sam tried. 'Of course, you'd be in deep trouble, but nothing you couldn't ride out in a few years. If you harm me, you might never get out. You're an intelligent man. Think it through. Don't make a stupid decision.'

Simon approached him, sneering: 'So I just let you go, say I'm sorry, bury my son and head meekly off to jail, for God knows how long?'

'Yes,' said Sam. 'That's what you do.'

There was movement. Sam flinched as he heard Simon's voice close behind him. 'I'm intelligent, you're right there. It's all planned out. All I need is forty-eight hours' start and you'll never get me back. And they'll never find you either, until and unless I tell them where you are. By the time they do, I'll be long gone.' He pulled hard on Sam's hair, jerking his head back. 'Or maybe they won't find you at all. Shame.'

'You're just going to leave me here to die, are you, like Dr Graham in that stinking shed?'

Buttler relaxed his gasp. He came around and pointed to a bag on the floor. 'There's water in there, if you can reach it. You can stay alive here for a while.'

'What if something happens to you?' said Sam.

'You'd better hope it doesn't,' he said, pushing on the heavy door.

'But we haven't got Buttler, have we?' said Pritchard. 'Where the hell is he? And how long are we going to keep the daughter before we tell her what happened to Rory?'

'We have to wait for the DNA result anyway,' said Bell, irritated by the reminder that this investigation was far from over. 'She doesn't seem to know much about anything.'

Maureen shook her head. 'Still not sure about that.'

On the screen they could see Anna get up from the table. A moment later she was beside them in the obs room, watching Caroline sit passively, as if someone had pulled out a plug.

'I'm going to ask about her mother,' said Anna.

'Her mother?' replied Bell, still irritated. 'What's her bloody mother got to do with anything? She left years ago.'

'That's what I want to ask about. If the man we're dealing with here is as ruthless as you two… we… seem to think he is, I want to know what happened to Wendy Buttler. She disappeared years ago, he reported her missing and then changed his mind, and there's some letter she apparently sent, saying she'd run off with someone else. The whole thing sounds dodgy and this is a good chance to check it out. We can keep Caroline another few hours, right, so why not use the time?'

Bell and Pritchard looked at each other. Anna pressed on. 'Look, Wendy left for a reason. Caroline told me that her mum and Simon had a row once about dirty money…'

'When did she say that?' Bell asked. Pritchard looked hard at Anna, willing her to be careful.

'Earlier on, when we were just chatting,' said Anna, without missing a beat.

'And when did Wendy leave?' Maureen asked.

'About three years ago, apparently. If we could find her, she might have more information than Caroline does. Too late to check with Rory.'

Bell leaned forward, excited. 'Maybe Simon set up Rory, killed him to keep him quiet.'

'No!' Anna protested, too loudly. 'No,' she said again. 'Caroline gives me the impression that Simon genuinely loves his kids.'

'I think Anna's right,' said Maureen hastily. 'If we can find Wendy, she could tell us more about this dirty money.'

'And if we can't find her,' Bell interrupted, 'we could get him on whatever he's done to his wife to shut her up. That'll do for a start. Give us more time to build the drugs picture. Good job, Anna. Can you carry on a bit longer? We should have something to show for our night's work when Sam finally gets back.'

He turned to Maureen. 'You get a few hours' kip now, then I'll knock off when Sam turns up.'

'Like a tag team,' she said.

Bell was pleased with himself, burbling like a school kid. 'Just like old times.'

Anna went back in to Caroline. She was sure that the girl was completely in the dark about Simon's affairs. It would come as a terrible shock when they told her about Rory.

'Do you need a rest?' she asked.

'I'm OK,' Caroline said. 'This is better than sitting at home, waiting for the phone to ring. I think Dad and Rory are off together somewhere, maybe on the boat. Sometimes it's impossible to get a signal out at sea.'

'While you're here, then,' said Anna, 'can I ask you about something else? You mentioned this before, but now the camera's going I need to check with you again.' Anna hoped to God the girl wouldn't refer to the time when they'd talked in the family kitchen.

'OK,' said Caroline.

'It's about your mum – Wendy,' said Anna.

Caroline shuffled uncomfortably in the chair. 'What about her?'

'Well, she's out there somewhere, isn't she? And sometimes we need our mums. When DC Pritchard brought you here, from that empty house, I thought this would be a very good time for your mum to come back into your life.'

Caroline pushed the chair back and looked away. Was this anger or sadness? Anna wondered. 'I know it's difficult to talk about her,' she said.

'She left us.' Caroline turned back, her eyes tired and moist. 'Dad gave us all a home and a good life, and she just walked out.'

'Do you know why?'

Caroline shook her head. 'Rory says she's a selfish bitch.'

'Is that what you think too?'

'What else could we think? She disappeared without saying goodbye or anything.'

'Did she and your dad have a row?'

Caroline looked curiously at Anna. 'I told you...' she began.

Anna interrupted her quickly, pointing at the camera. 'This is for the record, pet. If we try to find your mum, everything has to be a bit more official.'

Caroline nodded. How easy it was to dupe someone with 'official' procedures, Anna thought.

'She and Dad argued a lot anyway, but this was different. It wasn't just about the house or Rory being a pain. She screamed at him, threw money all over the place. It was scary. Even Rory was upset.'

'Do you remember what she said?'

'She said the money was dirty, that our dad was evil… all sorts of awful things.'

'And what did your dad do?'

'That was weird. He didn't get upset. Just picked up the money and told her off for upsetting us. He didn't hit her.'

'Had he done that before?'

The girl nodded. 'I think so. Mum cried a lot.' She sat still for a moment, thinking. 'There was one time, after we bought the boat. Mum and Dad and Rory had been out somewhere on it, and when they got back Mum was in bits. She kept saying "How dare you?" to him. He hit her then.'

'Did you see that?'

'No, but I heard it. And Rory did too. He said Dad had to do it, to shut her up.'

Anna went over the timeline in her head. 'So that was just before your mother left?'

'We bought the new house,' said Caroline, 'and then the boat, and Mum walked out a little while after that.'

'New house, new boat,' said Anna. 'That must have cost a lot of money.'

Caroline nodded. 'Yes. Dad said we were so lucky that someone left him the money, that lady I told you about before, Auntie Irene.'

'Irene Edwards?'

'Yes. Dad said she left him her house in Spain and enough money for us to buy our new house too.'

'But that didn't make your mum happy?'

'No, it made things worse between them. Why? Why was she so angry?'

'Did your mum get on with Auntie Irene?'

Caroline shrugged. 'Don't know.'

Anna looked at her watch then pushed back her chair. 'There's something I need to see to, pet. Can I get you anything? We won't be here much longer. There's a nice room where you can sleep when we've finished. OK?'

The girl nodded. 'Can I have a Coke?'

'Sure,' said Anna. 'I'll get you one.'

Bell was on his own in the next room. 'Pritchard's getting some shuteye,' he said. 'I have to say, Sergeant, you're doing a good job with this kid. Now we've got the Spanish connection on tape, and the link with Irene Edwards or Thornhill, the woman Nelly's always going on about. You reckon Wendy worked out where the money was coming from and did a runner?'

Anna was unsure. 'She must have been very scared or very angry to give all that up and leave her own kids.'

'Or else she was too much of a risk and Buttler bumped her off, is that it?'

'That's just it,' Anna said. 'We know he called off the misper inquiry before it had even started when a letter turned up, apparently from her.'

'And where is it now?'

Anna shrugged. She couldn't let on how she knew this. 'Maybe the girl knows.'

For the first time, Anna realised with a sinking feeling what a mess she was in. The man she'd trusted, liked, slept with, was now suspected of silencing his own wife and sending her son to his death, although she couldn't believe that Rory's death could have been anything other than an accident. But the boy wouldn't have been there at all, taking that risk, unless he'd been drawn into it by the dad he loved and admired. And now this same man could ruin her career too.

She went to find Caroline's Coke, then back to the interview room before her time ran out. She checked the obs room next door. Bell wasn't there. As she went back to Caroline, Anna stretched out and turned off the camera. It would record the gap, but it wouldn't be for long and she had to forestall any damage the girl might do.

'Just turning the camera off for a minute,' Anna said. 'I need to make sure we get it right. Procedure, you know.' She smiled reassuringly and Caroline smiled back.

'OK. Thanks for the Coke.'

'So,' said Anna. 'You and I have talked before, haven't we, at your house, but for the camera it has to sound as if we've never done that except here, in the police station. Is that OK with you?'

Caroline looked puzzled. 'So you've never been to our house, not been friends with our dad. You know...' She raised her eyebrows.

'That's it exactly,' said Anna. 'So I'll turn the camera back on now and we'll carry on, just a bit longer.

'Now then, Caroline,' she began, more formally once they were back on tape. 'Can you tell me about the letter that your mum sent, just after she went away? That was when your dad told the police not to search for her, wasn't it?'

'Well, it was addressed to him. I didn't actually read it. But he said she'd gone away with her boyfriend, and I thought that was true. I'd seen Mum with a man before, in town, and she'd kept very quiet about it.'

'Who was the man?'

The girl shrugged. 'They were in a café together, in White-haven, and they were talking very close, leaning towards each other. Then he gave her a big hug. They didn't see me, I was on the other side of the street.'

'Did you tell anybody?'

'I told Rory, but not my dad.'

'So when that letter came, saying your mum was with another man, you thought it was true?'

The girl nodded.

Anna leaned forward. 'Caroline, this is really important. Around the time your mum left, did anything else unusual happen?'

'Like what?' said the girl.

'Did your dad go anywhere?'

'The day Mum left, he was in Carlisle all day. Rory was still in school then, and Dad left me in charge at the office. He told me he was expecting an important visitor and I needed to be there. So I stayed at the office all day.'

'And did the visitor turn up?'

'No, and I was stuck there all that time. When I got home Dad was there, in the overalls he wears for gardening, not his suit, and Mum was gone. Her car, her clothes, everything.'

'Was your dad upset?'

'No, not really. He was very calm. He said Mum had gone, but everything would be all right.'

There was a knock on the door and Bell put his head in. 'Can I have a word, Sergeant?'

Outside in the corridor, he said, 'You reckon the wife, Wendy, could be crucial in nailing this bloke down?'

'Yes,' said Anna. 'But I'm not at all sure she's still alive.'

'Well, that's enough to get us a warrant. We need to search that house, turn it over for everything – prints, drugs, blood traces.'

'And the garden,' said Anna. 'Did you hear what Caroline just said?'

'About the overalls? OK, garden as well.'

'What about Caroline?'

'Don't have to do anything yet. Twenty-four hours after we brought her in, we have to charge her or let her go. Plenty of time left. Let her have some sleep, and we'll get organised for when Sam gets in. What time did he say?'

'Briefing at eight, I think.'

'Too late,' said Bell. 'We need to crack on.' He checked his watch. 'Gone midnight. Another couple of hours then I'll call him in.'

He looked at Anna. 'You should get some rest too. You've had a bumpy few days. One of the cells could be free, save you going home.'

Anna knew she was exhausted. And the house search? What would that turn up? She wondered how often Simon washed the sheets on his bed.

CHAPTER 23

In the hissing light of the paraffin lamp, Simon Buttler looked at his watch. 'That's it. I need to go,' he said.

Sam had to ask. 'Why did you help Mikey with Graham's body?'

Buttler shook his head. 'I should have told him to piss off.' He shrugged. 'I was in Whitehaven one day, minding my own business and the useless bugger stopped me in the street. Said he knew who I was, called me by my real name, out loud, in the street. I had to shut him up. So I took him out for a drink, somewhere no one would see us, and he asked me to help him. Said if I refused he'd make sure everyone knew that I wasn't who I said I was.'

'Would that have been so terrible?'

'Looking back now, maybe not. But then, I just wanted him to shut up. I offered him money and he took it like a shot, but that wasn't enough for him. He had to get rid of Graham's body and I had to help him.'

'Mikey's dead. But you know that, don't you?'

Buttler shrugged his shoulders. 'I didn't kill him, if that's what you think. He called me, said he wanted cannabis, told me where to meet him. I left the car and walked to where he said.'

'Where?'

'Near where the Gosforth road turns left towards Wastwater. Mikey was sitting there in Graham's car. I told him he was an idiot, but he was past caring. Don't know what he'd taken before I got there but he was half gone already. The hose was all set up. All he had to do was turn on the engine. He didn't need the cannabis. I think he just wanted someone to be there.' Buttler paused, shook his head. 'You still think I killed him?'

'Did you?'

'No need, but it was another loose end sorted. I cleaned the car up, just to make sure you couldn't place me there. I put the block of cannabis in his shed. Worth a try, I thought.'

Sam worked his shoulders, wondering if he was strong enough to overpower this man, and knowing that he wasn't. 'One more thing, before you go. Tell me about Irene Thornhill.'

'She was good to me,' said Buttler. 'Very good.'

The words hit Sam like a blow. Suddenly he was furious.

'For God's sake! Did she ever tell you, this woman of yours, what she did to Judith?'

'What about Judith?'

'Irene's miserable husband killed himself, I'm sure she told you that?'

'It was in all the papers. Of course I knew.'

'But before that, your precious Irene gave him the gun and told him to shoot Judith – my Judith. There was no good reason, Irene just wanted her dead. Because Irene was an evil bitch.'

Buttler stared at him. 'But Judith was OK.'

'Only because the miserable shit couldn't do it, could he? Irene abandoned him to take the flak and he shot himself instead of Judith.' Sam bowed his head, remembering. 'I don't think she ever really recovered.'

Buttler frowned at him.

'I didn't know that. Anyway, it was a long time ago. Now you and your fucking police buddies have come back to haunt me and I have to move on. Get used to being alone in the dark, old man,' he said. 'Once I've gone, you won't see me again. Ever.'

'What if I get free?'

'Your legs are chained, and what they're chained to has been here for a very long time. Padlocks, not knots. Your stiff old fingers won't help you with those.'

Sam took a deep breath. 'You're a sick man… Stuart. You think you weren't abused in that place, but you were. And the Thornhill woman – she used you, screwed you up, can't you see?'

He felt the blow as Buttler's fist smashed into the side of his head.

'Fuck you,' he shouted. Sam felt the spittle against his face. 'You know nothing about my life. I'm not Stuart, I'm Simon now and she loved me!'

'You're a fool,' said Sam. 'That woman loved herself and no one else. You could have led a proper life if she hadn't corrupted you, not this sham.'

He braced himself for the man's anger to explode again, but all he heard was the screech of the door. And then silence.

It was five-thirty in the morning. Still another hour before the eastern sky would begin to turn from black to grey. DI Bell was exhausted and angry. 'How deeply can a man sleep at his age?' he said, slamming down the phone. 'You and I kip with the mobile by the bed, right?'

'Under the pillow,' said Maureen. She'd snatched some rest in a cell and had no sympathy for the DCI's need to sleep in his own bed, however old he was. 'Do you want me to go and pick him up, sir?'

'Nay,' said Bell. 'We can get started without him. I've got the search team organised. Penrose and I'll get down there now. You bring the Buttler girl when she wakes up. I want her fresh. No way for the CPS or some clever defence brief to claim we've forced her to cooperate.'

'Do you think she will?'

'She wants her dad back, and she doesn't know what we know about him. She thinks we're searching the house to find out where he is. Keep it that way. We need someone there who knows where everything is. Get to Buttler's place at six-thirty, that should be about right. Can't start on the garden until it's light anyway.'

Maureen was driving, with Caroline in the back of the Audi, as they left the main road and headed up towards Hilton and the Old Vicarage. As they approached the house, the sky ahead of them glowed from the lights blazing in all the windows. Caroline craned forward to the limit of her seat belt, excited to be back.

Maureen was distracted, looking for the driveway, when an oncoming car's headlights suddenly flashed into her face. She braked hard and steered clumsily into the side of the road as the other car swept past them.

Caroline screamed. 'That's our car,' she cried, pulling at Maureen's shoulder. 'It's my dad.'

There was no time to call Bell. Maureen used the full power of the Audi's steering to turn around and force it back onto the narrow road, heading away from the house and in pursuit of the car ahead. 'What kind of car is it?' she asked, calculating how much speed she could get out of her beloved Audi.

'Big,' said Caroline. 'A Mercedes. It can go really fast.'

Maureen put her foot down, but even with full-beam headlights the narrow lane was unfamiliar to her and clearly well known to Simon Buttler. The Mercedes was drawing away from her, slicing corners. At this hour of the morning, drivers heading for the early Sellafield shift would be crowding the roads, half asleep, going through the motions of the daily commute.

In only a few minutes the narrow lane dropped down towards the main coast road, the A595, and a steady stream of cars and vans was coming onto the big roundabout from the right. Instinct told Maureen to brake, even though she knew full well that Simon Buttler would have barged onto the roundabout without hesitation. She was aware of the young woman in the back, already shouting for them to slow down.

'Caroline,' Maureen shouted back. 'Calm down! We need to talk to your dad. Do you have a mobile phone? Where is it?'

'In my pocket,' said the girl. 'Can I call him?'

'No,' said Maureen. 'Dial nine nine nine. Do it now. Now!'

'What shall I say?'

'Just dial and then hand the phone to me. No, just put it down on the front seat, close to me.'

A small black phone appeared on the passenger seat. A voice was already issuing from it and Maureen snatched it up, interrupting the terse request, 'Which service, please?'

'This is DC Maureen Pritchard, badge number nine one two five seven, needing immediate assistance. In pursuit of a car, probably heading north on A five nine five through Egremont. Dark blue or black Mercedes. Reg W seven five six, GHH. Driver could be armed and dangerous.'

'One moment, please. Connecting you now.'

'Traffic here. Any further information, DC Pritchard?'

'I have a civilian passenger. Contact DI Bell, Workington CID for details. Wait…'

She turned towards the back seat. 'Where's your dad's boat moored?'

Caroline didn't respond. Maureen could see her pale face in the rear-view mirror, staring dumbly at the traffic heading towards them while Maureen wove in and out of the left-hand lane, passing cars whenever she could without killing them both.

'Caroline, listen to me! Where's your dad's boat?'

'Maryport,' she whispered.

'Still there?' Maureen shouted into the phone. 'Did you hear that? Suspect may be heading for Maryport harbour.'

'Roger,' said the voice. 'Can you see the car?'

'No. No sighting since we joined the five nine five.'

'Could he have taken another route?'

'Damn! Yes... not sure.'

'Leave the phone line open. Stand by.'

Maureen glanced at the phone. The battery level was in the red.

'Have you got a charger? Caroline! Phone charger?'

'It's at home,' she gasped as the Audi screeched around the roundabout at the north end of Egremont. There was no clue as to where Simon Buttler might be, or which route he was taking, but the main road was the fastest option.

There was a mumbling from the phone and Maureen snatched it up. 'We have the details from DI Bell,' said an unidentified voice. 'Units mobilised all along the routes north. Any sighting yet?'

'Negative,' said Maureen. She had to slow down going through Bigrigg, aware of people and activity. 'No siren,' she said. 'Hard to stay safe.'

'Don't risk it,' said the voice. 'When we have a sighting, we can cover both main routes into Workington and across the river. Is the suspect alone?'

'Yes, from what we saw. No known accomplices.' Except the son, Maureen thought, but said nothing, aware that his sister was within earshot. She wanted to ask about the DNA result, but this was not the time. She could give up the chase and leave them to it, but she knew she wouldn't. This was a man who had poisoned too many lives. She wanted to be there when he was stopped.

'Where's Dad?' Caroline whimpered from the back seat. 'Why are you chasing him? Why did you say he might be dangerous?'

'We need to talk to him, pet. It's urgent.'

'What's he done? Tell me! What's going on?'

Maureen heard the confusion and hurt in the voice coming from behind her and turned to reassure Caroline. She didn't see the woman with a pushchair step out onto the crossing.

Simon turned off the main road towards Mirehouse and the old road into Whitehaven. He'd shaken off the Audi that had been pursuing him ever since he'd picked up the precious package from its hiding place in the wall outside the house and fled from the home that was no longer his own. His mind was racing. Rory was dead, the police had Caroline, Tognarelli was hidden away. What was there left to deal with? No one else mattered to him anymore. The boat was still there, fuelled up and ready. Plane tickets from Dublin to Tbilisi were in the car. The plan was clear, checked. Good to go.

All his life he'd worked and waited, taking opportunities when he could, scheming one step at a time. The ultimate goal of an easy life in Spain had been so close, then an old man died accidentally, a former mate tracked him down and all his carefully laid plans began to crumble. Bennett was a loose end for a while, but no longer. He'd come too far to stop now.

He checked the mental map in his head, realising that the escape plan would have to change. They'd be looking for him now, even if he could shake off the immediate pursuit. His boat was too slow, the coastguard would be faster, and they'd be watching the ports and harbours. Still, he could adapt. He'd done it before. The old passport was in his wallet alongside the new one, and there was another one too, just in case. Credit cards in all three names. He was always prepared. He just had to get free from this area, out onto the motorway: south to Manchester, north to Glasgow. It didn't matter.

And now he had Tognarelli's life in his hands too. How many times had he heard Irene curse saintly Sam and his red-haired bitch? Irene wouldn't have hesitated, he knew. She wouldn't have cared about an old man left to rot in an abandoned mine. 'Fuck them all,' she'd have said. 'You've got one life – live it. Save yourself.'

As the Mercedes passed Whitehaven cemetery, past the flashing warning of the speed limit, Simon didn't see the police car waiting by the gates until it appeared behind him, blue lights flashing, siren screaming. He pushed the accelerator to the floor and sped towards the busy town.

CHAPTER 24

DI Dinger Bell stood with the phone pressed to one ear, waiting for a response.

'What the hell's happened to Pritchard?' he asked of anyone who might be listening. All around him, and elsewhere in the Old Vicarage, officers in nylon coveralls were sifting through drawers, under beds, in cupboards, looking for anything that could tie Simon Buttler to the local cannabis crops, or to the Class-A drugs being smuggled into the county from overseas, or to the disappearance of his wife.

DNA results had confirmed the identity of the charred remains at the mortuary: Rory. Back at the station, Pritchard's task was to get as much detail as possible out of the sister, without revealing what had happened to him, and then bring her to the house to help them with the search. So where were they?

'And where's our blessed DCI, come to that?' roared Bell. Anna Penrose shrugged. She wasn't looking forward to the conversation with Sam that she knew was coming, but now that the new day was dawning she just wanted it over with.

As soon as Bell ended the call, his phone began to ring. 'What?' he bellowed into the mouthpiece, making Anna wince. 'Where? When?… Christ Almighty.' He checked his watch. 'We're just about finished here. Where's the DCI? He said he'd

be in first thing. We need him. I just rang but he didn't pick up…
OK, let me know. I'll get Brown to head back with the stuff we've
picked up here. Me and Penrose will head up to Whitehaven
Hospital… OK, OK.'

'What is it?' Anna asked, as Bell stood for a moment, head
hanging down. 'What's happened?'

'Maureen and the Buttler girl are both in hospital. They ran
off the road in Bigrigg, smacked into a wall.'

'Christ. On their way here?'

'No, they were heading north apparently.'

'North? How come?'

'Chasing someone, at speed. Simon Buttler. Now half the
county's trying to find him.'

Anna stood still, trying to work it out. Confusion and questions filled her mind. Maybe Simon had been trying to find
Caroline, to tell her about Rory? 'Where's Buttler heading?'

'That's it, we don't know.'

Anna needed to talk to Sam, urgently. 'And what about
Tognarelli?'

'Still no sign of him apparently. The Super's getting worried.
They're sending someone to his place to check. Not like him to
be out of touch for so long.'

'No,' said Anna, remembering the roasting she'd got for not
keeping in contact. Talking to Bell about sleeping with Simon
was out of the question. She could wait a little longer for Sam to
turn up.

It took only a few seconds for Simon to realise that he had to
change course. Even if he was confident that the boat was fast
enough to escape the coastguard, which he wasn't, there were
only two bridges that crossed the River Derwent in Workington

254

on the road to Maryport, and one of those was right next to police station. He wouldn't stand a chance.

Following the road map in his head, at the last possible moment he hauled the car round a right turn along the old coach road, which would take him away from the centre of Whitehaven, towards the chance of heading east and the motorway. There were so many routes to choose from, and he knew them all.

Fear and adrenalin pumped through him. He hadn't planned for this, but he would make it work. Turning right again at the end of the coach road up the hill on Inkermann Terrace, he decided which way to go only at the last minute. Not north on the 595, as the police might have been expecting, but south and then up the hill through the Hensingham housing estate, and cross-country along quiet lanes.

He smiled as he pushed the powerful car to its limits. He was calling the shots now. He had all the options, and they didn't have the manpower to keep up with him. So what if he wouldn't have time to make the call about Tognarelli? The old man would be OK for a few days, if he was sensible with the water. And if he died, too bad. He was old, expendable. Simon checked the rear-view mirror as he turned again, climbing higher up the hill that overlooked the town. There was nothing behind him on the road, no blue lights, no sirens.

The officer who'd watched him pass the cemetery was on his radio, admitting that the sudden change of direction had caught him off guard.

'He's going south?' Bell yelled into his phone, as he and Anna headed back to Hall Brow. 'What's he playing at? He knows we're after him. Get a helicopter up or we'll lose him completely.' He paused, listening, and then shouted. 'Cost? Who cares? Just fucking do it!' He turned to Anna. 'Get your bloody foot down, Penrose. This is a proper car, not that Noddy thing you drive around in. With the DCI missing, someone has to sort out this shambles.'

'Where is he?'

'No sign of him at his house. His car's there, but not Sam. Looks like he's not been home at all. Tyre tracks outside.'

'No one from our lot has picked him up?'

'We'd know that, wouldn't we?' Bell shouted at her. 'Use your head, Penrose. Someone's got him, and it's not us.'

'Who then?'

'How do I know? One of the ghosts from thirty years ago that he keeps going on about. Or else he's completely lost his marbles and just wandered off. We'll have to get on without him for now. One problem at a time.'

Anna felt a sudden jolt of fear. 'What if Buttler's got him?'

'Shit,' said Bell.

Sam must have dozed off, lying uncomfortably on the littered floor, with the chair still attached to his bent legs. When he opened his eyes, he noticed that a thin sliver of light was seeping in under the door. This gave him hope. At least he wasn't buried underground and would have a clue about the passage of time, for however long he was here. Eight hours had gone by already, he reckoned.

The bag that Buttler had left with him contained one big bottle of water. He'd struggled to unscrew the top and sipped a small amount at a time, and then only when his thirst was unbearable. He found he could stand, still chained to the chair, and move a few inches before the chains holding the chair to the iron pillar behind him pulled taut.

The tiny blessing of daylight enabled him to see where he was: at the entrance to the cage that had taken miners down into the pit. It was iron ore, not coal, and red was already staining his shoes and hands. There were dozens of disused iron ore mines in the area. He could be in any one of them. The mine shaft was inches from where he was pinned. Down below he could hear the pumps, diverting water somewhere, he didn't know where. What would happen if they stopped working? The shaft would flood, he thought, but this room was on the surface. He might die here, but he wouldn't drown.

He tried to work out what might be happening outside. He'd said he would be at work first thing, which probably meant about seven, and guessed it was earlier than that now. How long would it be before they checked his home? Would they find any evidence that he had been taken, rather than had left the house routinely? Bell thinks I'm past it, Sam thought. Maybe he'll assume I've had a breakdown, wandered off. Surely they'd find tyre marks, some trace of what had happened. Surely... Or could he trust Buttler to reveal his location as he'd said he would? Sam doubted it. The man was desperate and would put his own escape before anything else.

How far could he move, he wondered, now that there was just enough light to see by? Would there be anything lying around in the chaotic litter here that might help him break the chains of the padlocks? He had to do something to help himself.

He stretched down to the floor and stretched his arm and hand as far as he could away from him, groping for anything substantial that he could pick up. His fingers felt something and he strained to find a purchase, to get more than one finger in a position to manoeuvre the thing into his grasp. It was the piece of metal that Buttler had brandished at him in anger and then thrown down. Gradually, painfully, with wrist, elbow, shoulder stretched almost to rupturing, Sam managed with middle and forefinger to ease the metal bar towards his thumb, and then a little nearer. When the metal bar was finally within his grasp he fell back and collapsed onto the chair, which broke under his weight. As he lay, triumphant, clutching the bar, he felt the wet-ness under his body as the punctured water bottle spilled its contents onto the floor.

CHAPTER 25

Bell flashed his warrant card to the woman on reception at Whitehaven Hospital Accident and Emergency Department. 'You've got one of my officers,' he announced.

She looked up, registered the police ID. 'Oh, the car accident, yes. She and the young woman are both still here. We're waiting for test results. I can't tell you any more than that, I'm afraid.'

'Where are they? Come on, woman, we're in the middle of an urgent inquiry here. I need information from my officer, now, not when you feel like it.'

'No need to shout, sergeant,' said the woman, looking at him severely over her glasses.

'Detective Inspector,' Bell hissed at her. 'Now where's Detective Constable Pritchard?'

Bell barged into the warren of cubicles before accosting a white-coated figure emerging from one of them. He caught the woman by the arm. 'DC Pritchard,' he said. 'Where is she?'

'Are you a relative, sir?'

Bell waved his warrant card in the doctor's startled face. 'No, I'm her boss. Urgent police business.'

'I need you to lower your voice, sir,' warned the doctor.

Anna pushed Bell to one side. 'Sorry about this,' she said, 'we're anxious about our colleague – I'm sure you understand.

I'm DS Anna Penrose. We're in the middle of something really critical and need a word with DC Pritchard, please, if that's possible?'

Bell began to bluster but Anna put a restraining hand on his arm. The doctor looked at them both. 'Just for a moment then,' she said finally. 'Mrs Pritchard has been sedated, but I think she will be able to talk to you.' She turned to Bell. 'There is another police officer around somewhere. I'll get him to have a word with you. And you must keep your voices down in here or I'll ask you to leave at once, OK?'

Bell nodded.

In the cubicle, he hung back and Anna kept her expression as normal as she could while she took in Maureen's bandaged head and bruised face. Maureen put up her hand and Anna took it, squeezing her fingers gently. 'You'll be fine,' she said. 'You're in the best place.'

'Car's a write-off,' said Maureen. 'Is the woman all right?'

'What woman?'

'She was on the crossing… with a pushchair.'

Anna's stomach turned over. 'I'm sure she is,' she said, not feeling sure at all. She turned away, pulled Bell to one side and whispered to him, 'Can you ask if anyone else was hurt in the accident, apart from Maureen and Caroline?' She lowered her voice even further. 'Maureen thinks she hit a woman with a pushchair.'

Bell groaned. 'Oh, Christ. What a mess. OK, I'll check.'

Anna turned back to Maureen and wiped away a tear that was edging down her bruised cheek. 'What's the damage, do you know yet?'

Maureen shook her head slightly. 'My foot got stuck under the pedals. I couldn't move it. Smacked my face too, on the airbag. What about Caroline?'

Anna had no idea. 'I'm sure she's fine. Was she in the back?'

'Yes, and I made her put the seatbelt on.'

'So she'll be OK. Don't worry. Dinger's finding out about the woman on the crossing.'

'I don't think I hit her, but the pushchair...' Maureen's eyes filled up with tears again. 'We were going too fast, Anna. He was right ahead of us. I wanted to get to him.'

'I know,' said Anna.

Behind her, beyond the cubicle curtain, she heard Bell say, 'Penrose, out here.'

'Won't be a minute, Maureen,' she said, letting go of her hand. Outside she found Bell and a tall uniformed constable with a notebook in his hand. 'PC Plod here was at the scene,' said Bell. 'Tell the sergeant what you told me.'

'It was the crossing by the garage at Bigrigg, at...' the constable checked his notes '... six-fifty-four a.m. A dark blue Mercedes had gone through really fast, and I was just about to radio ahead about it when the Audi came along. The driver must have seen the woman on the crossing at the last minute and swung sharp to the left, away from her, straight into the wall by the Community Centre. Hell of a bang.'

'What about the woman on the crossing?'

'She just had time to pull the pushchair out of the way. Shocked, like, but she were OK.'

Anna breathed out heavily.

'One less disaster to worry about,' said Bell. 'What about the girl in the back of the Audi?'

'She was screaming,' said the constable. 'Couldn't get out of her seatbelt. Someone from the garage ran over to help. He managed to calm the girl down. We were more worried about the driver. She couldn't get her foot out. Ambulance came pretty quick. They managed to cut the driver out. The girl was still carrying on, shouting about her father. But there wasn't a man in the car, not when we got to it.'

Anna said, 'Her father was in the Mercedes they were chasing. Did it get away?'

'Her father was in the other car?' said the constable. Anna could see he was curious, but he didn't ask and she wasn't about to explain. 'Well,' said the young man, 'when the accident happened the Merc was long gone, but someone would have picked it up further on, if it carried on at that speed.'

Bell asked, 'Where's the girl now?'

'Cubicle at the end,' said the constable. 'I think they've given her a sedative or something. Want me to check?'

'It'll keep,' said Bell. 'You stay here, right? Don't care how long it takes. When the girl's ready, take a statement. You know how to do that?'

'Yes, sir,' said the constable gravely.

'Leave the driver to us, OK? We'll have to see what the bosses want to do. And radio in if there's any change.'

'We'll have to go,' said Bell to Anna. 'Tell Pritchard not to worry. We'll call her dad. Him or hubby will come down to be with her. Someone will take a statement when she's able to give it. I'm going to check with that doctor again.'

'Maureen?' Anna whispered, close to the DC's ear. 'The woman and the child in the pushchair were fine.'

Maureen squeezed her eyes shut. 'Thank God,' she said.

'We're asking your dad or your husband to come down now, so you won't be alone. Dinger and I have to go.'

'What about Caroline?'

'She's fine. Very shocked, that's all.'

'She knew it was her dad in the Merc. Wouldn't stop screaming.'

'Does she know about Rory yet?'

'No.' Maureen hesitated. 'Do you want me to tell her?'

Anna took her hand again. 'No, someone else will do that, when she's ready to hear it. Poor kid. First her mother, now this.'

'What about the mother?' Maureen's eyes widened. 'You think she's dead?'

'Could be. I should have said something earlier…'

Maureen said nothing, but Anna knew what the silence signified. 'I know, Maureen. As soon as Sam comes in, I'm going to tell him everything.'

Before she pulled the cubicle curtain across, Anna said, 'I'll be back as soon as we get Simon. You'll be fine until then. Just rest.'

In the car park, Bell was in the driver's seat of the car, revving the engine. 'Get in, woman, work to do!' he shouted, and they drove down the hill to the main road faster than was necessary.

Simon heard the thud of the helicopter's rotary blades, but it didn't linger overhead and soon he saw it, heading off to his right. Thank God he'd decided to stop when he did, ease the car out of sight under an overgrown hedge, take out the precious bag with all his documents, and take the van that was parked in a driveway just off the road. He hadn't lost his touch. One of the most useful skills he'd learned in Monty House was how to get into a car and start it up without a key. Didn't always work, but the Ford van was old enough to be vulnerable. Tank was about half-full – that should be enough. With any luck it could be a while before the owner reported its loss. It was a few minutes since he'd switched vehicles and he was still getting used to the Ford's geriatric gearbox. But changing cars had done the trick. The helicopter had clattered away out of sight.

Simon checked that his phone was still safe in his pocket and thought about Sam. The tip-off call could wait until he got to Dublin, if he bothered to make it at all. Irene wouldn't have.

263

Maybe he should do the same. Once he was in Tbilisi, he could go to ground there. He'd done it before, he could do it again.

He headed east again on the A66, keen to avoid the shorter route through Carlisle that could have snarled him up in the city before he could reach the motorway and the Scottish border. He slowed down to avoid drawing attention to himself. From the air and on the ground, for a while at least, he was anonymous. Maybe he'd swap cars again at a service station, keep them guessing. He was tired, but that didn't matter. Very soon he'd be sleeping for as long as he liked.

For a while the lack of attention paid to the van as he drove steadily on was encouraging, but pretty soon he began to wonder. They must know about the vehicle swap by now, surely, so what were they waiting for? Changing again would do the trick. He pulled into the North Lakes Hotel at the M6 roundabout. It would have CCTV in the car park, but he could disguise himself easily enough and could change vehicles and be away again before anyone would check.

Another Ford would do. What had the lad at Monty House told him: 'You could get into a Ford with a fork.' This time he found a Mondeo with a bit more poke.

Up and over Shap he went, shreds of cloud hanging on the bleak fells to either side and the familiar surreal towers of the concrete factory to his left. He wondered whether crossing into Scotland would make the police search for him more complicated.

Before he had time to think that through, he saw a warning on a roadside sign of bridge works ahead with a diversion at Junction 42. It's OK, he said to himself. It's normal, nothing to worry about. Just stick with it. The silly sod who'd left his car unlocked at the hotel might still be having his full English. You're ahead of the pack. The diversion was short, up the ramp and round the roundabout rather than straight under the bridge. No problem.

Simon didn't see the unmarked car on the bridge until it had started towards him. He veered towards the first exit, but that was blocked too. Cars behind him screeched to a halt, but not quickly enough, and as he was shunted forward, he spotted a space between an oncoming vehicle and the barrier on the bridge. He gunned the Mondeo's engine.

Twenty feet below, a watching traffic policeman flinched as the front of the Ford rose over the steel barrier, sparks flashing from its undercarriage. It tipped forward, creaking, then back. Flame was flickering under the crumpled bonnet as the chassis came to a halt, balanced precariously on top of the barrier.

CHAPTER 26

'They've got him,' Bell announced to the crowded room at Hall Brow. 'Junction forty-two. He went straight over the barrier on the bridge and got stuck. Car was on fire... hell of a mess. They pulled him out before the whole thing blew up.'

'Is he alive?'

'Still was when they got him in the ambulance, on his way to Carlisle Hospital, but only just.' Dinger looked for Brown who was on the phone at the far end of the room. 'Brown's got something about the tyre tracks found at the DCI's house. They think they're from Buttler's Mercedes, though they haven't found that yet. The Mondeo he was driving when he crashed belongs to a salesman from Leeds who's been staying at the North Lakes near Penrith. They're checking the CCTV there now. From that, we should know which car he was driving after he dumped the Merc. When we trace that back, we should be able to find his vehicle. Traffic cops swear the Merc wasn't on the A sixty-six. Apparently the chopper had a good look and didn't see it.

'Penrose... where's Penrose?' Dinger shouted, looking round. 'What you sitting back there for?'

Anna held up her hand but didn't talk.

'Get on to HQ at Penrith. Tell them we're an officer down and need some more help. Right? Got that?'

She nodded, willing him to turn away and bully someone else.

'Oh, and when you've done that,' said Bell, 'head up to Carlisle and see what you can get out of Buttler. Tell him his kid's dead, tell him anything you like, but we need to know what happened to the DCI. Whatever it takes, right?'

Another phone rang. Jason answered and listened, scribbling notes. 'Hold it,' he said, waving at Dinger. 'Bloke here reporting that his car's been stolen, near Eaglesfield, and he says there's a Mercedes in a ditch on the lane near his place. Cockermouth have patched him through to us.'

Dinger shunted his chair over to Jason's desk and snatched the phone out of his hand. 'Have you got the registration of the Merc?... OK, good. I'm sending an officer out now... be there in half an hour. Mr Driver, is it? We've found your van in Penrith... What? No, I won't call your boss, call 'im yourself!'

Bell slammed the phone down. 'Prat! Brown, get over to Eaglesfield – a Mr Driver, fourteen High Road. Get his story and wait there for Forensics. That's the car registered to Simon Buttler. It'll need checking. If Buttler took Nelly, we need to know everything we can about where he's been recently. And, Jason, get on to Carlisle Hospital. Check where Buttler is now and his condition.'

Anna was still sitting at her desk. Bell roared at her, 'What's up with you? Get a move on.' She gathered her things and left, dreading what she might have to do at the hospital.

Over the next hour, news accumulated at Hall Brow. Buttler still hadn't regained consciousness. Uniformed officers from Carlisle were with him; DS Penrose had just arrived there. Radio Cumbria was broadcasting news from the incident at Junction 42, and the crash in Bigrigg too, but weren't making any link between them.

'Won't take them long,' Bell said to Jason. 'They seem to sniff stuff out before we've told them anything, and if we deny things, they report that too.'

'How's Pritchard doing?' Jason asked.

'Sounds as if she could be out of action for a while. What did they say... broken bones in her foot, possible concussion... a right mess.'

'What about the daughter, Caroline Buttler?'

'They're keeping her in for now,' said Bell.

'Who's going to tell her about her brother?' Jason asked, relieved that it wouldn't be him.

The Intensive Care Unit at Carlisle Hospital was quiet, the hush interrupted only by the whirring and bleeping of machines keeping people alive. One end of the ward was curtained off and a policeman in uniform was sitting on a chair, reading a magazine, when Anna approached and held out her warrant card. Embarrassed, the PC got up, pushing the magazine to the floor.

'Sorry, ma'am,' he said. 'Not much happening in here, so I....'

Anna smiled. 'That's OK. I can take over here for a while. Why don't you go and get a cup of tea?'

'Yes, ma'am,' said the PC. 'Thanks.'

Anna waited a moment. She'd had a word with the doctor on the way in. Mr Buttler was 'very unwell', she'd been told. The head injuries were the most serious, but he also had damage to his chest and lungs from the impact, made worse by being dragged too quickly from the burning car, and there could be internal bleeding. The MRI scan was being analysed, but no results yet.

'Can he speak?' Anna asked. 'Will he hear anything?'

'He's coming round slowly,' said the doctor. 'He might be able to hear you, and to speak too. No way of knowing, not yet.' She looked questioningly at Anna. 'I understand he was being pursued by the police. Do you want information from him?'

Anna was doing her best to appear calm and professional. 'He's important to our inquiries,' she replied.

'Well, don't raise your hopes, Sergeant. He may not recover, despite all our efforts. I can't give you long with him.'

'Understood,' said Anna. 'Thank you, doctor.'

Before opening the curtain, she took a deep breath, relieved that she had the chance to be the first to see him but dreading what she would find.

Simon lay very still, his discoloured face in brutal contrast to the white of the surroundings. Both arms lay passive on top of the covers, hooked up to a drip and various monitors that glowed at the side of the bed. It was hard for Anna to recall her first feelings for him, and the hopes she'd had. And, painfully, she knew that some of those feelings were still there, even though he was a liar and a fraud.

She bent over him, listening to the sound of his breathing. His eyelids flickered. 'Simon,' she whispered. There was no response, but he might be able to hear her. 'It's Anna, I'm here. Can you hear me?'

She turned away, found a chair and pulled it up to the head of the bed. It was very warm in the enclosed space and she began to take off her coat.

'Anna?'

It was no more than a whisper. She threw her coat to the floor and leaned in close. 'Simon? Can you hear me?'

He didn't move but opened his mouth slightly, his tongue touching his lips. She looked around. A glass of water stood on a shelf by the bed and she dipped her fingers into it before touching them to his dry mouth.

'Again,' he croaked, and she repeated her action, feeling her stomach churn at the intimacy of it.

'You're in hospital,' she said, speaking softly into his ear. 'You crashed the car.'

A tear ran down one cheek. 'Rory,' he said.

She hesitated. Should she say what she knew? Would it be too much for him? Simon opened his eyes but didn't turn his head, staring at the ceiling above him. 'He's dead,' he whispered. 'My fault.'

She took his hand. It was cool and papery. 'No, not your fault. An accident.' She paused. 'Who told you?'

Simon closed his eyes tight and his breathing changed, turning rasping and painful. The monitors above them began to flash and a loud beep pierced the silence. He opened his mouth, as if trying to speak, and raised one hand. Anna bent towards him, her ear to his mouth. He made a strange sound – 'phuh, phuh' – but nothing more. Before Anna could react the curtains opened behind her. 'Stand aside, please,' said the nurse. She looked at Simon, turned and called, 'Dr Bopal, in here, please!'

Anna stepped back, away from the woman's urgent movements, and picked up her discarded coat.

'You'll need to wait outside,' said the nurse. Dr Bopal joined her at the bedside. 'Outside, now,' the doctor said sharply.

A large notice in the corridor said that the use of mobile phones wasn't allowed. Anna was running down the stairs towards the main entrance when she met the constable coming up, carrying two paper cups.

'What's happened, ma'am?' said the PC. 'Is he dead?'

Anna shook her head. 'I need to call in,' she said. 'Go back and stay there, but don't get in the way.' The PC nodded and

Anna continued down the stairs, pulling her phone from her pocket as she reached the main doors.

It took a few minutes for someone to pick up. 'Jason?' She recognised the voice. 'Is Dinger there?'

'On the other phone,' said Jason. 'What's up?'

'Buttler. He knows about Rory. Sam must have told him.'

'Where is Sam?'

'He didn't say,' Anna replied. 'He was trying to speak, but he's very sick, Jason. He might not be able to tell us anything.'

'So, how are we going to find Sam?'

She could hear the anxiety in Jason's voice. 'It'll be all right, don't worry. Can I speak to Dinger?'

'He's still on the phone. I'll tell him,' said Jason. 'Where are you now?'

'At the hospital,' said Anna. 'Buttler took a turn for the worse, they made me leave him, but I'll go back now.'

'Make him tell you,' said Jason. 'Dinger says Sam could be anywhere. And it's twelve hours since he went missing. He could die like that other bloke, that Dr Graham.'

'But Dr Graham was already ill,' said Anna. 'Sam will be OK.' She was not as confident about it as she sounded. What if there had been a struggle? And what had Simon been trying to say to her?

Anna went back to the ICU, taking the stairs two at a time. The young constable held up his hand. 'Don't go in,' he said. 'It's all kicked off in there.'

She brushed past him. Dr Bopal and two others were standing by Simon's bed, looking at him. The monitors were dark and silent. Dr Bopal looked up. 'We couldn't save him, I'm sorry. Did you know the man? He was asking for someone... Irene.'

Anna couldn't speak. She sat down heavily on a bedside chair and put her head in her hands.

CHAPTER 27

By the time Henny Brown found the address in Eaglesfield it was raining hard. A car with the unmistakable Mercedes outline lay in a ditch at the side of the road. Brown checked the registration plate. This was it. Buttler must have left it there under the overhanging hedge to hide it from the air, knowing that the helicopter would have joined the hunt for him. This bloke knows what he's doing, Brown thought. He knows we're after him, dumps his car, does his best to hide it in a hurry, takes another. Definitely not your regular estate agent.

He looked around. A man was standing at the window of the house just across the narrow road. Brown assumed he was the one whose car had been taken. He walked down the short driveway. The house looked uncared for, paintwork peeling and windows smeared. As he approached, he could hear a dog barking furiously on the other side of the front door.

Instead of ringing the bell, which would further enrage the dog, Brown turned and tapped on the front window. The man appeared again. He was unshaven and overweight.

'Control that dog!' Henny shouted. 'Shut it in the back.'

The man shrugged and disappeared. The barking receded, the front door was opened.

Brown held out his warrant card. 'DC Brown, Workington CID,' he said.

'Workington?' the man queried. He was local, from the way he pronounced the name. 'What's tha doing out 'ere?'

'You rang in,' said Brown, 'about your van, Mr...?'

'Driver,' said the man. 'Eric Driver. It were nicked.'

'Can I come in, Mr Driver?' said Brown. 'Very wet out here.'

'Bit of a mess,' said the man.

That was an understatement, thought Brown, as he followed Driver into the front room. The place smelled strongly of dog and urine. The carpet was covered in dog hairs.

'Just the one dog?' Brown asked.

'Aye. Had two but one died. And Adolf won't 'urt you.'

'Adolf?'

'The dog,' said Driver. 'He'll carry on for a bit, noisy like, but 'e's OK.'

'About your van,' said Henny, taking out his notebook. 'Can you give me all the details, please? Make, model, registration.'

'Found it already, 'ave you?'

'Not yet, but we expect to.'

'How come?'

'We have reason to believe the person who took your vehicle swapped it for another one, before he was apprehended.'

'Oh, so, you've got 'im, 'ave you?'

The man rubbed his hands together and looked pleased. 'Bastard. Cost me a day's wages.' He hesitated. 'Any reward, like?'

Brown shook his head.

'Just give me the information, please, Mr Driver.' He scribbled down the facts. 'And when did you see that your van was gone?'

'When it was time for work, about quarter to eight. Heard nowt. Keys were still in't kitchen – he must have fiddled about with it. Any compensation for damage?'

'You'll need to check your insurance,' said Brown. 'You do have insurance?'

Driver sniffed. 'Got it somewhere,' he said, without conviction.

'We have a Forensics team on the way,' said Henny. 'Have you touched the car at all, since you noticed it?'

'Had a look in, like,' said Driver, 'there's nowt in it that I could see.' He paused, thinking. 'And I checked the boot, but it was locked.'

'Any sound coming from the boot?'

Mr Driver looked shocked. 'Christ, what's in there?'

'So you didn't hear anything?'

'Nay, I'd have said or done summat. What's he done, this bloke?'

'Can't tell you that, I'm afraid.'

'Have you got 'im locked up?'

'Can't tell you that either, sorry.'

'Don't say much, do you?' said Driver. 'Funny accent that. Down south, is it?'

'You could say that,' said Henny.

They both heard car doors being slammed outside. They stood up. The narrow lane was blocked now by a car and a van. Brown noticed Tony Wong's dark head.

'Make sure the dog is secure, Mr Driver, and I'll talk to my colleagues.'

'CSI mob, is it?' Driver asked, looking interested. 'Watch all that stuff on the telly, I do. Magic.'

'Yes, and they'll be working there for a while. If you can do it without letting the dog out, how about getting the kettle on?'

'Aye, right,' said Driver. He opened the kitchen door an inch or two, cursing at the dog, before he mercifully disappeared and Brown could open the front door.

'Sorry, got lost,' said Tony. 'We'll get started on the Merc. Has the witness touched it?'

'He says not,' said Henny. 'But I reckon he'd have pinched anything that wasn't nailed down.'

'OK, let's assume he's not lying, but we'll get his fingerprints, just in case. Can we do that inside?'

Brown looked up at the sky, which was mercifully clearing, reducing the rain to a drizzle. 'Pretty grubby in here. Should be OK if you stay by the door. And watch out for the dog. It's called Adolf... you can guess the rest.'

Tony grimaced. 'OK. Tell the bloke to come out here, will you?'

'We need you outside when you're ready, Mr Driver,' Henny shouted through the kitchen door. 'Just you, not the dog.'

He followed Tony out of the front door and down the drive, pulling up his collar against the damp. Two men were struggling into coveralls. 'First thing to check is the boot,' said Brown. 'You know there's a missing person involved?'

'Rumour says it's the DCI,' said one of the men. 'Don't think he's in the boot, do you?'

Brown shrugged. 'We think the guy who took him is into drugs. His kid's died too. Who knows what he could do?'

'Boot first, OK,' said the man, taking a bunch of keys from his bag. 'One of these might do it, or else it's a crowbar job.'

At the fifth attempt, the boot of the Mercedes popped up and they peered inside. It was empty. A tarpaulin was hastily erected to cover the car while two of the three Forensics officers systematically began to examine it, outside and in.

Henny walked back towards the house, where one of the team was taking Eric Driver's fingerprints. 'Can you give us a DNA sample as well, sir?' he asked.

'Sure,' said Driver. He was clearly delighted to be part of the drama.

Henny walked back towards the car. The rain had almost stopped and he stepped down into the ditch to look at the car's tyres. The right side of the car was well below the left, and he wondered how easy it would have been for the driver to climb out. He used his torch in the gloom of the overhanging hedge to check for footprints in the muddy side of the ditch, noticing where Buttler must have slipped as he scrambled up.

As he regained his footing at the top of the bank, Henny caught sight of a pile of what looked like old clothes caught on a low-hanging branch of the hedge. He called to the man taking Driver's fingerprints. 'George, can you bring Mr Driver out here?'

Now there were three men looking at the bundle of clothes. 'Seen that before?' Henny asked Driver. The man shook his head.

'Find all sorts in that ditch that folk chuck out of cars, but not stuff like that.'

He started down the slope towards it but George caught his arm and held him back. 'Leave that to us, sir,' he said. 'Shall I get it?' he asked Brown, who was looking more closely.

'Could be anything,' said Brown, 'but let's get it out of there and have a proper look.' He pointed to the footprints below them. 'Go round the other side, George, away from these.'

George walked round the back of the car and pushed his way into the hedge, to approach the bundle from the far side. They watched as he unhooked it from the branch and put it in an evidence bag. 'Back of the van,' he said. 'We'll look at it there.'

The first thing they noticed when he pulled the bundle carefully out of the evidence bag was the colour, a dark red. 'Blood?' asked Henny. George shook his head. 'Right colour, wrong feel,' he said. He touched the material with a gloved finger. 'It's more like paint than blood. And it's not all over,' he added, stretching the material out on a plastic sheet on the floor of the van. 'Overalls, look. He could have taken them off when he got out of the car and chucked them in the hedge.'

He paused, turned towards the men working in the Mercedes. 'Harry, look at the driver's seat. Any sign of stains, dark red?'

'No,' called a voice, 'but looks like something on the passenger side. Need a sample?'

'No, I think we got the sample, thanks. Can you come and have a look?'

Three nylon-suited figures stared at the dark red overalls lying in the van. 'Hang about,' said one of them. 'Seen that before. My uncle Mike... that's what he wore for work, and the right colour too. He was a miner, haematite, in Beckermet, when I was a lad. It's shut now. There were dozens of those pits up and down the coast.'

Brown reacted fast. 'I'm calling this in,' he said, reaching for his phone.

'Tell me something useful, for God's sake,' said Bell, when Brown's call was passed through to him. 'All hell's breaking out here. Press have picked up that something's going on. How they found out that Buttler being at the motorway scene was connected to the accident in Bigrigg, Christ knows, but now we've got all the usual dumb questions about police chases, public at risk, blah, blah. And I'm carrying the can while Sam's in the wind. Wait till they get hold of *that* story.'

Brown held the phone away from his ear until the rant was dying down.

'We've recovered something from Buttler's car in Eaglesfield, sir, but I'm not sure how helpful it is.'

'What is it, man? Get on with it.'

'Overalls, sir. Looks as if Buttler got rid of them when he dumped the car. They're very stained. Looked like dried blood, but Forensics reckon it's the staining you get in a haematite mine.'

'Are they sure? What's Buttler doing down a pit?'

'No analysis yet, sir, but one of the Forensics guys recognised the colour and consistency. He says there's lots of iron workings all over the west coast area.'

'Well, he's right about that. And we think Buttler might have been in one since he took the DCI, do we?'

'It's a possibility, yes, sir. He could have killed him and dumped him somewhere well out of sight.'

'Or he could have hidden him away. But why? Sounds like a copy of what happened to Graham.'

Brown was silent. He knew that a response was not expected.

'You get back here,' said Bell. 'Penrith are dealing with the car theft at the North Lakes and the car Buttler was in when he crashed. Penrose is in Carlisle, but it doesn't sound too promising for getting Buttler to talk. Get a move on. It's like the *Marie Celeste* in here. I'm trying to get hold of Penrose, but she's not picking up.'

Outside the ICU, Anna sat still and quiet while the young PC went to fetch her something hot to drink. She didn't really want it but she needed to be alone for a while, away from the constable's excited questions. She'd seen dead bodies before, plenty of them, but never in such quiet orderly surroundings. Death was harder to accept when it was so clean.

Flashes of memory sparked through her brain. Mark's body in the ditch; Graham's in its shroud. The last time she'd seen Simon was in his bed, warm and passionate: now he was gone and no one but she knew what had passed between them. Would she have to explain? Would Caroline give her away?

Caroline... oh, God. First her brother, now this. For no concrete reason, Anna was sure that Caroline's missing mother was dead. There'd been no sign of violence, nothing, but people don't just disappear without trace unless they want to. Or unless they were no longer alive. Where was Wendy Buttler?

Chapter 28

For a long time, after Sam knew that all his water had gone, he lay quite still, not daring to move in case that made things worse. Why hadn't he drunk as much as he could while he had the chance? He thought of John Graham, imprisoned and dying slowly of thirst, losing hope, fading away.

Then the practical man he was reasserted himself. While the sliver of light under the door persisted, he must discover anything within reach that might help him. He had no idea where he was, but there was no sign or sound of human activity. He could hear birds outside and something had rustled in the darkness, but that had to be animal, not human. Was there any point in making a noise above the incessant throb of the pumps far below?

The rickety chair had collapsed, and the piece of metal that he'd managed to grasp had been knocked across the floor, out of reach. Sam was still shackled to the structure behind him. Searching for something to attack the chain and the padlocks with had caused the water calamity, but he had to try again. Carefully, systematically, he combed the floor within his reach, but there was nothing remotely useful.

Around the edges of the metal cage planks had rotted away. Fragments collapsed under his touch, rattling away to the bottom of the shaft, hundreds of feet below. He stretched the chain as far as he could, but still couldn't move it very far. Somewhere he could hear a steady drip. If he could find and reach it, it might be drinkable, but wherever it was in the echo of rock and metal that surrounded him, he could do no more while the chain bound him.

Once more, he turned his mind to where he was. Simon Buttler had said that the metal structure was the way into the mine, presumably the cage that went down the shaft, and said it didn't work anymore. So the mine must be out of commission. There were dozens of old mines and shafts in the area around Egremont and Beckermet. And would it really help to know where he was? The only thing that mattered was that someone else knew.

They must be missing him by now, have been to his house, seen where another car had parked, guessed that he'd been taken against his will. But after that, what? They would be looking for Buttler too. Maybe he'd been apprehended, told them what he'd done. Or maybe he was holding out, using Sam's life as a bargaining chip.

He rested for a while, regaining the sense he would need to help him decide what to do. And he thought about Stuart as he once was, and Mikey, and the other boys living at Montgomery House, placed there by people who presumably thought it was the best solution. The boys had made stupid choices, been rejected by their families and hardened themselves to survive, but none of them had deserved to be used and tormented and humiliated by Edwards and his cronies. The Thornhills had preyed on the abusers. They were all as bad as each other, and Judith had almost been their victim too. Sam would never forgive them for that. And what about Stuart Billings, the boy who'd played along? He'd been damaged too, by a ruthless woman who'd seduced and manipulated him.

Sam decided he needed to lie down, to conserve his strength, and used his feet to clear himself a space to lie in. Suddenly, he slipped and lost his balance on the wet floor.

Falling backwards, he felt his back hit the floor by the edge of the cage. The rotting timbers broke under his weight and he tumbled through the gap, the chain pulling taut, until he was hanging upside down, suspended by his legs. The fall made Sam shout with pain and shock. The sound echoed around the shaft yawning below him.

Outside the hospital, Anna called Bell.

'You still there?' he bellowed. 'Has he said anything?'

'He died.'

'What? Stop whispering, woman.'

She cleared her throat. 'Buttler died, sir, ten minutes ago. Doctor said there was nothing they could do.'

'Oh my God,' said Bell. 'Did he say anything? Anything about Nelly?'

'Nothing coherent.'

She heard Bell sigh. 'Well, no good staying up there now, is it? Get back here.'

'Where's Caroline?' Anna asked.

'Still in Whitehaven Hospital,' he said. 'Pritchard is out, but they kept the girl in. Hang on.'

Anna heard more shouting, then Bell came back on. 'They don't know what to do with the girl so she's still there, for now at least.'

'When you searched the house,' Anna continued, 'did you find any evidence about the mother, Wendy Buttler?'

'The woman you think he bumped off? No, nothing. Nothing in the garden either.'

'And the letter, the one from the wife that made him call off the misper report?'

'No. What we found were account books, loads of them, in a safe we had to blow open. Forensics have them. Looks like he's been bringing hard drugs in for years.'

'And what about Sam?'

'Still in the wind. Brown's coming back from where Buttler dumped his car. Looks like they found something, but don't know how useful it's going to be. We need you back here.'

'I'll be there,' she said. 'I'm leaving now, but I'm going to Whitehaven Hospital first. Someone has to tell that poor kid her brother and her dad are both dead.'

'Why you?'

Anna hesitated. 'Because I know her,' she said.

'You *know* her? From where? How?'

'Later,' said Anna, and rang off.

'We can't keep her here much longer,' said the ward sister. 'We need every bed we can get and Miss Buttler is well enough to be discharged.'

'But where will she go?' asked Anna.

'I'm afraid that's someone else's problem, not ours. We've called Social Services, they're trying to find somewhere. I understand the father's in some kind of trouble.'

Anna shook her head. 'Her father's dead, Sister. That's why I'm here, to tell her. Can you leave us alone for a few minutes, please? This will be difficult.'

'Oh, my,' said the sister. 'Yes, yes, go ahead. She's in the same place, but there's another patient in the room too. Do you want to take her somewhere more private? Go to the day room. I'll ask the staff to make sure you're not disturbed.'

'Thank you,' Anna said.

Caroline was sitting in a chair by the bed, a magazine on her lap. When she saw Anna, she stood up suddenly and started to cry.

'What's happened?' Caroline said. 'That other policewoman left, but she wouldn't tell me anything. One of the nurses said they were waiting for my dad to pick me up. Where is he, Anna? And Rory, have you found him? I kept looking on my phone but the battery's flat and they won't let me out. They've taken my clothes…'

The woman in the other bed sat up, caught Anna's eye and shook her head. 'She's been crying a lot,' she said. 'Can you do something?'

Anna took the weeping girl in her arms and held her close for a moment. 'We'll go for a little walk, Caroline,' she said. 'Come on. Somewhere a bit more private, OK?'

'Thanks,' said the other patient as Anna took Caroline's arm and led her out of the room and down the corridor.

In the day room the television was on and the sound of manufactured laughter issued from it into the empty space. Anna helped the girl onto a sofa before she turned the television off and sat down next to her. She took Caroline's hands in hers, looking into the girl's tired face.

'I have bad news, pet. You'll need to be very strong. I'm here to help you, any way I can.'

'What's happened? Is it Rory?'

'Yes. Rory had an accident. He died. We couldn't tell you straight away because we weren't sure it was him for a while. But now we know that it was.'

Caroline's eyes filled with tears. 'He's just a boy,' she said. 'He can't be dead. He's too young.'

'I know,' said Anna, putting her arm around Caroline's shoulders and pulling her in.

Caroline pulled back. 'And what about Dad? Was he in the accident too?'

Anna had already decided that there was only so much bad news she could share at one time. 'He's badly hurt, pet. He's in the hospital at Carlisle. We don't know yet, but he may not survive.'

The girl crumpled. 'No, no! Not him too. What will happen to me?'

It was enough. Anna couldn't say any more. She held Caroline in her arms, rocking her like the baby she'd never had. She couldn't hide the fact of Simon's death for long, but right now the truth was too hard to bear. It had to wait.

There was a tap on the door. Anna couldn't get up. 'Come in,' she called. The sister came close to her, looking concerned.

'I'm so sorry to disturb you, Sergeant, but there's someone outside who wants to see you. She says it's urgent but won't say any more. Can I send her in?'

'Is it police business? Couldn't it wait?'

The sister shook her head. 'I think she needs to come in, she's quite distraught.'

'No, I'll come out,' said Anna. 'I'll see her in the corridor.'

She whispered to Caroline, 'I need to see someone, pet. I'll be right outside, just for a minute.' Then she pulled away and walked outside.

Looking down the corridor, Anna saw a woman approaching. She was fair-haired, quite tall, well dressed. She looked anxious.

'Is Caroline Buttler here?' she said. 'I need to see her.'

Anna put out her hand and stepped towards her. 'Yes, she's here, but she's quite distressed at the moment. Can this wait?'

The woman pushed against Anna's hand. 'But I must see her.'

'Who are you?' said Anna. 'Are you a relative?'

The woman closed her eyes. When she opened them again, they were full of tears. 'I'm her mother,' she said. 'I'm Wendy Lilley.'

At Hall Brow, Bell was trying to hold it together. The room was crowded with CID officers drafted in from other teams and from uniformed branch too.

'Just so you know,' said Bell, 'we're treating the death of the young man, Rory Buttler, as accidental. No sign of foul play, apart from him trying to get rid of an illegal crop and making some stupid mistakes. That ID is now confirmed. His step-father, Simon Buttler, aka Stuart Billings, is also confirmed deceased by Carlisle Hospital, following the pile-up earlier today. There will be an inquiry into the circumstances of that accident, whether it was a direct consequence of the police pursuit. Nothing we can do about that, but there will be an investigation. Any questions so far?'

The room was silent. Rumour had already supplied all this information and there were no surprises.

'Far more pressing for us right now: we need to discover the whereabouts of DCI Tognarelli, who appears to have been abducted from his home sometime after ten last night. Looks like he arrived there in his car and didn't enter the house before he was taken. Forensics found a rag smelling of chloroform, or something similar, at the edge of the parking area. DCI Tognarelli could have been overwhelmed, pushed into a vehicle and taken somewhere, as yet unknown.'

He looked around. Some heads were down, taking notes. Others watched, waiting for more details. 'Any CCTV?' Bell asked.

A voice answered, 'Not much help, sir. Vehicle seen passing a garage on the Whitehaven Loop road at ten-forty-three that looks like a dark-coloured Mercedes, heading south, but no other details.'

'We know our suspect, Buttler, was driving a dark blue Mercedes, since recovered. More on that in a minute,' said Bell. 'No other sightings?'

'No, sir.'

'Well, at least we know it was going south. And that fits with some other evidence. Brown? Report on the Mercedes, please.'

DC Brown stood up and heads turned. Many of those in the room hadn't seen him before, and for one or two the last sighting of this tall good-looking man had been on the local rugby pitch. Two uniformed policewomen exchanged glances.

'The car was found in a ditch in Eaglesfield, just south-west of Cockermouth, and reported at around eight o'clock this morning by a Mr Driver. His van, a Ford, was missing and has since been found in the car park of the North Lakes Hotel, where Buttler obviously swapped it for the Mondeo he later crashed, probably to avoid being spotted by the helicopter.'

Bell interrupted. 'Penrith are dealing with all that, so cut to the chase. What did you find near the car?'

'Overalls were found in the hedge close by. These were stained with something dark red in colour, which has since been identified as iron ore. Looks as if Buttler had recently been in an iron ore mine, and we believe that may be where he's hidden the DCI.'

'Alive?' asked a woman's voice.

'No way to know,' said Brown. 'No trace evidence in the car to indicate that the DCI has been harmed. Looks like he'd been in the boot, but no visible blood there. Forensics expect to find evidence of his presence.'

'What about the car tyres?' someone asked.

'Forensics again,' said Brown. 'They're trying to pin down the exact area where the car might have been before heading off east. We believe the DCI was not in the car when it ended up in Eaglesfield.'

'So where do we look?' asked DS Carruthers, Bell's old side-kick whose permanent transfer to HQ at Penrith had been delayed to help with the search for Tognarelli.

'If we knew that, Bob, we wouldn't be here, would we?' said Bell. He hadn't yet forgiven Carruthers for climbing the ladder to HQ ahead of him. 'Turns out there's dozens of iron ore mines dotted all over the area south of Whitehaven,' Bell went on. 'We've got Quigley here drawing up a list of locations and contact people, and each of you will be allocated some of these to check. They're disused so the checks will need to be made in person. You'll be looking for any trace of recent vehicle activity as well as any sign of anyone hidden away, alive or dead. Bit of a needle in a haystack, but that's what we do. Get your assignments and get to it. If the DCI's out there, we need to find him.' He looked around. 'Any more questions?'

'Can Forensics pin it down by analysing the ore on the overalls?'

'They're on that now. There's some bloke who's an expert and they're in touch with him. If we hear any more you'll be informed, obviously. Anything we can do to reduce the size of the haystack. But for now, that's all we've got.'

'Wendy Buttler?' asked Anna. She glanced towards the door of the day room, making sure it was shut.

'Lilley,' the woman corrected. 'I changed it back when I left Simon. Changed everything – cut that man out of my life for good.'

'But the children?' Anna said, not ready yet to challenge the woman. 'How could you leave them?'

Wendy looked towards the door. 'Is she in there, my Caroline?'

Anna put her finger to her lips, warning Wendy to keep her voice down. 'Yes, she's here, but there's more you need to know before you see her. Not here, we can't talk freely. Please Wendy, can you wait a few minutes more, for Caroline's sake? Go back to the ward sister's office and wait for me. OK?'

For a moment, Wendy set herself as if she was going to barge past Anna into the day room. Then she stopped. 'You're with the police, right? You're not fobbing me off?'

'I promise you,' said Anna. 'I'll explain everything, and then you can see your daughter. She needs you, but you must be prepared.'

'Prepared for what?'

'Trust me Wendy, go and wait, I'll be with you in a minute.'

Reluctantly, Wendy Lilley turned and walked back towards the ward.

Anna went into the day room. 'I just have to go out for a few minutes, there's someone asking questions about the case. I'll be back in a minute, OK?'

Caroline was lying on the sofa, knees tucked up, as if yearning to be a child again. Anna left her and slipped out. In the office, the sister was looking annoyed. 'I know you have a job to do, Sergeant, but this is not a police station. I've had a DI Bell on the phone twice now, looking for you. I told him you were busy and he was quite rude.'

Damn the man, Anna thought. 'Sorry,' she said. 'There's quite a flap on, with another case. I'll ring him as soon as I can.'

'And what about this lady?' the ward sister said under her breath. 'Will this take long?'

Anna took the nurse's arm and turned her away from Wendy, who was fidgeting nervously. 'This is Caroline's mother. She should be able to take Caroline out of your way, but I have to tell her some things first. I'm sorry to inconvenience you…'

'No, no, carry on, Sergeant. That poor girl's needs come first after all.'

Anna joined Wendy and asked her, in a low voice, 'Will Caroline want to see you? You left them, didn't you? It's been a long time.'

Wendy was close to tears. 'I was afraid. When I knew what he was doing, I thought he would try to…' she hesitated, '… to harm me. I had to get out.'

'But what about the children?'

Wendy shook her head. 'I knew they'd be all right. Simon wouldn't harm them.' She took a deep breath. 'Before I left he poisoned them against me. Told them all sorts of lies. Rory believed everything, but he was just a boy and worshipped Simon. I thought Caroline would stick up for me, but then she said she knew I was having an affair, and I lost her too.'

'And were you having an affair?'

Wendy shook her head. 'That man she saw me with, that was my brother. He was helping me. He still is.'

'The letter you sent, a few days later…' Anna began.

Wendy shook her head. 'What letter? I never sent a letter. Why would I?'

'But…' Anna began again, then stopped herself. It didn't matter now. 'OK, before you see Caroline, I have to tell you…'

'I know about the accident she was in,' said Wendy. 'It was on the television, the car crash in Bigrigg. The local news said Caroline was involved, but I only saw it today. I thought she might still be here.'

'Have you heard anything else?' Anna asked. Wendy shook her head. There was no easy way to do this. 'Did you see on the news about the accident on the motorway earlier today?'

'I heard about it. A car was being chased, ran off the bridge… something like that.'

'Well, the driver of that car was Simon,' said Anna.

Wendy put her hand to her mouth. 'The police were after him,' she murmured. 'I told him that would happen one day. I warned him, but he wouldn't listen. He said that he'd paid for everything we owned with his "business" – that's what he called it. Said he'd give the children whatever they wanted and I should keep quiet or he'd make me sorry.'

Anna put her hand on Wendy's shoulder. 'Simon died, Wendy. I'm sorry to have to tell you. There was nothing they could do.'

'Oh, God. The fool, the fool! He pushed me out and took my kids. What about them now?'

Anna watched her grief and anger, and knew that there was worse, much worse, to come. She couldn't delay the shock of Rory's death as Caroline already knew about it. 'I'm afraid there's more dreadful news, Wendy, which you have to know. It's about Rory.'

It was the hardest thing Anna had ever had to do, but she told the woman only as much about her son's death as she could cope with. The full horrific details could wait. By the time Anna finally got away from the hospital and headed back to Hall Brow, darkness was approaching and she still hadn't found time to respond to Bell's calls.

CHAPTER 29

'About bloody time,' was his cheerful greeting when she arrived at Hall Brow. 'I've been calling the hospital, getting endless grief from some snotty woman there, and finally you turn up. What's kept you? Better be something important.'

'Depends what you think is important,' said Anna. 'Can we talk somewhere private?'

He looked at her, head on one side, then led the way to his office. She shut the door behind her.

'It's about the Buttler family.'

'What's left of it,' said Bell, checking the messages on his desk.

'I wanted to tell this to the DCI, but it's something you need to know, boss,' said Anna. She'd rehearsed what she had to say, but it was still hard. 'Simon Buttler and I were friends, before all this kicked off. I've been to his house, he to mine. I know his kids.'

Bell sat back in his chair, studying her closely. 'Ever occur to you that you should have taken yourself off the case?'

'I wasn't on it, not really, with being off work and everything. I waited, to tell Sam, and then he disappeared.'

'Kidnapped by your boyfriend.'

Anna stood in front of him, trying not to look as guilty as she felt. 'Sorry, sir,' was all she could muster.

'And now Buttler's dead,' Bell said. 'Were you with him?'

She nodded.

'I could say "Sorry for your loss", but I'd be a liar,' said Bell. 'And what about the daughter?'

'I had to see her. She has nobody, or at least I thought she had nobody. But her mother turned up, that's why I was so long at the hospital.'

'Bloody 'ell. The woman you told me was dead and buried in the garden, that woman?'

'Yes, sir. I'd heard about how she disappeared and I thought that, you know, something had happened.'

'Are you seriously telling me that you believed your boyfriend had bumped off his wife, and you didn't see fit to tell us?'

'But I did tell you,' Anna protested.

'While carefully not mentioning the other stuff.' Bell looked her up and down with a faint smile that turned Anna's stomach. 'How much of a boyfriend was he?'

She shook her head. 'That's as much as you need to know, sir. I know I've made a mistake, and I expect you to do whatever needs doing.'

'Don't have much choice, do I?' he said. 'I'll need to talk to the bosses, and there'll be more questions. Right now, we're short-handed enough as it is. As soon as we find the DCI, I'll take it further. Anything else you want to tell me now?'

She shook her head.

Bell checked his watch. 'Briefing at six o'clock. I've got teams out checking places Buttler might have taken the DCI. Don't suppose he told you anything about that, did he, before he snuffed it?'

Anna bit her lip, remembering *Irene* and a few disjointed sounds.

'We'll say nothing about this to any other officer, Sergeant, not until we have Tognarelli safely back. There's a lot of people well below your rank and experience busting a gut on this case, and I'm sure your absence has been noted.' Bell paused, choosing his words carefully for once. 'Frankly, it's about time you pulled your weight round here. And since you know the Buttler family so intimately, I expect you to offer us any insight at all that might be useful. If it makes people ask how you got the information, that's your problem, not mine, OK?'

'Sir,' said Anna.

As she left the office, people were gathering for the six o'clock briefing. One or two nodded, but no one commented or asked where she'd been. They probably assume I've been working on something, she thought. And they were right. She wanted to see a frightened young woman who'd lost her brother and her step-dad reunited with her mother, but none of that was any help with finding Sam.

Bell started the meeting without any preamble. It was a few minutes before Anna realised that all these people had been out for hours checking disused ore mines in the area for any signs of recent activity.

Suddenly, through the fog of all that had happened since, she remembered something she'd once been told at the Old Vicarage.

'It's the Florence mine,' she called out. 'Rory Buttler volunteered at the Florence.'

All heads turned towards her. She felt herself blushing.

'But it's a visitor place,' said Quigley. 'Why would Buttler put Sam somewhere there'd be people around?'

'It's closed Sunday and Monday,' another voice put in. 'Opens again mid-morning tomorrow.'

'And Buttler would know that,' Anna said. 'It's close to where they live.'

'Maybe he wants us to find Sam,' said Brown. 'Maybe...'

Bell interrupted them. 'OK, cut the chat. Who's checked the Florence?'

'It's on our list,' said one of the uniformed officers. 'But we thought it wouldn't be a runner. We left it till tomorrow.'

Bell jumped to his feet. 'Who's the contact person? Get them on the phone, now. Tell them to meet us there in half an hour. Brown, Penrose, you're with me. Jason, stay here, hold the fort, and tell the Super where we are.'

Ernest Longmire was waiting for them when Brown drove Bell's car up the short driveway into the yard of the Florence pit. 'What's all this?' Mr Longmire asked. 'Someone rang and said you needed to search the mine. What you looking for?'

Bell introduced himself. 'We have a missing person, Mr Long-mire. In fact, a police officer. And we've reason to believe that he may be somewhere around this mine.'

'Why here?' the man persisted.

'Doesn't matter, that's our information. We need your help now, and as quick as you can. If you were going to hide someone in this place, where would you go?'

'Main way in is down the ramp,' said Mr Longmire. 'We don't use the shaft anymore, not for years. Couldn't afford to keep the cage running.' He turned away. 'Ramp's up here, follow me.'

Longmire led the way through a small copse and along a muddy footpath, torchlight swaying as they walked. In front of a pair of metal gates securing an entrance, he put a large bunch of keys into the torchlight and picked one out. A minute later the metal gates swung open and they stood at the top of an incline. Brown shouted, 'Hello?' The sound bounced off the walls, but there was no response.

'Before we go down,' said Bell, 'have a look for signs of recent activity. When were visitors last down here?'

'Saturday, early afternoon,' said Longmire. 'We're closed Sunday and Monday.'

They shone their torches back along the path and onto the concrete floor. 'Anything unusual?' Bell asked.

Longmire shook his head. 'Not that I can see.' He flashed his torch down the slope. 'Plenty of places you could put someone down there.'

'What's that noise?' said Brown. 'Sounds like a motor running.'

'That's the pumps,' said Longmire. 'If they don't run, the mine floods. Water goes to Sellafield.'

'Can you knock them off?' asked Brown. 'We need quiet, so we can hear if anyone's shouting, and they can hear us.'

'How long for?'

'Minutes, no more,' said Bell.

'Important, is it?' Longmire asked.

'Don't question me!' Bell shouted. 'This is police business. Just do it.'

Longmire recoiled from Bell's anger and disappeared down the path.

Bell shook his head. 'Why would Buttler bring Sam here, knowing that tomorrow morning the place would be busy with people?'

'Unless he was already dead,' said Henny Brown. 'Must be plenty of places to hide a body down here.'

'Anna?' said Bell. 'You're very quiet. Did Buttler tell you about this place?'

She didn't answer. Everything she'd understood about Simon was imploding, overshadowed by regret at her own foolishness. If Sam was harmed...

Brown spoke before she could find any words. 'Maybe he wanted Sam to be found, but not for a while. Saturday to Tuesday – that's long enough for anyone to get safely out of the country.'

Bell nodded. 'They found papers in Buttler's car, passports in three names, plane tickets. Dublin to Tbilisi, but nothing to get him to Dublin.'

'Maybe that was planned as a boat trip,' Brown said. 'He could have been on his boat and across to Ireland before anyone knew Sam was missing.'

Suddenly, the noise stopped. For a moment the memory of it still rang in their ears, before a dark silence enveloped them.

'Hello,' Brown shouted.

They listened. He shouted again. There was a slight sound, something faint, right at the edge of their hearing. Anna prayed for it to be Sam, alive. Again, Brown called into the black hole, and again that sound came back, but not from down below. 'Out there somewhere,' he said, starting back up the ramp.

Longmire was coming back through the trees. 'Anything?' he said. 'Can't leave them pumps off for long.'

'What's up there?' said Brown, pointing towards a litter of buildings on the other side of the yard.

'That's the old mineshaft,' said Longmire. 'Haven't used it since we built the visitor ramp.'

Anna was already running. Brown quickly overtook her, leaving Longmire and Bell puffing in the rear. Brown looked around. Various dilapidated buildings flashed past under his torchlight. He called to Longmire. 'If you had to hide someone, where would you go?'

Longmire pointed to an old wooden door, heavily padlocked. A sign nailed to it read, 'Danger. Do Not Enter'. As they stared at it, Brown put up his hand. 'Listen! Someone's definitely in there. Can you open this door?'

Longmire examined his bunch of keys. 'It's not 'ere,' he said. 'Key's missing.' Brown flashed his torch around the yard then ran across, coming back with a small axe. He handed his torch to Anna and laid into the door, swinging the axe as far as he could to increase the force.

'Hey!' Longmire shouted, but Bell shut him up.

The door was heavy. It took several blows before the wood began to splinter apart. Brown kicked high at the small hole and more wood broke under the impact. On and on he kicked and swung with the axe, stopping finally to peer into the hole and shine his torch into the space.

He turned to Anna. 'Get an ambulance, quick!'

She hesitated. 'Is he alive?'

'Just go, woman,' Bell shouted. 'Find a signal. Call it in.'

Her heart sank. She ran.

Sam had heard the voices and tried to shout, but could manage only a dry croak. Moving his body might make a noise, but he daren't risk the final fall down the shaft. Then there was a violent sound and a light and a surge of adrenalin that forced a shout from him, and faces peered down at him from above.

Together, gently, Bell and Brown pulled Sam's body out of the hole, lying him on the ground, his ankles still tethered. When Anna got back she could see his hands and ankles, red with blood and the dark stain of the ore. He was moaning and she crouched beside him. 'We're here,' she said. 'We found you.' Longmire found a hacksaw and Brown patiently worked at the chain until it fell apart.

'Don't move him,' he said to Bell, 'not until the ambulance gets here.'

And so for a while they stood staring down at the man who lay at their feet. He was alive, but only just. Longmire fetched water and Anna dribbled it into Sam's mouth, which opened greedily to drink more, before he started to cough. Brown crouched down and gently bathed Sam's face, talking softly to him. Anna blinked away tears. Bell was outside, shouting into his phone, calling Forensics, the Super, anyone he could think of. It was over.

CHAPTER 30

Anna looked out of the window opposite the chair where she sat in the therapist's quiet room. Outside, early-morning sunlight picked out the colours of the few remaining leaves that had survived the first storm of the winter. It was only a day since Sam had been rescued, but the appointment with the therapist had been in Anna's diary for weeks. After the painful conversation with Bell about her relationship with Simon, she'd needed it more than ever.

'Are you still having the dreams?' the woman asked.

Anna nodded.

'The same?'

'No, not the same. Before, I could see Mark's face in the window of the plane before it crashed. He had his mouth open, screaming, but I couldn't hear him.'

'And now?'

'Nothing. The plane is there but the windows are empty, blank.'

'And with all that's happened here recently, how are you feeling?'

Anna thought about the question. 'I think…' she began.

'Anna,' the woman interrupted. 'I asked you how you are feeling, not what you're thinking.'

'How am I feeling? Numb. Stupid. I let someone deceive me. Maybe I wanted to be deceived.'

'But you couldn't have changed what happened, could you?'

'No, I don't think so. Simon thought only about himself, what he needed. He wanted to know what was happening with our investigation, so he befriended me, drew me in. I see that now.'

'Do you think he used you?'

'He did! Clearly he did. He used everyone.'

'When did you realise that, do you think?'

'It dawned on me gradually. And when I found out who he really was, I knew for sure then. I tried to tell myself it could be a mistake, but I knew, and everything fell into place. I should have told Sam right away, but I didn't.'

The therapist was silent for a moment. 'And now you've been suspended. How long will that last?'

Anna shrugged. 'I'm not sure I want to carry on anyway.'

'You want to leave the force?'

'It's one option. Or I could just move away, start again somewhere else.'

The therapist made eye contact. 'Anna, do you remember why you first decided to come and see me, months ago?'

'I said it was about work, but it was about me, too.' She hesitated, looking down at her hands. 'It was about me as a policewoman, because that's part of whom I am.' She glanced at the therapist, looking for a reaction but finding none. 'I should have known that Simon was too good to be true, but... I saw what I wanted to see, not what was really going on.'

She hesitated before she spoke again, avoiding the older woman's patient eyes. 'He was using me, like he'd been used himself when he was a boy. Sam told me how some of the boys in Montgomery House were brought into the circle of abuse, used to recruit other boys, given rewards, made to feel special.

301

That woman, Irene Thornhill – she did that to Simon… Stuart… and that's what he did to me.' She found a hankie and blew her nose.

Still the therapist wanted more. 'You said he had children?'

Anna nodded. 'Two. They were his wife's kids. He adopted them when they were young.'

'And are they OK?'

'One of them died,' Anna said, remembering the white shoes. 'Rory. He was just a boy, keen to do anything his dad wanted.'

'And the other?'

Anna thought about Caroline for a moment. 'I'm not sure. She seems OK, but…' She glanced at her watch and got to her feet. 'I have to go. Sorry.'

'We have another minute,' said the therapist. 'I want you to think about this man and the two of you together. We need to learn from it. Do you think he actively tried to harm you?'

Anna sat down again. 'I don't know. The first time, on the mountain, did he trip me up, just to get into my life, and then work on making me feel vulnerable? I felt ill after a meal at his house, but that could have been caused by anything. Anyway, he knew I was unhappy at work, and he played on that. I said more about the case than I should have done. Maybe he wanted me to leave the force. I don't know, and now I never will.'

'Can you put it behind you, move on?'

'What do you think?' Anna asked.

The woman smiled. 'It's your life, Anna. You know it's down to you.'

She sat still, looking out of the window again. 'I need to talk to Sam,' she said. 'He's back home now but I've been avoiding him.' She sniffed, wiped her eyes with the hankie. 'It feels like my fault that Simon was able to get to him. Sam could have died.

I should have stopped it and I didn't.' She looked up, vainly seeking reassurance in the other woman's impassive face.

'So what are you going to do?'

Anna got up to leave. 'I'm going to see him now. I have to talk to him. It's time.'

'When we meet next week, you can tell me what happened.'

'Yes,' said Anna. 'I will.'

She found Sam sitting in the garden of the house in Parton, leaning back in a wooden chair outside the back door, eyes closed, in the warmth of the low October sunshine. A walking frame stood by the chair. As her shadow crossed his face, he opened his eyes.

'Anna,' he said, and tried to get to his feet. She leaned forward to help him and felt the tremor in his arms. He winced. 'Still sore,' he said. 'It felt like a long time I was hanging there. I thought...' His voice tailed away.

'I know,' she said. 'Stay still. Can I get you anything? How are your legs now?'

Sam sat back with relief. 'Swollen, painful. Bad bruising where the chain pulled, but nothing broken. I'm having trouble getting about, though.' He rubbed his hand over his face. 'They've got me on painkillers. I hate them, it's like having a blanket round your brain. And that thing...' He gestured at the walking frame. 'Makes me feel like an old man, like those poor souls in the home in Bardsea.'

Anna pulled up another chair and sat down. 'But it won't be for long, will it?' she said. 'You'll be up and about again soon, good as new.'

'Not sure about that,' he said. 'I've been thinking it might be time to quit.'

'Leave the force? Do you want to go out like this, after all these years?'

'Have to go sometime, don't I? I've done my thirty years. I'm thinking about it.'

Anna knew what she had to say next. 'There's something I need to tell you,' she said. 'It's about Simon Buttler.'

'You were with him when he died, weren't you?' said Sam. 'Did he suffer much?'

Anna shook her head, remembering. 'He wanted to say something. I think he was trying to tell me where you were, in the Florence. That was just before he died. Maybe he wanted us to find you.'

'He could have killed me, but he didn't.' Sam shook his head. 'He left me water, but it got spilled.' He thought for a while, trying to remember. 'From what he told me, he didn't kill anyone. Not Graham – he said that was an accident. Not Mikey. And he could have killed me. It was as if he felt that killing was beneath him. You knew him better than me. Does that make sense?'

'He thought he was special,' Anna replied. 'You could be right about him. Killing was too sordid for someone like Simon. And now he's gone and we can't ask him, even if he would never tell us the truth about anything. Lying was at the centre of his life. I realised that when I found out he was Stuart Billings.'

Sam looked at her. 'When did you know that?'

'Before he took you. And I didn't say, I didn't tell you. I could have stopped all this. But I waited.'

'Why?' Sam asked.

'Because…' She hesitated. 'Because I thought Simon cared about me, and I didn't want to believe that he'd just used me to get inside information.' She looked up in appeal. 'I don't believe I told him anything important. But I should have been more careful, right from the start.'

Sam thought for a moment. 'Was he the special friend who looked after you when you were ill, the one from the Mountain Rescue Team?'

She nodded. 'That's where we met.'

Sam studied her. 'Did you love him?'

Anna looked away. 'Almost,' she said. 'For a while I thought we might have a future together.' She closed her eyes. 'I was such a fool.'

Sam put out his bandaged hand to take hers. 'Does Bell know?'

'Yes. Maureen had already worked it out and I had to tell Bell myself before she did. He talked to the Super and I'm suspended. They'll want to talk to you about it, when you're ready.'

He nodded. 'Is that why you've come today?'

She shook her head. 'No. I had to tell you, I feel so guilty about what happened.' She stood up, looking over the low wall to the sea beyond. 'Maybe I should just resign, get it over with,' she said.

'You could,' Sam agreed. 'But that would be a loss. Yes, it was a bad choice, but you could keep going in the police, somewhere else if not here. I had to do that, start again, thirty years ago.' He paused. 'I gave up the force for a while, after things went wrong. I was a postman.'

Anna looked back at him, smiling. 'A postman? Why?'

'I liked walking, and I liked the uniform.'

She laughed. 'Like being a constable on the beat.'

'Yes, and that's what pulled me back into the job, when things happened that I was curious about. It's more than just a job, Anna. It's a way of thinking.'

'We'll see,' she said. 'I may not have much choice in the matter.'

'What about the girl, Buttler's daughter?'

Anna sat in the chair again, feeling the warmth of the sun on her face. 'I've been thinking about that,' she said. 'Her mother turned up at the hospital, out of the blue. The plan is that they'll live together, after all Caroline's been through. That should be the end of it but…'

'But what?'

'Well, Bell says it's all over,' Anna said. 'With Simon and Rory both gone, and the drugs business being wrapped up, he reckons we should close the case.'

Sam smiled. 'No surprise, is it? He's been itching to get to the Drug Squad assignment since it was first mentioned. He knows that can only happen when this case is finished.' He considered Anna's expression. 'Are you saying it's not finished?'

She shook her head. 'I've been putting together what I know about Caroline, not just since this stuff happened, but before, when I saw her at home. There's something not right about her, boss. I think we need to do some more checking.'

'Where is she now?' Sam asked.

'As far as I know, she and her mother are back at the house in Hilton. Caroline said something about taking a holiday abroad, but that was planned before she lost her dad and Rory. What will she do now, apart from bury them?'

'Poor kid,' Sam said. 'She's been through a lot. How old is she?'

'Nearly twenty-one, but she looks older. Did Simon say anything about her, when you were with him in the mine?'

Sam winced. 'Some of that time's a blur to me – must be because of the pills. He did say something, I think, but I can't remember what exactly.'

Anna waited, watching Sam close his eyes, struggling with the fog in his mind. He opened his eyes. 'Yes. I asked him about Caroline and he said: "She knows what to do." It sounded as if there was a plan, as if she was in on it.'

Anna stood up suddenly. 'Sam, can you do something for me? Ring the office, get them to track down Henny Brown, and ask him to meet me at the Hilton house. We have to bypass Bell. If he knows, he'll tell me not to go. Please, Sam, override that if you need to. If I'm going to be disciplined anyway, just add this to the list of charges against me. I have to see Caroline again, before she disappears.'

Sam hesitated. 'Are you sure?'

She nodded. 'Just get DC Brown to meet me there, with back up, OK? I have to go.'

He made up his mind rapidly, like the Sam of old. 'Go,' he said. 'I'll square it with Bell. And, Anna, take care.'

Caroline Buttler let herself into the empty house and took a deep breath. She wanted to sleep, cry for her useless brother, take stock and decide what to do, but there was no time for any of that. It was already late in the afternoon and she needed to be away from here before anyone tried to stop her. That was something Simon had taught her. Make the plan ahead of time, and when you need to use it, don't hesitate.

Earlier in the day, she'd had to be careful for a while. Her mother had been clingy and tearful, and it had taken an age to persuade her to go home. 'You'll need to make arrangements for your brother, won't you?' Caroline had said, and it had done the trick. Wendy had gone, promising to come to her at Hilton the following morning.

Then there were the police still sniffing around, which was a worry. The fat man who seemed to be their boss, he was OK. He'd rung her at the B&B in Workington that the social worker had found for them, to tell her that as far as he was concerned the case was closed. Sounded like he was in a hurry to get on to something else. But she wasn't so sure about the two women, especially the younger one, Anna. Caroline knew why her dad had been all over the woman, but she'd hated it all the same.

She went through to the large room at the back of the house. It was hot from the afternoon sun and smelled of strangers. The whole house was a mess after the police search but it didn't matter. Anything she'd been able to find in the house about the drugs business was a pile of ashes in the garden before the search team ever arrived. The room was stuffy. She pushed open the bifold section of the glass wall and stood for a moment, enjoying the breeze. She would miss this place, but it was time for her to leave. They'd talked about it often, she and Dad.

'If anything happens to me,' he'd said, 'you know what to do. Everything you need to get away is hidden in the wall across the road, well out of the way of any search team. It's all there, for both of you. Rory might not understand, but you're the strong one. He'll do what you say.'

Caroline checked her watch. She was exhausted but she could feel the adrenalin bumping in her chest. She tried not to think about Rory. He was just a kid, hopeless, and it looked as if he'd made a mess of basic safety precautions. Ever since he'd learned to drive, she'd been expecting him to die, but not like that.

She left the doors open and sat down on a stool in the sun-warmed room looking out at the garden. For a moment all she wanted to do was close her eyes and blot it all out. Dad was gone. He'd always said that if anything went wrong, he would take his own life rather than go to jail. Maybe that's what he did, when they were closing in on him.

And now there was just Wendy to deal with. Caroline despised her mother. When she'd left them, Dad had been puzzled, but if he'd had any regrets about the situation the letter had finished them off. It hadn't been difficult to fake her mother's writing.

After that Dad changed his will, and now everything in the Swiss account would come to her, Caroline, and no one else.

She stood up and stretched her arms over her head. She had to keep going. First thing was to find the parcel of documents Dad had arranged for her. She opened the front door and listened. Everything outside was quiet. The narrow road was shaded by the lengthening shadows of the tall trees that screened the house from view. She scrambled over the low wall on the far side of the road and felt for the package hidden at its base, wrapped in plastic to keep the contents dry and safe.

She carried it back into the house and unwrapped it. Money in various currencies, passports and credit cards in three different names, Swiss bank account details, mobile phones, keys for the other car. And, of course, the gun. Caroline smiled, remembering those Sunday mornings with Dad at the gun club. Everything was ready. By tomorrow morning, when her mother was planning to arrive, she would be long gone.

Anna drove the familiar route to the Hilton house, thinking about what she needed to do. This was her chance to redeem herself before the wheels of the disciplinary process ahead of her began to turn. If she was wrong about Caroline, she would find her at the house with her mother, grieving and lost, and this unexpected visit would be viewed as a sign of concern from a caring police officer. And if she was right? Too late to worry about that now.

She parked the Land Rover in a passing place a few yards from the gateway to the Old Vicarage's drive and walked along the quiet road to peer at the house. It was quiet, no sign or sound of occupation. Caroline's car stood gleaming to one side of the gravelled drive. Anna's feet crunched on the shingle as she walked towards the front door. She pressed the bell, heard the sound as it rang, waited.

Footsteps inside. The door opened. Caroline stared at her, then smiled. 'Oh, it's you,' she said. 'I wasn't expecting to see you. Your boss said it was all over. And we have so many things to do… you know.'

Anna smiled back, trying to keep her eyes and mind steady. 'Yes, I know. I'm sorry to disturb you at such a difficult time but I wanted to make sure you're OK. Your mum's helping you here, isn't she?'

'Mum?' said the girl. She looked pale, Anna thought, but her eyes were clear.

'Is she here – Wendy?' Anna asked. 'I heard that she was coming back with you. You need looking after, with all that's happened.'

'Yes,' said Caroline. They were still standing, facing each other. Caroline was holding the door half-shut, looking around it at the unwelcome visitor.

'May I come in?' Anna asked, taking half a step forward.

Caroline didn't move. 'The place is a mess after the search you lot did,' she said. 'Mum's upstairs, resting. It's not really convenient.'

Anna hesitated. She could turn and leave, wait unseen in the Land Rover until the backup arrived. Instead, she took another step forward, pushed against the half-open door with one hand and guided the girl back into the hall with the other.

Caroline was taken by surprise and half stumbled as she was propelled out of the way. By the time she had recovered her balance, Anna was in. Caroline retreated across the hall towards the open door to the back room. Late sunlight streamed through the doorway and across the floor. The girl put out her hand to steady herself, holding onto a small table on which there was an opened package.

'You can't come in, I told you,' she began. Her smile had disappeared. 'My mother's asleep. We have things to do. You should leave.'

Anna took another step forward and held up her warrant card. 'DI Bell may have closed the case but there are still a few things I need to ask you about. I'm a police officer, remember?'

'Wait a minute,' said the girl. 'There's something on the stove. I need to turn it off.' She was out of Anna's sight for just a moment. When she reappeared the expression on her face had changed and she was holding something in her hand. It was small and shiny. She pointed it at Anna.

'Actually, Wendy's not here,' Caroline said. 'She's a stupid woman and I don't need her. I don't need you either. Get out of my house.' She waved the pistol. 'I know how to use this. Dad taught me.'

'So you were part of it all along,' said Anna. 'You're too clever to be an innocent bystander, I always felt that. All that stuff you told me in the interview... it was lies, wasn't it?'

'Of course it was. Why would I tell you the truth, about anything? And you fell for it, you and your fat boss. He said I was free to go.'

'We made a mistake,' said Anna. 'You're an intelligent woman, Caroline, but this is stupid. You're pointing a gun at a police officer, and that's a serious offence.' Caroline didn't move. Anna kept talking. 'You need to think hard. More police officers are on their way here. If you leave now, we'll find you. If you hurt me, the police will track you down and you'll spend half your adult life in jail. Is that what you want?' She held out her hand. 'Think, Caroline. Give me the gun.'

Caroline took a step back but the gun remained steady in her hand. In the momentary silence that stretched between the two women, another sound wafted through the open front door. 'Listen,' Anna said. 'Can you hear that? A police siren, with more officers coming here. I told you.'

Caroline's fixed expression crumpled into rage. She stamped her foot and reached for the bundle that lay on the table. 'Get out of my way, you bitch!' she screamed. 'I'll shoot you... Get out of my way!'

Anna lowered her head. On the floor of the hall where they stood, Caroline's shadow was changing shape. In the open doorway of the back room, a large figure blocked out the light. Caroline sensed the shadow and turned. As she did so, the figure launched itself at her. Two strong arms encircled her narrow frame and threw her to the floor. Anna crouched down, hearing the crack of the gun as it went off, the bullet smashing harmlessly into the staircase.

'You OK?' Brown asked. He had wrenched the gun from the girl's hand and slid it across the polished floor towards Anna, who picked it up carefully. There was one bullet left.

Caroline had stopped struggling and lay limp on the floor. DC Brown took handcuffs from his pocket and put them around her wrists, leaning on the girl to calm her down.

'We heard the siren,' Anna said, 'but it wasn't that close.'

'The rest of them were following me,' said Brown. 'I didn't wait. Tognarelli said to get down here in a hurry so I did. I could see your car, and the front door was open, but I didn't want to alert her so I kept off the gravel and went round the back. The door was open.' He stood up, pulling Caroline to her feet. 'Were you right about this one?' he asked.

Anna sat on the floor, breathing hard, looking up at them both. 'She's just a kid. Half-crazy. He used her, like he used everybody.'

The wailing of the siren grew louder and then stopped. Car doors banged, voices were raised, and Caroline Buttler started to sob, hanging like a broken doll in Henny Brown's arms.

If you've enjoyed this book, here are Ruth Sutton's other titles.

A Good Liar
Forgiven
Fallout
Cruel Tide
Fatal Reckoning
Burning Secrets